Heinz Hemken

Capture

Heinz Hemken

1

In some sense, Benita was paid handsomely to simply exist. There was certainly more to it. She had specific duties and had to hone and express specific skills, but ultimately the work she performed was her behavior itself, much more than whatever actually came of it. Every day she wore an instrumented bodysuit that captured her behavior in remarkable detail, which would later be imbued into the control software of virtual characters and most recently, in actual walking, talking robots. The substance of behavior was the accumulation over evolutionary time of genes, bodies, brains, minds, and culture, and their application towards fulfilling the quotidian needs and impulses of living creatures. It was a billion years of life sedimented into consciousness, and behavior itself was its sole outward expression.

This morning, she finished drying herself off with a bath towel, shaved the stubble from her head with an electric shaver, and returned to her bedroom. The behavior capture suit was neatly spread out on her already made bed, along with the rest of the clothing she would be wearing that day. The suit was a sheer two-piece bodysuit made of a material that felt similar to that of nylon pantyhose but was much more durable. She wore it under her street clothing. The surface of the suit was dotted with lentil-sized motion sensors interconnected with a network of fine wires, not much thicker than sewing thread. They all terminated at a thin elastic waistband that had connectors to join the top and bottom of the suit and another for a small electronic device that could be attached to a belt, or carried around in a pants pocket. Benita generally opted for a belt, of which she had quite a collection.

She chose a wig, one that she wore on dates when she wanted to make a particularly good impression. It was rust red in a cut somewhere between a "pixie" and what used to be called a "shattered bob." Today was a special day, and she wanted to make a good visual impression.

She took her specs from their base station on her night stand and put them on. They automatically paired with her bodysuit and synchronized timestamps with it, so that her body motion data and specs video and audio data were now in sync to within 4 milliseconds. Her every motion during the day was recorded, along with everything she saw or heard while wearing her specs. Every night while the specs and belt recharged, the data were uploaded to her employer's data centers.

The specs could do some basic reading of the diaphanous magnetic fields emanating from her brain, and could do a reasonable job of converting some of them into verbal commands and text, once she had been trained to do it. This was usually referred to as thought speech, private speech, inner speech, and so on. It was still quite controversial, even though these days most users had it enabled and constantly used it during the day. Most jobs required continuous communication with a variety of virtual characters that appeared in the specs, and it was far more convenient to converse with them using inner speech than by speaking to them out loud.

Finally, she put on her twiddle rings, sets of linked rings on the fingers of each hand. Like the rest of her behavior capture gear, all the subtleties of motion captured by the rings were duly recorded and uploaded. They acted as a substitute keyboard and pointing device, a means with which to interact with the items projected into her visual field by her specs.

"Suit's up and running, everything looks good," said Zag, as she pursed her lips a few times to even out the color of her lipstick. Zag was her current avatar for her personal Blam specs account, supposedly the most trustworthy specs account provider. He had appeared in her field of view behind her when she powered up her specs, and had been watching her indirectly through the video and audio data streaming from them, combined with the detailed model of her apartment and of Benita herself that was already maintained somewhere in Blam's limitless data centers.

There were several graded options to opt out of allowing user data to be used by Blam, and a small percentage of users actually did so. But not only did this mean that their service was no longer gratis, and could be relatively expensive if they opted out completely, it excluded them from the information and services that Blam provided through its virtual characters, like Zag. Sophisticated machine learning models derived from the simulations allowed Blam to provide timely and uncannily relevant information and assistance to users without their even having to request it or be aware of any need for it. Such was the fine grained predictive accuracy of the models. Characters like Zag appeared to act like an intimate friend, knowing what you needed and when, what things were going on in your life and helping out with them, sometimes even insightfully completing your sentences.

Benita had serious doubts about the privacy and security of her uploaded data, given that it contained practically everything she did, saw, heard, or said. Like everyone else, she knew in the back of her mind that Blam (and god knows who else) had detailed models of her and pretty much everyone else in the world.

In any event, behavior capture actors like her were a special case in which everything they did throughout the day was eventually uploaded to FfēFfē Automata anyway, in addition to Blam's data centers. She had long since lost any reservations. Their empire of data centers and artificial intelligence analysis undoubtedly knew her better than any human ever would. If anybody was peeking, she never wanted to meet them. Ever. Most people had the opposite problem. Their employer's data ended up contaminating their personal accounts, and this had given rise to litigation having to do with leakage of a large variety of confidential company information, imagery, audio, trade secrets, and anything else that could be deliberately or inadvertently captured by employees who were constantly capturing data during more or less all of their waking hours.

2

"You still have time for breakfast," said Zag over Benita's shoulder. "Your ride will be outside right afterwards."

Zag was only visible to Benita. He was effectively a video game character running on a Blam server out in dataland somewhere. She had set him up as a handsome young man about her age who came off as a really nice guy, very smart, very helpful, the kind of guy she wished she knew in real life. She had spent many hours tweaking things, adjusting the mix of personalities that Blam had available, choosing his wardrobe, adjusting his voice and appearance, and constantly changing him to suit her needs and whims. She had enabled the erotica package early on, and had spent a not inconsiderable amount of time adjusting that as well, although she was actually a fairly moderate user. There was a certain rather sophisticated electronic device that was paired with it, which she kept in a discreet box in her nightstand drawer. It was most satisfying, so much so that she made an effort to use it only under extreme duress for fear that relying on it would turn her into a social recluse or an *inchill*, an involuntarily childless person. At age 30, the clock was still running. In countries where specs use had become massive, birth rates were starting to dip into negative numbers as more and more people in their childbearing years found emotional solace in virtual characters paired with sex toys of various kinds. Yesterday's incels were today's inchills.

Zag and his ilk had been the first products created and marketed by her employer, FféFfé Automata. What used to be called augmented reality or mixed reality was now just "specs," and most of humanity was now connected. It was a world infested with phantoms of all kinds, used as assistants, companions, lovers, advertising vehicles, entertainment, telepresence proxies, gratuitously abusable victims, emissaries, spies, soldiers, swindlers, deities, propaganda, and for practically everything else a human entity had ever done, and for many things they hadn't.

They were primitive at first, like a mindless non-player character in a game, capable only of basic interactions and with a modest behavioral repertoire. Nevertheless, everybody wanted one, and they were surprisingly useful for managing calendars, providing timely reminders, and even engaging in simple open-ended conversation. Aided by people's unlimited ability and inclination to anthropomorphize inanimate objects and shape everything into a coherent story, these ghostly humanoids easily slipped into the collective psyche.

The current generation was far more sophisticated. Hundreds of thousands of hours of human behavior capture had been used to train their machine learning models, and many were now used to guide workers through complex procedures that would otherwise require highly trained employees.

That's what Benita did for a living. Benita's specialty had been working as an assistant to police detectives, intelligence analysts, and field agents. She had worked with security and intelligence agencies throughout the San Francisco Bay Area, in addition to a few of the big tech companies that needed to zealously protect their intellectual property.

"What time is it now, 7:30? I need to be at Dr. Thakkar's house in Woodside at 10:00, and it'll take me an hour and a half to get there.

After breakfast would be fine. I can hang out somewhere near his house if I'm there too early," she replied. She decided on just having a cup of coffee and a bagel, which she started to prepare. Setting up the trip and getting the timing right were simple tasks that Zag could do easily on his own.

"Done," said Zag. "A Scramb will pick you up out front and drive you to the CalRail station, five minutes later the train comes by and takes you to Redwood City, and from there another Scramb to Dr. Thakkar's house."

Benita lived in a town named San Martín, near the southern end of the CalRail commuter train line. San Martín was in the midst of an intense spurt of urbanization, especially around the CalRail station. An ambitious plan to build a European-style rail system connecting the San Francisco area to Los Angeles and San Diego had fizzled years earlier, but three separate lines from San Francisco to Hollister, Sacramento to Bakersfield, and Los Angeles to San Diego had gradually been upgraded and built out into light rail commuter systems that had resulted in powerful economic and technological corridors. It was currently San Martín's turn at gentrification and high density housing next to its CalRail station. It was far less expensive to live here than in Silicon Valley proper, so many people in Benita's demographic were ending up here.

Just as she was finishing her last gulp of coffee, the Scramb icon lit up in her specs alerting her to the imminent arrival of her car. A small video of it seemed to float in front of her about a meter away and to her right, conspicuously showing its appearance and license plate. She twiddled her acknowledgment and got up to go. The video disappeared.

"Let me check you in the mirror," suggested Zag.

She did so, and both saw that nothing was amiss. Benita grabbed her shoulder bag.

"You look good. Very professional," said Zag as he appeared to follow her out the door. Benita couldn't help but unconsciously hold the door open a bit for him.

As she reached the sidewalk outside, the car was just pulling up to the curb. It opened its door, and she took her seat. The car repeated her destination just to make sure, and set off. Benita was pleased that it was clean and fresh, and the AC had already been running. Zag sat across from her, gazing out the window. It was creepy how Blam knew where she was with enough detail for Zag to look like he was actually sitting there in the car watching the world go by.

There was a pall of wildfire smoke in the sky to the north of the CalRail station. Even this far south, the smell of burnt trees hung in the air. Acrid notes in that noxious bouquet indicated to Benita that homes were very likely going up in addition to trees and brush. As she found her seat on the train, a quick search in her specs confirmed that several small towns between Geyserville and Cloverdale in the wine country up north had been completely overrun by flames the night before, and all of the affected residents were now in shelters awaiting their fate.

"Oh," Benita whispered to herself.

"Yep, burnt to the ground, poor folks," said Zag absently. "I hope they don't all end up in tents." He was synced up to everything Benita saw or heard in her specs.

The train ride from San Martín to Redwood City would take the better part of an hour. She gazed absently at the intermittent tent encampments that lined the tracks between San Martín and the narrow pass between Morgan Hill and the southeastern tip of the San Jose metropolitan area. The authorities had been claiming for years that Green New Deal projects would gradually eliminate the tents and provide their homeless denizens more dignified incomes and dwellings, but progress was still slow. It didn't help that wildfires were a reliable source of new tent settlers.

Benita scrolled through the morning's news in her specs. The German Chancellor was in Washington D.C. on a state visit, and the president had commented on the snugness of the dress she wore as she arrived at the White House and jokingly disparaged the size of her breasts.

Benita switched from the news feed to a music channel.

3

The Crazy Ladies Agricultural Cooperative was located at the eastern edge of Watsonville, California, on a lazy rural dead-end road named Pequod Lane, one ranch short of the end. The paved road was just wide enough for the trucks and semi-trailers that came and went from the farm, but too narrow for it to be worth painting stripes along its center. It was unevenly shaded by trees, and in some spots trucks and trailers had carved short tunnels through the thick overhanging canopy.

Tavo Granados stood by his 15,000 liter water tanker truck he drove for the co-op. The farm had 3 such trucks, and each day they would all drive down to the coast to pick up full loads of fresh water from the desalination plant at Moss Landing.

These 45,000 liters a day of fresh water were crucial for the co-op. Without that extra water they would be unable to operate their greenhouses. Over the past 6 years or so, water desalination co-operatives had managed to fill the gap between what municipal water sources could supply, and what the local community actually needed.

Tavo was a child of The Riots. About a dozen years ago, the world seemed to be on fire. Along with ever more furious brush fires year upon year, the more desperate layers of society needed but a spark to burst into flames themselves. One fine August morning, at the $117°F$ peak of a two week heat wave, violence broke out in the largest contiguous tent encampment in Los Angeles over distribution of donated water and groceries. Shots were fired, and unrest spread explosively through every major city in the nation. During the next ten days, over 10,000 homeless people and random bystanders died, along with over 1000 police personnel and National Guard troops. Thousands more were injured, and swaths of destruction scarred the urban landscape. Long plumes of smoke were easily visible from Earth orbit. Panic over an imminent civil war seized the nation. World equities markets collapsed, and Japan, China, Russia, and most of the European Community went to their highest levels of military alert. The panic spread throughout the world, and massive social disruption along the lines of what had happened in the U.S. also flashed through other industrialized nations. It seemed as if the entire world teetered on the brink of violent civil insurrection. During those terrifying two weeks, over 300,000 people died worldwide of heat stroke and its complications.

It was a mid-term election year in the United States, and for the next 9 months the nation faced its most tumultuous social and political disruption since the Civil War. A wave of Green New Dealers was swept into both the House of Representatives and the Senate in a nation-spanning landslide. Almost half a century of tax cuts were rolled back, up to and including the Revenue act of 1964, in spite of intense and often violent resistance from the normally invincible American plutocracy. A far-reaching suite of legislation was passed that would profoundly change the practice of American Capitalism. It was one of the greatest and riskiest economic experiments the nation had ever attempted, and it had all occurred on very short notice. Co-operatives like Crazy Ladies and the desalinators were among the results of Green New Deal legislation forged in the aftermath of The Riots.

Tavo often lost himself in memories of those days. He was a junior in high school at the time, not far from where The Riots had started in Los Angeles. He lost an uncle in the unrest, two of his cousins were gang-raped, and half the block he lived on was burnt to rubble. His own immediate family, parents and younger sister Julia, were miraculously unscathed, and they still had their home. About a dozen displaced relatives came to live with them. Some were still there.

Tavo was waiting for his two fellow tanker drivers, Raúl and Sue. Raúl was probably still finishing his breakfast, and Sue was already walking towards Tavo, teeth freshly brushed and on display. Sue was actually Bahk Seo-yeon, but Sue was about as close as anyone could get. She had migrated to California from the small city of Chesterton, Illinois. Her newlywed grandparents had arrived there long ago with the help of relatives who already lived nearby, and the couple managed to set up and run a small neighborhood market. They lived the quintessential American Dream, building up their prosperous small business and putting their children through college, then retiring gracefully as their children became successful professionals serving the local community.

A quarter of the local farmland was now swamp, however, and the local economy was in tatters. Sue was part of a wave of thousands of twenty-somethings who were unable to afford a college education, and for whom the region had no jobs. Co-ops were tailor made for her demographic, and now here she was at Crazy Ladies.

Sue walked up to Tavo and gave him a hug and a kiss that raised his body temperature at least one degree. Celsius. Her eyes had a certain sparkle in them.

"*Vámonos, wey*," said Raúl as he jogged towards them from the main farmhouse. Raúl was born in Xochimilco, a suburb of the immense Mexico City metropolitan axis. His family was poor, and made their living selling flowers from a sidewalk stall outside of the local public market, *El Mercado de Xochimilco*. The Xochimilco public market had been in operation for hundreds of years, and Raúl's family had been selling flowers or produce in front of it since time immemorial. About 5 years ago, like many of his ancestors, Raúl left his hometown in search of employment and adventure, and had ended up in Watsonville. There were thousands of migrants like him here, each with a story very similar to his. Many had fled circumstances even worse than mere poverty, and hair-raising stories of escapes from drug wars, gang wars, and incipient local insurrection were the stuff of beer-fueled oral history sessions.

Each of the three climbed into their truck, the convoy drove onto Pequod Lane in single file, and then headed out to Moss Landing.

4

When Brenda Castro arrived at the antique shop in the morning, her boss Savion Bennington was already busy at his desk.

"Hey," she greeted from his office doorway.

"Hey," he responded. "Don't forget we're going shopping this evening."

"Yeah, I'm looking forward to it! By the way, there's a fashion event this week around Union Square that I think we should check out. Diva's and Goldiggers are both showing new clothes and accessory lines. I think there'll be a lot of cool new stuff," she said.

"Great! Remember, sexy but tasteful. I'm getting a few high end pieces today or tomorrow. The sales cycle may be a bit longer for them. You'll really need to patiently build up any potential customers," said Bennington.

"How much are we talking?"

"You'll be getting at least twice as much per piece as you did the last couple of times, with some of them even more. I'm expecting a couple dozen pieces over the next few weeks. I left some info on your desk with some new items that came in today. You'll be busy for a while, so make sure you get enough new things for several attempts per prospect. I'll leave the wardrobe decisions to your discretion?" he said. Try as he might, he could not avoid a creepy, libidinous undertone.

"Don't worry. I know what the customer wants, and how to shine at the Q'Boom. Repeat customers are always welcome. They spend more. Let me know when the stuff starts coming in," said Brenda.

"Will do. OK, be ready at around 5," he said.

Brenda walked to her desk, took care of some minor duties, and then went over to open the shop. The day was a bright and warm late autumn morning, and she couldn't help but be in a cheerful mood. She walked around the store a bit to see if anything needed attention. The thin layer of dust everywhere was annoying to her, but Bennington was too stingy to have people come in more than once a month. Two janitorial workers took the better part of the day to clean things up, and their hourly cost was not cheap. Bennington was leery of having outsiders prowl around the shop, especially during deliveries or shipments. The merchandise on the shop's shelves and floors was not much of a moneymaker. The most profitable deals made at the shop were, to say the least, informal. Bennington did not want to have any auditable or subpoenable data lying around in anybody's specs, nor did he trust the janitorial workers not to snoop around. Every time a cleaning crew came, several items disappeared from the shelves. He even had video of some of them *in flagranti*. Hence, carefully scheduled human workers were brought in as infrequently as he could justify to himself.

Brenda went back to her desk and started looking through the paper documents Bennington had left for her. Why he insisted on hard copies was beyond her, and she assumed it was just out of Savion's constitutional paranoia. She'd have to give them back to him later in the day so that he could shred them. Of course, everything she looked at was captured by her specs, and she would be able to look at it all again as often as she liked. It didn't make much sense, but she played along.

There were several file folders, each describing a piece of handsome jewelry, supposedly with genuine, high quality diamonds and colored gemstones. These were small and easy to transport, and her usual class of customers always brought thermal and spectral testing tools to check the authenticity of the gems, as well as jeweler's loupes and the like to judge their quality. Bennington always used them on new shipments as well, and Brenda had learned to use them long ago. She always carried a set of portable tools with her when she delivered the goods to clients.

Each file folder was from a different one of Bennington's partners, and Brenda could recognize each of them. Among her duties was to follow up on delayed shipments, call back about shipment issues or discrepancies, and to relay messages for Bennington. She had established a working rapport with her counterparts at most of these places, and she and her peers had established their own discreet trading network of jewelry and small *objets d'art*. She surreptitiously sent text messages via her personal specs account to each of her counterparts represented in the files asking what else was new. For the moment, there was no need to send any official communications in Bennington's name.

Next to the file folders was a box containing a dozen or so pieces of jewelry, each carefully wrapped in soft chamois. One by one she carefully unwrapped them to have a look. They were clean and ready for sale, beautiful gold and platinum pieces with a variety of emeralds, rubies, sapphires, and diamonds. It was fairly standard stuff, but some of the centerpiece stones were large enough to considerably raise their value. She carefully packed them up again and put the box in the large bottom drawer of her desk.

Over the nearly 3 years she had been working with Bennington, she'd developed a reputation at the Q'Boom Qlub where she found most of her customers. She had a number of regulars, along with frequent trustworthy recommendations from them, and she had sold this sort of jewelry to most of them. Bennington had met her at the club at a time when she was doing primarily sex work and building up a trade in expensive stolen goods she was able to obtain from some dubious sources who also regularly plied the club. She was a much more enticing sales person than they were, and she developed an excellent reputation among them as well. Bennington was among these early partners, and he gradually monopolized her, mainly because he had a steady source of high quality product to sell. Now she was basically full time with him, and even had her own desk here at Bennington's Antiques. It was here that she had met Rashaun DuPont, Bennington's jack of all trades. She had developed an intimate friendship with him, and for the moment she was satisfied with life.

A wheeled delivery drone entered the store with a large box, maybe half a meter long and almost as wide and deep.

"I'll get that," said Bennington as he walked out of his office and towards the drone. He twiddled his fingers to sign for it and carried the box to his office, closing the door after him. Brenda knew better than to investigate. If it had to do with her she'd eventually know about it and probably make some money. If not, it would eventually be discreetly handed off to another courier, or Bennington would send DuPont out to deliver it. Either way, no questions asked.

Almost an hour later, she heard Bennington walk out of his office towards the loading area behind the showroom. There was some rustling, then the careful opening of the back door. She quickly twiddled her fingers to bring up the feeds from the rear surveillance cameras into her specs. Bennington had opened the delivery van's side door and was putting a couple of boxes inside, each somewhat larger than a shoe box. He closed the van and came back into the building closing the door behind him as quietly as he could manage. She pretended to be examining the jewelry files he had left her.

"So, what do you think?" he said as he passed by on the way back to his office. Was it possible that he was unaware that Brenda could watch his every move, or that it would be recorded? Bennington was a big fan of "hiding in plain sight," so perhaps this was his way of bulking up the background noise. She'd have to think about the pros and cons of such a strategy.

"They're beautiful," she said, and she truly believed it. "They look pretty expensive."

"They are. I'm going to try adding more high end items to our repertoire and see how it goes. Think you can handle it?"

"Of course! Some of my clients have been asking for more expensive stuff. For most of them it's an investment, not a fashion accessory. I used to think they bought them for their wives or lovers, but a lot of it ends up in safe deposit boxes, or so they tell me."

"Yeah, these days it's just another asset class, not art or jewelry. Either that or a way to clean up illicit income. *C'est la vie,*" he said, and went back to his office.

He paused and turned back.

"By the way, sorry for the late notice but something came up. Do you think Rashaun could take you up to The City for the shopping? Use your company expense account for everything. Make sure you file the receipts."

"Sure, no problem. Anything wrong?" she replied.

"No, no. Everything's fine. I have to meet a contact at the Q'Boom. They may have something we're interested in. I may talk about it with Eddie. There might be, you know, something mutually beneficial, and at any rate it may take a few hours," he said looking at his watch for no good reason.

"Sure, I'll let him know right now. Is he at Eddie's warehouse?" Brenda couldn't help but look pleased. Going with Rashaun instead of Savion would be a welcome pleasure.

"Uh, yeah, he's helping pack something up for the Gliese people. He should be free after lunch," he said.

Whenever Savion dissembled and provided extra pointless information, Brenda had found that it meant he was either hiding something or just plain lying. Undoubtedly it had to do with the boxes in the van, and more than likely with that new girl he had been hitting on lately at the club. She assumed that he had already made some headway with her. The girl looked almost half his age, as usual.

5

Benita had become a talented and experienced actress, though few would ever see her perform. Her work was mixed together with that of other actors, and distilled into an immense blob of numbers that drove the behavior of robots, both real and virtual. She had never studied drama, nor had she ever acted in a play or a video. In fact, she had studied chemistry and biology in college.

Her acting career began soon after she could only find employment as a lab technician in a biotech company near South San Francisco. After about half a year, she felt that she was drifting into depression from the long, monotonous hours and overly aggressive production goals. The switch to acting started on a whim after hearing snippets of conversation at a local café. FfēFfē Automata was holding large scale auditions open to anyone and everyone, to gather data for the training of virtual characters. That sounded potentially interesting, and when she looked it up she found that the salaries were unusually generous, bordering on lavish. Certainly more than she was making at the time. Now, seven years later, she was an experienced behavior capture actress specializing in security, surveillance, and intelligence gathering.

It had gradually accustomed her to enjoy more and more of the finer trappings of life. Some oenology courses a few years ago had equipped her to accumulate a closetful of wines well above supermarket grade. The commercial posters of her college years had long since been replaced by original works by local and even international painters, sculptors, and illustrators, or at least by signed archival prints of some fairly well-known artists. On her frequent art gallery outings, she could hold her own with the owners and had even occasionally outbid others for pieces she found particularly interesting.

Benita gazed out the window as the CalRail train she rode slowed down to a stop at the Redwood City station. People waiting to get on were milling around on the platform. A scruffy-looking sixtyish woman was carefully examining the contents of some trash and recycling bins.

"Your car will be here by the time you're off the train," said Zag through Benita's specs audio. He was standing outside on the platform more or less where she had been looking. He was wearing a beige trench coat and some chic sunglasses, like a modern day private eye.

It would be about a 15 or 20 minute ride to Rameshwar Thakkar's home in the genteel town of Woodside, California, in which scores of billionaires and several trillionaire contenders made their homes. Now old and infirm, he and his protégé Joe Zheng had founded FfēFfē Automata about a dozen years ago, when Thakkar was already 62 years old. At the time, Joe was a 36 year old rising star at a video game company both had been working at, and ended up doing most of the heavy lifting at their new startup. Now Zheng was 48 and chairman of the board.

As far as Benita knew, Thakkar was now dying of cancer and was confined to a wheelchair, a fate that even the ultra-wealthy such as he could not always buy themselves out of. He still managed a small research and development team at FfēFfē, working on making the virtual characters and robots more and more capable of generating intelligent adaptive behavior with deeper and deeper specialized knowledge. These days he was too weak to go to the office every day, but strong enough to still attend teleconferences with his team and hold in-person business meetings at his luxurious home. He was the sort who would rest when he died, and no sooner.

It was just before ten in the morning on a warm, sunny, late October day, not yet chilly enough to merit a sweater, when Benita's car pulled up in front of the Thakkar home. The foothills in the distance were a mottled green and golden brown, and maybe a third of the trees on them were dead from years of on again, off again drought and the resulting carnival of tree parasites. It was a landscape of tinder waiting for a spark. Like many residences in Woodside, the home was more of a compound. Several acres of greenery seemingly immune to the surrounding drought framed an expansive two-story vaguely Craftsman-style home.

Across the street, in front of a similarly plutocratic estate, a young man carefully polished an expensive-looking bright red gasoline-powered sports car, the kind that she presumed required skill and tenacity to operate. From the open front door she could see pedals, levers, knobs, and other controls that one would need to monitor or manipulate at the high speeds the car could undoubtedly achieve. Benita had never learned to drive one of those old cars, and never really felt the need or the interest in doing so. The young man was athletic and attractive, with closely cropped curly red hair, freckles, and the hypertrophic musculature of someone who spent far too much time in the gym, and consumed an unhealthy quantity and variety of nutritional supplements. He glanced at her with perfunctory interest as she got out of the car, and was still studying her as she turned to walk up to the Thakkar house. This bolstered Benita's confidence in preparation for her imposing meeting.

She walked along the gently winding cobblestone path that led through the large and well-tended front garden to the front door. Two icons appeared in her field of view, and she twiddled each one. The first allowed her to identify herself, and the second was akin to a doorbell.

A robotic butler opened the door, presumably a beta version of a model being readied for its market debut by her employer. He was somewhat taller than she was, with a vaguely athletic build and a fortyish looking mannequin face. She was unaware that they would have such finely crafted bodies. The overall look was indeed that of a butler, with the outer covering alternating between a warm charcoal finish that looked like a woolen suit, and an understated off-white with a texture of finely woven linen. Some of the external fixtures, such as certain exposed sensors, small button or switch panels, access hatches, and the like, were colored and textured to give the impression of cufflinks, a bow tie, pockets, and other butlery accessories. What corresponded to his exposed skin was ivory-colored plastic that had a fine, satiny finish. A high end product, no doubt about it. The early adopters were undoubtedly the sort of people who lived in places like Woodside. Not too many others could afford them, this early on.

He motioned her in, and she was now in a spacious and sumptuously appointed foyer. On the left wall, above some beautiful antique chairs and cabinetry, was a large painting of an apparently Hindu mythical scene. A beautiful blue-skinned goddess floated above her earthly sword-wielding and monkey-faced female champion, who was attempting the rescue of a frightened-looking damsel, who in turn found herself in the process of being carried off by some truly wicked-looking demons. The demon leader was a formidable male with multiple heads, who appeared to be bellowing angrily at the simian heroine and waving a fearsome sword. A swarm of lesser demons was fanning out from the kidnapping scene, some towards the heroine and the rest out to the forest in all directions. Some forest animals looked on with expressions of worry bordering on panic.

"Do you like the painting?" asked the robot.

"It's beautifully done," she answered. "I'm not familiar with the mythology, though." The robot nodded silently.

Past the foyer, there was a gallery with a staircase on the right hand side that curved up to a mezzanine level. There were paintings, sculptures and fine furniture everywhere, all carefully placed and visually appealing, a splendid pageant of elegance and good taste, like something one might find in a catalog of expensive home furnishings. In fact, most of it looked unused, as if their purpose was almost exclusively decorative. The residents of this beautiful home evidently sat in chairs, read books, or opened drawers only on special occasions.

The dominant painting here was a life-sized portrait of her host, Dr. Rameshwar Thakkar with his late wife Tiffany Chen. He looked to be in his mid-40s, and she couldn't have been older than 30, about Benita's age. Both were dressed in formal attire. They were standing on cobblestones surrounded by a richly appointed garden, with a stone arch and some stone benches in the background. The setting provided a sense of timelessness to the image, but it was their eyes that drew her attention. Sharp, coal black, not quite stern, an expression somewhere between the eyes of monarchs who were fully aware of their station in life, and those of seasoned professional grifters together evaluating a potential mark. The painting must have been at least 20 years old. Tiffany Chen had been killed during The Riots, when their daughters were still young.

Out of the corner of her eye, Benita saw a young woman approaching. She looked to be about 20 years old, but Benita was not sure. The robot butler was suddenly nowhere to be seen or heard, nor was anyone else.

The girl was slender, with a hint of athleticism, and not especially tall. She wore a close-fitting one-piece dress with enough of a neckline to show some modest cleavage, in spite of her petite curves. The soft-looking fabric of the dress was like a second skin.

She came up close to Benita, and at the last moment seemed to trip and fall against her, and Benita had to catch her to keep her from falling. The girl's short and puffy hair had a gentle, lilting scent, like that of a cactus flower, and unlike any shampoo or conditioner Benita had ever used. As the girl raised her head up close to Benita's face, her half-opened eyes were dark and mischievous, like those of a cat preparing to hunt down a mouse, behind a pair of sleek and very expensive looking specs. She smiled, her unpainted lips the color of aged Bordeaux. Her golden complexion nonetheless seemed drained of color.

"Oops! Thank you," she said, pulling up slowly, and grinding herself against Benita as she slithered to her feet. Her lithe body slid through Benita's hands and undoubtedly generated a wave of signals in Benita's body suit.

"No problem," replied Benita, steadying the girl perhaps a bit more than necessary.

The girl's eyes were locked onto Benita's. A constant rhythm of barely perceptible saccades were scanning Benita's every movement, gesture, and breath.

"Strong. Who are you?" the girl said. Benita shrugged.

"A random person," replied Benita.

"Hmmph!" was the reply. The girl slowly pulled away from Benita, running the tip of her tongue along the rim of her lower lip, never breaking her gaze.

"Are you police?" asked the girl.

"No, I work at Dr. Thakkar's company. Were you expecting the police?"

"Hmm," she said, standing straight for a moment, looking Benita up and down with her eyes. She paused briefly on the shoes, with a fleeting look of puzzlement. Disdain?

"Is your father in?" Benita by now assumed the girl was one of Thakkar's famously spoiled daughters.

The girl ran her right hand through her hair, turning almost completely around and finally looking away so that Benita could get another look at her. Who knows? Maybe this time she'd see something she liked. Benita looked, but didn't show as much interest as the girl expected.

The girl faced her again, with a perverse smile, grunting a strange, staccato, quiet laughter. She went limp and fell towards Benita once more, this time with her full weight. Benita struggled to keep her from falling to the floor. She had gone completely rag doll. If she was faking it, she was doing a stellar job. Benita looked for a chair or something, and dragged the girl to a nearby loveseat and set her down on it. She seemed completely unconscious, breathing raspily.

As Benita laid the girl down and started to panic, the robot butler calmly entered the room and approached them. Nothing in his manner indicated alarm, which Benita found unusual. Practically every model of FféFfé's virtual characters was trained to take command in an emergency and make sure everyone, especially customers, got all the assistance they needed. She assumed the physical robots would be even more driven.

The robot was followed by two of his fellows, who were preparing to pick the girl up and take her somewhere. The other robots didn't seem concerned either. This must not have been the first time. They waited a few moments for the girl to regain consciousness, then two of them assisted her up the staircase.

"The professor will see you now, Ms. Garcés." said the remaining robot.

"Who was that?" asked Benita, still a bit jostled.

"That is Miss Pari Thakkar, Ms. Garcés, Dr. Thakkar's youngest daughter."

"Interesting girl."

The robot politely ignored the accompanying smirk and proceeded to lead Benita to Dr. Thakkar.

6

Sue, Tavo, and Raúl backed their trucks into filling stalls at the desalination station. It would take about an hour to fill them.

"Well, back to sleep," said Raúl, winking at Tavo. He got back into his truck, put his seat back, and placed his farmer's hat over his face before pulling his door closed.

Sue looked at Tavo with an impish smile and flicked a lock of hair away from her forehead. Unlike the other two trucks, Tavo's had a double cab, with colorful little curtains on the side windows. He drew her close, and they kissed languidly. She led him into the rear cab of his truck, and he shut the door behind them. They had the better part of an hour.

*　*　*　*　*

Ten minutes later, another tanker truck backed into the stall next to Raúl's. It was from Gliese Genetics, coincidentally the farm at the very end of Pequod Lane, just past Crazy Ladies. Another two Gliese trucks filled the remaining berths and began filling their tanks as well. The three drivers, two women and a man walked across the parking lot to a restaurant that overlooked Elkhorn Slough, each of them wearing a company issued beige baseball cap. They ordered coffee and chatted among themselves in a glass enclosed dining area. The brisk weather left the deck area outside practically empty of people.

Gliese Genetics was more than a company. It was a privately held intentional community with an ideology whose leftward leanings belied its highly profitable business model. Gliese didn't have employees, it had members, much like a co-operative. It did not fall under the Green New Deal co-op legislation because it was privately funded and chose not to receive the kinds of tax-deductible contributions that most other co-ops received. The Gliese community members were of a somewhat older demographic than most coastal California co-ops, thirty-somethings as opposed to twenty-somethings. Co-ops with older age groups tended to be further inland where resources were less expensive and life was less exciting, but Gliese Genetics was a high tech purveyor of genetically modified plants and animals, some of them rather heavily modified, so they stayed near the coastal tech scene.

They were noticeably cliquish, and kept mainly to themselves. To outsiders, their internal dynamics were definitely cultish, with their days full of organized group activities and communal living. A small executive team of three people managed the business and oversaw the community's affairs. They made sure that social cohesion was maintained and everyone's concerns were always satisfactorily addressed and resolved. It was rare for a person to want to leave, but when they did they were sent to one of Gliese's sister organizations elsewhere in Northern California, Oregon or Washington state, usually never to be heard from again. Gliese itself had occasionally received such individuals who had not been satisfied at one of these other communities, but still wanted the social dynamics of the group-oriented culture and the greater care taken in the selection of prospective community members as compared with other co-ops. As far as they were concerned, Green New Deal co-ops would take just about anyone, whereas Gliese ensured that each new recruit was a good fit for the community. A few dozen people went through the lengthy interview process each year, but only a 2 or 3 were selected, if that.

Like any other co-op, the staff was small because most of the administrative work was done by software. The people at Gliese were guided continuously in their duties by means of the beige baseball caps, supposedly made at one of the sister sites. Through them, virtual characters and other information appeared in their minds as if in a dream. They were like specs, but were a completely different system that none of the conventional co-ops had, and the imagery was more like a hallucination than a digital overlay. This allowed reasonably intelligent people without advanced degrees to operate sophisticated scientific apparatus, synthesize complex chemicals and genetic material, maintain plant and animal tissue cultures, and carry the organisms through from the petri dish to a living plant or animal, guided by human figures within the dream world. These virtual beings were much more articulate, knowledgeable, and insightful than those in the average corporate specs account. Gliese members' ability to create wealth was thereby fabulously magnified, so it was quite a profitable little company. The dream world was known to the community members as The New World.

The extensive use of software guides and assistants made for low stress and high productivity, and was not unique to Gliese. It was like being part of a social club with a few duties that were easily taken care of. The ghostly software made sure that everyone fulfilled their duties correctly and in a timely manner, and most day to day background operations were carried out by a team of skilled virtual managers. Automated company management and operations formed the foundation of a massive wealth-creation engine that was gradually expanding throughout the nation and the world. The Riots of a dozen years ago were a rapidly fading memory, especially for twenty- and thirty-somethings, unless they had been directly traumatized by the violence.

*   *   *   *   *

After a while, Tavo and Sue got out of his truck with breathless smiles on their faces. They slowly walked hand in hand towards the restaurant. It was a beautiful day if you didn't mind the cool ocean breeze, and they were in such a great mood that they didn't mind it at all, chatting and tittering their way across the parking lot.

As they entered the glassed-in dining area, they caught sight of the Gliese folks, and the Gliese folks saw them. Sue nodded a greeting at the guy, who nodded back, and Tavo did the same with the two women.

There was no further contact between the water tankers of The Crazy Ladies Agricultural Cooperative and those of **Gliese Genetics**.

Sue and Tavo sat near the lengthy window facing the ocean, at the opposite end of the room relative to the Gliese drivers, who were by now oblivious of them. Outside, about a half dozen small boats of various kinds lazily plied the inlet from the ocean, which formed a small network of fairly deep channels lined with a variety of aquatic parks and businesses. A few seagulls diligently patrolled the restaurant from the air. On a warmer day people would be sitting outside and the birds might have gotten a steady stream of food scraps, but not today. A sea lion could be heard loudly complaining about something in the distance.

Tavo could see the Gliese people sitting at their table, chatting over coffee and some food. They looked friendly enough. He wondered why they all so conscientiously avoided contact with the Crazy Ladies staff. Contact between the two farms was rare. Tavo had never spoken with any of them, and as far as he knew neither had Sue. He never recognized them at local co-op parties, and rarely ran into them in public. In fact, the desalinators might be the only place they crossed paths.

Tavo and Sue each got a cup of coffee and headed out for their trucks.

"We should be friends with the Gliese folks. We see each other practically every day," he said.

Sue wrinkled her nose a bit.

"They're kind of snotty. I've tried to start conversations with them but they always break them off. They always sit far away from us."

"Has anyone ever talked to them? You know, been friends with them?"

"Not really," she answered. "There was this one girl, she was older than us. In her thirties. I think she used to be in the military or whatever. Alice, I think was her name. She worked in the greenhouses near the fence on the Gliese side. People say they tried to ignore her, but she just kept on trying. There was one guy there that she was interested in, and he didn't mind talking to her. Then she started going over there, and sometimes was missing at dinner time. Then one day they said she left Crazy Ladies and we all started seeing her on the Gliese side. She does stuff off site, because you can see her drive in and out with that same

Gliese guy. People say those two have something going. I'll point her out next time I see her."

"So what's the deal over there? People say it's a cult or something," asked Tavo. Tavo had only been at Crazy Ladies for about a year. He had been at a similar co-op in Orange County for about two and a half years, and before that he had been an automated freight vehicle technician at a large parcel delivery company in Los Angeles for a little over three years. There was plenty of work in that field, and he was able to pick and choose among several co-ops. This was the first time he had lived in northern California.

"They're some kind of socialist capitalist crazyist cult that has to do with wearing baseball caps and being really polite all the time. They're like Mormons, only they don't go out and try to convince you to join them. Basically, they *don't* want you to join them. Supposedly it's really hard to. It took Alice a few weeks to get in there. They're part of some network of anti-Green New Deal co-ops or something weird like that." She was fairly dismissive and disinterested, but Tavo's curiosity was piqued.

"Also, those baseball caps they wear? It's like their own private specs world," she said, "at least that's what people say. They never let anyone else put one on. It's a really big deal to them."

7

The robot led Benita out through a set of French doors in the back of the gallery into a xeriscaped yard the size of a small city park. They walked along a path that led to a house-like outbuilding, one of three that she could see. They entered, passed through a small receiving area, and into the main part of the structure, which turned out to be mainly one large room that seemed to have been used as an artist's studio for many years. Large windows on the wide south facing side let in plenty of sun, and the studio was much warmer than the outside gardens.

There were some dressing room dividers and other kinds of partitions that divided the space up into regions. One area had a couple of easels and work tables with shelves full of painting materials, canvases, bottles, cans, and so on. Another had a variety of materials, power tools, and work surfaces for carpentry. Yet another had electronic and mechanical parts, including a few finished and half-finished toy-like robots. Here and there were an espresso machine, a wet bar, reading areas, a ping pong table, and a billiard table. The odd thing about the place was that it all seemed to have been unused for a long time. The espresso machine and billiard table had plastic covers, the bar had visible dust on it, and the ping pong table was folded up. The painting area was neat and tidy, and there was no smell of linseed oil or paints. What few canvases there were stood leaning against a wall, covered with dusty drop cloths.

The light was bright but had a stale stillness to it, as if the room wasn't really a room, but a distant nostalgic memory of one. The room had died and was now not much more than an old photograph of itself. Finally, at the far end of the space, in an area that must have at one time been used for birthday parties and other celebrations, sat Dr. Thakkar in an easy chair wearing a compact and unobtrusive geriatric exoskeleton. There were a couple of other exoskeleton sets nearby, and a variety of tablets and other electronic devices on tables here and there. He appeared to be wearing a full behavior capture suit much like her own under his clothes. She couldn't bring herself to ask why. A folded wheelchair was parked near the window.

Although she had never actually met him, Dr. Thakkar couldn't have been much older than his early seventies or so, by Benita's calculations. The person in the chair looked much older. He was thin and wiry, and looked too frail and weak to get up on his own without the aid of a geriatric exoskeleton. His swarthy skin had turned sallow, and was mottled by discolorations. He sat hunched over, seemingly alienated and embittered, until Benita noticed that he was smiling at her and weakly holding out a hand to greet her. He was a living photo within a photo. *That's my grandpa, right before he died*, might say a grandchild, pointing him out in the picture. *I never knew him, he died before I was born.*

Benita and the robot stopped in front of him and the robot said: "This is Ms. Garcés, Dr. Thakkar."

Benita shook his hand carefully, gently, as one might pick up a hummingbird barely alive after having been clawed out of the air by a cat. He motioned that she sit down in a comfortable chair facing him. The exoskeleton was surprisingly quiet and responsive.

"Wilkins, bring us some refreshments," said Thakkar, raising an eyebrow at Benita so that she might request something specific.

"Mineral water, very little ice," she said.

"Some lime juice?" asked Thakkar, his voice creaking like the door of an old cabinet.

"Yes, please," said Benita, some genuine pleasantness in her voice.

"The usual for me, Wilkins, thank you," he said and turned towards Benita. Wilkins the robot bowed like an old-time movie butler and went off.

With noticeable effort, the old engineer prepared to say something. Here was the man, who together with Joe Zheng founded FfēFfē Automata the old Silicon Valley way, out of a suburban garage with little more than a handful of credit cards and a few patents that Zheng had filed on his own, at no small expense. The rest, as the cliché goes, was history. Each of the men was worth billions of dollars, and FfēFfē had been filling the world with a wide variety of intelligent, friendly, and useful virtual characters for over a decade, and now they were bringing them into the physical world in the form of robots like Wilkins.

"The usual, for me, is chicken noodle soup," he said finally. "A lot like the canned stuff, but with real chicken and real noodles." A staccato vocalization reminiscent of his young daughter scraped out of his throat, and Benita took it to mean that he was chuckling at his own joke. She smiled warmly as well.

In spite of her light clothing, Benita was starting to sweat. There was a small pile of paper napkins on the coffee table next to her chair, and she took one to start dabbing the sweat from her face. The sunlight streaming through the windows had made the room a greenhouse.

"Yes, it is warm in here," he observed. "Everywhere else I'm shivering cold. I sleep back there." He signaled with a glance and an index finger towards a small area behind an antique Japanese partition where there was a bed, a night table, a couple of dressers, and a wardrobe.

"Years ago I would have asked Wilkins for some wine, but..." he raised his hands in a *what can I do* gesture. "As you might already know, I have cancer, and it is well advanced in the process of getting the better of me," he said. "Sadly, I have learned that all the money in the world is not enough to stave it off."

Just in time to interrupt the grim news, Wilkins arrived with the refreshments, and set the tray on the coffee table before them. He gave the mug of soup to Thakkar, with a spoon in it, and a glass with just the right amount of ice in it to Benita. It had a teaspoon in it as well. Before she could say anything, the butler handed her a small shot glass of freshly squeezed lime juice, Mexican-style. He waited for her to pour it into her glass then handed her the opened bottle of chilled mineral water. Benita poured the water into the glass with a bit of stirring. She sipped it, and it was good. A minor luxury that she realized she had never had.

The butler turned towards Thakkar, who gave an abbreviated nod, and the butler went off again, taking the tray with him.

"This room," he motioned towards it with his free hand, "is my final resting place. What comes after, is of no concern to me."

"Why did I ask for you, specifically?" he began again. "We've never met, but many have noticed you, at the company. Your work has been very valuable. You do it very well. The behavior you've generated for us is a critical part of many of our products. It will be in our new surveillance and intelligence robots as well as a mix-in for the consumer virtual characters. News of your skills has made it all the way out to me, and now I need the services of someone just like you."

Thakkar had fixed his gaze on Benita, and she now saw that the portrait painter had captured it very well. It was steady and penetrating. It was the gaze of a predator, waiting for the right moment to take its prey. Like his daughter a few moments ago, he was watching her and constantly gathering telemetry from her.

8

"So, what, exactly, can I do for you?" asked Benita.

"I need you to gather information. You'll wear your rig and gather very detailed information. I will review everything you capture, and it's very, very important that you pull no punches, ever. Whatever is out there, no matter what, no matter who, I want to see it," he said. He leaned forward about as much as a person could in his circumstance, aided by the exoskeleton. "I really can't emphasize that enough. There will be things that you may not want me to see, but I have to see them. For your sake, I guarantee the utmost discretion and confidentiality. I will not judge you. If you knew me, you'd know I cannot judge you. Only my small team, a few of my machines, and I will see the material. For my sake, you must never, ever shield me from anything."

"Will this be 24/7 or only during actual work?"

"It will be continuous, as long as you're wearing your gear. Your private life is your own business, of course, and it will be respected just as it has always been," he said. "Your feed will now be routed to us instead of your usual team. It's all been arranged."

Benita was used to having her every move uploaded to FfēFfē Automata's boundless data empire, at least while she was wearing the company behavior capture suit. When she wanted more privacy, she wore suits of her own and switched the specs to a more personal mode, which she assumed went only to her Blam account and not to FféFfé. You could never really tell, of course.

"Anyway, I trust your judgment. You aren't the first person doing this, by the way," he said. "Your predecessor is married to my oldest daughter, Aradhya. His name is Mohan Bakaya. He works at FféFfé, same as you. Does behavior capture as well. You may have met him?" He seemed hopeful for an answer.

"The name vaguely rings a bell," she answered, "but no, I don't think I ever have. What section was he in?"

Thakkar shrugged, as if it didn't matter.

"I need you to see what's going on at a little shop in San Mateo. Antiques and *objets d'art*, supposedly. Much more than that, I believe. Much more."

Benita raised an eyebrow.

"Nothing illegal or dangerous," he reassured her. "At least nothing beyond a bit of the gray market trade, maybe some stolen goods. They're secretive, sure. Paranoid maybe, and of course you'll have to be on your toes."

"Can I meet with your son-in-law, Mohan? Get up to speed on what he's found so far, maybe see some of his video capture data?" she asked. "If I have to be armed or anything..."

"No, no. Nothing like that. Do you own a firearm or a taser or anything?" he asked, seemingly out of curiosity. "I assume you have company issue. If not, Wilkins will provide whatever you need. Unfortunately, it seems that Mohan has run off with another woman." Deft change of subject, almost in mid-sentence.

Benita wanted to backtrack a bit.

"Have you met my daughters? Have you heard any gossip or rumors about them? They are probably all true," he said, with a detectable note of bitterness. "Truth be told, we're not a good family. We're not really nice people. People like me are the ones who make a lot of money. Not nice people. The Thakkars are good at getting what we want. Mohan wasn't a very good fit with us."

"I met a young woman just now, Pari?"

"Aha. My youngest. That brings us more to the point. She's involved with this little 'antique shop'," he air-quoted the latter. "Seems like the owner has been brainwashing her, and exploiting her. She's involved in whatever little mysteries they have going on out there. That's also part of what I need you to find out."

"About Mohan," she started.

"Mohan, yes," he broke in, pretending to wax nostalgic, "A very likable young man, a charmer. He spent a bit of time in Jammu and Kashmir some years ago, apparently fighting in the hills," he recounted. "On *our* side," he emphasized, looking directly at her. She assumed that this meant on the Indian side.

"He was here illegally for a while, overstayed his student visa. We hired him as a behavior capture model, put his papers in order, and he eventually met Aradhya, my eldest daughter. They fell in love, I assume, and a few months later they got married. We got along very well, and at some point I asked him to look into this shop. Meanwhile, Aradhya got bored with him, as she always has, and things went sour. Now he's gone. Ran off with some skanky member of their dubious circle of friends, from what I gather."

"Did he leave any notes, or media? May I see what he got for you?" she asked.

He shook his head solemnly. "We had the same arrangement I'm proposing to you. Absolute confidentiality. You know how personal these things can be. In any case, I want fresh eyes. I want to see what correlations and discrepancies you find. We'll provide you with enough material to give you context."

Benita finished her drink and set it down on the coffee table. She ran her gaze along the diverse objects in the different partitioned regions of the room. It was as if they were halfway packed up to be moved into storage.

"Of course," he began again. "There will be additional compensation. As far as FfēFfē is concerned, you're on a special project and will be making twice your current salary for its duration. Plus expenses, which will go on an account you will be provided. No expense reports, by the way." The last part was intended as some kind of rhetorical maraschino cherry.

"So, nothing from Mohan? Any other information I can use to start out?" she asked.

Thakkar shook his head. "You'll have a robot at your disposal. One of the new ones, specialized in surveillance and intelligence gathering. You'll also have next year's capture gear. Believe me, it's improved."

"So when do we start?" she said.

"Starting now, if you're up for it. You'll deal with Wilkins, mainly, and machines in his crew. They'll provide a lot of background, some of it from Mohan," he answered. "Authentication, authentication, authentication," he said emphatically, again looking her directly in the eyes. "This is all extremely confidential."

"Of course. I'm a stickler myself."

"Good," he replied. "Your first task is today. No need to beat around the bush. You'll be conducting a search of a private residence in San Mateo. It belongs to one Savion Bennington, the owner of the antique shop. We believe he's in possession of materials that pose a significant national security threat. It'll be your job to find them at his home. He will be out until late tonight, so you'll have at least a two hour window in which to work."

"A residential search? Will I be accompanied by law enforcement?"

"No, you'll go in on your own with an avatar we'll provide. You'll be supervised at all times and in constant contact with us through the avatar. Don't worry about the legalities. FfēFfē has all the requisite authorizations to operate as a private law enforcement agency at the local, state, and federal level. As long as we share all evidence we find, eventually, and abide by the pertinent statutes, we're fine. We're basically on contract with the federal government for a variety of projects."

"Nobody will be home?"

"No," said Thakkar, waving it off as unimportant. "He lives alone, and we have intelligence indicating that he'll be in The City buying work clothes for one of his assistants."

"What, a work uniform? Office attire? He has to go to SF to buy that?" asked Benita.

"No," he answered, "The assistant does some, shall we say, one-on-one sales of his merchandise to wealthy clients and needs to dress the part. They're going to some fairly high end shops."

"And how do you know these things? Do you have people in the field on him?"

"Not at the moment. It's mostly electronic intelligence. We don't have anyone on the ground. That's precisely what *your* role is going to be."

Benita saw Wilkins enter from the door on the far end of the great room, heading their way. Time to go, apparently. Benita stood to leave.

"I want you to know, I appreciate your help very much. If there's anything you need, and I mean *anything*, let Wilkins know. He and his crew are at your service." he said, standing from his chair and extending his hand to bid farewell. Benita shook hands with as much daintiness as before, but it probably wasn't necessary. Either he was stronger than he made himself out to be, or that was one high-tech exoskeleton.

"If you find anything else I need to know, please send it my way," she said, by way of good-bye.

Thakkar bowed his head, and Benita followed Wilkins back to the house. Already some new icons had appeared in her field of vision.

Once in the gallery, under the all-seeing gaze of Thakkar and his late wife, Wilkins paused and turned to her.

"We've sent some information to get started, and access to an account from which you can draw for your expenses. Use whatever you need, we'll let you know if it's too much. Don't worry about it," he said.

"He said something about a robot?" said Benita. She had not yet had a chance to work closely with any of the new prototypes. Now *that* would be interesting.

A voice called from the mezzanine.

"Excuse me, a word? Please?" asked another young woman. This must be Aradhya. Wilkins turned to look at her, then at Benita, and left the room. Aradhya turned and started to walk away from the railing, and when her head was about to disappear past it she stopped and paused to look at Benita. Spoiled rich girl? Check.

Benita headed up the staircase.

9

Just over two years earlier, months before being diagnosed with liver cancer, Thakkar had taken on the role of Emeritus Director of Frontier Technology. The post had been created by FfēFfē just for him. He felt that the word "emeritus" in a title added aromas of "annoying old fart being kept out of people's way," or "retiree who can't figure out what to do with his time." In practice it meant that he had a small technical staff, access to the full technological might of the company (including its extensive staff of skilled behavior capture actors), a substantial budget, standing invitations to important meetings, and freedom to explore whatever he wanted. It turned out there was a project he had wanted to work on for quite a while.

One of the original insights he and his co-founder Joe Zheng had had at the start was to capture certain biometrics from the behavior actors, create machine learning mini-models out of them, and then feed their outputs into the main machine learning model that drove the virtual characters' movements and vocalizations.

As the data were repeatedly ground through the algorithm, a landscape began to appear in the initially formless mass of numbers. Not a landscape of mountains and valleys, but one in which the mass of numbers began to resolve the myriad features of human behavior. Subtle movements of the body, meaningful gestures, sly looks, soft voices and shouts, a run of conversation, the skills of walking or serving a cup of coffee, and countless other shards of human behavior sculpted the mass of numbers into an abstract landscape of features.

As wave after wave of data came in, the features on this landscape of numbers grew finer still, each spark of human experience taking its place as a grain of sand or a pebble, a petal on a flower or a vein on a leaf in a pastoral scene. The billions of numbers ceased to be a formless mass of randomness, and gradually became the intricate web of a human body's movement through the world, of its voice speaking, of its furtive glances to its fellows, of skills and activities, and of intuitions and innate understandings of some part of the world of *Homo sapiens*. The numbers became human behavior in the same way that stacked sheets of numbers became images and videos. Their smudges of pixels were themselves tiny numerical clumps standing in for fine gradations of hue and value that swam organically through time to form a moving image. That the smudges represented the iris of an eye or the wing of a bird was a matter of subjective interpretation.

To describe the content of this mass of numbers would be a fool's errand. Theirs was a deep and unfathomable encoding, a mystical representation, an enigmatic simulacrum of body and soul. The scientists and engineers who plumbed these numbers, the psychologists and choreographers who guided the actors through thousands of hours of varied and repetitive behavior, all were magicians summoning a mysterious spirit and capturing it in the form of a digital avatar, the sacred rites of ancient conjurers harnessed for FfēFfē's and Blam's filthy lucre.

Capturing human behavior at this level of detail was a quantum leap for Blam. In the market economy realpolitik that drove and ruthlessly weeded out tech companies, no stone could be left unturned, and no detail of consumer or enterprise behavior could be left unexamined. Anything short of complete and total modeling of the human species was simply not enough. The avatars would be their tireless explorers and faithful missionaries, weaving their way into people's lives and into the deepest recesses of their day to day activities.

The algorithm also received biometric data from sensors on the body suit that gathered electrocardiogram, electroencephalogram, breathing, and body temperature data. Thakkar and Zheng needed a way for inanimate virtual characters and robots to have some kind of emotional tone. They invented the biometric mini-model for this, a touch of pure magic.

The mini-models took the same inputs as the main model, but instead of producing behavior as an output, they reproduced the biometric data gathered from the human actors. One mini-model reproduced an electrocardiogram trace, another the rhythms of the actor's breathing, still others reproduced several channels of electroencephalogram, and body temperature at various locations. When these mini-models were fed into the virtual character's main machine learning model, in addition to sights and sounds and movements driving the virtual character's movements and speech it was also receiving a distillation of the human actor's emotional tone, as represented by the biometric signals. Things that got the actor's pulse racing got the corresponding mini-model's pulse racing. Things that got the actor's breathing to accelerate or to slow down, did the same to the breathing mini-model. The same was true with EEG activity and body temperature.

The coursing of blood, the beating of hearts, a breathless gasp, a change in mood, these could now become part of the model. Whether this meant that the virtual characters had real emotions or even real consciousness, as opposed to being only clever machine simulations, was a raging discussion that had spilled over from academia into general popular culture. Most users gave free reign to their natural tendency to anthropomorphize anything that resembled a person, and so developed more and more intimate bonds with the virtual characters as the sophistication of their behavior increased.

Thakkar wanted to push it to the next step, one that had been impractical and prohibitively expensive in prior years. He wanted to capture a higher resolution reading of the human actors' minds, to go beyond the low resolution information that came out of conventional electroencephalograms and gather something much closer to reading the actor's thoughts themselves. He and Zheng had discussed the possibility since the very beginning, but until now it had remained a dream. Now, such a thing existed: small lightweight probes that measured the extremely weak but information rich magnetic fields that surrounded biological brains. These diaphanous emanations were the mind's twin, its shadow, its very spirit. Everything that went on in the mind was reflected in them.

Thakkar's team was able to build a dozen prototype magnetometry caps and integrate them with the rest of the sensors the actors usually wore. Like the caps with only EEG electrodes, the new version covered most of the head, leaving the face uncovered, like a swim cap.

The virtual characters would have an additional mini-model trained with the human magnetometry data that would generate simulated magnetic field measurements. These signals would then be fed into the main virtual character control model, just like the other mini-models for heart rate or respiratory frequency. This mini-model, hypothesized Zheng and Thakkar, would be the most detailed simulation of the human mind ever created, and it would help drive the behavior of their virtual characters and robots.

Now, two years later, these mini-models were part of the new line of walking, talking, physical robots.

10

FfēFfē's behavior capture process was vast. The company had well over a thousand actors on staff in several sections, each section devoted to different kinds of human activities. In those early days of the magnetometry project, Thakkar only had 25 actors at his disposal. That would give him maybe 25,000 of hours worth of data in a year, compared to the millions of hours that were going into the next major release version of the virtual characters. He had 3 talented machine learning engineers doing all sorts of cheats and tricks to leverage as much of the existing behavior capture data as possible to bootstrap the new models, but there was no substitute for the real thing.

The team used a variety of offices, homes, and even retail businesses to capture data, spread out all over the San Francisco Bay Area. The actors were divided into teams covering 2 shifts per day 7 days a week. This provided the large amount of variety and redundancy needed to train usable machine learning models. One such area was a stretch of El Camino Real in San Mateo, between 25th and Borel Avenues. Other than a FfēFfē behavior capture site they often used there was nothing particularly interesting in the area. A couple of strip malls and a variety of mom and pop restaurants and shops on either side of El Camino Real were surrounded by a residential area. The actors liked it because there was a locally famous ramen joint and a respectable barbecue place in the neighborhood.

It soon became clear that the magnetometry data was distorted somewhere in that area and nowhere else. At this point the new caps and support equipment were working pretty well, so there was no escaping the conclusion that there was something weird going on nearby. It seemed to occur at random intervals and locations in that small area, usually at lunch time. Sometimes the effect was weak, and sometimes it almost completely obscured the signals being captured from the actors' brains. They were seriously thinking about avoiding the area to prevent having to discard any of their precious behavior capture data.

Thakkar and his engineers were piqued, however. The incoming distortion wasn't random noise, nor was it the monotonic hum of some standard industrial process or restaurant equipment. To their magnetometry equipment, the interfering signals looked exactly like the measurements they were gathering from the actors. It was as if there was an invisible human brain haunting and harassing them like a poltergeist.

It was a puzzle, alright. Thakkar and his crew, and maybe only a handful of people around the world, were starting to take these new sensors out of the lab and out and about in the world. Readings like these had never been done, because nobody had ever had cause or the equipment to do so. This was unexplored territory. Was this a natural phenomenon? Was it some kind of weird effect originating from certain people? Were there certain kinds of people who generated far more powerful emanations than others? Were there superheroes among us? Those last two possibilities were pretty goofy, and Thakkar and his team only mentioned them after a few beers had been consumed. Nevertheless, they were greatly intrigued. The only constant was a beige baseball cap worn by some of the locals. Could it be that the cap itself was somehow broadcasting human thought? It seemed almost as silly as believing in superheroes.

Thakkar and his crew had taken to calling the distortion in San Mateo "Tycho Magnetic Anomaly 1," or TMA-1, after a subplot in an old science fiction story. They were loathe to use the magnetometry caps to investigate, losing precious hours of behavior capture, so they used some of the electronic equipment that was used for setting up and tuning them. The instruments were capable of not just detecting the distortion, but also of providing a rich trove of analytical information about it. They examined these measurements with the video and audio data coming from the behavior capture gear, and within a few days, they had identified the mysterious source. They concluded that it was indeed the baseball cap-wearing people who occasionally sat near the actors, walked past them on the street, or drove by in their utility vans. A few times, they would be sitting at a restaurant eating lunch and some of these cap-wearing people would sit in an adjoining booth or at a table back to back with one of the actors, and the distortion would be constant until they were gone.

Over the years, there had been several reports in the scientific literature, and even in the popular press, of devices that could generate magnetic fields near a human's head and influence that person's behavior. There were cases where electroencephalographs and even magnetometers similar to those being used by Thakkar had been used to capture signals from one person, the signals then transmitted to some kind of magnetic coil worn on another person's head at another location, sometimes miles away, and the person at the receiving end would move a finger or a limb in the same way as the person at the transmitting end. In the case of transcranial magnetoencephalography, receiving subjects were even able to distinguish sounds and images that were being viewed by transmitting subjects. One researcher even tested the ability of users on the receiving end to guess what Zener card a person wearing the magnetometry sensors was looking at, the famous ESP cards of popular culture. They were able to guess the card almost 100% of the time. This caused quite a stir among students of paranormal phenomena, because Zener cards had been used for decades in the search for demonstrable extrasensory perception. Nobody had ever been able to show anything before, and yet here was a device that finally seemed to endow users with some kind of genuine telepathic power.

What if the same could be done with these mysterious magnetic anomalies? Could they be recorded somehow, then passed through a coil next to a person's head, and thereby inject intelligible information into a person's mind? What about the information captured by the FfēFfē magnetoencephalography sensors? Were they now sitting on a powerful read/write system for the human mind? What about the baseball caps? Was somebody already using such a thing out in the wild?

11

During that same time, Thakkar managed to get his hands on some of the magnetic field transmitting headsets used by scientists working in that branch of neurology, and had his engineers build a few headsets of their own, with coils matching the locations of the sensors of the FfēFfē behavior capture magnetometers. The idea was to emit magnetic fields at the same locations of the head where they had been originally captured. Same data, just send it back in at the same locations. Would the wearer sense what the original actor had going through their mind at data capture time?

In order to allay misgivings, Thakkar volunteered to be the first guinea pig. This was utterly unethical, and most likely illegal on several counts. Human experimentation was nothing to toy with. There was nothing in the growing scientific and medical literature that indicated any danger, however. In the course of obtaining the magnetometry gear and know-how, Thakkar and his team had been in lengthy meetings with the researchers who had been doing this kind of work for years. The first time was always kind of scary, though.

The system was set up in such a way that the coils were set to transmit at the same magnetic field strength as a typical behavior actor's brain, which is to say a very weak field indeed. He could adjust the strength with an app in his specs from that level all the way up to several orders of magnitude greater. He could move all the channels up evenly, or tweak each one independently. It had already been tested and calibrated with instruments. He would be the first person to actually try it on.

They were going to play magnetometry data captured from one of their actors walking down a street. There would be no video or audio provided to Thakkar, nothing but the magnetometry data captured from the actor's head. He'd have to guess where it was and what the person was seeing and hearing. His crew were watching and listening through their specs to the video and audio that had been captured at the same time as the magnetometry data. Thakkar was not clued in, so he had no idea what to expect.

"Here goes," he said, at the moment of the test.

They turned it on, and Thakkar sat there, straining to see if he felt anything, but he felt nothing. He twiddled the intensity up a notch. Nothing. More twiddling, more nothing. He was about half way up the scale, and nothing. This was disconcerting, and he hoped it wouldn't be a bust. He twiddled again.

Now there was something. He seemed to remember something, like a distant memory. A childhood memory? It didn't fade like a normal memory, though. It wasn't fragmentary. It continued, persisting in the distant fog somewhere at the edge of his consciousness. Up another notch. He was about ⅔ of the way up the exponential intensity scale.

"It's sunny, it's warm," he said, "There's shade over there, on the other side of the street? I'm a teenager?" More twiddling, at about ¾ of the way up the exponential intensity scale. According to the scientists, the whole scale was safe. He hoped they were right.

"I know where this is, I remember," he muttered, and yet, he couldn't quite pin it down. He'd been there not long ago, maybe a few weeks? More twiddling, around 85% of maximum. The hairs on the back of his neck stood to attention. His skin crawled. His mouth fell open.

"I'm walking on University Avenue in Palo Alto. I'm walking past the old Stanford Movie Theater. I'm looking at the marquee, they're playing *Forbidden Planet*. I'm passing a window with the movie poster. It's a gaudy painting of an old-fashioned Hollywood robot carrying an unconscious woman," he narrated. He was fully aware of the people in the room, and of the app he had been cautiously twiddling in his specs. He was fully present in time and space with his team in their little hardware lab. And yet, he was having a simultaneous and very vivid daydream, one that he didn't need to switch back and forth from, dividing his attention between the real and the imaginary. They were both there, sustained and fully present. It was like some kind of virtual reality running in parallel with his own consciousness, in a separate channel.

"Whichever one of you recorded this data is getting pretty excited about that girl in the red t-shirt," he said, and gently lowered the intensity back to zero. "I foresee serious privacy concerns with this stuff," he said, grinning.

The team was in awe. It hadn't really clicked in their heads that they already had half of what was needed to read and write to a human mind. Now they had the whole setup. The room was silent. Thakkar took the device off and surveyed the room. Everyone was silent, still watching the video produced by a behavior actor walking down the street, some with furrowed brows. They all had specs face, the blank, thousand-yard stare people have when mesmerized by something in their specs.

"Anyone want to try it? It doesn't hurt," he offered. For a moment, nobody responded. Some exchanged glances, especially with the now deeply blushing actor who had been the source of this behavior capture data.

"OK."

"Sure!"

"I'm after Wei Xien!"

"Let's make a sign-up sheet!"

By the end of the hour, everyone had had a try.

"OK, now let's try one of the TMA-1 samples, and see what that's about," said Thakkar. A sudden hush, and then the last person to try the headset handed it over to him. Would it be dangerous? What if it wasn't really from a person? What if it was something psychotic? How would it work spreading the same single channel all around the head on all of the little coils he had just tested?

There was only one good, clean, high quality recording, a fairly brief one where a FfēFfē cap had been deliberately placed almost back to back behind one of the beige-cap-wearing people at a deli on Borel Avenue in San Mateo, only a few blocks from where they had first starting detecting it. The actor had taken off his own magneto-encephalographic cap and put it on the high back of a chair nearest to one of the beige baseball cap wearers as he ate lunch.

Thakkar started the playback, and slowly tweaked up the intensity, as before. Soon he was hearing voices and seeing images. It seemed flatter than the sensations from their behavior capture sensors. It was like comparing a live performance to a small, low-resolution video.

His point of view was of someone eating lunch at a restaurant. He was sitting at a small table, with one other person sitting across from him, also wearing a beige baseball cap. There were two other people sitting at the table in the remaining two chairs. They were not wearing caps. The four of them were conversing, but Thakkar couldn't quite make out what they were saying. Either the audio channel was of poor quality, or perhaps they were speaking in a foreign language. He did feel he was getting the gist of what they were saying. Something about how together they would change the world. Soon it would be a better place. There was some strange notion about spirits or angels or avatars or something from a different plane of existence that would be brought down to earth, and they would fix everything. Thakkar took off the headset.

"How many people were at the table when you recorded this," he asked nobody in particular. "There were two people with caps, right? Nobody else?"

"Nobody else," answered one of the engineers. "Have a look." The young man shared a video capture, and Thakkar viewed it in his specs. It was from the point of view of the behavior capture actor sitting across the table from the chair with the FfēFfē cap that had captured the baseball cap emanations. At the next table in front of him were the same two cap-wearing people and nobody else. He put the headset back on and could clearly see four people sitting around that table. There was a time lag between the two, but there was no disputing that it was the same scene. In the specs video there were two people, and in the magnetic anomaly video there were clearly four.

"It's some kind of augmented reality device, like specs, only via magnetic fields," he said. "Two additional people are spouting some kind of inspirational propaganda to get people to work together in solidarity to bring some kind of spirits into the world. This was made by people. Or *for* people, at any rate." It soon ended and he took the headset off.

"Anyone else want to have a look?" he asked.

12

Once Benita had reached the mezzanine, Aradhya turned and walked into what appeared to be her bedroom. While technically correct, the word "bedroom" seemed to diminish the space in which Benita now found herself. This was a luxurious living room with a matching bed at one end. The upholstery of the small couch and two easy chairs was a rich chestnut-colored leather, with a texture that approached suede. Unlike the other furniture in the house, it definitely looked lived in, but by no means worn or scuffed. The visible wood grain of the furniture had an almost crystalline glow beneath its satiny surface. To her right, on a credenza, was an antique sculpture that looked like classical Greek. To her left, a floor to ceiling abstract sculpture that looked mid-20th century, it reminded her of Louise Bourgeois, whose work she had found intriguing in college art history class. There were several paintings on the walls in styles that Benita seemed to recognize, as well as many other small sculptures here and there. It was a small fortune in art.

There was a spacious, handsome desk near a window, and the bookcase next to it was filled with an intriguing variety of tomes. Unlike the impeccable books in the gallery, these looked like they received occasional use. A couple of small stacks were on the desk itself, next to a large computer screen that looked like a large wafer of dark stone. In front of the screen was plenty of room to manipulate objects in her specs.

Aradhya was dressed in an elegant, business-like dress that just passed her knees. Snug where necessary, the design allowed her to be framed in small, loose, understated drapes of fabric, a shimmering silk darker than blood red. Her specs were made of a deep red material to match. Benita wondered how many pairs of specs this woman might own. Maybe as many as she had shoes, which was undoubtedly quite a few. Aradhya sat herself on the couch, and languorously crossed her legs.

Like Pari, she was a raven-haired beauty, but Aradhya was not attempting to be some kind of sexual diva. She carried herself like a well-educated and very successful venture capitalist might, exuding power and influence from her bearing and gaze. Benita knew the type. FfēFfē was crawling with them on board meeting days and formal office celebrations. Money attracts more money, and more money attracts these peculiar creatures.

Aradhya sat looking at Benita for a few moments with a calm, neutral expression. "So, are you a private detective?" she asked finally. "Would you like a goblet of wine? I opened a nice Malbec last night, it should be at its best right now."

Benita nodded and sat in an easy chair to Aradhya's right.

"Lety, please bring the wine from last night." Lety, a prototype housemaid robot, was just then entering the room. She bowed her head slightly, and turned to fetch the wine. Like Wilkins, Lety's finish was stunning, and beautifully complemented Aradhya's bedroom *décor*.

"I'm not a private detective. I work at FfēFfē. I'm a behavior capture model in the security and surveillance section," said Benita.

"Oh, you do security guards?" asked Aradhya.

"And a variety of other things. I assume you have several of them here at the house, maybe even with my content in them," answered Benita.

"I believe they're all male, though. I wasn't aware they were going to come in female, but I suppose that makes sense. I hadn't thought about it. I do venture capital in biomedical, so that sort of thing isn't my field." Bingo. You can spot these people a mile away.

"So, what brings you here? Are you doing some 'security and surveillance' for my father?" continued Aradhya, with the spoken version of air quotes.

"Your father and I have discussed some activities I'll be working on. You understand that he holds me in his confidence", answered Benita. Aradhya raised an eyebrow.

"He holds you there, hmm?" she answered. As before, the drinks came at an opportune moment.

Lety poured the wine and handed out the goblets, left the tray on the coffee table before them, and went and stood at the far end of the room awaiting further orders. Only now Benita noticed another robot identical to Lety sitting in a chair in the shadowy corner opposite Benita. Nice choreography and additional data capture.

"My father can be a bit stern," said Aradhya.

Benita shrugged. "He was pleasant enough," she answered.

"He was quite friendly with Mohan, my husband. Did he mention him?" explored Aradhya.

"Briefly," answered Benita, "Mohan is not on my plate. This is an unrelated matter. I gathered that there was some kind of friendship between your father and Mohan." If it was a fishing expedition, then she might as well grab a pole herself.

"Mohan disappeared on me," she bit her lip a bit. "He went off with someone else and hasn't been seen again. Didn't even have the balls to file for divorce."

Benita wondered whether the wine was from last night or from earlier this morning. It went down well though. A curious interplay of berries, jam, and just a whiff of baking spice, with tannins discreetly in the background. Definitely out of her price range. Nice finish.

Benita nodded, not wanting to interrupt the flow.

"Mohan was fun," she said, "more than fun, actually, and he got on very well with my father. I hope Dad can find him." She looked at Benita expectantly, with those penetrating Thakkar eyes.

"Well if he does, it won't be thanks to me. I've got nothing to do with that," answered Benita.

"He mentioned him, though, you said."

"He did. He's not on my plate, though," said Benita, meeting Aradhya's gaze.

"Did he at least ask you to keep an eye out for him? Ask around?"

"No, that has nothing to do with the project," replied Benita. She was starting to actively repress an urge to make a snide remark. "You could report a missing person if you want. You could have one of your undoubtedly numerous lawyers look into it, if only to finally get a divorce. Is that the concern?"

"Perhaps it isn't obvious to you, but this is a delicate family matter, a private matter. We aren't going to spin up a bunch of people to go poking around, raising all sorts of suspicions about us." Now she was turning icy.

"Still, it's not on my docket," said Benita. She stood up to leave.

Aradhya motioned her to sit down, Benita stood where she was.

"I'm sorry, I'm sorry," she said, shaking her head apologetically. "You're right, of course. Happens all the time. Silly me, just another woman betrayed by some macho asshole. Please, sit. Lety?" she said towards the robot, still standing loyally on watch. Aradhya wiggled her empty goblet, and Lety came by and refilled them both. Benita gestured to only have a half goblet.

"Without knowing any details of what you and my father are focusing on, please bear in mind that you may come across information pertaining to Mohan and his whereabouts and activities. I would be very interested in being kept in the loop, at least with regards to that," said Aradhya, sounding every bit the venture capitalist. "Very interested," looking directly at Benita.

All roads lead to Mohan? That's a bit odd, thought Benita.

"What exactly did he do?" Benita sat down again.

"One day he drove off in the morning, and didn't come back," said Aradhya with a furrowing brow. "He was doing something for my Dad as well. He went to work and didn't come back. No calls, no messages, no updates, pictures, nothing. All of his devices are offline. He must have changed all of his accounts."

"What if something happened to him? Where did he work, exactly?" asked Benita.

"I don't think he's dead, if that's what you mean," answered Aradhya. "I simply can't imagine not finding out about that, in this day and age. People know him. People know *us*."

"Where does he work?" Benita asked again.

"He was at FfēFfē doing behavior capture before he started doing a few things for my Dad. I believe he did what they call 'interstitial engagement,' a fancy term for interacting with people while not doing any useful work."

"I don't think I ever met him," said Benita. Interstitial Engagement was where all of the party animals worked. That wasn't a crowd Benita ever hung out with. Aradhya gave her a puzzled, somewhat suspicious look.

"But then, my team does some fairly specific kinds of work, not general human interaction. I don't really know anyone in that section. We're on a separate campus," continued Benita.

It was starting to sound as if Mohan was one of those people without any marketable skills beyond being a very good behavior capture model. She knew of plenty of people like that at FfēFfē. They were paid well, and led wild, diffuse lives. They had gotten nothing from higher education, so it seemed, even though more than a few had advanced degrees. Sex, drugs, partying, and non-stop socializing were what they lived for.

The behavior you got from them was always charming, always engaging. They had a repertoire of consistently pleasing body language, and uncanny abilities to say the right thing at the right time all the time, especially after having been coached by the Structured Behavior staff. They were gushing fountains of human behavioral filler. They were what virtual characters and robots were expected to do when dealing with people, and not yet doing anything that required any specific knowledge or a particular skill. They were the foundation of machine empathy, of human warmth and engagement embedded in an otherwise non-living automaton. It was they who did the heavy lifting to imbue the illusion of sentience, the ghost in the machine, and they did it very well indeed. Their captured behavior, once instilled into the virtual characters, is what drew people out. It's what allowed the characters to get to know their users and learn about the subtleties of their lives, and for Blam to compile fine grained profiles of them. Hence Blam's and FfēFfē's prodigious fortunes. It was the unreasonable effectiveness of embodiment.

They were artists of real life, in the sense that real life itself was both their stage and their medium. They were impossible to live with, notoriously fickle, constitutionally unable to maintain intimate relationships or lasting commitments, and (or so Benita had heard), they fucked like bandits.

Was this what Aradhya was after? She missed the sex? If it were someone else, Benita might suspect so, but that just didn't come across. She was fishing for something, but Benita couldn't begin to guess what it was. Aradhya was silent. Her eyes slowly swept the floor around them, from one side across to the other. After a few moments, she looked back up at Benita.

"I would have hoped you could ask around? That perhaps you had mutual acquaintances? Occasionally crossed paths? Let me know if you come across any information from his last whereabouts?" Aradhya stood up abruptly, evidently the meeting was now over. Benita stood up as well.

"It was a pleasure speaking with you," said Aradhya. Her work was done. She had finished injecting whatever she had hoped to put in Benita's mind, vague and ambiguous though it seemed.

"My pleasure," answered Benita politely, then turned to leave. Aradhya did not follow, and Lety discreetly closed the door behind Benita.

13

Wilkins was waiting for her, at a diplomatic distance from Aradhya's door.

"Thank you, Ms. Garcés, we'll be in constant contact. As I was saying earlier, your robotic assistant will find you," said Wilkins as they walked down the curved staircase, then past the ruthless and ever-vigilant gaze of Rameshwar Thakkar and Tiffany Chen.

As they approached the damsel painting, Wilkins noted her interested glance.

"It's not a real mythical scene, in the sense that it doesn't accurately represent an ancient Hindu story. Dr. Thakkar had it commissioned by a well-known Indian painter of traditional Hindu scenes. He dictated the content to the painter in some detail, and had to overcome the artist's reticence to diverge so much from established canons. The artist felt it was close to heresy, that it was a corruption of one of the most cherished traditional stories. Dr. Thakkar eventually found a threshold of payment that fully assuaged the painter's concerns. We only received it a couple of weeks ago."

"It's a beautiful painting," said Benita, wondering why Thakkar had done that, and why Wilkins had thought to explain it. "Magnificent."

"Would you like a print?" asked Wilkins. "Dr. Thakkar had some museum quality giclées made up. I'm sure he'd be pleased for you to have one."

"I," stammered Benita, "don't want to impose." Her eyes said *Yes please!*

Wilkins made a convincingly avuncular gesture to indicate that it was no problem at all, *how could you suggest such a thing*. He motioned to another Wilkins who was already approaching with a flat plastic bag containing a large print already mounted on a board and framed in a charcoal gray mat. The other Wilkins handed it to Benita with a brief polite bow as she stood in the doorway.

"Thank you!" said Benita. "I, I really appreciate it."

"We're pleased that you like it. I hope you enjoy having it in your home. We'll be in touch. Thank you for visiting us!" he said as he closed the door behind her. Benita could see a few more icons appear in her peripheral vision. Homework already. Wilkins was surprisingly articulate, at least as much as any virtual character she had ever seen. His movements and gestures were a sublime decoction of the many actors whose behavior was instilled into him. The robotic mechanism itself was a walking, talking work of fine art.

She walked along the lengthy path towards her car, which waited dutifully for her at the curb. Zag had called it back from wherever it had decided to wait. The sky was deep blue, and fluffy white clouds were scattered about, teasing the landscape that one day there might be rain, if the stars and planets aligned just right. She basked in the warm sunlight as she walked. The neighborhood somehow managed to escape the pall of smoke from the wildfires raging in the wine counties up north.

"I see you got some swag," said Zag. He was now walking alongside her. "Beautiful painting. It doesn't exactly match any specific Hindu myth, though. It looks like it might be the kidnapping of Sita if there was some fabled Hindu equivalent of Lesbos."

"Whatever," said Benita. "I was kind of embarrassed to take it, but I really like it. Where can we get it framed?"

"We can stop by a place in San Martín not far from the train station. It might be a bit pricey, though."

"I just got a raise, so I can splurge just for today."

There was a faint odor of horse manure on the tepid breeze, mixed in with the delicious, dreamlike smell of the woods that surrounded the homes, but not enough to be unpleasant. On the contrary, it made for a bucolic, storybook mood. To call these palatial estates "homes" was, of course, merely a figure of speech. This was where the big money lived. The really big money. Billionaires like Thakkar were among the average joes of this neighborhood. "Neighborhood," too, was a word that came up short.

The car opened its side door to let her in. She had splurged on a car much fancier than her usual rides, one of Scramb's quasi-luxury models, and had it wait nearby instead of getting another one after her meeting. She didn't want to be too easily mistaken for a maid interviewing for a job.

Once in the car she sat back, hands crossed on her lap, fingers going to work. She had a look at what Wilkins and crew had sent. There were a few icons pointing to documents that required her signature, and she had to wave her authentication ring next to her goggles a few times to legally agree to terms, to set up secure credentials, and to be added to some private quantum-encrypted ledger chains. Strictly hush hush. Even Zag had to be upgraded to a higher level of security than he already had.

"Wow," said Zag. "Cloak and dagger."

"Did it feel good?" asked Benita. Zag simply laughed.

Another icon proved to be information about the antique shop. Imagery, historical information, a database of comings and goings she'd have to examine in more detail later, brief dossiers on people somehow connected to the shop, information about the building itself, the surrounding streets, details about surveillance devices in and around the building, and a wealth of other information. A few items were behavior capture feeds. At least one person wearing behavior capture gear had been snooping around. It might have been two. She noted slight differences in movement. Could one of them have been Mohan? How many people had worked on this? She couldn't tell from the audio or video, which were carefully excerpted from the original feeds, and she didn't recognize the gait or other body movements. Quite a bit of audio and video came from devices hidden in public places like restaurants, fences, landscaping, etc., as well as drones and specs. It was a lot of material. The car dropped her off at the Redwood City CalRail station.

Back home, after about an hour examining the materials, she dropped her duffel bag on an easy chair and plopped herself on the couch. An icon changed color in her specs. The behavior capture data from her specs and bodysuit was being downloaded to her local cache for eventual upload to FfēFfē. The caching server did some preprocessing, merging the various media and motion capture feeds into a single multi-channel streaming media file, among other things. She assumed that Thakkar and his people had changed things so that it all got sent to him before being sent to the general behavior capture data queue where it would ultimately end up. Would they forward the original data or a curated version? She heard a CalRail train whiz by on the tracks behind her building.

"Falafel wrap for lunch?" asked Zag. Benita nodded, for the better part of an hour she had been thinking of a wrap she had eaten at an outdoor market in Gilroy during the summer. It had been glorious. She remembered that there was a place in San Martín that made them almost as good, but she didn't feel like riding for 20 minutes to get one. What was it called? Phelps? Flep's?

"Pleff's?" asked Zag. Benita nodded eagerly. "It'll be here in a few minutes," he said.

She saw her doorbell ring in her specs and twiddled her fingers for the street door camera feed to come up. It was a humanoid robot. It didn't look as stately as Wilkins, though, but otherwise fairly similar. The finish looked like the interior of a not too expensive car, or the enclosures on some high end electronics. Nice, but more or less commercial, at least on video. It had a nice forest green and off-white color theme. An actual robot knocking at her door!

"Yes?" she asked over the intercom.

"Dr. Thakkar sent me," it replied, or rather, he replied. An authentication icon that Wilkins had provided her brought up a small dialog box indicating that this machine was trusted. She twiddled for the door icon to buzz him into the building. A few minutes later, there was a knock on her door. She examined him briefly through the peephole of her front door, and had him re-authenticate. All was well, apparently, so she let him in.

"Hello, I'm Brad," he said, holding his hand out in greeting. She shook his hand.

"Benita," she said. *Brad?* Somehow that didn't seem like a very robotty name. The robot nodded his reply. She saw that he was pulling a piece of rolling luggage. It was larger than a carry-on. She motioned for it to come in.

"Who the fuck is *this* guy? This... *thing*?" asked Zag. Luckily, Brad could not hear him. Zag stood slack-jawed next to the door as Brad walked in.

"What's in there?" she asked expectantly. No doubt some cool new cloak and dagger toys.

"Some things we'll need. You'll need," he replied. "May I?" he asked, motioning towards the kitchen table.

"Sure."

14

Savion Bennington was finishing a late lunch as he scrolled through images and videos of prospective merchandise. Fine jewelry was his specialty, but he was not averse to the wide variety of fine art pieces that were in circulation. He was cautious, though. Counterfeit art was plentiful, and at the prices he usually dealt in the quality of the forgeries was high. In general he only traded with people with whom he had built up a great deal of trust over the years, people who were generally forthright about the authenticity of their merchandise.

Bennington was the proprietor of Bennington's Antiques in San Mateo, California, about halfway up to San Francisco from Woodside, and a good hour and a half or so north of Watsonville by car. He had purchased the business about eight years ago from an elderly Chinese couple who had been running it for most of their adult lives, and had finally decided to retire. During the due diligence, he saw that they had been doing fairly well, but in the previous few years business had gone down somewhat. He pounced on that to haggle the price down, and eventually got what he thought was a reasonable deal.

Business had continued to slide, but Bennington wasn't terribly concerned. They sold enough of the kitschy stuff left by the previous owners to pay the rent and the overhead, and even make a decent profit. He paid Brenda's modest salary from there. He retained the previous owners' suppliers, and everything continued to move along more or less as before only somewhat less so. Bennington thought it likely that as the economy improved, volume would pick up and the business would more or less run itself under the control of the shop's retail software, just as it had for the Chinese couple, with only a modicum of tweaking. By now he had met all of the previous regulars, and knew what demographics to target some advertising to, and what sorts of items they were willing to buy. He was friendly and charismatic, and the mainly East Asian clientele continued to come, along with faddish ebbs and flows of non-Asians.

His main money maker was an informal trade in largely one-of-a-kind high-end jewelry pieces, along with a variety of other small but high-margin items that flowed through his network of contacts. Most of them had small shops like his, and also made most of their money on these private placements. As an antiques dealer, he was a member of several networks of police and insurance company alert systems, and he used these to gauge the viability of trading each individual piece. A surprising number of people did not insure such valuables, even very expensive items. The reasons were many, such as laundering money, hiding assets from spouses, or avoiding attention from professional thieves who also had access to these services.

Once an uninsured piece was stolen, however, it was usually lost for good. The former owner would of course not collect insurance on it, and was invariably unwilling to contact police, who would start an audit trail that would soon show that the piece was stolen merchandise that had been paid for with unreported or ill-gotten income. Those pieces then entered the informal antiques market, and dealers went to some lengths to make sure the piece was resold far away from its initial point of entry. If an occasional former owner stumbled upon their stolen item on the market, disputes were always settled privately, and usually amicably. Hostile dispute resolution was an occupational hazard, though, and there was no shortage of violent horror stories. Bennington was a fairly cautious sort, and went to considerable lengths to avoid being beaten senseless or shot.

He had just left some information on Brenda's desk about a series of pieces he had purchased. It was probably the largest single investment he had ever made, and he expected to reap his largest profit ever. He had spent quite a while searching for them in every venue he could, to make sure they weren't known to either the various levels of police authorities or insurance companies, and therefore not too hot to be worth the risk. These were fine pieces from the late twentieth century, several of them dating back to the colored gemstone craze of the 1970s. This lot would have several large and clean pink tourmalines on rings and earrings, a platinum necklace with an arrangement of topaz in a gradient from pink to red interspersed with diamonds, a set of matching necklace and earrings with numerous finely colored peridot, and a variety of pieces featuring tsavorite, tanzanite, faceted alexandrite, and lapis lazuli, in different combinations of gold and platinum. All of the gemstones were supposedly close to flawless.

It was an ambitious project, and he was relying on Brenda to unload them on the very wealthy customers that frequented the Q'Boom Qlub in Burlingame, California, a leisurely fifteen or twenty minute drive north from San Mateo. Burlingame was on the eastern border of the small enclave of Hillsborough, which had been jostling among the top ten wealthiest communities in the United States for decades. Billionaires were a dime a dozen, and a few contenders for trillionaire supposedly lived there. If things went well, there would be plenty more pieces like these to be had through his network.

He had also come across some items that were well outside of his usual specialties. Two months ago, one of his contacts in Texas had gotten hold of a small lot of semiconductor chip prototypes that weren't even on the market yet. A shipment of them had been stolen from SuperTango Semiconductor, a chip design and prototyping company on the outskirts of Austin. His contact said they were the next big thing, that they would be very expensive once they hit the open market, and that no doubt people in Silicon Valley would sell their grandmothers to get their hands on a few. Bennington, in spite of his evident technical illiteracy, was this person's only contact in the high tech world.

They were Flash Programmable Quantum Gate Arrays, or FPQGAs, and of course Bennington hadn't the slightest idea what that meant, although having the word "quantum" in its name sounded pretty sexy. He had looked up what those things were, but could not make heads or tails out of it beyond the fact that they were expected to be incredibly powerful computer chips, supposedly with tens of thousands of times more computing power than anything currently being sold in computers, specs, or robots. Bennington supposed that whatever the word "quantum" denoted, it made the chips mighty indeed. From what he could glean from his contact and from his research, these parts could fetch quite a bit of money from the right customer. He relied on his business partner, Eddie Wu, to shop them around. Wu was the owner of the Q`Boom Qlub and of an industrial consignment warehouse not far from it that specialized in scientific and technical instruments and equipment. He was also a minority partner in Bennington's antique shop. Wu's many contacts among the upscale clientele of the Q'Boom Qlub were a steady source of lucrative deals for both his consignment company and Bennington's antique shop.

The chips had come in this very morning, along with some jewelry pieces he had been expecting for Brenda's current sales projects. Wu had lined up a customer for the chips, who seemed quite excited about them. He had been supplying a company named **Gliese Genetics** with a variety of used biotech and automated manufacturing equipment and materials for about fives years now. More recently, they had been buying parts to build a customized artificial intelligence computer, and Wu had mentioned the availability of the parts to them. The Gliese people kicked it back to someone in Watsonville over their specs, and within the hour they got back the decision to buy as many as Bennington could find. This was two weeks ago. It took that long to carefully move the significant amount of cash around and get the chips sent out from Texas as discreetly as possible.

The Gliese people had seemed so anxious about the delivery, and had been pestering Wu about it almost every day since, that Bennington had gotten seller's remorse. He suspected that he could have been paid much more for them. He had asked his contact if he could get more, and apparently there was another lot becoming available in the next few days. Bennington decided to hold some of the chips back and try to shop them around for a better price. He had to be very careful, this wasn't an area of expertise for him. There was a fellow antiques trader he knew in Palo Alto who had a lot of contacts with high-tech start-ups that were always desperate to move faster and get their products out the door sooner. High end AI was pretty hot, and there was always a shortage of people, equipment, time, and practically everything else. Everything, that is, except money. If there was anything that was plentiful in Silicon Valley's techie start-up land, it was money.

Bennington decided to take the chips home with him, and give half of them to the Gliese people in a few days. He'd stall them for the rest until he got the next shipment. If he got a better offer from his Palo Alto friend and the other shipment fell through, he'd just refund the Gliese people the difference and say *c'est la vie*. Worst case, he wouldn't be able to get anything more for them, and he'd just deliver them to the Gliese people later than expected.

"Sav, we're leaving. I'll see you tomorrow," said Brenda. She and Rashaun DuPont were standing at Bennington's office door.

"Great! See you folks later. Send me pictures of you in the new clothes if you can," replied Bennington.

"See ya, Sav," said Rashaun, and the two left to go shopping at some of San Francisco's trendiest boutiques.

Bennington decided to close up shop early and go home to celebrate the receipt of the mysterious quantum chips. He'd stop by the Q'Boom Qlub to pick up his latest lover, a young woman he had been plying for a couple of weeks now. He had access to practically every psychotropic substance known to man through his network and was able to supply her with anything she asked for. He was able to do whatever he wanted with her, and she generally had only a vague recollection the next day. He was happy to fill in the details for her.

He went out the back door, locked it and got into the delivery van, where the chips were hidden under a tarp, then headed on out to Burlingame to pick her up.

15

Brad had placed several things on the kitchen table, including a brand new pre-production prototype of the latest behavior capture gear, the latest FfēFfē-customized specs, and an odd-looking thing with a handle attached that looked like the black blinder on a stop light. It was a stubby, matte-black tube about 15 cm in diameter and 30 cm long. Inside, a thinner concentric tube with a dark glassy end cap extended almost to the end of the outer tube. Behind that, Benita could see miscellaneous electronic components. The handle looked more like a stocky version of a glue gun than a firearm. Benita took it in her hand. It was heavier than it looked, but well balanced.

"Be careful with that," said Brad. "It's pretty destructive. Don't turn it on until the last minute."

"What is it?" she asked.

"It's a maser. Like a laser beam, only with microwaves instead of light. You're going to use it to knock out Bennington's home network and surveillance system."

"I'm going to microwave his router?" she asked.

"It's tuned to act like an electromagnetic pulse. It'll fry the electronics of whatever is in the beam's line of sight. It's actually several beams that you can adjust slightly to cover a small area," replied Brad. "You'll park in a shady area near his house, aim it through your specs, and pull the trigger when you get the green light. The user interface is pretty straightforward."

"Do I get to practice first?" she asked. The robot looked at her for a moment and shook his head.

"Won't be necessary. You'll see."

She put the ray gun on the table and picked up the specs. They looked more or less like hers, like those used by millions of other people to exchange messages, watch videos, post things onto their favorite media venues, etc. The frames and rims were just a little thicker, and looking more closely she noticed a few extra sets of lenses and additional small holes for microphones.

"You now have stereoscopic forward looking infrared and military-grade night vision that you can layer on or off as needed. You also have a few other icons that will light up when they sense things like gamma radiation, and selectable ranges of radio waves and magnetic field frequencies. You'll hear them as vague buzzing noises, and will at least be able to tell whether they're coming from the left or right, front or rear. Roughly."

"Can I try them on?" she asked. This was a large part of what she enjoyed about this job. That and working with new generations of FfēFfē virtual characters. Now she was working with Brad, an actual humanoid robot. She could already sense that he was clearly more articulate than the current virtual characters, including Zag, with finer use of language and a more detailed awareness of his surroundings and his activities. They had sent him instead of a person to train her in the use of the new generation of behavior capture gear, and even this strange-looking spook weapon, in her experience the kind only highly trained and experienced intelligence field agents tended to have. Usually she was brought up to speed on work techniques and equipment by precisely those kinds of human experts. Thakkar had delegated the task to a robot!

"Sure! They'll replace your current ones. You'll have to sign into your identity, but everything else is all set up."

Zag sat at the kitchen table and said nothing. He wasn't exactly pouting, but he remained silent.

Benita removed her specs and put on the new ones. She tapped the specs on, and went through the brief activation routines to add her identity. The resolution of the overlays felt higher than those in her current specs. The icons looked finer, crisper. The text was smaller but more legible. These could probably fit more items in her field of view, or at least have things more out of the way and less cluttered.

"Nice?" asked Brad.

"Wow. The audio."

"You have a couple more audio channels," he continued, "Per ear. They fit more snugly and the transducers are carefully shaped and located to enhance your ability to locate sound. You have this new bone conduction collar." Brad pointed at a necklace-like device that looked flatter and more flexible than the one she was wearing. She swapped it for her old one and paired it with her specs.

"Go to the sound menu and activate 'Visual Location,'" he said.

She activated it, and Brad said "testing, testing, 1,2,3, testing..." lowering his voice with each utterance. Benita looked around. The usual sound location indicators were smaller but just as visible. They glided around more responsively as she moved her head around and still accurately located Brad even when he was barely whispering. The audio felt deeper and gave her a much more accurate sense of Brad's location. She could feel more background noises.

"Nice!" she said.

She carefully unfolded one of the sensor suits and held it up before her. It looked a lot like hers, a bodysuit made of a thin, sheer fabric dotted with lentil-sized sensors interconnected with delicate zig-zaggy wires. The crotch and *derrière* openings had smooth and comfortable-looking hems, like expensive lingerie. If there was anything that annoyed her about her current sensor suits, it was the thickness of their hems and seams. They weren't quite elastic enough, either. While not a show-stopper, sometimes when you were sitting down, or walking, or at other random times, they sort of drew attention to themselves. She had no doubt that this added noise to the sensor data, and had even filed a bug about it a few months back.

There were several bodysuits. They looked more densely populated than her own. There were new sensor-laden caps as well. They looked different from the ones they usually used, with several electroencephalograph electrodes that had to touch the scalp. This was why most behavior capture actors chose to wear their hair short, or just shave their heads bald every day or two. You had to apply a special electro-conductive gel to the electrodes before putting the cap on so that they could capture electrical signals from the skin. Aside from those, these caps also had some larger flat sensors distributed over the inner surface, but that did not appear to need direct skin contact. The cap was slightly bulkier and heavier than the regular one, but it fit more comfortably. *Finally*, she thought.

The interface they all connected into was part of a snug belt, which was itself covered end to end with interconnected boxes the size of small, curved candy bars holding batteries and other electronics to store the stream of data coming from the sensors. They didn't look much different from the ones she already had.

"What are all of these new things?" she asked, holding up one of the caps.

"They're a new kind of sensor that captures far more data from your brain," he said.

"As if they weren't getting my entire life already. How much more?" she asked suspiciously.

Brad shrugged. "They capture the magnetic field around your head. It's a lot like the EEG, only with a lot more resolution. It's just more data." He was pulling a robot charging station out of his rolling luggage. "Where can I set this up," he asked.

"What is *that*?" she asked.

"It's my charging and data upload station. It unfolds into a chair. It needs to be near a power outlet and your router. Do you have wired network sockets?"

"I think so. In the second bedroom," she answered, pointing. "The small office." The smaller of the two bedrooms in her apartment was a sort of home office. He went over and set up the charger next to a bookcase. When he came back, he noticed Benita's piqued expression.

"That's where I'll be spending the night," he said, somewhat sheepishly. "I won't bother you. It'll be as if I'm asleep. It'll work with any other robots they send. It's like the base station for your specs, only it's for my data and my batteries."

"What's that other stuff?" asked Benita, directing her gaze at several boxes still in the luggage.

"It'll come out in due time," he replied. "As needed. Wilkins will let us know."

She knew better than to press the point. It was all company stuff, and it was up to her supervisors to give her access to things. Knowing when to play ball and when to be sneaky had gotten her plenty of privileges and extra pay. If she found an opportunity to con Brad into pulling it out, though, she'd take it. He was turning out to be a fairly cagey fellow, though. She wondered how well her usual virtual-character-cajoling tricks were going to work on him.

"Want to go out someplace and check out your specs?" suggested Brad.

An icon flashed in Benita's peripheral vision. It was the falafel wrap Zag had ordered when she got back from Woodside.

"I think it'll have to wait until after lunch," said Benita.

"No problem, we can test them now. Go to the video menu and switch on the FLIR, it's sensitive to a lower frequency of infrared light, which allows it to make images based on how much heat is being emitted by the objects in view," said Brad. "Set it to a low sensitivity since it's still daytime."

Benita saw that there were a few more entries in the video menu, one of which was FLIR, and the menu indicated that it meant "Forward Looking InfraRed." She activated it and looked around. The FLIR image was an overlay of wispy orange and blue in her field of view. Her hands glowed bright orange as if they were coated with fluorescent paint under a black light. Brad had orange hotspots where his electric motors and warm circuitry were, but the rest of him looked either neutral or bluish. Her front door glowed slightly blue compared to the rest of her apartment, probably because it was cooler out in the hallway than it was inside. The glow from her windows was blinding, so she put it on the lowest sensitivity setting. That got rid of the glare. She could still see where Brad's interior mechanisms generated more or less heat, and her own skin still glowed noticeably.

She opened her front door to retrieve her lunch from the street door. The hallway was both dark and cool, and the overlay gave everything a transparent cobalt blue tinge. As she approached the outside door, she could see that the small delivery robot had orange hotspots, contrasting with the slightly bluish interior hallway. Both the food compartments and the area around the wheels were bright orange. She twiddled her finger for her food compartment to open, and her food glowed even in the afternoon light, especially a bag of french fried potatoes. The street in front of her house now had a new ghostly life overlaid on it. Passing cars had orange stains around their motors, and more so the people riding inside. One person appeared to be drinking from a decidedly blue container. Sidewalks and buildings were tinged with orange in varying degrees where they had been warmed by the sun, and areas that were in shadow went from neutral through a range of bluishness. She wondered what temperature corresponded to neutral, in which the overlay was colorless and the underlying image was unchanged. No doubt there was a tool in there somewhere to get temperature estimates from the image.

She took her food and went back up to her apartment. From the outside, her door glowed visibly more than the hallway wall, although the faint glow in the wall itself seemed to stop where her apartment ended. The neighbors must not be home at the moment, because their outer wall and their door were both bluish.

"Wow. That was interesting. It's like a superpower," she said as she sat down to eat.

"For your first mission, Dr. Thakkar wants us to retrieve something from someone's house," said Brad.

"So he said. Isn't that illegal? Breaking and entering?" asked Benita.

"I gather this wouldn't be your first time, for FfēFfē."

Benita shrugged, and put some hot sauce on her wrap.

"I've always been with actual police officers," she said.

16

Bennington parked the delivery van under a carport on the driveway side of his house. He took the two boxes he had hidden under a tarp and went inside, into the kitchen. His specs alerted him to a call.

"Pari? Hi!" he said. He put the boxes down on the floor, not far from the door. "I'm on my way. Yes. Sure, no worries, I'll be there in an hour or so. OK, Bye!"

He was running a little late, but Pari was not yet on her way to the Q'Boom Qlub from Woodside. They'd probably get there at about the same time. He took a quick shower, and put on an ivory colored linen shirt, leaving the top two buttons undone, warm gray corduroy pants, and a lightweight wool jacket of a darker shade than the pants. A full length mirror next to his bedroom closet reflected his meticulously contrived appearance, and he decided he looked like a hip gallery owner. He carefully preened himself so that his hair looked fashionably uncombed, and applied a few drops of expensive Italian cologne he had gotten through his network.

From the top left drawer of his dresser, he pulled out a small enameled box from Guatemala. Inside was a collection of pharmaceuticals from which he would later draw in order to maximize his enjoyment with the young socialite. He removed a small plastic bag from the box, containing some capsules he had prepared himself, and emptied them into a small velvet pouch he kept in his jacket pocket. He placed the box on the dresser, next to a sandalwood carving of a scene from the Kama Sutra. There were some other custom-mixed drug cocktails there ready for use later in the evening.

In his specs he could see that he was running late. There would be no time to switch to his own car at the antique shop, he'd have to drive directly to the club in the delivery van. He took one last look in the mirror and went out the side door to the van. The sun was low in the sky as he drove off.

Once in Burlingame, he parked the van across the street from the club's parking lot. He nodded a smiling greeting at the burly bouncers sitting by the main door of the former dive bar that had been the original club venue years ago. He kept them supplied with tips and trinkets, and they let him come and go as he pleased, looking the other way when he managed to get some wealthy and naive young woman to go off with him. In his specs he saw that Pari was still on her way, maybe 5 minutes out.

"Hi Gayle," he said to the hostess. "Can I still get a booth?"

"Of course!" said Gayle, also the occasional recipient of his little gifts. She guided him to a booth near a corner of the bar, from which he had a commanding view of the whole room, and would see Pari as soon as she came in.

"Could I get a *yerba mate*?" he asked the waitress. She nodded and headed for the bar.

The Q'Boom Qlub was on a side street in the small city of Burlingame, a safe, well-patrolled area where the wealthy could come and be as naughty as they liked. Many patrons felt safe enough to leave their security details on call nearby, rather than bringing them to the club, or not bring them at all. The club had grown from this small one story dive bar to take over the larger two story building next door. There was now a small upscale restaurant, several bars, two fairly intimate dance floors, a casino, and a few sections of private rooms accessible via some dark and conveniently labyrinthine hallways. Brenda knew that area well.

Sometimes it was necessary to provide potential customers with sexual incentives of various kinds, which Brenda did not find objectionable, as long as the price was right. She was a sultry, charming, beautiful temptress. She knew it, and played her part with skill and *éclat*. Hence the occasional shopping trip to provide her with up to date work attire, which is where she was at this very moment with Rashaun DuPont. It was money well spent.

DuPont did a variety of work for him, driving the delivery van, doing inconspicuous pickups and drop-offs of dubious merchandise, and helping Brenda behind the scenes. He was always nearby to keep her safe. He was a smart, reliable and resourceful fixer and jack-of-all-trades. He was always on the lookout for poorly secured valuables, and had skimmed his share of loot from the antique shop. He was discreet about it, and not greedy.

DuPont and Brenda had an ongoing relationship of sorts. As far as DuPont was concerned, Brenda's duties *vis-à-vis* the Q'Boom Qlub and its patrons were strictly business, not something he'd lose a wink of sleep over, or so he told himself. Bennington's relationship with Brenda was dispassionate and professional. While Bennington certainly appreciated her smoldering allure, she wasn't his type and he wasn't hers. Both Brenda and DuPont knew quite well who Bennington's type of woman was, and it turned out that Pari was just that sort of girl. Bennington liked rich, unattached, naïve, free-spirited young women, bored out of their wits and willing to try anything. His routine was to build himself up as some sort of hip and adventurous underworld player, and ply them with whatever pharmaceuticals they were looking for. Later, he'd slip them a particular benzodiazepine he knew of and then leisurely rape them once it took effect. Eventually the girls would catch on, and he'd never see them again. If they complained, he'd show them surreptitious videos in which the girls played conspicuous leading roles. There were always more like them at the Q'Boom Qlub, though. Pari had been his latest find. DuPont and Brenda always looked the other way. To them, the filthy rich were like antelope on a savanna. Like them, Bennington was just one of many predators that lurked at the Q'Boom Qlub.

The waitress brought his *mate* and as she left he saw Pari enter the bar and scan the tables searching for him. She wore a snug black dress, silk or perhaps satin, bright red stockings, and black ballet flats. A furry red bolero jacket matched her stockings. It was more of an ornamental accessory than something that could actually keep her warm. Her jet black hair framed the crimson-lipped golden-skinned face of a beautiful young woman, anxiously looking for her date. She spotted him, and made her way to his table.

"Hey!" she greeted, planting a kiss on his forehead, and sat down next to him. He breathed in her gentle yet intoxicating scent.

"Hey!" he answered. Her eyes never left his, and seemed to constantly scan the upper part of his face.

"Want a drink?" he asked.

"Sure! Did you bring anything interesting?"

He discreetly looked around, and saw that nobody was paying attention to them. Everyone else was intently focused on their own mischief. He extracted the small velvet pouch the color of concord grapes from his inside jacket pocket and put it on the table in front of her. She picked it up almost reverently and peeked inside. There were two yellow capsules of the sort that usually contained some kind of medication, but which she knew concealed something more interesting than vitamins or antibiotics. The capsules looked as if they had been prepared by hand, and were larger than normal. She looked at him quizzically.

"These will enhance colors and geometric patterns. They'll seem to jump out at you. It won't be too speedy, and there's some THC in there to give it a sensual vibe."

"One for each?" she asked. He nodded and smiled. She popped one into her mouth and took a couple of gulps of the *mate,* and he did the same with the remaining one. They ordered some more tea and chatted for a while. When they realized that the drugs were finally kicking in, they headed for one of the club's dance floors.

17

"OK, it looks like everything is working as expected," said Brad.

They had spent a couple of hours reviewing the materials related to Bennington's home, and into late afternoon getting Benita used to the new behavior capture gear. There was always some adjustment needed to get them to fit each individual actor and calibrated against the previous suits. There were some buttons and laces that could be used to ensure a snug fit. Brad had used some standard FfēFfē software to make sure all of the sensors were working as expected and that the readings could be reliably intermixed with Benita's now voluminous body of existing data. The new skull cap in particular was more sensitive than the older one, and it had to be adjusted more carefully. They tested it with each of Benita's sizable collection of wigs. A few of the older ones would have to be retired due to metal parts or wires in the scalp. They interfered with the magnetometers. The body suit sections were noticeably more comfortable than the older ones, and Benita was able to do light calisthenics and some standard yoga moves in them without screwing up the sensor readings. The older suit would have been too constricting for that. The new hems were fantastic.

"I'd say you're ready to roll," said Brad.

"Sure you can't come along? The buddy system is always better," said Benita. Even on a breaking and entering mission as simple as this one, it was uncommon to go solo. If there was a chance of anyone being there, they'd probably send a small team of at least two people.

"I'll be in your specs. It's better to travel light," he said. "You can run me as a virtual friend. Whatever you see, I see. If you have another one, it might be best to switch it off for the mission."

"What!" exclaimed Zag in her specs. Benita had had him on for a while, exchanging snarky remarks about Brad in secret speech with him.

"I'll tell you all about it later," she told him privately, and twiddled him off.

"I think I have time for a quick shower," she said to Brad.

Benita went to her room. She had been wearing nothing but the sensor-laden bodysuit, a bra, and some underwear. It was partly out of laziness, since she had been changing bodysuits and clothing a lot during the sensor adjustments, and partly to see how Brad would behave, especially when she was between sensor suits and entirely unclothed. Nothing much out of the ordinary, but she thought she'd caught him stealing more than a glance or two. It was an odd side effect from using human behavior to train machines. There wasn't much Brad could do about it, but evidently he was a fan of the female form.

She showered quickly and then put on the all-new gear. It fit deliciously, even after she was fully dressed. She wore a pair of black jeans, a black sweatshirt, and a pair of her sneakiest sneakers, all tested with the new gear, just to be on the safe side.

"OK, I'm off," she said as she entered the living room.

"Good luck! Switch me on and I'll be with you the whole time," said Brad. "I'll probably be in my charging station when you get home. By the way, I've called a car for you, from a more private and trustworthy service, not Scramb! or Gógogo. FféFfé uses Coché for this sort of thing."

Benita had heard of them, vaguely, but had never used them. She had the impression that they were fairly costly and had a much smaller fleet than the others, which made for longer waits. In her specs, she found an icon among those that she had gotten from Wilkins and twiddled the virtual Brad to life. He stood standing in front of her, next to the real Brad who was still seated at the kitchen table. There was a comical note to it, but she said nothing.

"OK, let's go," she said, as she picked up the duffel bag. When she had gotten outside, she saw that the Coché car was pretty ordinary looking. Evidently luxury wasn't their only selling point. The virtual Brad was right there with her.

The car already had the address. Bennington lived in a small and secluded neighborhood just off of Skyline Boulevard near Highway 92. It was halfway between San Mateo and Half Moon Bay, and a good hour and a half away from her apartment in San Martín.

18

The Coché parked in the staging area that according to the materials she had been studying, was invisible from the house but had a view of most of the house's facade through the shrubs and trees in the front yard. It was now clear to Benita that part of the invisibility was due to the fact that the spot was in pitch black shadow. No street light shone on it, nor any lights from the few nearby houses. Once the car's lights were off, she was effectively invisible.

"Now activate the interface for the maser in your specs," said the virtual Brad. He was sitting in the car seat across from her, also examining the house. Benita twiddled it on.

"Open right rear window," she ordered privately, and the car complied. She flipped on the maser, and waited for the interface to come up in her specs. The device had some cameras in front, facing in the same direction as the microwave sources. She raised it and pointed it at the house. On the overlay in her specs, it painted a cluster of red dots on whatever surfaces would be hit by the beam. She twiddled her fingers a bit and managed to bring up another overlay that mapped a three dimensional diagram of the house and its contents onto the actual scene in front of her. The lines were soft and wispy, like watercolor brush strokes that shot through the house and sketched out some of its internal details. She twiddled some more and filtered out everything but the house's surveillance and wireless networking equipment, which came up as soft lines and a smudge that was presumably the router. All of this must have been obtained by surveillance and scanning from outside of the house, the detail was low. Her vantage point was ideal for hitting the router, which was in a closet just behind the right side of the wooden facade, near the edge.

More twiddling, and she had a list of all nearby wireless access points, including Bennington's: "ArfBowWow." It was the one with the highest signal strength since she was parked right in front of the house. Her field of view felt clean and uncluttered, thanks to the higher resolution and higher sensitivity of the new specs.

"OK, now hit the charging button and wait for the green indicator," said Brad. "After that, fire whenever you're ready."

She pressed the charging button. It filled a capacitor with electric charge that would blast out a burst of energy when she pressed the trigger. A quiet, ascending tone was produced as it charged, and a red targeting overlay appeared in her specs. She braced her upper body on her car seat backrest, and rested the maser device on the window edge. She had a quick look around with FLIR enabled on her specs to make sure nobody was nearby. She carefully shifted the maser to make the thin red line of the targeting overlay coincide with the router, and held the red dots centered directly on it. When the "Charged" indicator went green, she gently squeezed the trigger, keeping the dots on the router. The gun grunted audibly and hummed for a moment, and the "Charged" light went off. ArfBowWow was still there on the access point list. An odor of warm circuit board and ozone wafted from the gun. She examined her hands to make sure they hadn't gotten cooked. Her hands looked fine, but the gun was noticeably warmer, glowing a little more orange than before in the FLIR overlay. The wall outside of the router had gone from cool blue to neutral.

"It'll probably take a couple of shots," said Brad. "You've still got two left."

She waited for a few seconds, but the network stayed up. She hit the charge button again to repeat the process. The capacitor took noticeably longer to charge this time. She braced herself again and fired. Another buzzing grunt. A small amount of misty orange steam came off some ivy on the house's outer wall, around the spot she was aiming at. ArfBowWow was still there. It disappeared for a second or so, then came back. The black cylinder of the gun was lukewarm, noticeably more orange, and there was more circuit board odor. This thing better not blow up on her. She checked her hands and fingers again.

"Third time's the charm," said Brad. "If it doesn't work we have an extra battery."

"I hope I brought it with us," said Benita privately to Brad.

Once again she hit the charge button, and this time it took easily twice as much as the last for the capacitor to charge. Another grunt, and a little more steam than before seemed to waft from the ivy. She hoped it wasn't going to leave a mark. A tree branch near the line of fire also let off a bit of vapor. It looked like the actual beam was wider than what the interface indicated. The wall near the router was now definitely warm, an orange stain on the otherwise blue-tinged house that coincided with the smudge that represented the router in the house diagram overlay. She glanced at the available wireless networks, and ArfBowWow was gone. She stared at the list for a while, expecting it to be back up at any moment.

Two loud popping sounds rang out from the house, and Benita froze. Did the router explode? Did she start a fire? No smoke could be seen, nor any light in the windows. The FLIR thermal overlay showed no new sources of heat. Now that she looked closely, she realized that there had been a dim light in a window behind some vegetation, not the flickering light of fire, but the soft glow of a living room window. At least one heat source was moving around in it.

"Did you hear that?" she said to Brad. Brad's figure nodded, still looking out at the house, even though he wasn't really there.

The front door flew open, and a glowing orange man ran out. He looked to be in quite a hurry, quickly running out of sight down the street and around the corner to Benita's left, and in a few moments she heard a car door slam closed. A dim red glow appeared, then quickly faded with the sound of a car noisily speeding away. The street was silent, not even a neighbor's dog barking. She twiddled her fingers and got rid of the maser interface, and put the device back in the duffel bag. She spent a few moments scanning her surroundings, but saw and heard nothing, even with the new specs' sensitive settings. Now here's a neighborhood where people mind their own business. Being inside the car muffled much of the sound outside, though. That was part of surveillance lore. The heat source she had seen in the window through the bushes was gone. It had probably been the man who ran off.

19

"We should go in and see what we can find," said Brad. "I've let Wilkins know how things are going so far."

Benita looked at his ghostly image, then turned back to study the house. Most of the way from the car to Bennington's front door was in shadows.

"What if there's somebody there? What if they're armed? Those pops were gunshots," said Benita.

"Nobody came out after him. There were no more gunshots. If there was anyone there, they'd show some activity."

"There must be somebody in there. What else would he be shooting at? What if someone was shooting at *him*?"

They waited for a long minute. Nothing else stirred in the house, so she decided to go have a peek, and see if she could complete her mission. She twiddled some more to swap out the house's surveillance and networking overlay, since ArfBowWow was still gone, and replaced it with the local surveillance coverage. It showed estimated regions of high and low visibility from neighborhood surveillance and security equipment.

The path all the way to the door was clear, none of the few nearby homes could see anything. Most of the property was shielded by vegetation.

"Looks like it worked," said Brad.

"Are you sure about this?" she asked. "There's probably someone there."

"It's covered."

That meant nothing to her. Part of her told her to abandon the mission, while another compelled her to go in. She sat perfectly still, watching the house. The orange stain on the wall near the router was quickly fading. ArfBowWow was still down. Nothing appeared to be happening. The neighborhood was silent, even to her sensitive new gear.

"Open right side door," she said privately to the car, and it unlatched softly. She put on a pair of latex gloves, pulled a military-grade taser out of her duffel bag, just in case, and put on a dark matte plastic wig that was unlikely to leave any fibers behind. She got out, told the car to quietly close the door, and walked swiftly across the street to the first big shadowy area under an avocado tree. Brad's translucent figure was close behind. She looked around carefully. There were a few small glowing orange shapes here and there, skunks or rabbits or something. Cats, maybe. Nothing seemed to be moving in the house. The miscellaneous sounds of the night were now clearly audible. She made her way from shadow to shadow, taking care not to step on anything that would make noise. The last three meters or so were lit by moonlight, but there was shadowed area just to one side of the open front door. She strode over as quickly and silently as she could. From there she peered into the living room, and saw no evidence of activity. She moved towards the doorway, and heard a brief, low guttural cough, and some nasal sputtering. From further inside, she heard someone mumble a couple of incoherent words, a woman's voice.

She braced herself for a sprint back to the car, and craned her neck to look inside the living room, pointing the taser ahead of her. There was a glowing figure lying on a couch, and another on the floor next to it. The thermal image obscured too much detail in the dim light, so she turned it off. She could see that the person on the couch was a woman, and the one on the floor a man. The house seemed smaller than the models and diagrams had suggested.

The woman on the couch looked to be either half asleep or extremely intoxicated. The man on the floor was lying still, save for an occasional gurgling cough. Benita crept in quietly, taser in hand, quickly shifting her gaze and her taser aim between the two figures. Neither of them was paying attention to her. She stood still, looking around, listening for any kind of activity in the rest of the house. There was nothing but an occasional creak of the house's wood frame and the humming of a refrigerator somewhere.

Pari Thakkar was splayed on the couch, one leg dangling off to the side, incoherently mumbling something as she tried to raise her groggy head. She was naked, save for some blood-red stockings and black ballet slippers. Her groin glistened with moisture that matted down and smeared her thick black pubic hair. Alongside the couch lay a man, trousers around his ankles, snorting and gurgling up blood from his nose and mouth, with two growing red stains spreading across a neatly pressed off-white shirt. At the rate the stains were growing, he'd bleed out in ten or fifteen minutes. His glassy eyes pointed at her through his specs, but Benita sensed he saw nothing. It was Bennington. He was as smeared as Pari around a loyal erection that would very likely remain with him even after death. Benita put the taser away, for the moment.

Pari looked at her, and her mumbling seemed to get more animated. She was blinking and trying to push herself upright. Her red lace underwear was on the couch next to her, and a skimpy black silk dress was on the floor. There was a crimson-colored furry bolero jacket on the nearest couch armrest, which fashionably matched the color of her stockings and panties. All this was being recorded, and would eventually be seen by Thakkar. He said he wanted to see everything, so here it is.

Benita grabbed Pari by the arm and sat her up. She looped the underwear around the woman's feet and struggled to hoist them all the way up, leaning the half-awake girl on her shoulder and raising her up to get them on. Not quite, but close enough. She grabbed the dress and put it over Pari's head and tried to put her arms through the thin but surprisingly sturdy straps. Pari was wasted almost to unconsciousness, but tried to help as best she could. Benita pulled the dress down to cover Pari up. The dress went on smoothly and snugly, every square centimeter quickly finding its proper spot. There were no wrinkles or creases. It was as if the thing was actively trying to fit her. Way out of Benita's price range.

Benita pulled her up again, leaning Pari against her shoulder while she finished adjusting the dress, and Pari wrapped her arms around Benita as she struggled. Once again Pari's scent filled her nostrils: sweat, sex, and desert flower. The young woman's body rubbed intimately against her as she worked. Benita was all the more annoyed as she sensed a trickle of wetness coming on as she stood with Pari pressed against her. When they came eye to eye for a moment, Pari rolled her head back, looked into Benita's eyes with her own barely coherent gaze, and clumsily tried to press her slightly drooling mouth against Benita's. For a moment the girl's warm scent was overwhelming, and Benita savored the girl's wet lips.

"Stop it," whispered Benita abruptly, giving Pari a firm jostle. The young woman relented. There was something curiously wild in her eyes, like a small forest animal, a fox or a bobcat, yet devoid of hostility.

"Can you stand?" she asked Pari crossly. The young woman looked at her with eyes that didn't fully agree with each other, and moved her head in a way that Benita took to mean yes. Benita grabbed the little jacket with her free arm, and managed to thread it onto Pari.

"Stand!" ordered Benita, who then scanned the area, and recovered a small pouch that must have been Pari's purse.

"We need the specs," said virtual Brad. He was standing near the door, as if supervising the operation.

Both Bennington and Pari were still wearing their specs. Benita bent down and was barely able to grab Bennington's. She would have loved to check the rooms, but given the soon-to-be-late Mr. Bennington lying at her feet, it seemed unwise. She carefully scanned the living room with her specs, then once again with the thermal imaging on. At least they'd get that.

"Let's go," she mumbled to Pari, and pulled her along. They went outside and went from shadow to shadow over to Benita's car, much more slowly than Benita did on the way in. Pari was stumbling along, barely able to walk, but they made it without her falling to the ground or crashing into anything. She was on the full auto mode that only experienced drug users were able to muster. They got into the car, where Pari finally fell clumsily onto the floor.

"Thakkar residence," she told the car as she latched the door as quietly as she could. She pulled up the wireless network list, ArfBowWow was still down.

"We have to check the house," said Brad quickly. "That's why we're here."

The car was starting to pull away from the curve when she said "Wait! Back to the same spot!", and the car complied. Through the trees and shrubs, she could see the back of the gray delivery van peeking out of a covered carport on the far side of the house's facade. Search and retrieve, that was the mission. Was there anything in there? Would Pari try to escape if she went over there to check? Would there be anything in plain sight in the house? Would the police arrive at the worst possible moment? She wasn't entirely convinced that FféFfé had that fully covered. It didn't make much sense. She hadn't signed up for getting involved in a murder. The taut, hyper-alert tension of the mission was becoming tinged with anger.

"Open the door," whispered Benita to the car, and got out. "Child lock, all doors." She heard the click as she set off to retrace the dark path back to the house, with low-light and thermal imaging back on. The street was still deserted. She pulled her taser out again.

She carefully peered around into the carport before approaching the van. Nobody around, save for a couple of house cats cautiously examining her from the back yard, eyes and bodies aflame in her specs. Beyond them, there was a small garage at the end of the driveway, probably flush against the back fence. The garage door was closed, and no light or heat was leaking out of it.

The van looked empty. She walked around to look in through the rear windows, but there was nothing of any interest in it except a tarp that didn't look to be covering anything. She looked through the window of the side door on the carport side of the house. There were two shoebox sized parcels on the floor inside, one on top of the other. She tried the door. Unlocked. She had another look at the wireless list, ArfBowWow was still down, and went inside. She intended to go in just far enough to grab the boxes, and make her way back to the car, but she was already here and might as well have a more complete look. She stood motionless with specs at full sensitivity, but heard and saw nothing out of the ordinary. She noticed that water seemed to be running somewhere in the house. The image painted in her eyes by the specs was bright and detailed, but she knew her surroundings were dimly lit. She had her taser ready to fire.

Benita went inside, and cautiously walked around the single story bungalow. Bennington was evidently a neat and tidy person. No clutter in the kitchen, living room, or anywhere else. She approached the bathroom with the taser ready to fire, and pushed the half-open door with her foot. The water was running in the tub, and it was almost full now. There were half a dozen lit candles here and there. No doubt a romantic bath had awaited Pari and Bennington. The water glowed bright with warmth in her specs. Unsure of what to do, she turned the water off.

She made it a point to take lasting, steady glances as she methodically walked through every room, just as she had been trained to do and had done on-site many times. Her captured behavior and that of many co-workers had been instilled in virtual characters like Zag and now in a line of surveillance robots much like Brad and Wilkins. The techniques were designed to maximize feature extraction and object recognition, and to gather long snippets of forensic audio and video. Virtual Brad was following close behind her, but had stayed silent so far.

"Should we check the closets? The dresser? The bed?" she asked Brad privately.

"I think we're pushing it a bit as it is. Let's take those boxes in the kitchen and leave," he answered. "According to the FLIR, there's nobody else in the house."

There didn't seem to be anything of obvious interest, so she made her way back to the kitchen. The two boxes were heavy, like small appliances, and didn't rattle as she moved briskly out the side door. She paused, still heard and saw nothing, and went to the back yard for a quick look. She noticed that the metal door of the circuit breaker panel was warm in the FLIR overlay. The gas meter below it was hissing slightly, as gas passed through the pipe and into the water heater behind the warm wall. She looked up, and saw that the water heater vent on the roof had hot orange air billowing out. The novelty of the thing hadn't yet worn off.

The large back yard had a nice patio, a small pool, and a lot of landscaping, but nothing stood out to her. The garage had a side door that was locked. She peered in through the window, but there was a curtain on the inside and she could not see into the darkness beyond. She walked to the main garage door and saw that it had no windows or cracks that would allow a look inside. The boxes were getting heavy, so she went back to the car.

"Open the door," she whispered, and the car let her in. Pari seemed asleep where Benita had left her. Or passed out. She put the parcels on the floor next to her and said "Thakkar residence" again as she buckled up. She really and truly hoped that rescuing Pari and exploring the house didn't turn out to be a stupid decision. The same could be said for this entire little adventure. She did her best not to list the number of felonies she had just committed.

"So far, so good," said the imaginary Brad seated across from her. Benita only glared at him, then twiddled him off.

There was a sparse but steady flow of cars coming back from Half Moon Bay on Highway 92 and, like her, most of them merged onto highway 280 south. It was probably best that Pari was lying on the floor. A clearly intoxicated, lolling young woman leaning her face against a car window would draw attention. At least she was fully dressed. She noted that the red stockings were in fine shape, no tears or runs, no stains or smudges, not even a drop of blood that she could see. Lights along the freeway shone on her intermittently, creating momentary vignettes of a young woman on the floor, leaning against a seat. The close-fitting dress draped on her as if she was in a fashion photo shoot with a kidnapped ingénue theme, and a team of assistants had made sure that her clothing was carefully staged for maximum effect.

Benita twiddled her fingers and started a call to Wilkins through a special app that was encrypted and supposedly misrepresented itself in various ways to the outside world.

"Yes?" said his voice.

"I'm coming by with Pari. She happened to be there. I should download at your place. I'll need some help with her." It had better be encrypted, anyway.

"Brad mentioned it. We'll be waiting," he said calmly, after a moment's pause.

*   *   *   *   *

"Drive up to the side entrance," Benita told the car. Wilkins and a couple of other Wilkins were waiting for them just outside the door under a dim light. Were they the same ones as before, or different ones?

"She was pretty intoxicated. Bennington's dead. Someone shot him and ran out while I was parked outside. He's still lying there, as far as I know," she said as she got out of the car. Wilkins looked inside the car, then turned and looked at one of the others, who immediately went back inside. The remaining two managed to get Pari half awake and help her out of the car. These lesser Wilkins helped her stumble into the house.

"Don't worry about Bennington. We'll deal with the authorities," said the main Wilkins. "Those boxes?"

"The gray van was there. It was empty as far as I could see," she said. "These were just inside the side door of the house. I didn't want to risk looking around too much, so I just brought these back. There's some video and audio of the scene." He motioned to another Wilkins who had just come out to take the parcels into the house.

"There wasn't supposed to be anyone there, Wilkins. Bennington's been murdered, and I was at the scene," she looked at him sternly. "I could really get shit for this. I fucked up a crime scene."

"Don't worry about it. You won't be mixed up in it. We'll take care of it. You saved Pari. You can't imagine how grateful we are for that," he assured her. He sounded confident. Then again, he was a robot. Who knows whose behaviors he was trained with that led him to say that.

"Did you get his specs?" he added.

She looked at him in the eye for a few moments. She was good at judging virtual characters by their vocal inflections, which were pretty rich and human-like. They were, after all, the product of putting thousands and thousands of hours of actual human behavior and speech into their machine learning models. They were constantly updated with more behavior, much of it carefully staged to fill in gaps, fix glitches, choreograph unusual situations, add missing vocabulary and idioms, and whatever else occurred to the folks at FfēFfē.

Facial expressions were a different story. Like their virtual forebears, robots had a noticeably limited range of facial expressiveness, which gave them an air of inscrutability. They smiled at the right times, and were serious at the right times, and the direction of their gaze always made sense, but they weren't nearly as expressive as the actors that gave them life. Their faces had only a few movable control points, fewer even than the virtual characters. You might make something out of the head cocked to one side, or a furtive glance, but in people these gestures framed the face, and it was the subtlety of facial expression and eye movement that told the tale. Virtual character and robot faces were barely sketches.

"They're on the car seat," she said. "Shall I download here?"

"Please do. We've prepared a late night snack for you, if you like," he said, and led her inside and into the nearby kitchen. Another Wilkins was just serving a freshly prepared potato and leek soup on the kitchen table, accompanied by what smelled like a freshly baked batard. She handed him her specs and sat down to eat. Another Wilkins served her a goblet of golden pink wine. There was a charging station on the kitchen counter next to a video tablet. She assumed they didn't want her to feel there was some kind of bait and switch going on, as if that could matter. Much of the information was being lifted from the small data storage array in her belt, anyway.

Most of the way through her bowl of delicious soup, she became aware of some commotion going on outside the kitchen. The two Wilkins noticed as well, and both left the room together, only to be replaced by Aradhya, who came in and immediately fixed her gaze on Benita. She sat at the table across from her, but said nothing at first. Did she seriously expect Benita to explain herself?

"I don't know if there's any soup left," said Benita, feigning a glance into the kitchen. There was still a pot on the stove. She hoped she wouldn't have to share her little loaf of bread. Aradhya's gaze didn't waver.

"Well, thanks for giving Pari a ride home," she said finally.

"No problem," answered Benita. She dipped a crust of bread in her soup and bit off the soaked end. It was masterful. She wondered if the robots had prepared it.

"Did you run into her in town?" asked Aradhya. Benita met her glance, as calmly as she could.

"Aradhya, please drop it. It doesn't involve you," she replied.

"She's my sister!"

"Then perhaps you can discuss it with her in the morning." Aradhya's eyes were starting to show anger.

"I have a right to know about the goings on in my own home! This is my family!"

"Again, you'll have to take it up with them. I have no obligations to you." *That's it*, thought Benita. *Dinner's ruined. Too bad, it was truly well executed, like something a skilled and loving grandmother would prepare.* She got up to leave. The download could finish at home.

"OK, you're just going to leave? You coward! You're just in it for the money, aren't you!" said Aradhya. Benita walked towards her, showing no intention of stopping. Aradhya tried to pretend she wasn't intimidated, but started to back away. Benita managed to corner her against a nearby bar stool, which almost toppled over and Aradhya with it.

"Next time, *you* take care of it," said Benita in a low, firm voice, her face inches away from Aradhya's. "And yes, I'm on the clock. Lucky me." She turned and headed for the side door, where her car was. Aradhya didn't follow.

"We've spoken with Brad," said Wilkins as he showed her out. "He'll be of assistance when you get home. Please resume the download as soon as you get home. Sorry you couldn't finish your meal." Benita waved it off.

"I'm good," she said, and got in her car.

20

Benita rode back silently, watching the bucolic, plutocratic neighborhood go by. Warm windows well away from tree-lined streets, large yards with all sorts of landscaping, a peaceful community out of a storybook. No tent encampments, nobody getting ready to spend the night on the sidewalk, no motley lines of vehicles that doubled as dwellings, nothing that looked even slightly out of place. Just a crisp autumn night, and the nostalgic smell of fireplaces instead of wildfires.

Bennington wasn't the first murder victim she'd ever seen, not by a stretch. She had done about a dozen internships with police departments and investigative agencies over the past 5 or 6 years, doing on the job behavior capture for FféFfé Automata as they tried to sell customized virtual assistants to those same agencies. She and maybe 10 or 20 fellow behavior capture actors at each site would work at these places for a few months, enough time to gather the behavior necessary to embed into their virtual characters and have them start doing useful specialized work. Even more actors would re-enact a lot of the activities in-house with extensive subtle and not so subtle variations, and the customers would contribute quite a bit of additional after-the-fact content to improve the scenarios.

After about a week of training by the client, the actors would be out in the field assisting real agents on real cases. Property crimes, domestic disputes, witness interviews, depositions, undercover work, stake-outs, lots of surveillance, site searches, foot patrols, and negotiating with or arresting people spanning the full range of cooperation with the authorities, or lack thereof. There was more than the occasional break-in, generally covered by one kind of search warrant or another, and every month or two the elaborate ceremony of dealing with the recently or soon to be deceased. The virtual characters were expected to be general assistants that kept track of everything that went on, and to whom the agents could delegate any kind of information request, so that's what the actors did. The agents would ask for something, ask that somebody be informed of something, request authorization for unexpected additional field activities, and a variety of other information-related tasks, and the virtual assistants would be expected to carry them out while the agents stayed focused on their field work. This turned out to magnify the agents' ability to do quick, effective, and accurate work. These were high-margin products and services for FfēFfē with a lot of recurring revenue.

Homo sapiens' capacity for mischief, and in particular their always simmering inclination to inflict harm on their fellows seemed both limitless and infinitely varied. Bennington's was a plain vanilla shot-twice-in-the-chest bread and butter homicide. Nothing to see here, citizen.

Brad was waiting for her when she got home.

"Did you get anything off of Bennington's specs?" she asked. The killer would have to be there, in glorious high-res video.

"Before we get to that, you may want to see this," he replied. An icon appeared in her message list, and she twiddled it on. It was a news video, not even half an hour old, of a home burning off Skyline Blvd., near Highway 92. It was burning ferociously, and the authorities reportedly suspected the fire was caused by a blown breaker in the house's main electrical panel, which in turn ignited a leak in the gas meter next to it. Even the gray van was fully engulfed in flames.

"Poor Bennington. Was he still there?" she said twiddling it off.

"Presumably," shrugged Brad.

"So, did we see who did it? I doubt that it was an electrical fire. You can watch the video from my specs. There was nothing wrong with the breaker panel, and I didn't smell any gas. I walked right by the meter."

Another icon appeared, and she twiddled it on. The snippet began with an extreme close up of Pari's face, grunting and looking confused, her face moving up and down in a vigorous rhythm. Bennington was going at it full bore, and Pari's eyes were already starting to disagree with each other behind her specs. The video was from Bennington's specs, which Benita had managed to bring back, and it was spooling out the evening's events from his point of view.

Pari looked quite intoxicated, and Benita doubted that she was fully aware of what was going on around her. A muffled noise, made Bennington turn his head suddenly. A man was standing just inside the front door. Had he been watching for a while? He looked familiar, but there was a lot of movement as Bennington got up from the couch and turned to face him. His movements were unsteady, and Benita remembered that he had his pants around his ankles at that moment. By then the intruder had a gun pointing at him, and this stabilized the scene quite a bit. Bennington stole a glance to one side. Towards the kitchen? Some spot in the living room where there might be a weapon?

"Who the fuck are you? How long have you been there? Get out of my house!" said Bennington, turning back towards the young man.

The man looked at him, nervously moving the fingers with which he gripped the gun.

"What do you want? Get out!" repeated Bennington. He was standing in front of the couch facing the young man, who was still silent. Bennington took a step forward and nearly fell.

"Don't move, you slimy piece of shit!" said the young man through his teeth, extending his gun arm towards Bennington's chest. He too took a step forward. He wasn't much more than a couple of meters away from Bennington. His face was now better lit. It was the young neighbor of the Thakkar's who had been polishing his car that morning. His hair was unmistakably red, and Benita thought she recognized the sweatshirt. The boy next door, with a gun.

"You fucking pervert! You goddamn deviant scumbag!" growled the young man, glancing at Pari. "Look what you've done to her."

Bennington looked towards Pari, still splayed on the couch with her legs spread wide and a look of confusion on her face. She seemed oblivious to what was going on around her. She reached with her right hand to scratch an area near her navel, her left arm remained limp on the couch cushions.

Bennington looked back at the young man.

"Look what you've done to her! Do you have any idea who she is? You think you can just go around raping whoever you want? You fucking asshole! You fucking piece of shit! You fucking... fucking..."

The young man was enraged, half sobbing, barely able to articulate his thoughts. He now allowed the pistol to speak for him, and fired two shots into Bennington's chest. The image shuddered violently with each impact, then some blurry movement as he fell, and finally a static examination of the ceiling. The young man stepped closer and into Bennington's field of view, suddenly looking terrified, and then disappeared. The video snippet was fast forwarded a bit, and Benita came into view where the young man had been before. She looked like a dentist sizing up the fifth patient of the day. Disturbingly business-like, she thought. She hoped to god the police would never see this. The rest of the video fast forwarded to the moment Benita put the specs on the car seat before they drove away. She must have been a block away when the young man had entered Bennington's home.

"I've seen that guy," she said, after twiddling it off. "He's a neighbor of the Thakkars. He watched me go in the house the day I spoke with Dr. Thakkar. Why would he do that?"

"Yeah, we were able to identify him," he said. "He had a crush on her in high school. She toyed with him for a while, the better part of a summer as I recall, then dropped him when she went off to college. I gather he never got over it."

"Where is he?" she asked. "Did he come back to set the fire? Wait, you weren't around back then." Somebody who *had* been around back then had apparently gotten quite a bit of behavior content into Brad's machine learning model.

"We don't know yet, but as far as we can tell he hasn't turned up in San Mateo or Woodside. He'll eventually reappear. Have a look at this. It's more interesting." She twiddled the icon.

A video snippet showed Wilkins or one of his crew opening the parcels. One of them had several bundles of cash in high denomination bills, and some labeled glassine bags with pieces of jewelry in them wrapped in a cloth that looked like suede, along with a smaller box. Bennington evidently had a healthy back-channel trade with his network of fellow antique traders.

"Looks like a bit of skimming on the side?" she asked.

"Looks like," answered Brad. "We've got a few bugs in his shop. He was supposed to have been shopping for clothes with Brenda. DuPont went with her instead. We're assuming he decided to squirrel these away for later, then celebrate with Pari afterwards."

In the video, the robot hands separated out some items that were not cash or jewelry. There were three sealed jars with some irregular metallic lumps or beads in them. The labels were unreadably terse, like some kind of inventory code. In the smaller box there were several black stackable plastic trays with electronic components nestled inside them like eggs in a carton. They were all of the same kind. There were 10 components in each of 6 trays.

The second box was larger, and had two of the boxes with electronic components in them, with some cash and jewelry used basically as packing material to keep the smaller boxes from moving around.

"OK, that's no accident. He definitely took those deliberately. What are they?" asked Benita. She assumed they'd figured all that out by now.

"They're programmable quantum gate arrays," answered Brad. "Those are state-of-the art, very high capacity and high performance parts. They're very expensive and hard to get, even for electronics companies. They're still in the sampling phase, not even on the open market yet. The only company that has a reasonably reliable supply of them is Blam. You have to be pretty well connected to get your hands on that many of them. Military and intelligence agencies are all over this stuff, not to mention pretty much every Asian intelligence agency and smuggler. It's hard to fathom where a random smuggler like Bennington got them and why there aren't spooks all over this. Even FfēFfē has to twist arms to get a steady supply of them, and we can only get them from Blam. This is more than FfēFfē has received in months."

"What are they for?"

"You can make any kind of conventional computing device you want with them, with the important additional feature that you can connect it to quite a few quantum computing gates right on the chip itself," replied Brad. "They're specifically designed to make state of the art hybrid quantum computers for applications that can be significantly accelerated with quantum computing gates. This stuff is far more valuable than the jewelry, money-wise, and even more valuable as contraband for whoever was expecting to receive it. They won't get too many chances to order more of them, so they'll be looking to get them back."

"What does FfēFfē do with them?"

Brad turned to face her.

"You know that FfēFfē has been making all of its money from software-based artificial intelligence products, right, in partnership with Blam? Virtual characters and assistants of various kinds? Well, we also help Blam make big back end AI systems to make the characters much more knowledgeable and useful to customers. With enough back end computing behind them, those characters can be pretty powerful in terms of the things they can do for customers."

Benita nodded.

"Yeah, that's the whole point of capturing my behavior, to put it in those products. I know they can mix in behavior from several people, right? To mix their skills together?" she said.

"That's right, but the more behavior you mix in, the bigger and more complicated the machine learning model, and the more compute power you need to train it. It takes a truly huge amount of compute power to train the model with behavior from lots of people, which is where Blam's huge data centers come in. Conventional computers are too slow to be practical. To do it at the scale FfēFfē and Blam are doing it requires far more power," he replied. "These exact parts are going into the next generation. It's expected to be orders of magnitude more powerful than our current product. Thousands or millions of times more powerful, who knows? It's still hard to say how much. This is the heavy duty stuff, a whole new paradigm."

Benita's face was locked in perplexed incredulity. Thousands or millions of times more powerful? She knew about the back end AIs, but had never had any direct contact with them. She knew that back end systems of some kind were what powered the virtual characters, and that big companies were replacing certain kinds of specialized corporate employees with them. They could interact with people exactly as people interacted with each other by phone, in their specs, or in video-conferences. The really big ones, the ones that combined the behaviors of many people with different but complementary skills, were arcane and very expensive products that only large companies and high-level government ministries used because they needed massive amounts of computing power, and massive amounts of behavior capture from skilled and experienced experts. Such people were hard to convince to constantly wear the behavior capture gear during their everyday work. They chafed at the often irritating and disruptive procedures, and at the burdensome practices they had to follow to make sure their personal lives were separated from their professional activities during behavior capture.

This wasn't the sort of thing that caught the public eye, and it didn't get into the popular press that much, beyond shallow repetitive videos of virtual robots talking and doing miscellaneous activities in a virtual corporate setting. Or maybe it did. Benita didn't know much about it. The public was scandalized enough already by the virtual characters in people's specs that had started flooding the world about 6 years ago, and the massive spread of augmented reality specs and active rings just a few years before that. There was only so much that people could deal with at any one time. It was like living in separate but overlapping realities, one overlaid on top of the other. She strongly suspected that Blam and other interested companies produced all sorts of distracting bells and whistles to keep people from thinking about such things.

Most people were overwhelmed by the layers and layers of virtual characters and virtual worlds that could be overlaid onto their everyday lives, right inside their field of view. Everything was a quick finger twiddle away from being placed right in front of them. You could be standing in front of a real person and have no idea that they're private-speaking to a whole group of other people or virtual characters, their avatars crowding around you, watching you, hearing you, carefully examining you, maybe mocking you or doing all sorts of degrading things at your hapless expense. The constant stream of data being uploaded from people's specs to their spec hosting providers like Blam was terrifying enough already. What did those companies do with the detailed contents of your everyday life? Was it really as protected and confidential as the law required? Did they have detailed models of every single subscriber? Were we all reduced to heavily instrumented laboratory animals, pushed this way and that by an invisible realm of machine learning models and AIs? Were ever larger and more inscrutable artificial intelligences increasingly running the show? What was the show really about, anyway?

And yet, almost everyone had specs, and almost everyone uploaded some or all of the data they captured, day in and day out. If you uploaded everything, the service was free. If you uploaded nothing, aside from defeating the entire purpose of the specs, the service was fairly expensive. If you also subscribed to third parties and uploaded a copy of the stream to them, there were prizes, discount coupons, exclusive content, and myriad special offers. If you opted into receiving advertising, there were still more prizes and more discounts. The more virtual characters you allowed into your specs to promote products and services, the more incentives you received. Consumers couldn't resist.

Of course, there were hackers as well. Each additional character, and each additional subscription brought with it the risk of having someone or something invade your entire life. Not just your contacts, your finances, and everything you saw or heard every day, but your entire life. Everywhere you went there might be some contrived situation set up in your specs to pull you into some transaction, some activity, or some group of people, real or virtual, that could carry you away and dominate your life without you realizing the degree of manipulation to which you were being subjected.

Benita was in there somewhere. By now FfēFfē had amassed thousands of hours of her behavior. Some of it, along with behavior from hundreds of other FfēFfē employees and partners, was in the virtual characters, the back-end AIs, and now the robots. How much of her was in Brad, she wondered.

"Our new line of physical autonomous robots, such as myself, have live feeds coming from data center AIs. That's why I couldn't go with you to Bennington's house. The charging station in your office has a high-bandwidth connection through which I get a stream from a pretty large AI at FfēFfē. It receives my sensor inputs via a live feed and sends back a stream that feeds into my main machine learning model. Outside, 6G network coverage is still spotty, and it's pretty saturated in places. The node I connect to has the equivalent of about 2 to 4 of these chips, but in a unit the size of a refrigerator. It's interacting with all of the Wilkins models, about 5 of them, as well as 2 of me. We've been using that system for about 6 months and..."

"Wait! Wait! Hold on. 4 of these chips control 7 walking, talking robots?" interrupted Benita.

"The equivalent of 4," said Brad, "Maybe fewer. And they don't actually control them, they feed complementary data into the robot's main control systems. There are closer to a dozen or so robots connected at any given time, along with varying numbers of virtual robot sessions going on. These chips are a lot smaller and more powerful. The ones we have require several rack-mounted computers to get less compute power than a single one of these chips."

"How many of these are they planning on putting in each robot?"

"Maybe 4, or so."

"So the robots will be maybe a dozen times as powerful as now, right? I'm not sure how to calculate that."

"Not really. Other processes are also running on the big AI, so that consumes cycles. More importantly, though, is that you eliminate having to send and receive huge amounts of data over a network, and you won't have to switch among lots of competing processes and dealing with lots of different characters or robots. The chips will be dedicated to just one robot with direct connections to the rest of its systems. Also, it won't just feed into the main control system, it will *be* the main control system. On top of that it will still be communicating with other AIs over the network, only those may eventually have scores or even hundreds of these chips. So it's hard to say how much faster or more powerful they'll be," explained Brad.

"But they'll be more powerful than you? Much more?"

"Oh yeah, no question. Hundreds or thousands of times more, supposedly. Maybe millions."

"How many systems like that does FféFfé have?"

"More than one, that's all I can tell you. They've sold a number of them over the past few years to several large customers," said Brad.

"Like what customers?" she asked.

"You know I can't go into details there. Three letter agencies, among others."

"Blam?"

Brad said nothing.

"So what was Bennington doing with this stuff?"

"Looks like there's someone out there looking to make a big AI behind everyone's back."

"You mean like, a criminal organization or something?"

"Good question," he answered.

"Do you know who it is?"

"We think so."

21

Sue and Tavo were waiting at their trucks for the morning's water run. Raúl was fashionably late as usual. Their neighbors at the end of Pequod Lane opened their gate and a car drove off at unusually high speed. Someone was clearly in a hurry. Sue and Tavo watched them drive by.

"That's her," said Sue. "The girl in the car? That's the girl I was telling you about yesterday. Alice something."

"Do you know the guy?"

"Nah. I don't know anyone over there. I only know her because she used to be with us," said Sue. "Maybe it was the guy she was trying to hook up with. People say they're always together."

"So what all do they do over there? I know they do tissue culture and cloning and whatever. But I don't even know what that is. They don't have enough greenhouses to make much money selling plants."

"Oh, dude, they make piles of money. A lot more than us, and look at all the land and greenhouses and vertical farms we have," she said, sweeping her arm across the expanse of the Crazy Ladies Co-op. "They do scientific stuff to make new breeds of plants, and make them resistant to bugs, germs, drought, and all sorts of stuff. They even make new strains of wine grapes and fruit trees for the hotter weather. All sorts of stuff like that. Even animals."

"You only need a few greenhouses for that?" he asked.

"They just do the scientific stuff here. Besides the greenhouses they have a few portables with labs in them. You can sort of see them behind the second treeline," she said, pointing at something behind the trees. Tavo looked more carefully. There was a line of trees between Crazy Ladies and Gliese, a large farmhouse, a parking area, and some greenhouses and small buildings after that. Beyond was another treeline, and some two-story temporary-looking buildings beyond that. They were hard to see.

"Wow. I don't think I'd ever noticed them. What do they do there?" he asked. Sue shrugged.

"They do something with plants and animals to make them grow in petri dishes. They treat them with chemicals and radiation, change their DNA, mix it up with DNA from other things or that they designed in their labs, and other stuff to make new kinds of plants and animals that didn't exist before. Basically they design new kinds of plants and animals. Supposedly they're making new kinds of pigs and chickens, but I haven't seen any."

"Have you seen their plants?" he asked.

"Yeah. You know those new citrus trees we planted a couple of weeks ago? Those are from Gliese. Supposedly we'll be making twice the profit from them," she said. "Also some of our vegetables and salad greens. They're pretty much guaranteed to grow big and healthy. The arugula's pretty good, so are the heirloom tomatoes."

"And how do you know all this?" he asked with some skepticism in his tone.

"Because the founders all used to work at the same plant tissue culture company when they started Crazy Ladies. Not at Gliese, another one that eventually got bought out by some big corporation. That's when they all got laid off," she said. "Haven't you watched the videos?"

"Uh, yeah, it just didn't stick I guess. I don't know anything about biology and stuff."

"You work on a farm, bro!"

"Yeah, but I drive and fix trucks! I don't do anything with plants or animals, or whatever," he replied. "All I do here is mechanical stuff."

At that moment, Raúl finally came out for the water run.

"Come on, you guys, let's go!" he said, as if he had been patiently waiting for them. They all mounted up and drove off towards Moss Landing.

While they waited for the trucks to fill at the desalinators, they walked around the desalination buildings themselves. The passive solar desalinators were the most interesting ones because you could see everything inside of them. Each was a 6 story glass enclosed structure with another slightly smaller glass building inside. The outside set up a greenhouse effect inside and protected the interior structure from the often chilly breezes. The inner building was where the main business occurred. The greenhouse effect in there, on a bright, sunny summer day could get its interior temperature up to 50 or 60 degrees Celsius at its peak, quite a hothouse.

Sue and Tavo stood mesmerized as the water streamed from one broad surface to another in small waterfalls. Here and there multicolored water-powered mobiles of various shapes and sizes spun around for decorative effect. Towards the bottom, crusts of salt grew on the edges of everything. Some evenings, after things had cooled off, co-op workers went in and cleaned things up, scraping off kilograms of salt and minerals and carrying it all away in wheelbarrows.

A couple of busloads of tourists were walking around looking. There was a tour of the desalinators, and some of the visitors could be seen walking through the outer glass buildings, where the heat was barely tolerable but much lower than in the inner chamber. Outside, where Tavo and Sue were, they were buying hot dogs, ice cream bars, and other seaside snacks.

"I'll be right back, I need to go to the bathroom," said Sue. She walked towards the restrooms in the restaurant on the other end of the parking lot.

As Tavo watched her walk away, he twiddled an icon in his specs to bring up the overlay from the HunterGather matchmaking app. The service at first identified other users for initial test dates based only on the new user's initial profile. Regular users who made themselves available for these initial dates earned points that could be exchanged later for exclusive offers or premium features. After each date, the new user had to have an interview with a HunterGather virtual character about the experience. The service had a panel of machine learning models constantly updated with data obtained from the interviews and from data captured from users during the dates. These models attempted to predict what potential dating partners would result in a positive experience on the next date. Scores appeared in the user's specs through the HunterGather overlay summarizing the predictions. After the initial test dates, new users became eligible for dates in the general user population.

"Oh naughty boy!" said Cin. She was Tavo's Blam virtual character, a sexy young female figure he had configured to change her appearance at random intervals, within a range of attributes he enjoyed fiddling with. The base character was a smart and athletic British archaeologist and adventurer who enjoyed exploring mysterious ruins, castles, underground labyrinths and the like. There were several game packages available where both she and Tavo could share adventures, some of them convincingly overlaid onto the real world.

"I hope Sue doesn't catch you," she said, smiling.

"She won't."

The overlay in the specs highlighted potential matches as logged-in HunterGather users moved around in public places. There were enough tourists here that Tavo felt he should have a look and see if there were any good candidates. He had already gone on a few hundred dates over the years, and dutifully had the success interviews after each one. At this point, the dates tended to be fantastic matches, as long as he stuck to the ones with high confidence scores. Occasionally there were women with lower scores who he couldn't resist selecting, and the results were generally mixed. Nevertheless, these experiences tended to enrich the models that HunterGather maintained about him, and constantly improved and expanded the population of users that it recommended to him.

He walked along the main walkway among the desalinators, but only a few people had HunterGather callouts next to their heads, an overall average score with a pop-up you could twiddle to expose a panel of 12 scores ranging between 0 and 100. Twiddling over those would show even more details about the likelihood of scoring highly on the date interview for things like empathy, friendliness, mood, overall experience, sexual compatibility, conversation, fun activities, taste in food, taste in euphoric substances, personal interests, a variety of "gut feeling" criteria, and other traits. Each of them could be drilled down on still further for more detailed summaries. The average score in the callout was usually pretty reliable, and most people tended not to drill down much. Anything above 90 would be very enjoyable, and even the high 80s tended to be great. Below 80 was hit or miss, but even those dates had a few interesting results that he would highlight in the interview afterwards. The lowest average he had ever dated was in the low 70s, and by then things were not so great. Down there, things could be downright frightening. There were definitely some crazy wild folks out there.

In order for the callout to be visible next to a person's head, they would have to be actively signed into their own HunterGather account, effectively advertising their availability. There were extensive rules governing how contact could be made, and HunterGather was pretty strict about people following them. Nobody wanted to be kicked off the service, but there were occasional nut jobs who broke the rules. The app was the only way to do it correctly, and it guided users through a multi-step process, which the receiving party could authorize or not at their discretion. It had a reputation for safety and security, earned the old fashioned way through trial and error, with periodic episodes of intense public controversy. There was even a stealth mode where users could see other logged in users, but the others would only see a green dot next to the stealth user's head.

A group of Asian tourists had a couple of girls in it with moderate scores, but he didn't really find them that attractive. As they passed by, he could hear them speaking a rapid fire Chinese, and he doubted he would be able to communicate very well with them. A lone woman about 10 years his senior was about to walk past him from the opposite direction. She wore sunglasses, but he could tell she was studying him intently. She scored in the high 80s, and he surmised she was seeing the same thing attached to him. He definitely found her alluring, but let her walk past.

He heard or felt a buzzing sound towards his right, his specs alerting him to something just around the corner of the visitor center.

"Bandit at three o'clock," said Cin. She was currently dressed as a mid-twentieth century military aviator with a snug V-necked flight suit.

It was a HunterGather alert letting him know that someone with an average score over 90 was nearby. As he rounded the corner, he saw a young woman about his age who was frozen in mid-motion, replenishing the soft drink cans in a tub of ice on one side of her falafel wrap cart. She was also looking expectantly to see who was about to walk by. Their eyes met for a moment, and then she continued with her work. Tavo kept walking, and twiddled on her scores to have a look at them. Her average was 93. She had nothing below 88. He initiated the contact process and pretended to carefully examine the solar desalinator across the path from her. In less than a minute he was authorized.

"Hey," he twiddled a message in private speech.

"Hey yourself," came the reply a few moments later.

"I see what you're doing," came a voice from behind him. It was Sue, who must have also had her HunterGather overlay on and could see that he did as well. She must have switched it on and off quickly, because there was no score next to her head, not even the green stealth dot.

"That was sneaky," said Cin. "I didn't even notice her do that."

"Just looking around. I was waiting for you," he said. He bookmarked the girl, whose name was Carol.

"Uh huh." Sue was piqued, more than a little jealous that Tavo would go on the hunt at the drop of a hat. "Find anything? I wouldn't want to intrude," she said sarcastically.

"Nah, not that many people here," he replied. He felt his face blushing. Cin smirked at him and shook her head.

"OK, let's go, man," came a voice message from Raúl. They turned and walked back towards their trucks.

22

A specs-faced DuPont leaned against the wall in Brenda's bedroom, vaping and checking for messages in his specs as she carefully examined the new clothes now hanging in her closet for about the eighth time. They had just had a light breakfast, the morning after an enjoyable evening of shopping, followed by drinking, dancing at the Q'Boom Qlub, and a prolonged romantic interlude here at her apartment.

"Did Sav comment on the photos you sent?" he asked her idly.

"Nope. I haven't heard from him. You?"

"Uh-uh. He was going to let me know if we were moving some stuff from Wu's warehouse to the shop today," he said. "Weren't you going to work the club tonight with some new jewelry?"

"Supposedly," she said, closing the closet. "That's what we went shopping for, right? Yesterday he showed me some new stuff that's going to be coming in. We should be getting a few things today." She came up close and leaned on him lightly, parting her lips for a kiss. They cuddled for a bit and then she said "We should go, I have to be at the shop in about 15 minutes."

When they got there, the shop was still closed. They parked in the rear of the building, and saw that the van wasn't there, but Bennington's car was.

"That's weird. Is he here or not?" said Brenda. Bennington wasn't exactly a morning person, but the shop opened at 11, and he was generally there well before opening time.

"Whoa! Check this out!" He twiddled his fingers to share a news video with her. They watched the brief report in silence. It was unmistakably Bennington's house and the gray van engulfed in flames the night before.

"Should we go up there? Call him," she said somberly. DuPont tried to call him, but nobody answered. He sent a text asking "Hey, what's up?"

At that moment, a gray van like the one they just saw on fire drove up to the shop's loading dock. It was a couple of folks from Gliese Genetics, a man and a woman DuPont had seen a number of times before. He didn't know their names, and had the impression they were some kind of security staff. They got out of the van.

"Opening time?" asked the woman. She was athletic-looking, with short spiky hair peeking out of her beige cap. She might have been ex-military, or maybe an ex-spook. She and the guy looked at DuPont and Brenda expectantly.

"Yep, about that time," said Brenda, trying to play along. Did these people know about the fire? Brenda twiddled the back door open and all of them entered. Bennington was not in yet. As soon as the door closed, the spiky haired woman spoke.

"I don't know if you know yet, but tragically, Bennington's passed away. His house burned down, and on the news they said he was in it," said the woman rather coldly. She waited to see what effect the news had on Brenda and DuPont, who stole a brief glance at each other.

"Yeah, I saw the news. Poor bastard. Was it really him? Have they identified him?" said DuPont. He didn't think he could play for time. Better see what these people knew. It couldn't be any less than he did. If the rich girl was also burned to death, there would be a big mess to deal with. Or to escape from.

"Doesn't matter, at the moment," said the man. "He still hasn't delivered a few things. We're here to pick them up."

Brenda thought of the boxes that Bennington had taken in the van. She doubted they had been sold to anyone yet, and had no doubt that the rich girl would have been Bennington's first priority last night. The boxes were most likely just charred debris in what was left of the van. These people were serious, and it looked like the boxes were valuable enough for them to make a rare personal appearance at the shop. Brenda sensed they'd be better off not getting wrapped up in this.

"Bennington was skimming stuff from the store," said Brenda. "He took the van last night with a couple of small boxes in it. That's the last we saw."

This took DuPont by surprise, but he nodded at the visitors with the best ignorant dumb-ass face he could muster.

The pair from Gliese looked at them steadily, studying their faces and judging their degree of nervousness, but Brenda and DuPont were seasoned con artists so this was unlikely to get them much.

"We'd like to have a look, if we may?" said the woman. They were both already on their way into the shop.

"Knock yourselves out," said DuPont, invitingly holding his hand out towards the showroom. Brenda looked at him, and he tipped his head slightly towards a spot near the back door. They quietly walked over.

"You knew he was stealing shit?" asked DuPont.

"Please. That guy couldn't sneak a pack of gum *into* a supermarket without getting caught. There's always been a ton of stuff that's not on the books, and he's not very good at sneaking things home," said Brenda. "I took a few things in my day too. Nothing these people would care about. Didn't you?"

"Yeah, nothing major, though. Not as much as Bennington. That guy probably had a little warehouse in his closet," he joked. He froze. Brenda looked at him intently for a moment, her mouth shaped like *Oh!*

"Have you ever been to his house? I can't remember if he has a shed or anything. I think he had a garage in back?" whispered Brenda. "His closet's probably gone. Anything that was in the house is probably gone."

"He does have a garage, or did have, whatever. He had an ancient Porsche convertible in there at one point. It was in pretty good shape, by the way. You went out there?" asked DuPont.

"When he first hired me two, no, three years ago. He drove me up there after work one night and tried to get me to suck him off, and when I didn't he tried to drug me. A couple of times actually, the creep. The second time, I swapped the drinks and he ended up drooling and blubbering on his couch. I had a quick look around, but he was always stumbling after me. There was a door off the kitchen which might have been a basement, but I couldn't check. I got him to finish his spiked drink and then served him some more out of the bottle. Some fancy brandy, as I recall."

The pair from Gliese Genetics discussed something briefly, but DuPont and Brenda couldn't make out what they said. They were systematically going through the whole store.

"I gave him a slow strip show, and told him that with every gulp I'd take something off," continued Brenda. "Luckily, he more or less passed out after about 2 minutes. I was running out of things to take off pretty fast. I didn't want to risk the job, so I straddled him on the couch, shook his specs off, made sure they were looking down, dragged him to his room, pulled his pants off, and left him on his bed. I made it look like we had a grand old time. The empty booze bottle, empty glasses on the floor, bed covers all over the place, music still playing, and I left my underwear next to his face as a souvenir. I had to sneak out through the living room and grab my clothes, hoping his specs didn't catch anything. Next day it was as if nothing had happened. He never invited me again."

DuPont took it in for a second. Was he jealous?

"We should go up there. Let's wait for these people to leave and go check it out," he said.

"What if they go too?" she asked.

"Maybe they would have checked it out on the way over. It's kind of out of their way, though."

The folks from Gliese were back, empty handed. They didn't look happy. Whatever it was they were looking for, they really, really wanted it.

"Where else would he keep our stuff?" asked the woman.

"Back here, either here on the loading dock or on those shelves," answered DuPont, pointing at a few shelving units. They were empty, and there wasn't anywhere anything could be hidden. It was a fairly small and sparse area. "I'm pretty sure I delivered everything we had the other day."

"Except for what Bennington had in the van," added the guy.

"Well, sure, but I wasn't the one who loaded your delivery," said DuPont.

"Who did?" asked the woman.

"We order out for manual labor. It's different people every time. I'm not sure what company," he replied.

"It's *Logistics La Lupita*," said Brenda. "I'm the one who usually calls them. They're in Redwood City." The Gliese guy smirked.

"Well, if you find any leftover boxes, it's *very* important that you bring them on out to the farm," said the woman. She sounded like a president considering the release of nuclear weapons.

"Will do. Definitely," said DuPont. Brenda nodded gravely.

"OK," said the woman, and the pair left without further comment. They got in their van and drove off.

"Let's wait a few minutes and call a car," suggested DuPont, "I don't want to use mine for this."

"What if the stuff is gone and these people get all worked up about it? Should we talk with Eddie? You know him better than I do," said Brenda.

"As far as he's concerned, we're Bennington's crew. Bennington owns this shop, so he owns us," he said. "Owned. Somebody must have been financing it all, though. Did Bennington set this up with his own money? Where are his files? Do you know what was in those boxes he took? Did he get them through Wu? They're partners or something, right?"

Brenda's eyes lit up, and she led DuPont to Bennington's office, inside a door behind Brenda's reception desk.

The Gliese folks had been in there. The closet door was open, as were all the drawers of the filing cabinet. Some boxes were on the floor with their lids removed. They had been systematic, but not messy. Brenda sat at the desk and twiddled her fingers to log into the store's system.

"Will your account be able to see everything?" asked DuPont. Brenda shrugged.

"One way to find out," she said. She opened up the accounting app, and looked through the ledger that appeared on a desktop screen. Lots of irregular payments, a number of monthlies to banks, insurance, utilities and the like, and one consistent monthly payment, a rather hefty one, to Magical Elements, LLC.

"That's it. That's Eddie Wu's holding company. We occasionally get checks from them. That's a lot of money, and pretty regular," she said.

"Paying a debt?" asked DuPont. "Would those boxes show up somewhere?"

"They'll show up, but with bogus descriptions in case his systems ever got subpoenaed. Only Bennington would know what's what," she answered.

"Anyway, let's go check out Bennington's garage. We can see Eddie later," DuPont said. He twiddled for a car, as they walked out the back door. He retrieved a duffel bag from his own car, and the nondescript silvery gray ride arrived a few moments later.

23

As they approached Skyline Blvd. from Highway 92, they saw the Gliese people in the gray van turn back onto 92 in the opposite direction, towards the coast.

"Damn! They beat us!" said DuPont. "Makes sense, I guess."

"Let's check anyway. Maybe they missed something," said Brenda. DuPont shot her a doubtful look as the car turned left onto Skyline.

"Turn onto Hawkins Road, and keep going all the way around back to Skyline," DuPont told the car, in case the authorities were still working the site. "Drive at 30 KPH on Hawkins."

They drove past Bennington's property, and saw that the house was burned to the ground, but the garage in back was intact. The delivery van was totaled as well. Its tires and windows were completely gone, and the remains of the carport had collapsed on top of it. There were still a police car and a red fire department pickup parked out front, the rear guard of an underfunded and overstretched municipality. A single cop and a single fireman stood on the sidewalk chatting as they stared at the burnt ruins.

"I bet they're going to drive around for a while and wait the cops out," said DuPont. As they approached Skyline at the other end of Hawkins, DuPont told the car to park at the corner.

"We can see when the cops leave from here. I can see the other end of Hawkins Road," he said. It was over half an hour before both vehicles passed them and turned left onto Skyline to leave the area. They passed the time finishing off the last of DuPont's vaping cartridge and fretting about Bennington's death and their own immediate future. About 20 minutes later, the police and fire department vehicles drove by and turned towards highway 92.

"Go back to the address," he told the car. It obediently turned left and went back into the other end of Hawkins Road. "Park 20 meters past the address," he ordered.

Now there was nobody parked near the burned house. The street was clear, so they got out and walked casually towards it. DuPont had his duffel bag slung over his shoulder. There were no neighbors looking at the ruins, which seemed odd. They knew that surveillance cameras were watching, so they acted as if they were just going for a look at the newly incinerated home. Not much else to be done about it, just a couple of random disaster tourists.

Once at the driveway, they walked under the police tape and walked towards the carport. They couldn't see any other houses from here, so most likely they wouldn't be directly in the middle of a video feed. The van was burnt out completely, and they didn't see any evidence of burnt packages inside. It didn't look like the fire department wasted any water on it, either. The house itself wasn't worth looking through. It was a soggy mess of ashes and charred building materials lying on a concrete foundation. It was starting to smell, an unpleasant, stale rankness.

"Where would that door you saw that might lead to a basement be?" asked DuPont. "I doubt there was one. The house would have collapsed into it."

Brenda shrugged.

They went back towards the garage, which appeared to have been untouched by the fire. There was a door on the side. DuPont got some latex gloves and lock picking tools out of his duffel bag. Both the door lock and the deadbolt were set, but in a few moments he had them open.

The Porsche was still there, with a dusty canvas cover over it. They walked around it, looking for boxes or storage areas. There was a workshop along one side of the garage, with a few antiques that Bennington was presumably working on. Woodworking tools hung fairly neatly on a pegboard above the workbench surface. They looked in the cupboards and storage cabinets set into the wall on either side of the work area. It didn't help that they had no idea what they were looking for.

On the other side of the garage were shelves that had the sorts of old useless stuff that populated most garages, then a washer and dryer and another cabinet with laundry soap, bleach, and other such things. DuPont noticed that the canvas on the front end of the car had been moved. It was wrinkled and less dusty, with what might be finger marks. He lifted it up, but there was nothing but the smooth surface of the car, and a chrome decoration on the hood that looked a lot like a handle with a Porsche logo on it. The hood was ajar. Too bad. The finish on the car was immaculate, the chrome handle shiny and unblemished, the Porsche logo stately and richly colored. You'd think Bennington would have fixed the latch. DuPont was about to try and push it closed, just out of instinct, but lifted it to have a peek at the engine.

To his surprise, there was no engine. It was the trunk. Of course! These cars had their engine in the back! There were some dirty rags inside piled in an old box with road flares, cans of motor oil, and a grimy jerry can. There were two new-looking cardboard boxes next to it, about the size of shoe boxes.

"Brenda," he said. Brenda had been looking at some antiques that were in boxes shelved along the back wall of the garage. She turned and looked at DuPont, then at the boxes.

"There's nothing up here," she said.

DuPont pulled one of the boxes out and slipped the top off. It wasn't even taped shut. There were several plastic trays inside, stacked on top of each other. The box looked tailor made for them. Each tray had two rows of fairly large flat objects that were probably computer chips of some kind. Bennington did not traffic in this sort of thing, as far as either of them knew. The trunk of the car must be some kind of hiding-in-plain-sight cache in a locked garage. They took the two boxes and inside of 60 seconds were on the sidewalk, calmly walking back to their car. DuPont had the now stuffed duffel bag over his shoulder.

As they drove off, Brenda saw in the rear-facing camera view that the gray van from Gliese was just then parking in front of Bennington's former home.

"Shit," she muttered.

*   *   *   *   *

The pair from Gliese effectively retraced DuPont and Brenda's steps, except that they didn't waste as much time looking around the garage. They had a tag reader with them, and could look for the tagged boxes far more efficiently. The woman started scanning the workbench and storage cupboards, while the man noticed that the car cover in front was less dusty and more wrinkled than the rest of it. He lifted it, and saw that the hood was ajar. He lifted it and looked inside, but saw nothing.

"Give this thing a scan, will you?" he asked his partner. She came over and waved the wand inside the trunk. There was some beeping, and she soon pulled out an old box of oily rags, road flares, and other automotive miscellany. Under the rags, there were a couple of small boxes. She slipped the top off of one, and found a circuit board with two large chips, each covered by a respectable heat sink. They exchanged glances, and she nodded approvingly.

"Someone's been in here," he said. "Something tells me these weren't the only things here. The car cover was moved, it wasn't as dusty on this end. It was opened recently."

"It could have been when these were put in here," she speculated. "They were only shipped out here a week ago."

"Maybe, maybe not. If these are here, you'd expect it all to be here. They may have missed these because they were under the rags." They spent another 20 minutes carefully searching the garage, but found nothing else.

"Let's just take these back," she said.

24

"You never did tell me how that fire got started last night," Benita said to Brad as she sipped her morning coffee. Brad was sitting opposite her at the small kitchen table.

"I'm giving you the gift of plausible deniability," he answered. "In case you're ever asked about it."

She took this to mean that Thakkar and his crew had somehow been involved, and yes, she was probably better off not knowing anything. It was small comfort knowing that at least he had already been dead.

Her front door icon lit up. It was Aradhya. *Give me a fucking break*, she thought.

"Yes?" she asked, through the icon.

"I'd like to apologize about my attitude last night. I would like to chat a bit about a few things. I promise not to be, um," she trailed off. "I promise not to insist on anything inappropriate."

"You really shouldn't be here, Aradhya. I don't work for you."

"I know, I know. I'm concerned about Pari. There are a few things you need to know about her. I don't know if my father has filled you in on them."

Goddammit, thought Benita. If this was some sort of ruse, she would break Aradhya's nose then call the cops on her and say she had become threatening. It would be hard to make the specs videos plausible, though. She buzzed Aradhya in through the building's front entrance.

"Aradhya Thakkar?" asked Brad, surprised.

"The same."

"What does she want?" He quickly looked around to make sure none of their equipment was visible. He had by then put it all neatly away in the duffel bag, which at the moment was next to his charging station in the second bedroom.

Benita went to let Aradhya in when the door told her she was there.

"You shouldn't be here," Benita told her. She stood aside for Aradhya to enter, and motioned towards the kitchen. "Please, have a seat. Coffee? There's still some left."

Aradhya walked to the table but didn't sit down. She was casually dressed to the extent that people like her understood the notion of "casual." Her blouse was a hip-length dark red silk faux cheongsam, lightly embroidered with gold-threaded floral designs, worn over charcoal gray jeans that had some barely visible smoky gold stitching to match the blouse. Some pricey-looking gray sneakers with a red highlight finished the set. She looked at Brad, then at Benita. "Could we speak privately?"

"Brad is working with me on your father's project. He's fully read in."

"Brad? His name is Brad? Seriously?" She scoffed. "I'd prefer it just be you and me."

"Brad, would you mind going to your charger? I'll get you later."

"No problem," said Brad, and got up to go. This was a standard virtual character response. If the owner or client wanted them to switch off, they had to do it graciously and without question. Evidently it also applied to robots.

Benita served Aradhya a cup with the remaining coffee and both sat down.

"Sorry about last night. I really mean it," began Aradhya. Benita waved it off as unimportant. "Pari is ill. As I recall she had a minor seizure when you visited my father."

Benita looked puzzled.

"She lost consciousness in your arms."

"That was a seizure?"

"She doesn't have *grand mal* seizures, she just loses consciousness for a moment or two then comes back. She falls occasionally, but she says she can generally tell when it's about to happen," explained Aradhya. Benita remembered Pari falling into her arms. She had thought the girl was faking it.

"OK," said Benita. "Is that it?" She realized too late that she may have come off as curt or impatient. Aradhya looked at her coolly.

"No," she answered after a moment. "There's more." She thought for a second, preparing her words.

"Pari was involved with some people, some fairly shady people," she began. "She was getting drugs from them, and from what I've been told, being abused by them."

"Abused how?" asked Benita. "Told by whom?"

"She was being sexually exploited by some prick she met at the Q'Boom Qlub, a place in Burlingame. Do you know of it?"

"It rings a bell. I don't think I've ever been inside," she answered. "It's a somewhat fancy place, no?"

"It is. Hillsborough types, people from other affluent enclaves," answered Aradhya. "You know, dancing, gambling, drinking, smoking, carousing, you name it. Swindlers and predators of various kinds lurking in the shadows."

"What was she doing there? Is she over 21?"

"She's 23," said Aradhya. "What does *anyone* do there? She was there for fun and excitement, to be with the cool crowd and the hot guys and hot girls, to get the hip new drugs and have wild experiences. She leads a pretty dissipated life."

"Sounds fun," said Benita dryly. "Is that why *you* go?" Aradhya bristled a bit, then tried to hide it.

"I'm friendly with the owner, Eddie Wu."

That name, and the club, there was something about it in the materials she had gotten from Thakkar. Something about scientific equipment and shady deals. The antique store was also mixed up in it, and also something about a magnetic field, now that she thought of it.

They were related in some way, otherwise she wouldn't have been given that information. Wu owned some kind of used industrial and scientific equipment company, and Bennington was his partner. Something along those lines. Was Wu involved with the quantum computing chips she picked up from Bennington's house?

"*Friendly* friendly, or just friendly?"

"Just friendly. It's not like the guy is my boyfriend or anything. I'm a married woman," answered Aradhya.

"Whose husband is no longer in the picture."

"We're still married," said Aradhya without blinking.

"And yet he ran off with somebody," added Benita. Aradhya's eyes narrowed, just perceptibly. She was definitely trying to be nice, and here was Benita, taunting her. "Do you know with whom?"

Aradhya examined the back of her right hand, looked towards the kitchen area, taking in the cramped panorama for a moment. She looked towards the living room and noticed the giclée that Wilkins had given her on the faux mantel leaning against the wall above the faux fireplace, still in its plastic bag, then looked back at Benita.

"I see that Dad gave you a print of that hideous painting," she began. "I've been told that Mohan is with a woman named Myrna. Myrna de la O. Her last name is the letter 'O,' if you can believe that. I should mention, at this point, that she was Eddie Wu's flame for a while. He's looking for her as well." Benita raised her eyebrows, one noticeably more than the other.

"And you've been friendly with *her* ex-flame. I like the symmetry."

"Mohan and I went to the Q'Boom fairly often, for a time. We got to know Eddie and Myrna while they were still a thing. She used to sing there a couple of evenings a week. Quite a talented jazz vocalist, I have to admit."

Admit wistfully, noted Benita.

"Was Pari part of your group, or did she go separately?"

"She was with us at first. One day there was a guy named Sav at our table, a friend of Eddie's. Has an antique shop in San Mateo, and occasionally has dealings with Eddie from what I gather. Eddie has a big industrial consignment store in Burlingame, not far from the club. Sav occasionally helped him find or dispose of old and antique industrial equipment. He also sells gray market jewelry and whatnot at the club. He has an ex-hooker do the selling to wealthy older men. I suspect most or all of that stuff is stolen."

Did that include state of the art electronics? Were these guys moving high tech contraband? How did the place near Watsonville figure into this?

"Sav as in Savion?" asked Benita.

"Yes Savion Bennington."

It was Benita's turn for a thoughtful pause.

"Bennington," said Benita, almost to herself.

"Do you know him?" asked Aradhya with genuine curiosity.

"The name rings a bell," she feigned. "Let me check something." She twiddled to find the news video of the fire. "Ah, here it is. I thought the name sounded familiar. Here, have a look at this."

She sent the link, and Aradhya spent a moment watching it in her own specs. Her mouth opened enough for Benita too see the top edges of her teeth, upper and lower. So neat and even they seemed carved by a skilled artisan. Her face showed something akin to surprise, but mixed in with something else. Maybe it wasn't such a huge surprise.

"Oh my god," whispered Aradhya, "Oh my god..."

"Sorry to be the bearer of bad news," said Benita.

"This happened last night?" asked Aradhya. "Where were you last night? Where did you find Pari? What's going on? Did you have anything to do with this?"

"No. I've never met Savion Bennington," she said. Strictly speaking, it was true. "As to Pari, you'll have to ask her."

"She's my sister! I'm the only person she has who is looking out for her! She is *ill*!" Aradhya was losing her composure, in spite of valiant efforts to the contrary.

"Look, I'm sorry. I'm sure you are," said Benita, trying to be more soothing. "I really can't talk about it at the moment. One day I may be able to, but not right now. Please understand."

Aradhya was starting to tremble, and struggled visibly to bring herself back.

"OK, right. Sorry," she said. "I want us to be on the same side. I need us to be. I want to keep Pari safe." As an afterthought, she added "And I want to find Mohan."

"Look, I'll do what I can. I won't let Pari come to harm, not if I have anything to do with it. I'll see if I can find out anything about Mohan, but he isn't really on my radar. If something comes up, I'll let you know, but it's not an active priority for me. Please understand."

"OK, OK, sure. I understand. Sorry to be so insistent, but it's something that's on my mind. Constantly," said Aradhya apologetically. "There's something else."

Benita cocked her head slightly.

"Eddie Wu and Sav had dealings with a small biotech company in Watsonville. They sold them some used genomics equipment, incubators, organic chemical synthesizers, spectroscopy equipment, computing systems, and quite a lot of other things. Also respectable amounts of specialty chemicals, solvents, and other lab supplies. In my experience, far more equipment and materials than a tissue culture company really needs, and rather more varied than usual. I assume my father mentioned *that*."

Benita said nothing for a moment, looking into Aradhya's steely gaze.

"As I mentioned before," said Benita slowly, "my work with your father is confidential."

Aradhya got up to leave.

"Well, thank you for your time. I know you've got things that need your attention. I'll certainly appreciate any help you're able to provide. Please help us keep Pari out of the Bennington thing," she said, extending her hand to Benita.

Benita shook her hand as a friendly gesture.

"Of course," she said. Aradhya led the way to the door, thanked Benita, then turned and walked down the corridor.

25

It was mid-afternoon and Brenda and DuPont were sitting in his car, parked on the topmost level of a parking structure at 2nd and El Camino, in San Mateo. They had made sure to park near the middle, well away from street view. They had stopped by a drug store and were now sharing a vape.

"We could just dump this stuff. Leave it here in the parking lot and let some other poor schmuck take the heat," she said.

"Or make a million bucks," he responded. "Maybe less."

She looked at him, noting his doubt.

"Would Wu give us anything if we turned them in to him?" asked Brenda. DuPont shrugged.

"We're basically nobody to him. The store is probably his now, but we're Bennington's crew, not his," he said. "Plus, who knows how much this stuff is really worth. The Gliese people are pretty excited, but maybe it's more about whatever they want them for than for the things themselves."

"Or maybe it'll help us get in with him. You know, loyal workers or whatever. We play dumb. We don't know if these things are valuable or not. We got them back so that he can give them to the Gliese people."

"We probably should have left them at Bennington's," said DuPont, shaking his head. "Too late now though. We'll be the prime suspects no matter what."

They smoked for a while, in silence. Finally, DuPont blew his last billowy white plume of opaque vapor out of the car window.

"You're right. We should give them to Wu. We have to show him we're not trying to steal from him or from Gliese. We're basically going to throw ourselves at his mercy. At the mercy of some fucking crook," he said bitterly. Brenda looked out her window, and blew out her own dense white cloud. After a few moments, she turned to him and asked, "So where would he be now? At the warehouse?"

"One way to find out," he answered. "Adrian Road," he told the car. He'd been going there regularly enough that the car was able to remember the exact address.

*   *   *   *   *

"Park here," he told the car. It had just turned onto the last block of Adrian Road, which dead-ended less than a hundred meters further ahead, just past Wu's industrial consignment warehouse. The pair sat in the car, still unsure of the plan. They could see Wu's expensive sports car in the warehouse parking lot from where they sat.

"What if he tries to do something to us?" she asked.

"The guy isn't some kind of murderer," said DuPont, "At least not as far as I know. We'll probably get shit for it, but we'll get rid of the chips, and he won't have anything on us anymore. Maybe he'll let us run the shop for him." He turned to look at her. "You were more or less running it already, right?"

She shrugged. "The thing pretty much runs itself, but I know where everything is. The software takes care of everything except the black market stuff, and there's ways to get that into the system. Bennington was the guy who did all the hookups for it. We'd have to figure that out. I know all of his friends' assistants, at least online. I think I could ramp it back up. *We* could." She looked at DuPont.

"Let's just do it," he said. Each one took a box.

They walked in through the main entrance, and were greeted by the receptionist, whom DuPont knew fairly well.

"Hey, Sami, the boss around?" he asked.

"In his office. You can go in, I don't think he's busy," answered Sami cheerily.

"Thanks," answered DuPont with an amiable smile, and the pair went into the building's small office area. DuPont knocked on the frame of the open doorway. Wu was there with a couple of his crew, two stocky-looking Hispanic guys who always seemed to be with him. DuPont had always assumed they were bodyguards. As far as crooks went around here, Wu was more than a few notches above Bennington, no question about it. Wu's face froze for a moment when he saw them. He looked each in the eye and saw the two parcels, then instantly went into full-blown sincere condolences mode.

"I'm really sorry to hear about your boss, really. It was a tragedy," he said, motioning them in. "Please sit down."

He indicated some chairs in front of his desk, just now vacated by his associates, who quietly left the room.

"If there was any foul play, we'll work with the authorities and get to the bottom of it. Rest assured that you're still part of the team. I'm going to count on you to keep the shop running until we find another antiques buyer."

So that's what Bennington was, thought both Brenda and DuPont. Neither of them could afford to make any snarky comments about it, however, not even in private speech.

"Thanks, we really appreciate it," said DuPont. "By the way, some folks from Gliese stopped by earlier. They mentioned something about some items missing from their last shipment."

Wu's gazed turned more serious.

"Yeah, they mentioned it to me," he answered. "Any clues?" He carefully pretended not to have noticed the boxes they had with them.

DuPont hesitated, so Brenda jumped in. "We drove past Sav's house after the firemen were gone. The garage was still there, so we had a look to see if Sav might have stored anything there temporarily." Nice whitewashing, thought DuPont.

"So, did he?" asked Wu. "May I assume it's those two boxes you have with you?"

DuPont placed his on Wu's desk, and Brenda followed suit. Wu slipped the top of one of them, and lifted the topmost plastic tray to see the chips. He did the same with the other box.

"The rest are in your car?" he asked.

Brenda's and DuPont's faces went blank. Wu studied them closely, trying to judge if they were about to bullshit him.

"This is all we know about," said DuPont.

"Bennington had them in the van yesterday afternoon, when he left. We found them in an old car he has in the garage," added Brenda.

Wu considered this carefully. There were still two boxes missing, and the Gliese people were getting insistent. They strongly suspected DuPont and Brenda. He didn't want to spook these two, though. He had to track down the rest of the chips and calm the Gliese people down. He knew what they were capable of.

"OK, well, thanks for bringing them, I really appreciate it," said Wu. "I'm glad you thought quickly and found them. Good job!"

"We can scour the shop for the rest of it. They may still be there somewhere," offered DuPont. Brenda nodded in agreement. Wu was undoubtedly aware that Gliese people had already done that.

"Good idea. I'll give you guys a call later, sound good?" Wu said and got up to indicate they were done.

"Sure, no problem," said DuPont. A round of handshaking, and the pair left.

On the way back, both of them were in much better spirits. Wu had seemed positive and remarkably non-threatening.

"We definitely have to go through the entire shop. No telling what Sav may have been hiding in there. Do you know of any secret hiding places?" asked DuPont.

"I know of a few. I know of a couple that Sav used to use."

"Really? You didn't mention it this morning," said DuPont. Brenda shrugged.

"It didn't occur to me then. I thought those two boxes were all there was."

"We should get on it," he answered, "Get this over with."

"I have a job tonight at the Q'Boom. I need to go get ready for it. I've got something at my apartment that I was supposed to deliver today. Could you please drop me off on the way? We can search for more stuff tomorrow," she said, trying to be sweet and regretful at the same time. DuPont scowled at her.

"Don't tell me, computer chips?" he asked. "Sav's dead! How can you still be working for him?"

"This is *my* stuff!" she replied, "I managed to grab a few things every now and then, I already told you. I actually do know some of Sav's contacts, and I usually did the final ordering from their assistants. We helped each other out whenever we could."

DuPont stared at her.

"Jewelry, Rashaun!" DuPont turned and looked out of his window for a while. He told his car to stop off at Brenda's.

26

The Woods was a cafeteria-style eatery that was set up in such a way that patrons carried their trays from food station to food station all around the periphery of the dining area, which was roughly a 6 by 6 grid of tables arranged asymmetrically with respect to each other. In the middle of the room were coffee and espresso machines, as well as tea, milk, cream, pastries and other desserts. The idea was clearly to provide plausible excuses for people to parade themselves around, weaving through the tables and lingering at the food stations, so that anyone who had their HunterGather overlay switched on could get a good long look and leisurely examine their scores. It was pricey compared to other places, but the food was OK and most people there were indeed studying each other's HunterGather metrics as they ate. Practically everyone was always logged in, and only the newbies were in stealth mode. The room had excellent sight lines and was well illuminated by shaded, glare-free lighting.

Benita was no exception. As she feigned disinterest in her surroundings while eating a complex salad composed of kale, arugula, Mexican *esquite*, goat cheese, tomato, quinoa, and sunflower seeds, all bathed in a lime juice vinaigrette, she kept her eye on the scores that surrounded her. They were custom calculated for her based on her experiences on HunterGather dates. It was uncommon for her to find scores here much beyond 80 or so, in spite of already having gone on well over two hundred HunterGather-selected dates, and promptly attending the success interviews afterwards. She was a loner, and always had been. Her social skills were not great, and she quickly became bored and impatient with people. As a result people found her to be boring, laconic, and not a little bit weird. She didn't find people here that often, but there had been exceptions, once in a blue moon. She had no doubt that they were all 90s to each other. What she was looking for was a mystery even to herself. All she knew was that the search had so far been interminable.

This was the new San Martín gentry, people from diverse pasts and generally humble beginnings who had managed to place themselves in the chronically overheated Silicon Valley economy, educated thanks to Green New Deal largesse. They were newly-minted engineers, scientists, economists, MBAs, and the many other professions whose attention the tech economy maintained by throwing increasingly large amounts of money at them. Some may have lived in old gasoline-powered vehicles or in tent encampments at some point, perhaps recently, or had grown up in urban ghettos or run-down formerly middle class homes. Now they dressed in the height of fashion and rode in high-end Scrambs, and they carried themselves about like glamorous video characters.

She finished her salad and got up to get some coffee. She went the long way, as people did, going all the way around via the second concentric ring between the tables, cutting towards the coffee and dessert area only after going almost the whole way around.

"79 at 9 o'clock," said Zag. It was one of the highest scores currently present.

Zag was synced with Benita's HunterGather account and could scan the scores of everyone in the room without actually having to look at them. She slowly turned towards her left, pretending to examine the posters and diverse knick-knacks strategically covering the walls for this very purpose, briefly dropping her gaze down at the end to see who he was referring to. A man was seated at a table with a woman, both about Benita's age. Both had average scores of 79, although when she drilled down she saw that there were notable differences. They were hot, though.

"Which one did you mean?" she asked Zag in private speech.

"Take your pick," he replied, "or do both. You know you want to. That's why we're here. It wouldn't be the first time."

"It took me a month to get over the first time. 79 is way too low."

She saw that both scored relatively highly in "friendly," "outgoing," "extrovert," and "talkative," albeit low in "talks too much." Their scores in "interesting conversation," and "thoughtful" were in the low 70s or high 60s. "Nerdy" and "geeky" dipped into the low 50s, a red flag for Benita. Several educational, socio-economic, and sex-related scores were in the 80s, which explained their otherwise highish score. She'd had dreary experiences with such people. Sexual and educational compatibility weren't enough to overcome her shyness with strangers, and the dates didn't tend to go very well.

She kept in contact with a handful of mid-90s she had managed to find over the years, and they were each other's *de facto* social circle, even though they were dispersed far and wide in the Silicon Valley area. None of them was less than a 45 minute drive away. She fantasized about being able to have a nice lunch at *The Woods*, choose among several 90-plus candidates, and take one home to her flat just two blocks away.

After a leisurely cappuccino, she walked back home. She still had to clean up after Aradhya's visit earlier. Pari's epilepsy thing seemed dubious, but Benita wasn't a neurologist. The young woman *did* seem to go convincingly limp for a moment the second time. The first time was still in doubt in Benita's mind. Aradhya's visit had been strangely brief. As she carried the cups to the dishwasher, she saw that Aradhya's was still practically full. Had Benita spooked her, or was that all she had wanted to say? Pari was ill, and she had gotten caught up with Bennington. She wanted to find Mohan. That was about it, except for the oddly specific bit about the Watsonville site. She had checked the materials provided by Wilkins and saw that Gliese Genetics was ostensibly just another plant and animal tissue culture company, but Thakkar and his crew had some kind of keen interest in it. The Gliese people bought an unusual amount of specific kinds of lab equipment, as if they were making large amounts of specialty chemicals or something in addition to their tissue culture business. Mohan was the connection, somehow. Mohan had been working on the case before her, and now it turned out that Aradhya was interested in Gliese. How did she know any details? Had she and Mohan discussed it? What was Aradhya's interest in it all, Aradhya the biotech venture capitalist?

She remembered that Wu owned the nightclub Aradhya had mentioned as well as the industrial equipment consignment warehouse. She and Brad had reviewed it all last night before the visit to Bennington's home, although they had focused mainly on the house, its surroundings, and its surveillance coverage. If there were any "magnetic anomalies" detected around either the warehouse or the antique shop, she couldn't recall.

"So, anything interesting?" said Brad as he sat at the kitchen table.

"What's the connection between the antique store and Eddie Wu again?" she asked, in lieu of looking it up herself.

"Wu and Bennington have business dealings with each other. They buy and sell used and antique items, from home decor, jewelry, and fine clothing, to old electronics, lab equipment, and industrial materials and machines," said Brad. "Bennington was more on the antiques side, Wu is more on the industrial side. There's some overlap, though."

"What's the deal with the magnetic fields? I didn't look at that very closely."

Brad looked at her for a moment, his servo-driven eyes looking into her own.

"Magnetic fields have been detected around the antique shop and its general area," answered Brad. "Not just any magnetic field, but one that's exactly like a human brain's. Some people that frequent the shop have devices that broadcast human thought. They're from one of the shop's steady customers, a company in Watsonville."

Benita looked at him steadily for a moment with furrowed brow.

"The tissue culture company? I don't understand what that means," she said. "Broadcasting thought? That makes no sense."

"As you may or may not know, FféFfé has been developing another biometric capture system to go with heart rate, breathing, body temperature, and so on that you're wearing right now. There are sensors in your new head gear that are able to capture the very weak magnetic fields that surround biological brains. Since there are tiny electrical currents moving along the huge number of nerve fibers in your head, there is a magnetic field around the brain resulting from the sum total of all of those little currents."

"Right... right..." she said slowly, "electrical currents generate magnetic fields. I think I remember people mentioning it at FfēFfē about some future product. I think marketing has a phrase like 'the mind's twin, its shadow, its very spirit' that they're going to use at some point, right?"

"Right, something like that."

"But why broadcast it? Is someone receiving it? Can anyone walking down the street receive it?"

"There are certain people who wear caps on their heads that generate the fields. It turns out that you can induce mental activity with magnetic fields, including playing back someone else's recorded thoughts as if they were a video," explained Brad. "That sort of thing is still in the research phase, though. These people are already using them in the field."

"These caps are made by FfēFfē?" she asked.

"No, they're made by someone else. This is very sophisticated technology. It's actually well ahead of the state of the art."

Benita's eyes narrowed, something didn't entirely jibe.

"How can it be well ahead of the state of the art if someone's already using it? In the field?" she asked, "That would mean that it *is* the state of the art. It defines the state of the art. That's what FfēFfē has, right?"

"Whatever. Dr. Thakkar is extremely interested in the technology. The next generation of FfēFfē robots have a mini-model in their machine learning algorithm that uses data captured from that new cap I brought you," he said. "I have that new mini-model in my own system, by the way. It simulates the magnetic fields that a person's brain would be generating if it was seeing and hearing what *I'm* seeing and hearing. That goes into my main control model, and simulates detailed human thought in far greater detail than the older EEG sensors you're also wearing."

Brad was obviously holding back on her. She suddenly realized that he had been doing so all along. This wasn't just some cheerful, competent, and loquacious yet servile machine. This thing had depth, forethought, a deliberateness that seemed un-robotlike. It was clearly holding a variety of concepts in its head, and making determinations as to how and when to dose information to her as needed. No doubt he was following orders, and no doubt there was some kind of communication between him and Thakkar's systems even as they spoke, but his grasp of the moment was entirely new to her. It was something more than the typical virtual character. It was sneaky, almost cunning.

"Brad," she said, and paused. After a moment, he turned to her.

"Yes?" he said after another moment.

"Why use the new magnetic field detectors if the EEG already gives virtual characters and robots a credible emotional profile? How much more is really needed, especially given the additional costs all the way up and down the product pipeline?"

"It's not for the emotional profile, it's for the cognitive profile. The magneto-encephalographic sensors capture several orders of magnitude more data than the EEG sensors. The models that are built with that data are rich, black box simulations of the human mind at a much deeper level. They simulate human thought, human creativity, and human imagination. If you put data from several human actors into a single machine learning model, you essentially have the makings of a super-intelligence. If you put the data from a hundred or a thousand human actors into a single model, as will be possible with these new quantum computing chips, you get something that we can only imagine right now."

"We? Are you 'the makings of a super-intelligence'? How many human actors' magneto-encephalographic data are in *your* model?"

"More than 10, depending on how you count them," he answered after a long pause. "That's why I have to stay near the charger. It's too much data to send over the public data networks, even on 6G. There's too much traffic on them."

Benita uselessly studied Brad's face. It was pointed at her, and she could see that he was looking at her as intently as she was looking at *him*, but she was still not good at reading robot faces. For some reason, she was better able to read Zag's facial expressions than Brad's, even though they were probably based on very similar data. Maybe it was easier to fudge virtual characters than robots.

"And what does 'ahead of the state of the art' mean?" she asked. "Don't bullshit me."

Brad was motionless for a moment. He gently tapped the table with his right index finger a few times. She knew that gesture and recognized the cadence. There was a woman at the Palo Alto Economic Intelligence Office who did that at meetings. Benita couldn't remember her name, but she had occasionally spoken with her. She was one of the folks on the customer side who also wore behavior capture gear. Serious woman, upper management, an old wolf.

With the virtual characters, Benita still felt confident and in control. The characters were at her service, and she still had to provide reminders and prodding when they inevitably started to lose focus on long or complicated tasks or conversations. Now she wasn't so sure. If the robots were going to be filled with the behaviors of upper management, of senior people, of experts in sophisticated arts and sciences, of ninja-like detectives, now what? The finger tapping was a tip-off, a tell, the beep of a timer finishing its interval. Did she have Brad, or did he have *her*? Who was at the service of whom?

"You have to decide something, Benita. We chose you because you're good at what you do, at gathering information, at snooping around, at going the extra mile and finishing the job, at dealing with virtual characters and reporting our flaws and shortcomings. We like your judgment calls, even under duress," he started. "We need that."

It was Brad, and not Brad. It was as if something else was speaking through him, albeit in his voice and still with his casual tone, something that suddenly felt deep and incomprehensible. Benita shuddered, fine hairs on the back of her neck and on her forearms came erect.

"Who, who are you?" she asked, an edge in her usually placid voice.

"I'm many people, as you know, and I'm a machine. I'm made of you, and of many others. You're in me. Much of the work you've ever done for FfēFfē is in me, in machines like me..." he paused. "You have to decide something Benita. We want to assign you a task that is far more important than you can imagine. It is also very dangerous. Your predecessor has very likely been killed in its service."

"What? Mohan? He's not with Eddie Wu's lover?" she asked in alarm. She stared fixedly at his glassy electronic eyes, behind which there were no doubt a variety of video capture devices. "What happened to him?"

"In the collective opinion of our team, and based on what evidence we've gathered, Gliese Genetics, one of Wu and Bennington's customers, are operating a research station in Watsonville. They're in possession of these magnetic field generators in the form of beige baseball caps worn by their human staff. Bennington and Wu have been quietly supplying them with a variety of materials and equipment for some kind of sophisticated biological experiments," said Brad. "We believe that your colleague Mohan, was either captured or killed while trying to approach the site."

"How, exactly do you know this?"

"One of our prototype robots was there. An early beta model. They don't have your skills. It wasn't armed. There was nothing it could have done. We only know all of this because it managed to come back. Barely."

Benita shook her head involuntarily. She was no novice to violence on the job. She had faced lethal danger before. During the 18 months she had worked with the San Mateo County Industrial Espionage Unit, the teams she had worked with had frequently faced armed cut-outs, the desperate fools recruited by foreign intelligence officers to do their dirty work in-country. There had been gunfire a few times, and on one occasion an agent on her team had been standing next to her, almost touching her, when a stray round hit the agent in her upper chest, blasting out half of her shoulder blade on the way through. Benita was the one who gave her first aid and helped keep her calm. Luckily, the bleeding wasn't life threatening, but the injury was serious enough for her to give up her career as a field investigator. She'd known a few others, over the years, who had gotten shot, deliberately hit by moving vehicles, beaten, or otherwise injured in the line of duty. She herself had been lucky.

"This wasn't part of the deal," she said.

"Benita, you know that's *always* part of the deal. This is what you do, what you do well," he said. "Yes, it's dangerous, like most of the work you've done over the past few years. This time you'll have better backup. Much better. You'll be working with me."

"I'd feel better with a competent human. Somebody with more experience than me, not less," she said. "Someone who won't have to stay home."

"I have that experience, Benita. Dr. Thakkar has managed to gather behavior data from all of our most important security and intelligence customers here in the Bay area," he said, trying to be reassuring. "San Francisco. Palo Alto, San Jose, up and down the peninsula and much of the South Bay. On top of the hundred thousand hours of non-magneto-encephalographic behavior data from the virtual character product line, I have about 3 dozen of their best field agents, an average of 1000 hours each, and over 3000 hours each from 10 of their managers. You know them. You've worked with them. They were capturing data right alongside you."

She studied the wooden surface of the kitchen table. It was showing its age. A few food stains, some scuffing, some white discoloration of the varnish in places. She should think about getting a new one.

"I have over ten times the processing power of the virtual characters. Almost 5 times longer short term memory," he continued.

"Spare me the sales pitch," she said, holding one hand up, palm towards Brad. "OK, fine."

She should have expected this. The compensation had been too good to be true, suspiciously so. She thought she'd be doing some minor snooping around for a doddering old man. She thought it would have been a sabbatical of sorts. She really should have known better.

"So what's next?" she asked. *What the hell, right?* she thought.

"I'll tell you in the car," he replied. "This time I'm coming with you. You'll need to dress up a bit, though."

Benita frowned.

27

By what charm of magic or summoning of demons did Brad come to exist? Truth be told, the answer is *by cheating and trickery*.

Old-timers could recall a day when teams of programmers spent hundreds or perhaps thousands of hours writing reams of complex computer code to make their employer's products work. Whether it was the firmware in a car or an airplane, an operating system, or a human resources department management tool, quite a lot of code had to be written. That code was invariably full of design errors, misunderstandings, bad assumptions, and plain old bugs. Hence, a similar team of software quality assurance engineers was needed to find those flaws and report them so that they could be fixed.

When the project was young and the software was starting to do all of the things that were expected in version 1, there was much excitement and rejoicing. A half dozen years later, few if anyone on either team knew the full details of how the software actually worked. Many of the initial authors and testers had by then cashed out their stock options and moved on to greener pastures, and it was now painfully clear that no amount of money could pay for enough people to keep fixing the things that were not working and adding the new features constantly demanded by customers and company executives.

Such an approach was essentially intractable for developing something as complex as a virtual character capable of simulating a human being, let alone an actual physical humanoid robot. The time, money, and inclination to do it the old fashioned way no longer existed. Years earlier, a clever means to cheat had been developed. Gather large amounts of data that accurately represent what outputs are expected from the software when provided with specific inputs, and build a black box that consistently did exactly that. Machine learning algorithms derived from software neural networks suddenly became practical thanks to a handful of computer software and hardware advances that more or less coincided in time.

Years later, after even more advancements, Joe Zheng and Rameshwar Thakkar realized that the time was right to tackle the imposing problem of simulating complex human behavior. The cheat? Instead of treating it as a code-writing project, they devised a way to capture behavior from hundreds of actors at a time, and use that data to train a machine learning algorithm. This way, nobody would need to understand how people walk or talk, why they laugh sometimes and sometimes not, what "friendliness" is, how to keep robots from hurting people, how not to constantly stumble over chairs, how to neatly and cleanly serve several cups of coffee, and the myriad other things that people do without a second thought. In essence, they had figured out a way to steal the innate and learned behavior that *Homo sapiens* had accumulated over millions of years of biological and social evolution. Quite the computer science hat trick.

Now, years later, there was Brad. He was a composite of many people's behavior, carefully composed by FféFfé employees who were now experts in the black art of human behavior blending.

As the years rolled on, the behaviors became more and more complex and nuanced. While the early models of virtual characters were barely able to do basic personal assistant duties and painfully simple conversation, the latest models were able to help children with homework, provide adults with solid financial advice, and carry on lengthy, seemingly intelligent conversations with most users. The amount of carefully planned, gathered, and curated behavior data behind them was prodigious indeed, thousands upon thousands of person-hours.

This was why the Flash Programmable Quantum Gate Arrays, the FPQGAs, were so greatly anticipated and in such short supply. The amount of behavior that could be embedded in a single robot could be scaled up from the relative handful used for characters like Zag or Cin to the equivalent of scores of human experts, each in a separate field. Data from the architect group could be combined with data from the structural engineering and civil engineering law groups, along with data from the graphic designers, clinical psychology, and social worker groups. The resulting virtual character or robot would be all of those experts in one. It would be more than an artificial general intelligence, an entity capable of behaving like a normal human being in a wide variety of tasks and contexts. It would in effect be an artificial super-intelligence, an entity able to do significantly more than a normal human being. Blam was already making money with these from very large customers. They were connected to huge data centers over extremely fast networks, and already they had several products that combined the talents of up to 5 expert human beings.

The FPQGAs would allow them to combine the talents of more human experts than that in a single robot, and to allow the robot to roam freely through the world without having to be attached to a high speed network. They would be fully autonomous, like Brad.

*   *   *   *   *

Thakkar got the itch for immortality about 6 years ago, when the first virtual characters for enterprise customers started to display sophisticated behavior. He immediately started wearing behavior capture gear every day, and continued to do so even after he became ill. He managed to set up a special project in which a few virtual characters would be gradually trained using data representing his own behavior. It would be mixed in with the minimum number of other actors needed to get the machine learning model to work reasonably well, and these actors would be carefully chosen from among those whose behavior data statistically clustered most closely with his. Mohan Bakaya turned out to be one of them, as did Benita Garcés. About a third of the actors who clustered most closely with him were women. In most activities, Benita clustered close to Thakkar, rarely hovering away from the nearest 10 actors who also clustered with him. Mohan was generally in the same ballpark as well. Thakkar's secret interest in the two was entirely due to the similarity that their captured behavior bore to his own.

Now, years later, some of these experimental behavior mixes were fairly well advanced, and had been modified to be used in physical robots. Wilkins and all of his peers were one of the mixes, and Brad was another.

Thakkar had been systematic about skewing his behavior towards "immortality," to the extent that it could be called that. He encouraged his daughters to continue living at home, and had created trust funds whose disbursement was contingent on their spending the night at home at least 15 days per month. He had meals with them whenever they were available, and occasionally went out with them for lunch, dinner, coffee, or drinks. He was scrupulously kind and tolerant, even when discussions ranged well away from his comfort zone. They looked through old family photos and videos together, and discussed them extensively, pointing out who was whom, where the location was, and what had happened. All of his presentations and meetings at FféFfé and elsewhere had been captured, often surreptitiously. Before he was ill he tinkered in his home workshop and painted in his home studio. Frequent outings with friends to museums, galleries, concerts, and other places were recorded, also with his friends not always being aware of it. Sometimes he would visit the same gallery or listen to the same music with different friends in order to layer in more detail and improvisation.

Now that he had a few Wilkins robots, he was able to converse with them about the things in his life that most interested him, and which most other people would find boring or tedious. Even rambling unstructured conversations were able to draw out parts of his past and of his more intimate inner life.

Part of the upkeep of a virtual character or a robot consisted in recording its own behavior. Whether the movements of the body were in the virtual realm of a game engine somewhere in the cloud, or produced by sensors present on the robot's body, these were identical to those of the human actor. A trained virtual character or robot continuously generated spontaneous context-dependent behavior in the course of its everyday functions, and this was recorded, just as the actors' body suit data was recorded. This data could be fed back in and used to continue training the machine learning model, so that it could continue learning about the environments in which it went about its activities. This training could occur on a variety of schedules, but mostly it occurred at night, while the character or robot was effectively powered down. In the case of robots, this coincided with battery charging.

Lengthy and frequent conversations between Thakkar and his robots, much like any user's conversations and activities with their Blam virtual characters, resulted in the robots learning more and more about Thakkar. Unlike the average Blam user, however, Thakkar's body suit data was also fed into his robots' machine learning models. Not only were the robots learning more about their environment and their place in it, like a normal Blam virtual character, but they were also being trained on even more data from Thakkar's body suit. The robots were becoming both more like themselves and more like Thakkar, and this was about as close to immortality as he expected to get.

Brad was a separate experiment. He, too, received data from Thakkar's behavior data cluster, but it was tuned more towards Benita. It received data both from Thakkar and from actors who most closely clustered with Benita. Many of those actors worked in security, surveillance, and related activities because their similar behavior and individual inclination and ability towards that line of work got them clustered together in the first place. Quite a few others came from a variety of professions and backgrounds, with the arts and sciences unusually well represented.

Benita was in Brad, as were many of the people she had been working with over the years.

28

DuPont parked behind the antique shop and went inside. He thought he saw a light go out somewhere in the front of the store, and froze where he stood. He strained to see if he could hear anything. He twiddled to have a look at the security camera feeds, but he was locked out. Brenda had changed the access key, and had sent him the new one a few days ago, he now recalled. He quietly made his way to a shadowy corner near some shelving, which was unfortunately empty so it afforded little cover, and twiddled to search for her message with the new key. There was a key in a message that looked older than he remembered. Still locked out! Where was that damned key?

"Come out DuPont, let's keep this business-like," said a familiar woman's voice. The lights came on and the same man and woman who had been there that morning walked into the shipping and receiving area. Each had a pistol in one hand pointing down towards the floor at their side, as non-threatening as you could be and still have a gun in your hand.

"Hey, man, I'm here for the same thing as you. We found a couple of boxes at Sav's place and gave them to Eddie Wu. He said to look for more here at the shop."

"So we heard. We've been over the place twice and haven't found shit. Is there something you know that we don't?"

"Brenda said there's some hiding places that Sav used to use," replied DuPont.

"Do you know where they are?"

"I know of a couple."

"And where might your lovely friend be at the moment?" asked the woman. Both started walking towards him.

"She had to work at the club tonight. She's got a customer for some jewelry."

"Jewelry? Does she run some kind of a jewelry business? Like a specs app or something?" asked the woman. They were right in front of him now.

"Maybe she runs an antique store," smiled the man, "An antique jewelry store. You guys sell any jewelry here?"

"I don't know, man. I mainly just do pickups and deliveries."

"It seems your fetching accomplice knows more than you do," said the woman. "Maybe we should invite her over. Maybe it isn't just jewelry she's selling. Did you see this *alleged* jewelry?" The woman tapped DuPont's chest with the tip of her gun.

DuPont shook his head, and noticed the man make a quick arm movement. He got a very brief look at the man's pistol, from up close. It looked a bit scuffed.

*   *   *   *   *

DuPont was now lying on the floor of a moving vehicle. The man and the woman were looking down at him from their seats. He soon discovered that trying to turn his head by even a small amount was enormously painful. The left side of his head was throbbing with pain, all the way down to his neck. His hands were bound at the wrists with twist ties. Nobody spoke. After a while, the car got off the freeway, and DuPont recognized that they were now in Burlingame, undoubtedly heading towards the Q'Boom. His specs were smudged and powered down. They didn't fit right, and they might not even be his.

"OK, time for some adult entertainment," said the man as he got out of the car. The woman followed him, and they were kind enough to help him out of the car. He could handle it, as long as he didn't make any sudden moves, especially from the neck up.

"We're going to cut you loose, but you're going to have to be cool. We have lead, and we have high voltage, and we'll be judicious in the use of either," said the woman. The man snipped the twist ties off. DuPont was a thief, not some kind of special forces commando. He'd have to play it cool. The man and the woman took off their beige Gliese baseball caps and put them in the woman's shoulder bag. They both kept their specs on.

They went in through the back door of the dive bar side of Q'Boom, which faced the parking lot. Inside was the usual party atmosphere, people flaunting their expensive clothing, socializing, networking, preening, bragging, parading their wealth for all to admire, making shady deals, sowing and cultivating erotic liaisons, and generally seeing and being seen in this strange little habitat, all sprinkled liberally with booze and cannabis consumables from the bar, and a variety of other substances obtained less formally.

They walked through the cramped and crowded space and into the adjacent main building through a short passageway. This area was less crowded and had a more refined vibe, a demographic that skewed noticeably older. His current escorts walked him towards a bar that was Bennington's favorite, and by extension Brenda's. They went directly towards the first empty booth they could find and sat down, DuPont wincing as he settled between them with his back to the wall.

He looked around and quickly spotted Brenda at the bar on a bar stool, talking to a fifty-something man with graying hair. She was being more than friendly and conversational, maintaining a sultry gaze on her target. She was wearing a deep violet satin dress that beautifully exhibited her luscious figure, and short enough to make the crossing and uncrossing of her stocking-sheathed legs a minor cultural event, at least for the man she was chatting with. She was too focused on her customer to have noticed DuPont enter the dimly lit bar with the Gliese crew. He was hoping to somehow signal to her to get the hell out of here.

"Don't do anything rash, DuPont," said the woman calmly. "She doesn't look like she has any merchandise with her," she said to her comrade.

"Maybe she's got it stuffed in her bra," leered the man.

"I don't believe she's wearing one," said the woman, pretending to crane her neck in Brenda's direction. "I don't imagine anything really valuable would fit in that purse."

Brenda had a small purse that matched her dress lying on the bar near her elbow. That was all she had with her. DuPont knew there'd be some pepper spray in there, maybe a small one shot taser, and not much else. The plan was usually to lure the guy to an apartment rented just for this occasion, make the sale, sweeten it with some erotic artisanship if needed, and then both would go their separate ways. The guy could always come back here to look for her if he wasn't satisfied, or conceivably even go to the police, but the Q'Boom Qlub was always quick to eject troublemakers, and the police would certainly note that receiving stolen merchandise didn't come with an enforceable warranty. In any case, this crowd didn't tend to play it that way, and Brenda was giving him a good enough deal on some hot goods that there would be no unsatisfied customers, especially if there was any sweetening involved. She had a hard won local reputation to maintain, after all.

"Drinks?" asked a waitress cheerfully.

"Club soda, with lime juice, low ice," said the woman.

"Same," said the man.

"Give me the darkest and hoppiest of whatever you have on tap," said DuPont glumly. The young woman went off to get the drinks.

Brenda sipped her drink and slowly re-crossed her legs, to her client's brief but rapt attention.

"Can we assume that guy's the mark?" asked the woman. "She's really got him hooked."

"Most likely," said DuPont.

"How long does this usually take?" asked the woman, glancing at her watch. "You've seen her do this, right? So you have some sort of sense of the timing? I assume you're a grifter yourself. Can you read the guy from here?"

Go fuck yourself, you self-impressed bitch, thought DuPont. He craned his neck, pretending to try and get a better look at the guy, but didn't get very far from the pain. Luckily, the waitress arrived with his beer.

"He's definitely interested," said DuPont.

The woman stared at DuPont as he calmly took a sip of his ale. It hurt a bit to swallow, but the cool, creamy drink was soothing. DuPont had another look at the guy. Yes, he'd seen her work many times before. There were tells that could measure her progress. How tipsy was the guy? Had he touched her deliberately near the knee yet? How interested did he appear during her occasional leg crossing and uncrossing? Was he getting fidgety?

"As soon as the guy gets fidgety, especially after getting a flash of thigh or whatever, he's probably ready to buy. She may take him someplace private for the actual transaction. He looks pretty close already."

Brenda said something that her mark evidently found very funny. He rocked back with his laugh, and on the way back his hand just happened to give her a friendly squeeze on the knee, accidentally slipping further up her thigh. She looked to one side and pretended to wave at somebody across the room as she leisurely re-crossed her legs, partly to get his hand off. She had already let him see the lacy tops of her stockings a couple of times. This would be the charming third. Her mark couldn't help himself, and took advantage of her supposed distraction to take in the marvelous view, almost all the way up, but not quite. She judged that he was ripe for the picking. Brenda set her glass down on the bar and asked him something. He responded most agreeably, picking up a small shoulder bag and getting off his bar stool. She led the way, weaving him through the crowd with one or two well-timed come hither glances.

"Looks like the mark's got a purse," said the man. "Is the cash in there?"

"It's never cash, it's always some kind of crypto-transfer," replied DuPont. "He's probably got some gem testing gadgets in there to make sure the stuff she's selling him is legit."

"Smart guy," said the woman.

29

"OK, we're moving," said the woman to nobody in particular. She got up, and looked at DuPont to get him going. The man was soon at her side, both of them waiting for DuPont to take another gulp of beer and gingerly slide himself out of the booth. The throbbing was gradually subsiding.

Brenda and her client got into her car and drove off. DuPont and his captors managed to follow them in theirs, though not without some car-scolding and instructions to drive more aggressively. The car dutifully complied, and soon Brenda's car was in sight. DuPont sat between the Gliese people, who faithfully donned their baseball caps once more. He couldn't help but roll his eyes.

The trip was brief. Brenda parked her car in the driveway of a small bungalow in a not so fancy part of Burlingame. The Gliese folks had their car park discreetly under the shade of a large tree about 10 meters further down the street. They had a clear view of the bungalow. Brenda and her mark were already inside by then. A dim living room light went on, but drapes obscured any view from outside.

The three sat in the car silently, hoping for something to be visible through the curtained window. The pair must have been in another part of the small house, because there weren't even any shadows visible.

"Should we go in and grab her?" asked the man after a while.

"We should try to keep the customer out of it. The club is a valuable resource. We don't want to spook the clientele," answered the woman. "Does she live here?" she asked DuPont.

She didn't, and DuPont tried to think quickly.

"Yeah, this is her place," he lied. With any luck it would throw them off her trail, if only for a little while. She'd have a few weapons hidden here and there in case the customer got unpleasant. It wouldn't be the first time.

"Does she have any weapons?" asked the guy.

"She's got a few. I'm not sure how many or what kind," replied DuPont. "These guys can get rowdy sometimes."

"Let's wait until they leave," said the woman. "Will they go back to the club?"

"It varies," he answered. At that moment, an empty car approached, parked directly in front of the house, and powered off. "That's probably his car."

After a tense 10 minutes or so, Brenda's mark strolled out of the bungalow with a smile on his face and a small box in his hand. He got in his car and drove off.

"That was fast," said the man, "Looks like he got what he wanted, though. Happy endings all around."

"Cool. Time to have a chat with your lovely assistant," said the woman. She pulled out her black pistol and chambered a round.

"Or your lovely boss," said the man.

"What are you doing?" asked DuPont, alarmed. The woman looked at him impatiently.

"She *will* come with us, and she *will* show us all the hiding places. We'd better find the missing stuff, for both of your sakes."

The man ordered the car door to open.

"Let's go," the woman told DuPont, motioning towards the door with her pistol. DuPont hesitated a moment. He had no trust in these people. He and Brenda were in grave and imminent danger.

"Car," said the man. The woman lowered the gun, out of sight. All watched as a car drove by. One of those fancy new robots sat inside, apparently fiddling with something. Once it was past, the woman nudged DuPont with the tip of her gun. DuPont moved to exit, but quickly reached around with his left hand, grabbed the woman's wrist, and pulled as hard as he could. With his free hand, he tried to grab her pistol. The man reached in to pull DuPont's arm away from the gun just as the gun fired, and the man was thrown back onto the sidewalk. The woman pulled away from the scuffle and then shot DuPont in the chest. He fell to the floor of the car, the wind knocked out of him by a hot piercing pain, like a red hot crowbar slammed into his chest. He tried to gain a foothold on the sidewalk outside with his dangling leg, but he felt weak, very weak. He couldn't catch his breath. He felt he was suffocating.

The woman stared in shock at her partner, who lay motionless on the sidewalk next to the car.

*   *   *   *   *

Inside the bungalow, Brenda had been gathering up a few small weapons that she had hidden in various places in case the client became aggressive, which thankfully did not occur. The customer checked the stones with his own gear, so she hadn't had to pull her own gem testing tools from her duffel bag. The agreed upon funds had been transferred, she gave the client a box with an antique diamond and emerald necklace, and after some quick and skillful fellatio the smiling man had left.

A snap outside made her instinctively freeze. She listened, but heard only some rustling. Another snap, and she realized that there was gunfire outside. She threw her purse and her expensive pumps into the duffel bag, looked around one last time to make sure nothing else was left, zipped it up, and ran to the back door. The yard was empty, and she heard nothing more. She opened the door as stealthily as possible, and examined the possible escape routes as she padded outside in stocking feet. Just the one, a walkway around the little house to a fence gate that opened onto the front lawn, near where the gunshots had been fired.

The back fence was just high enough that she had to stand on tiptoe to peek over it to the neighboring house. It was dark and silent. She hit the fence a couple of times to see if there was a dog, but nothing else could be seen or heard, even with her specs at their most sensitive settings. With the help of an old tree stump, she managed to hoist herself up, and make it over the fence with the duffel bag over her shoulder. Some roughness on the wood caught her stockings, and tore the front her dress.

She ignored the damage and carefully made her way through the shadows, and up the house's walkway towards the front. The gate was half open, and she peered through the opening. Nothing. She twiddled for her car to come around the block to pick her up. She stood in the shadows behind the gate and took stock of herself. Her stockings were totaled, and there were droplets of blood dotting a scrape on one shin. Her torn dress exposed half of her chest. Still breathing heavily, she waited, holding the flap of ripped fabric against her. The night was brisk, but not cold.

Once the icon indicated that the car had turned onto this street, she opened the wooden gate just enough to make it through. A short but alarming squeak came from its hinges, and she walked swiftly to the car that was now stopping at the curb in front of the house. She twiddled her fingers as she walked to get the door open as quickly as possible. She told the car her address, and they were off. She looked all around her, but saw and heard nothing. No doubt she was captured by a few surveillance systems, though. As she took stock of herself once more, she failed to notice a car that had turned onto the street behind her.

30

"We'll be talking to Eddie Wu," said the physical Brad as their car pulled away from the curb. "We want three of the caps the Gliese people wear. More if he can get them, and whatever related items he can provide. We also want information. We want to know who those people at Gliese are and what they're doing."

"Why would he cooperate with us?" she asked. "Money? What would he even know about them? Does he sell them the caps?"

"He already has money. We'd have to make a significant offer. We have something much better, more compelling," said Brad.

"The chips?"

Brad nodded.

"Did we bring them?"

"No," he replied. "It would be easy for his people to take them and get rid of us. We need to negotiate a deal first, and make an exchange at a neutral location." He turned to her and said, "You've done this before, right?"

Benita had been a part of more than a few exchanges like this, where terrified cut-outs were convinced to rat out their handlers, or the handlers themselves were duped into exposing their operations. The cut-outs were more often than not ordinary people with workplace access to valuable information. It wasn't difficult at all, in Silicon Valley, to find people living well beyond their means, in some stage of a messy divorce, deeply in debt and in need of fast money, or naive enough to be easily seduced. The time-honored intelligence techniques of generations past were as viable today as they ever were. The professional agents were the grifters, and the cut-outs their gullible marks.

Benita had herself been trained to negotiate such deals, and had participated in several out in the field, increasingly often as the lead negotiator, always in full behavior capture gear. A few times she had played the role of a potential cut-out, and she and her team had caught more than a few professional agents that way. It didn't stop the business, though. Where there were extremely valuable trade secrets and early stage technologies, there would be highly motivated people trying to steal them. Capturing them was at best a Darwinian selection filter that culled the less competent from the herd, and made the cat and mouse game ever more challenging as the years rolled by. The many thousands of hours captured by her and her fellow FféFfé actors were already infused into virtual assistants used by police and intelligence services, and evidently were already being deployed in physical robots like Brad.

"How do I get some face time with him?" she asked.

"Tell his people to ask him if he lost anything that ends in 6509," said Brad. "It's the last 4 digits of the chip model number."

"Will he know that?"

"If he doesn't, one of his people will. We're sure he's under a lot of pressure to find those chips," said Brad.

"Do we have backup? Chase teams?" she asked.

"We have some people in the area," he replied. "They can't kidnap you without us stopping them a block or two away. No cops, just us."

Benita twiddled an icon and the basic details that Brad had just sent came up. 180 chips, and 100g each of elemental germanium, indium, and gallium. There were a few photos of Eddie Wu.

"This stuff isn't radioactive, is it? Or toxic?" she asked.

"No. The jars are sealed, and in any case you'd have to be exposed chronically for years. They're bubble wrapped, so when the time comes, you'll be safe. You may not even be the person to drop them off."

"We're just going to hand the stuff over?"

"If he gives us what we want, yes," answered Brad.

The car parked in the spacious rear parking lot of the Q'Boom Qlub, which was hidden from street view by an ivy-covered brick wall. They got out, and walked to the front entrance. Benita had chickened out at the last minute and instead of heels wore flats that looked like ballet slippers. She wore some loose black velvet pants, the same burnt orange silk blouse she had worn to Thakkar's house, and a thin black open front cashmere sweater over that, which barely kept the evening chill out. She looked attractive, intriguing perhaps, but not sexy.

"No robots," said one of the two burly men at the door. Both of them had dense tattoos on the visible parts of their neck, chest, and arms. He had some kind of Eastern European accent. Benita looked him in the eye.

"You get a lot of robots trying to get in here?" she asked.

"Robots don' eat or drink, they just take up space," said the other, by way of an excuse. Another Eastern European.

"No problem, I'll wait in the car," said Brad, and walked away. *Great*, thought Benita. He could have just stayed home.

"I'm here," said the virtual Brad, who was already past the bouncers.

"What you want with robot, anyway? What can robot do for *you*?" asked the first man as he waved her in. The second one chuckled an obscene guttural laugh.

She walked inside. The evening was still quite young, but the place was already getting packed. Plenty of background noise, continuous conversations, the occasional burst of laughter, background music low enough for people to chat and high enough to be reasonably private, unobtrusive lighting just good enough for HunterGather. She flipped it on, and saw that easily half the room had it on as well. A hostess at a podium fake-smiled in her direction. Benita approached her.

"Hi, I'd like to speak with Eddie Wu?" asked Benita.

The hostess pretended to look around the room.

"I don't think he's here right now, would you like to leave him a message?" she replied, as if looking around this one room informed her that Wu was nowhere to be found in the entire building.

"Yes, I have an urgent message," said Benita. "I believe I know where his missing 6509s are. Could you please have someone let him know? I suspect he'll be very interested."

The hostess continued the fake smile with a contrasting blank look in her eyes as she private spoke the message to someone higher up the chain.

"Alrighty! I'll let somebody know!" she added after a long moment, with fake smiling eyes to match her fake smiling mouth. Benita did not envy the young woman's job.

"I'll have a drink meanwhile," said Benita.

"Sure!" said the young woman.

Benita approached the bar and ordered a goblet of the house Merlot. She was unpleasantly surprised at the price when it popped up in her specs for authorization. Nevertheless, she left a 20% tip, not wanting to draw attention to herself. *This had better not be supermarket plonk*, she thought.

She slowly walked around the room as she sipped at her drink, taking in the view. The wine was too sweet and without depth, but had some nice barrel notes that kept it drinkable. The crowd spanned the gamut of Silicon Valley society, from people who were not much more elegantly dressed than she, to people who would be more than competitive with Aradhya or Pari. Apparently this is where normal people came to offer themselves up to the local plutocracy. For what, Benita didn't want to speculate. The place reeked of ostentation and unseemly wealth.

"Yikes! The place is crawling with fucking 90s!" said Zag suddenly. "Half the room is high 80s!"

Virtual Brad looked puzzled.

Zag was standing beside her at the bar, next to a guy who looked like a fancy real estate agent with a hairy chest and a partially unbuttoned shirt that looked pretty expensive, but whose score was a mere 72. It was true, though. She twiddled the overlay to show the scores in a brightness gradient according to average score, and there were at least ten 90s in this very room. She couldn't recall ever being in such a place in the past two years, except for the one time her little circle of friends had a barbecue last summer.

"Come on!" said Zag, and he led her around the room in a path that would allow her to examine them all, Brad following along behind them. Like clockwork, everyone above 90 made it a point to make eye contact, and she trembled inside. Aradhya wasn't kidding about the hot guys and hot girls. There was smoldering yearning in their predatory gazes, and she recognized something in them that she seemed to be searching for constantly and never finding it. The contact icon pulsed as she passed each one, and she shelved them for later as they came in. Her pulse raced, her skin became clammy, and she felt the urge to put in a panty liner, or at least darken her specs. Male or female, each moment of eye contact sent a shiver through her body, and she had to make an effort to walk steadily. She hadn't expected this. Why were they all gathered here? What had she been missing? How could she have been so consistently in the wrong places? As in an epiphany, the appeal of the Q'Boom Qlub was now clear to her.

On the other side of the room, a broad archway led to an adjoining bar, just as large and as full of partiers. She entered, and the music here was different. It was pop music on the side she first entered, and more jazzy on this side. She noticed the demographic here was older, with more silvery hair in evidence. The more mature men and women tended to be matched up with people as young as those in the other room. More 90s. If there was a promised land, she was now strolling through it.

"Let's do another pass in here!" said Zag.

"Not now," she answered privately.

"Look over there," said the virtual Brad, looking towards the bar.

Benita saw the young woman seated at the bar, chatting with a fifty-something gentleman. She was chestnut-haired and stunningly beautiful, dressed in an alluring, deep violet satin dress that fit like a second skin. Quite effective, judging by the attention she was getting from the older man. She scored a 90, with an impressive number of reviews. Benita switched HunterGather off. It was becoming a distraction.

Benita thought she recognized her. She looked away to not draw the woman's attention, and twiddled an icon to pull up some of Thakkar's files. There she was, Brenda Castro, Bennington's assistant, with several photos to confirm it. Benita slowly walked towards the booths opposite the bar. There was a small two-seater next to a larger one with a man and a woman who seemed to be avidly people-watching, and a glum-looking guy sitting between them. She sat in her booth, which placed her at the edge of Brenda's peripheral vision. She dried the skin of her face with a napkin. She didn't want to look nervous with Wu.

A waitress came by and delivered some drinks to the booth next to hers, then approached Benita and bent down to whisper something.

"Please come with me," said the waitress, and then walked off. Benita followed her to a carpeted staircase, and both of them went up. At the top they followed a hallway off to one side and the waitress stopped at the door of an office. Benita paused at the door, and saw that the man sitting at the desk on the far side of the room was none other than Eddie Wu, who stood up from his chair smiling and effusive, motioning her to have a seat in front of his desk.

"Please! Have a seat," he said jovially, as if they were good friends who hadn't seen each other in months. The chairs in front of his desk looked comfortable enough. They shook hands, and she sat down. Zag and virtual Brad stood at the doorway of the office.

"Thank you for seeing me," said Benita. Wu made a gesture indicating that he was more than happy to do so.

"So, what brings you here, Miss..." he started.

"Grossberg. Romi Grossberg," said Benita

"I understand you have some kind of information?" he said, sitting back in his chair. He had a distinct Hong Kong accent, but spoke English quite fluently.

"Yes. Cutting to the chase, your missing 6509s have been found, and the finder is willing to return them."

Wu looked at her for a moment, perhaps choosing from a handful of possible gambits or listening to an assistant, human or virtual. He was not exactly in a position to draw things out and either get the lowest possible price or simply take them by force, his preferred strategies.

"Did the finder mention something expected in exchange?" he said slowly.

"They did, in fact. You're in a position to obtain an item they would like, something that frequents your antique shop," she replied. A moment of concern flashed across Wu's eyes, but he quickly recovered his jovial poker face.

"They're interested in some antiques?"

Benita continued to look at him calmly for a moment, allowing the pause to answer him.

"Could you be more specific?" he asked.

"They would like three of the beige baseball caps used by your customers from **Gliese Genetics.**"

Wu's eyes went wide, briefly. Benita was grievously challenging his poker face skills.

"I'm not sure what you're referring to," he said, feigning concern by furrowing his brow.

"Yes, you are," she said. "We also want spare parts and documentation describing their operation, communications protocols, and so on. In exchange, you will receive the 180 6509s that the finder came to possess."

Wu scoffed, almost snorting.

"'Came to possess'?" repeated Wu. "How did *that* happen?" It was undoubtedly a rhetorical question.

"Mr. Wu, do you feel that this is an attractive offer?"

Wu scanned the items on his desk. He didn't have to check his coffee mug to know that it was empty. It was too late to get more, otherwise he'd lose even more sleep tonight. The desk was messier than he would like. Who were these people? How much did they know? Who or what could back them up? Were the chips in this woman's car? How would he get his hands on the caps?

"Are you in possession of the chips?" he asked.

"Do we have a deal?"

Wu considered Benita. She looked serious. She looked like a moderately younger version of the hard bargaining women he often had to deal with in the Valley. He sensed that she wasn't going to budge and that she knew herself to have the upper hand, at least for the moment.

"What you're asking for is impossible. I might add that you don't seem to appreciate the seriousness of your request," he said slowly. "I don't own any such caps. I don't have any to trade. I have never even seen any protocols or manuals or spare parts for them. They're baseball caps, not gene sequencers."

"I'm sure you can obtain a few, one way or another. Would the owners prefer to avoid trading a few caps or would they rather recover the chips? Perhaps they wouldn't even need to know about the trade."

Wu wanted to ask who she was, or who she represented, but it would be a pointless question that would show weakness, perhaps even fear or incipient panic.

"If such a thing were to occur, how would it be arranged?" he said, trying to stall.

"Place the caps, spare parts, documentation, and any attachments or other accessories needed to make them work in the shipping and receiving area of the antique shop. Leave the rear door unlocked, and have your people evacuate the area. Send a message to this location."

She sent him a contact to which he could send the message. Brad had provided it. It would be very difficult if not impossible to trace, and would be destroyed once the transaction was successfully completed.

"Confidentiality is critical, and any attempt to pursue our staff or vehicles will be considered a breach of trust," she continued. Would tomorrow be a good day for the pick up?"

"Tomorrow? Are you serious?" he scoffed again. Of course, getting the chips back by tomorrow would be fine thing indeed. "Maybe by evening. When and how do we get the chips?"

"We'll leave half of them there, and let you know when to come by," she answered. "Once we've verified that the devices work, you'll get the other half."

"So, I have to give you the caps, and trust you to give me the chips without having any clue about who you are? How do I know you even have them?" At that moment Wu was interrupted by a flashing icon in his specs. He twiddled it up, and there was a photo of all the chip trays fanned out on a table, as well as the three jars of rare earth metals. The surface of the table was plain and white, as was the wall in the background. No doubt the metadata of the photo was scrubbed, and it was sent from some bogus location. Wu would have his people check, but he didn't expect to find anything of use.

"So, do we have a deal?" she asked again.

"Fine. 6 pm tomorrow," he answered, raising his hand dismissively. "We'll send a message when they are ready."

"Great! I'm glad we could make this work," she said and got up to shake hands. "Please power down the entire shop and keep all of your resources at least 2 kilometers away. We'll be patrolling the area by land and air all day, and keeping tabs on local communications," she continued as they shook hands.

"Sure, fine," said the now dour-faced Wu, waving his hand dismissively. He needed the chips.

Benita left him in his office, and walked down the hallway back to the bar.

"I'm following some people from Gliese, who are following Bennington's assistant and her client. Get a car and I'll let you know which way they go," said virtual Brad.

"Got it." She twiddled for a Coché to come pick her up. There was one less than 3 minutes away. She went down the stairs and the three waited by the bar, near the front door. She was taut and on her guard. Wu's people could ambush her at any moment. An icon indicating her car's arrival soon flashed.

"Is the robot girl!" said one of the bouncers as she walked out. "You miss your robot so soon? He have good *attachments*?" His fellow bouncer maintained a background of lascivious chuckling. Benita wondered if they were this rude to the rest of the clientele.

"Fucking gypsies," said Zag.

"I believe they call themselves 'Roma,'" said Brad.

The car parked directly in front of the door, a white-curbed passenger loading area. There was another car there disgorging more rich-person-wannabes.

"Here's the address," said Brad. The address appeared in a small box in her field of view. She forwarded it to the car as she got in. The address was nearby, still in Burlingame. The car quickly and deftly made its way through the evening traffic. She was beginning to like Coché.

31

Robot Brad had parked a block down the street from the Gliese people and their companion. His car's headlights washed over them for a moment as he passed, and Brad saw that the man was one of Bennington's people. It was DuPont, who made deliveries for the antique shop, among other things. They were parked in the shade of a tree and looked like they were getting out of the car.

Brad had the car kill its lights and park in the shade of a tree at the end of the block, then switched seats so that he could see them. They were scuffling as they got out of the car, and he saw the flash and heard the dull report of a firearm, at which point the man from Gliese crumpled to the sidewalk. Soon another shot caused DuPont to fall to the floor of the car with one of his legs hanging out through the open door. The woman froze for a moment, apparently considering her next move.

Porch lights came on in a couple of houses across the street, surprising the woman. She started pushing DuPont out of the car with her feet, and the car started to move. It was already driving away before DuPont was fully out of the car, and he was dragged a few feet alongside the curb. Brad saw that the Gliese man was still wearing his cap. He looked around at the newly lit windows in the houses across the street, but nobody was even peeking through the curtains. It didn't look like anyone had heard the shots. Maybe the lights came on coincidentally or automatically, and the woman was needlessly spooked. He got out and walked briskly toward the men, moving from shadow to shadow along the sidewalk. Local surveillance cameras probably wouldn't be able to make him out clearly unless they had low-light sensors, which most did these days. Still, there was plenty of foliage.

He stood above the Gliese guy. Both men were still alive, but probably not for long. They were breathing spasmodically and DuPont was coughing up blood. The three of them were in the broad shade of the tree, so Brad took the risk of picking up the cap, taking both of their specs, and walking as briskly as before back to his car. He messaged Benita not to come by, that they would meet back at her apartment, and told the car to drive off.

Benita got the message as she turned onto the street Brad had indicated, and told the car to go to her apartment instead. As she drove by the address, she could just make out the two men lying in the shadows.

"What happened?" she asked Brad over the phone.

"They went after Brenda, Bennington's assistant. When I got there they were getting out of their car and started to fight. The Gliese woman shot them both, her colleague accidentally, I would guess. Then she pushed DuPont out of the car and drove off. She must have panicked."

"Where's Brenda?"

"No idea," said Brad. "I assume she's in the bungalow."

Benita ordered the car to go around the block a few times to have a quick look. On the other side of the block, a car had just pulled away from the curb. She twiddled the zoom function in her specs, and a small window appeared to one side of her field of view. She activated the low-light function in it. Benita was able to see the side of a woman's face as she manipulated something on the car seat next to her. She had the same haircut as Brenda had, and Benita compared some stills of the feed with pictures she had gotten from Wilkins.

"I think I've got something. Someone on the next street got in a car, it looks a lot like her from behind. I'm tailing her," said Benita. "Convoy with that car at 20 meters," she told her own car.

Both cars were soon on a busier side street, then on the well-trafficked California Drive. Brenda's car continued on, apparently oblivious of being followed. She stayed off the freeway, eventually crossing over to El Camino Real in San Mateo and continuing south for a good 15 or 20 minutes to an apartment complex on Davey Glen Road in Belmont. Brenda's car dropped her off in the parking lot, and Benita told her car to park in a visitor's spot. She watched Brenda get out of her car and walk towards the stairs. The young woman looked like she had been dragged on the ground. She was holding part of her dress together with one hand and a duffel bag in the other. Benita watched her go up a flight of stairs and emerge on the second floor, entering the third door past the stairwell. Benita decided to go have a chat with her.

"I'm at some apartments on Davey Glen Road. She's in the third door to the left as you exit the north elevator on the second floor," she dictated to the messaging icon in private speech. "Send me photos of the victims if you have any."

"Got it," said Brad. "I'll meet you back at your place afterwards."

Benita put on her shoulder bag and went up quietly, listening at the door for a moment when she arrived. The drapes were drawn on the windows facing the courtyard and parking lot. A light was on inside. She tried amplifying the sound, and heard only rustling and intermittent footsteps. Benita pressed the doorbell button.

No answer, so she pressed it again.

"Brenda, I know you're there. We need to talk," she said, not so loud that any neighbors might easily hear. She knocked again. Some rustling near the door. Benita knocked softly on the door yet again, standing to one side to avoid any gunfire. You really never know.

The door opened a crack with the chain on. Benita slowly peered in. Brenda stood there watching her like a cat. Neither of her hands were visible.

"I'm just here to talk," she said slowly raising her hands and putting them into view. "A few things have happened that you probably need to know about."

Brenda stared at her with a stern yet difficult to read gaze. She closed the door, unhooked the chain, and let Benita in, her hands still not visible. Benita kept hers in view. Once Brenda had shut the door, Benita saw that she had put on a sweatshirt over her dress and had a small pistol pointing at her.

"May I sit?" asked Benita.

"Drop the bag and sit over there."

Benita complied. She sat in the easy chair of a bland living room set that may well have come with the apartment. Brenda sat in the middle of the sofa, turned towards Benita, still pointing her gun.

"What things happened?" said Brenda icily. "Who the hell are you and what do you want?" She gestured with the gun as she spoke.

"Let me send you a picture," said Benita twiddling for the images Brad had just sent.

"Send someone over here and they'll only find you," said Brenda, "Lying on the carpet." She twiddled with her free hand to see the pictures and gasped. It was DuPont lying in the street, a few feet from the curb, in the shadow of a tree. The scene was painted in the eerie, washed out shades of Brad's night vision mode. DuPont's eyes were open and vacant, a puddle of blood seeped from the folds of his sweatshirt. Tears rolled out of Brenda's eyes.

"Did you do that you fucking bitch?!" she said angrily, holding the gun out and pointing it squarely at Benita's center of mass.

Benita shook her head slowly, and waited for Brenda to watch the video snippet. Brenda gasped again and the tears stopped, but her face reddened visibly with both anger and terror. It was the moment of the scuffle, where the Gliese woman shot both DuPont and her partner. She lowered her gun hand involuntarily to her lap. Her shoulders slumped, she covered her eyes with her free hand under her specs, and sobbed. Benita didn't move. Brenda tried to grieve as intensely as a person could in 30 seconds or less.

"So what the fuck do you want?" asked Brenda, finally recovering some composure. Her gun hand was still on her lap, but the gun was pointing at Benita.

"You were there, Brenda," she said. "You were in the house when it happened." There was some speculation there, but she left it to Brenda to fill in the details.

"How do you know my name? Who are you? What do you want from me?" demanded Brenda.

"Why were those people following you?" asked Benita.

"You seem to know everything. You tell me," she said, wiping mascara-laden tears from her face with her free hand. "Oh fuck it," she said, and got up to fetch some napkins from the kitchen table. Benita stayed put, avoiding any sudden movements. It would be nice to have her shoulder bag within reach, though. She'd feel a lot better with some pepper spray in her hand. She had a pistol in there as well.

Brenda sat down again, pistol next to her thigh, doing a much better job of tidying up her face and blowing her nose with the napkin.

"They were looking for some things Sav took from them. You know Sav? Savion Bennington?" said Brenda, calming down gradually.

"I know who he is. Or was."

"Did you people burn his house down? Did you at least kill him first?" said Brenda, a note of bitterness in her voice.

"No. He was shot by a neighbor kid of Pari Thakkar. Do you know her?"

"Who? I assume that's the little rich princess he was hitting on. Some spoiled Indian bitch," answered Brenda.

"Sav was drugging her and raping her. I suspect the neighbor kid had some objections to that."

"Well, that's Sav's M.O. What can I tell you. The guy was a fucking creep."

"He did that a lot?" asked Benita. Brenda rolled her eyes.

"A lot?" she snorted. "He'd try it with any woman whose drink was near enough for him to spike," said Brenda. "He tried it on me a couple of times when he first hired me."

"And you stayed on?" asked Benita.

"I swapped the drinks the second time," she answered. "He didn't try it again. I know how to deal with assholes. I do it for a living. How would *you* know who shot him?"

"I was outside of his house when he got shot. I was going to go inside and have a look around. We had a tip that he would be taking you shopping and that nobody would be home, but it didn't turn out that way."

"Who the hell is 'we'? What did you people want with Sav?"

"He's involved with some people we're worried about. That woman who shot your friend is one of them, as was the other guy."

"You didn't say who's 'we'."

"I'm not going to tell you, Brenda."

"No?" Brenda raised her gun.

"Brenda, you know you don't want to do anything like that. You're still not in any official trouble. I'd suggest you keep it that way."

"You a cop?" asked Brenda, lowering her gun to her lap again. Benita shook her head.

"I'm in trouble with the Gliese people, that's for sure," said Brenda. "Which reminds me. I have a plane to catch. I'm not sticking around for this shit. You people, whoever the fuck you are, are on your own. I just worked at that damn antique shop. I didn't run it, and I didn't deal with the Gliese people. Sav did, and now the sleazy piece of shit is gone. And so is Rashaun." Brenda stood up from the couch, pistol pointing downwards, next to her thigh, tears welling up again.

"OK, well, thanks for the chat. I'm really sorry about your friend. Good luck," said Benita. Benita walked over, picked up her shoulder bag and let herself out. Brenda was still standing there as she closed the door.

Benita sat in her car. Only two days in, and 3 people were dead. The whole project was a mess. And what had happened to her predecessor, Mohan?

32

Brad stopped by the Thakkar home in Woodside on the way back to Benita's apartment. It was a small detour, but Thakkar and Wilkins wanted the cap he had recovered from the now presumably deceased Gliese security operative. As Brad's car pulled up to the side entrance, both Thakkar and Wilkins were already waiting. No sooner had the car opened its door, than Thakkar had his hand extended. Brad handed him the baseball cap he had retrieved.

"As it turns out, gentlemen, I'm the only one here who can actually try this thing on," said Thakkar. "I'll have to ask the hardware guys how much time it would take to hack up some way to record it and put it into your control model. Maybe through the new brain sensors." As he spoke he walked back into the house, unable to take his eyes off the cap, like a little boy with a piece of birthday cake.

The cap! Finally! The artifact he had been coveting for months, the single most important clue that could support his hypothesis. He took a seat at the kitchen table, and turned it over in his hands. It wasn't exactly a normal baseball cap. The material looked like spandex or some high-tech sweat-wicking material. That made sense if the user would have to wear it during their entire waking hours. There was a double layer of material, with stitching around some hard flat objects held in fixed positions between the fabric layers. They seemed to be all the same size, spaced equally around the wearer's head, much like the magneto-encephalography sensors that FféFfé was now using.

By then, Wilkins had sat down in a chair next to him.

"It could be dangerous to try that on. We don't know how strong it is or what it may be transmitting," said Wilkins. Thakkar eyed him impishly.

"I think we know enough," replied Thakkar, and he put the cap on. Initially, he felt nothing, and even wondered if the thing was still powered on. As he looked around the room, a few things suddenly appeared out of thin air. He was wearing his specs, but these new objects were different, and seemed garbled or hard to interpret visually, as if he was intoxicated and unable to see correctly. He was seeing them through his own eyes, not as an overlay created by the specs. It occurred to him that he should think or say "configure auto-adjust field capture," and was quite puzzled by the thought.

"Configure auto-adjust field capture?" he mumbled. Wilkins was ready to snatch the cap off of Thakkar's head, but Thakkar waved him off.

Now the strange objects resolved themselves. He was aware that the cap was using the local city data network, and felt an urge to pair the cap with his specs to significantly increase the bandwidth. It was now obvious that saying or thinking "configure change of network portal" would start the process. It took some conscious effort to resist the urge, even though a small panel of labeled push buttons appeared and disappeared a few times on the surface of the kitchen table.

There was something that looked like a map marker, seemingly far way in the distance, kilometers from his house, and yet he could see that it was there in spite of the walls that surrounded him. As he focused on it, he knew that it was Alice Woods driving down highway 280 in her car. He didn't guess it or reason it out, the knowledge was simply *there*. It hadn't been there a moment ago, but now it was, much like the phrase "configure auto-adjust field capture" had suddenly popped into his head. There were icons around him in his field of view, some of them next to his specs icons. The new icons seemingly arranged themselves next to their specs counterparts, as if they somehow knew they were there. He sensed something next to him, opposite Wilkins. There was somebody else sitting at the breakfast table with them. An actual flesh and blood woman.

"Who are you?!" he asked, momentarily startled.

"The question is, who are *you*?" said the woman. She paused for a second, looking directly at him. "Rameshwar Thakkar, correct? What's your address?"

Thakkar said nothing, but couldn't help but think of his address.

"3360 Mountain Home Road, if I'm not mistaken," said the woman. She was vaguely Eurasian in appearance, thirty-something, and had a short haircut that reminded Thakkar of his late wife Tif, around the time they had gotten married. Suddenly, yet in a most subtle morphing of features, she looked exactly like the young Tiffany Chen, as if that had been her face from the beginning. Thakkar's pulse raced, and he was unable to speak for a moment.

"Well, well," said the woman, her voice seemingly zeroing on Tiffany's youthful voice, "With any luck I can get you to keel over right now."

"Who made these caps?" asked Thakkar as soon as he could speak. "Where do you come from? Why are you here? What do you want?"

"I don't think we're playing on the same team here, do you?" she answered. "Maybe you could tell me a little more about yourself."

Try as he might, Thakkar could not avoid the distraction of seeing his late wife as she was when they were deeply in love so long ago. It was as if he was looking at her, sitting across the table from him. It *was* her, it was *exactly* her. As old, long unused memories flooded back it was without a doubt *her*. For him she had been the most beautiful woman in the world, a brilliant young scientist that dazzled him from the start with her immediate understanding of what FfēFfē Automata was all about.

"Mm-mm!" said the woman, a lilting expression Tiffany Chen often made when she was in a mischievous mood.

She rose slowly from her chair. A tan silk sheath dress hugged her body as if it had been tailor-made for her. Thakkar remembered a similar blue and white dress that Tiffany once had, and some skimpy lingerie she often wore with it when she was in the mood for romance. The woman's dress transformed into that remembered blue and white dress, and Thakkar had the sense that this hallucinated woman had been wearing that dress all along. He briefly wondered what it might look like in tan, but he definitely preferred this one and immediately forgot about the other color, whatever it had been. She walked slowly towards him as she undid the zipper by pulling the shoulders of the dress apart, also something Tiffany used to do. By now Thakkar was not at all surprised that she was wearing the lingerie he remembered, and which he had always found unbearably sensual. The woman slipped out of the bra, then the undies, then sat on the table before him. She was close enough to touch, but he didn't try. Every blemish, every curve, every shape, and every color, together were the Tiffany of his memories, the Tiffany of his dreams. He could smell her, the same shampoo, and the same lemony scent from the bars of soap she had in her dresser drawers. A whiff of the natural odors of her body made him inhale deeply, slowly, and tremulously. Above and beyond any other odor or fragrance, it was the scent of Tiffany Chen. She shifted her position on the table to slowly spread her legs as wide as she could. She leaned forward to look into his eyes, and the sensation was overwhelming.

Thakkar jerked the cap off, and she was gone. He was sweating, breathing hard, his heart still racing. He looked around the room. The marker tracking Alice Woods was gone as well.

"Good thing you pulled it off. It looks like your magnetic detectors were starting to drop out for some reason. It looks like they're slowly coming back online, though," said Wilkins. "What did you see? Who are they? What did they tell you?" Robot or not, Wilkins could not conceal his suspense, his intense curiosity of what this strange artifact was, and what role it played in the game.

Thakkar shook his head, unable yet to compose a reply.

33

"Go back, Alice! We have to save Cliff!" said Rita, a New World woman who was now sitting in the car across from Alice. Alice and Rita chatted often in New World. She was an informal mentor.

The New World was the realm that users experienced while wearing the beige caps. These devices had been patiently developed over a few hundred years by work units that were the ancestors of Gliese Genetics. It was no simple thing to learn how to make a device that could read and write images and sounds into a human brain with enough quality and accuracy that it seemed like a dream-like twin of the real world. Once that had been achieved, an even more ambitious task was to build a communications system to read what the user's sensorium was receiving from their surroundings and compose a scene that made sense to the user, with all the virtual entities correctly placed. Many users were recruited over the years, and hundreds of prototypes were tested. During the first century, little progress was made and the human test subjects more often than not had terrifying experiences, frequently with lasting psychological damage.

Eventually, a working system was developed, and what remained was for New World to gradually synchronize with prevailing culture and make use of well-known archetypes, idioms, commonly held beliefs and traditions, and awareness of social, political, and economic context. The loose federation of work units of which Gliese was a member were linked together by the New World.

It was quite literally a continuous, coherent, consensual hallucination generator.

Rank and file work unit members like Alice only interacted with the virtual characters for two main reasons. First, the location of other work units was a closely guarded secret, and it was a practical certainty that members would soon compile an accurate picture of the sites and their locations if they were to communicate with each other.

Second, the New World was at its core an ideological support system that did double duty as a labor support system. The federation of work units recruited people who bought into a social, political, and economic vision centered around a resource based economy where money would one day be abolished, and everyone's needs would be met through the use of automation and careful use of resources. Everyone had a productive role in society and wealth would remain distributed among all members of society rather than being funneled up into the hands of a very small number of ultra-wealthy individuals, families, and cronies. Government bureaucracy would be a thing of the past, and war, poverty, crime, and hunger would be obsolete.

That was the plan, anyway, and the avatars in the New World maintained the ideology in subtle ways as well as through frequent team activities at each site. It wasn't particularly different from the practical results of using specs and conventional virtual characters to run greenhouses or take care of day to day company management, but between the hallucinatory immersiveness and the inspirational ideology, certain types of people bought into it like a religious cult.

Most of the characters in New World were virtual characters not unlike those marketed by Blam and other companies. Blam's characters had been around for less than 10 years. The refined characters of New World had been around since the middle of the 19th century.

Alice had spent years searching for community, somewhere to fit in, at one place after another, and was now a New World true believer. Rita was her most trusted friend and confidante there.

*　　*　　*　　*　　*

They were only two blocks away from the bungalow, and Rita managed to calm Alice down enough for her to tell the car to go back. How could she have left Cliff there? It had been a moment of panic. A primal terror had boiled up from within her, one she had thought she had left behind years ago. Suddenly she felt hunted. The hunter was near, almost upon her, meaning to hurt her, to violate her, to mutilate her, and finally to kill her. Alice recalled an incident in her youth, in a distant foreign country, where that same panic had also resulted in tragic deaths that had emotionally crippled her and her companions for the rest of their lives. Was she once again being visited by tragedy? She realized that she'd been crying.

"He'll be OK if we help him," said Rita.

The car parked in the same place, next to the motionless bodies. She opened the door and got out. Cliff took a spasmodic breath as she kneeled over him, searching for a pulse. Their eyes met, and Alice's heart filled with hope. Another spasmodic breath, and Cliff's worried eyes seemed now to examine the tree branches above him. Alice could barely see what was going on through her tears.

"Let's get him in the car," said Rita, who was now standing next to Alice.

Alice dragged him by his feet into the car, trying not to hurt him. She gingerly put her hand under his back to get him all the way in. The hand came away covered in blood. It was rough handling for someone with a bullet inside. Alice told the car to close the door and go back to Watsonville. Cliff drew a slower, shallower breath.

Alice tried to wipe the tears away with her sleeve, but they kept coming. Cliff drew another shallow breath.

Why was this happening? How could she have shot the one person in her world that was close to her, the one person she never had to go search for with some meat-market specs app? Should she get him to a hospital? She checked in her specs, and the nearest emergency room was in San Mateo, maybe 5 minutes away.

"We can't go to a hospital," said Rita. "They'll ask too many questions. They'll find out about us. They'll either put him in jail or let him die. They'll put *you* in jail."

"What should I do?!" cried Alice.

"Try giving him CPR to keep his heart going."

Alice got down on the floor and checked for a pulse, but couldn't find one. She started to bear down on his chest hoping to get his heart going again, but there was a raspy gurgling noise under his shirt, and she saw a sudden flow of blood come through it and puddle on the inside of his jacket. His eyes were open and not looking at anything in particular. He hadn't breathed since a minute or so before she tried to get his heart going.

"No!" she said softly through still more tears, "No no no no no..."

"Try giving him mouth to mouth," said Rita. "If his heart is still beating that will get more oxygen into his system."

Alice pinched his nose with one hand and pressed her mouth against his, and forced air into him. She did it a couple more times, but didn't dare try to press down on his chest. More blood had accumulated in his jacket. Maybe his heart would start up on its own? She forced several more breaths into him, but he was unresponsive.

She knelt next to him, watching him. She remembered friends and fellow soldiers, fellow operatives, half a world away, half a life ago. Lying on the ground staring vacantly at nothing. Brothers and sisters in arms gazing down upon them in somber silence. The cold recognition of finality, of helplessness. The random background sounds that would haunt them all until their own end of days.

It had nearly drained the life from her, over those years, and during her transition out of it, her escape from it, she had lived in a series of tents set up on railroad rights of way or in the parking lots of abandoned buildings. Weeks and months and years in one chemical daze or other, living a miserable existence in the parallel world below ordinary human society. She was one of the many whose lives were saved from the tents by some random co-op job.

Alice lost herself in time, keeping a numb vigil over Cliff, until Rita let her know that she was back at Gliese. As soon as the car stopped someone was at the door, tapping on the glass.

34

It was fairly late when Tavo headed back to Crazy Ladies. Carol, the falafel cart girl, had turned out to be a wonderful person. He couldn't resist the temptation to see her, and had invited her for lunch in Santa Cruz while he was on an errand for the farm. They spent a few hours getting to know each other, flirting, and realizing that, once again, HunterGather had brought two kindred souls together. He had rented a modest, one-room beachside bungalow between Santa Cruz and Watsonville for a day, in a line of weathered working-class houses on the crest of a hill overlooking Highway 1 and the Pacific Ocean beyond. They spent the late afternoon there, and watched the sun set from the living room, where they fell into each other's arms and into each other's passion. Later he had dropped her off at an apartment complex near downtown Watsonville, where she lived with two other young women, all three refugees from one disaster or another, some impoverished town or ghetto, fleeing worlds of chronic hopelessness and desperately trying to jump-start their young lives.

For seven of the ten years before The Riots, massive flooding of some areas along the Mississippi, Missouri, and Ohio rivers had left large swaths of countryside flooded year-round, essentially converting what was once some of the most productive farmland in the world into worthless swampland.

The girls hailed from Kentucky, Iowa, and Indiana, states that even 10 years after The Riots still had legislatures that were doing everything they could to block the formation of Green New Deal cooperatives, in spite of the economic crises that plagued them ever more mercilessly. The three of them were currently working odd jobs as they waited for acceptance to one or another of the local co-ops. Tavo said he'd try to help her get into Crazy Ladies. He wondered himself if that was true. He wondered if she believed him.

That night, Tavo was driving one of the farm's pickup trucks back, bringing an order of packaging materials purchased earlier in the day for the leafy greens that were about to be harvested. They almost filled the truck bed, as could be seen through the windows of its enclosure in back. He had been worried that someone from another farm might try to break in and steal them while he was with Carol, but the evening had been uneventful.

It was near midnight and the roads were largely empty, and yet Tavo saw that someone had been trailing him for about 5 minutes. He was still about a kilometer away from the farm. At a stoplight, the car came up near enough for him to see who it was in his rear view mirror. At first he didn't recognize her, but then he remembered Sue pointing her out that morning. It was Alice something, riding a car from **Gliese Genetics**. She seemed to be kneeling on the floor facing him, visibly distraught, and even in the harsh sodium vapor street lights she looked as if she might have been crying.

He drove on towards the farm, glancing at her occasionally. On Pequod Lane, he dawdled a bit in the Crazy Ladies driveway and watched her drive past. The gate opened to let her car into Gliese and slowly closed behind her. He parked the pickup and decided to unload it in the morning. Tavo bunked in a refurbished bus that had been converted into a sort of dorm room for 8 people. It was permanently parked near the main farmhouse, next to an old motor-home and a couple of large Airstream trailers, all modified as sleeping quarters for as many people as could be comfortably packed in. As he walked toward it he could see that beyond the farmhouse and the treeline behind it that divided the farm from Gliese, there was a minor commotion going on. Animated whispering barely under control, car and house doors opening and closing, and red flashlights appeared to be centered around Alice's arrival. It was hard to tell, but it looked like several people were examining her car.

The path around the dorm bus, on the other side of it relative to the farmhouse, was dark under a crescent moon. He walked silently towards the tree line from there, until he came up to an old fence made of decaying redwood boards, still in the shadows. He could peek between them and not be seen by the 3 or 4 visibly agitated Gliese folks flitting between Alice, her car, and the nearby farmhouse about 5 meters beyond the fence. For each person that went back inside, it seemed another came out to see what was going on.

A woman was escorting Alice back to the house. Alice was barely holding back her sobbing, and soon a man joined in to help escort her back to the house. Meanwhile, 2 people were pointing red flashlights into her car while another two struggled to extract something. It turned out to be the limp body of a man. Tavo couldn't see the face, although it might not have mattered since he didn't know anyone at Gliese. The body was carried into the farmhouse and everybody went inside after it. It all took less than 3 minutes, and now only the sounds of the night remained, some rustling in the underbrush, two owls calling back and forth in the trees, and the gentle backdrop of crickets.

Lights were still on in the farmhouse, in what was presumably the kitchen and the living room. Curtained windows obstructed his view inside. He stood there looking and listening for a minute or two, but not much could be seen or heard. He walked back towards the dorm bus and quietly got in, so as not to disturb his roommates. He changed into his pajamas and had a quick peek behind the curtains of his bus window. He was in the upper bunk, and had only about 20 centimeters of window peeking above the level of his thin mattress. Between the limited window access and the treeline, he could see nothing.

The next morning, he was the first to arrive at the tank trucks. Nothing out of the ordinary could be seen or heard at Gliese, at least nothing he could detect through the trees. Faithful to his reliable tardiness, Raúl walked towards him from the farmhouse a few minutes after they should have already been on the road. Sue walked beside him.

"Come on, man, let's go!" said Raúl.

"Hey," said Tavo, mainly to Sue.

"Hey," she said coldly, walking past him towards her truck. She didn't even meet his gaze. Raúl said nothing and got in his truck.

"Icy," remarked Cin. She had been standing next to Tavo, dressed again as a vintage airplane pilot, goggles and all. The flight suit's snug fit didn't look period accurate.

"You deserve worse. You know that, right?" she said.

Tavo was the last to get on the road, and last to arrive at Moss Landing. By the time he was out of his truck, both Raúl and Sue were halfway to the restaurant across the parking lot. The drive to the desalinators gave him plenty of time to turn over and over in his head that Sue was angry and hurt because he had gone out with Carol. He could respond that there was no formal relationship between Sue and Tavo, even though they spent a lot of time together and shared quite a bit of romantic and sexual intimacy, that each was free to see other people, blah, blah, blah, but he knew it would only make matters worse. He had acted like a horny and inconsiderate teenage asshole, betraying her obvious love for him by casually going off with a stranger he had just met. A 93 point stranger, but a stranger nonetheless.

Speaking of whom, he flipped on the HunterGather overlay and started walking towards the spot where Carol had her falafel cart.

"Is she around?" he asked Cin privately. She was walking next to him dressed up to explore a jungle, knife in hand.

"She doesn't seem to be anywhere near here. It looks like she's not logged on," she said. "You're quite a character, you know that?"

"Shut up," he said morosely, no doubt reinforcing whatever conclusions the AI behind Cin had been drawing. Among the many configuration options he had tweaked, he had set her to be a trusted friend and confidante and provider of good advice.

Tavo rounded the corner of the visitor center, and someone else was tending the cart. A guy. He logged off of HunterGather and walked back towards his truck, dejected. He wished Sue wasn't mad at him and he wished he hadn't gone off with Carol. He wanted to discuss last night's goings on at Gliese with her, knowing that she would certainly be interested. Now their friendship was in doubt, and he'd have to climb a mountain to get her to speak to him again.

He stood by the truck for a few minutes. There was still a good half hour remaining before it was full. It was a warm and sunny October morning, with only a light ocean breeze. He walked towards the restaurant, intending to sit with Sue and Raúl and start paying his dues. He didn't want to lose Sue's friendship. On the drive over it became clear to him that she was the person he was closest to at Crazy Ladies, and frankly anywhere else.

"You're going to throw yourself at the mercy of the court?" asked Cin. "Good man!"

Now she was handsomely dressed as a 19th century British barrister, wig, top hat, breeches and all.

"Shut up," he replied.

35

Wu sat stewing at his desk. Giving these people Gliese caps seemed like an insane and dangerous ploy to get the chips back. Sure, he'd get the Gliese people off his back, but they'd undoubtedly be outraged. Neither did he trust the woman to simply hand over the chips as promised. He wasn't about to hand anything over and end up with nothing to show for it. He got up and went downstairs to the bar, even though we has in no mood to socialize.

He walked at the periphery of the crowds, smiling and waving, and having brief small talk conversations with a few of the many people he knew here. He'd had all sorts of business with quite a few of them, each individual or group and their dealings with Wu were neatly and discreetly compartmentalized. The nightclub itself was an informal business incubator, a place where the rich and powerful from all over Silicon Valley, the Americas, Asia, Europe, and points in between came for privacy and security. His security staff was invisible but ever-present. There were several discreet conference rooms, bedrooms, communications rooms and other facilities in the building besides bars, dance floors, and a restaurant. It was part of a network of such places around the world. He, too, had investors to report to.

He was looking for someone in particular, and he found her on one of the small dance floors. In the darkness, flashing lights, and loud music, he was able to watch her dancing wildly in a dark corner, alone and looking lost in her own little world. At this hour, everyone in the room was probably peaking out on an endless variety of chemically-induced euphoria, and Pari Thakkar was no exception. Through his specs, she was lit up plain as day in the infrared view.

Wu stepped outside for a moment and messaged a couple of his people to come up. A female plainclothes security staff member soon arrived, and he whispered something to her off in a discreet corner of the alcove that separated the dance floor from an adjacent bar. He twiddled for some images to be sent to the young woman, then went back to his office to wait. On the way, he alerted a few more of his security staff.

The woman went into the dance floor and casually approached Pari.

"Hey, you're Pari, right? Sav's friend?" she asked cheerfully as she started swaying to the music. Pari looked at her blankly, and reduced the intensity of her dancing.

"Pari? Pari, right? Sav's in a booth at the bar waiting for you, were you waiting for him?" she repeated loudly, over the music, with a friendly smile.

Pari had stopped dancing, and nodded at the woman with a puzzled expression, but said nothing. Colored lights swept over the woman's face, and her skin looked like that of a magical creature, changing its colors in successive waves, like waves of color on a seashell but in motion. The colors seemed to go deep. Beauty is only skin deep, but the colors went further, all the way in. The glow came from within. She felt she could trust this smiling stranger, but at the same time she knew it was just the drugs. That was one of the things they did. She liked it, but she knew it could be an illusion. There was a pattern of red dots on the woman's white shirt, small ones, hundreds of them, and they pulsated with the light and the music. She looked more closely at them and saw that they were getting bigger and smaller, bigger and smaller in a subtle way that you'd have to examine carefully to notice.

"C'mon! I'll walk you down if you want," she said. Pari nodded again slowly, *No! don't go*, she thought, and the two left the dance floor through a door that was behind a large black partition near where she had been dancing by herself. Pari squinted at the light as they went into the more brightly lit hallway, one she wasn't familiar with. She couldn't recall ever coming off the dance floor through that door. In fact, she wasn't aware there even *was* a door there.

Someone came from behind and grabbed her, wrapping strong arms around her and pinning her own arms to her sides, and a hand clasped itself tightly over her mouth. A dark hood made of some stiff, thick material came over her head as the woman who had been helping her calmly looked on. Was that the shadow of a sneer? A smirk? She twiddled to look up synonyms of "smirk," but her specs seemed to be offline. She couldn't recall the last time that had ever happened. Something was keeping her mouth shut, like duct tape or something. Each of her legs was grabbed by a different person and stretched out. She couldn't shake them free or even bend them. A hand pulled up one side of her skirt and a needle went into her right thigh, then the dull ache of some liquid going into a muscle. That frightened her, and she tried to struggle as hard as she could. Her own body was struggling, and yet someone else's in the darkness below was struggling as well. She could see nothing in the blackness, but she knew as plain as day that there was a young woman down there, just like her, struggling against her captors. Or was there? She could no longer remember. A thick layer of even more blackness covered everything below her, and she couldn't recall what the question was. All around her, in the darkness, the red dots pulsated, bigger and smaller, bigger and smaller, swirling around like bees, only now on a deep black background.

*　　*　　*　　*　　*

It took close to half an hour, but eventually an icon flashed at the edge of Wu's view. Pari was now unconscious in a car headed for one of Wu's safe houses, a discreet bungalow in the seaside town of Pacifica. Now he had collateral, and a deep sense of relief.

Next, he had to get some caps in less than 24 hours.

36

The next morning, Wu was at his warehouse earlier than usual.

"What happened? Did you fall out of bed?" joked Sami, his receptionist.

"No, I just got up early for some reason. Couldn't get back to sleep," he said amiably. "Is Meg here yet?"

"In her office," said Sami.

Wu went down the short hallway on the office side of the warehouse and peeked into Megan Kao's office. As the operations person, she made sure all of the merchandise they dealt in came and went in an orderly fashion. She was very good at her job. He knocked on the door frame as he went in.

"Good morning!" she said, not quite concealing her surprise. "Slow night at the club?"

"Nah. Couldn't get back to sleep this morning. Figured I'd just come in to work."

"Well, I hate to disappoint you. Not much going on at the moment. The Gliese people are picking up some synthesizers and attachments before noon. They're also picking up some boxes we received from one of their mystery suppliers."

One of the reasons Gliese had been dealing with Wu and Bennington was because they often sent and received shipments to and from suppliers whose identities and locations were hidden from both of them. They were effectively dead drops by anonymous private couriers, authenticated only by a code word that Bennington or Wu would confirm with someone at Gliese. Wu and Bennington were more than happy to deal in gray market and even black market goods, no questions asked. It was a premium service. DuPont had also become an expert at picking up and delivering merchandise at ever-changing drop points. Gliese relied heavily on such discretion and was more than willing to pay well for it.

"Yeah? On the loading dock?" he asked. "Is DuPont delivering it?"

"No, it's just waiting for the Gliese folks to come and take it away."

"OK, Thanks for the heads up. Coffee?" he asked.

"No, I'm still nursing this one, thanks."

Wu headed for the loading dock. He had two choices: see if the boxes from the mystery suppliers had any hats, or somehow take hats away from the Gliese people who came to pick them up. The latter choice might require violence of some kind if he wasn't able to cajole or bribe them into giving him their caps. There was a possibility that only one person would come in for the pickup, and he needed 3 caps.

The shipment for Gliese was already near the main door of the loading dock. The synthesizers and their attachments were in large shipping crates. There were 2 cardboard boxes on top of one of the crates. They were not too big nor too heavy for him to carry to a work table behind some shelving units. Nobody else was there.

He shook them, and from the sound of it there were separate parcels inside each box. The boxes had been reused a few times, so he decided nobody would know if he opened them up and resealed them.

One box had some bubble-wrapped jars containing dull metal lumps with subtle differences in color and luster, other jars contained powdered chemicals with long multi-part names interspersed with numbers and oddly placed punctuation. There were also some circuit boards, and some chips that looked different from the ones he was trying to get back. The second box had more chemicals, a couple of items that looked like attachments for a larger device, and a smaller cardboard box. He opened the small lightweight box, and to his great surprise and relief, found 6 new-looking beige baseball caps packed together as if they had just been manufactured. Wu let out a deep sigh of relief.

What was special about them? He knew the Gliese people wore them with such unfailing consistency that bordered on fanaticism, but why? On the outside they looked like regular baseball caps. They seemed a little thicker, though. He took one and unfolded it from the rest and had a closer look. Between the layers of fabric he could feel a network of wires interconnecting some flat things the size of large coins and only slightly thicker. Under the brim, along the right hand edge, was what looked like a small flat pressure switch. He pressed it, but nothing happened. He tried the hat on to see if it was comfortable enough to wear all day.

As soon as it was settled on his head, his field of view became populated with hallucinations of small inanimate objects of various kinds, and he could clearly hear noises that some of them were making, as well as a cheerful voice that had launched into some kind of corporate greeting.

"Welcome to Gliese Genetics! To configure your new cap, think or say 'configure'," said the voice. There was a woman standing in front of him, on the other side of the work table, and Wu was startled enough to jump back and hit the back of his head against a shelving unit behind him. She repeated the suggestion, then 5 seconds later, repeated it again. Wu looked around. There were symbols, text, and some moving icons in his field of view. They were sort of like the visual and aural iconography he was used to in his specs, but unlike those they seemed completely real. There was never any mistaking the information provided by his specs for real entities. The caps produced a different effect altogether. His eyes seemed to be actually seeing the objects in the overlay as if they were real objects in his surrounding environment.

The smiling, patient woman kept repeating her suggestion every 5 seconds. He walked up to her, close enough to reach out and touch her. She slowly turned to keep facing him, and the light on her skin and clothing changed exactly as it would if she were a real flesh and blood woman. His reached out to touch her, his hand entering her body through her sternum, and he felt some tingling of the skin on the part of his hand

and arm that were inside her body. She was unperturbed, and kept patiently repeating her suggestion. He moved both hands and arms around crossing in and out of her body. The only indication that she was there was the tingling on his skin whenever it was inside of her.

He looked around to see what else the cap was telling him. There was some iconography that was apparently waiting for him to configure the cap. A small panel of buttons had appeared on the table in front of him, one marked "Configure Cap" was blinking to draw his attention. In the distance, which he could sense as if he could see through the walls of the building without actually seeing through them, an icon had been slowly approaching. No sooner did he think the thought of what it might be (not the words "what might that be?" but the primordial thought that might a moment later engender the worded question), than the thought arose in his head that some Gliese people were coming to pick up a shipment. A man named Liam and a woman named Jenny. That knowledge simply popped into his head like a neutrino from a distant galaxy. He took the cap off immediately, and started packing everything back up the way it was and taping everything shut with the packing supplies that were on the work table. Everything except the box with the half dozen caps.

He put the two boxes back on top of the crates on the loading dock and took the small box of caps with him out to his car as discreetly as he could, then got in and told the car to go to the club. As it turned onto Rollins Road a few blocks away, he saw the delivery van coming in the opposite direction, with a man and a woman in front, each wearing a beige cap. They made a point of looking at him with curious expressions as he drove by. He touched his head after they passed to make sure he wasn't still wearing the cap. He wasn't, but he now remembered that he hadn't turned it off. *Shit!* he thought. He pulled over to the side, and grabbed the box of caps. The one he had tried on was haphazardly packed against the others. He put it on again and saw and heard the astonishing landscape of icons, lines symbols, sounds and the voice asking yet again if he wanted to configure the cap. The woman was sitting next to him in his car, her legs crossed and her hands casually folded on her lap. She was an attractive woman, of some indeterminate Eurasian stock, perhaps 10 years younger than Wu. She seemed cheerful and patient, and he was sorely tempted to start the configuration process, whatever that might entail. He felt for the button along the brim, and pressed it. There was a strong and quite unpleasant snapping sensation inside his head, accompanied by a flash of vertigo and a moment of nausea. Not enough to throw up, but it definitely had potential. It took him a minute or so to calm back down. The strange hallucinations were now gone, including the woman. He took the cap off and put it back in the box with the others.

"To the club," he told the car.

37

Thakkar was sipping the last of his breakfast coffee, reviewing a digest of the previous night's activities. Bennington's specs had provided them with recordings of his entire last day, but Cliff's had provided much less. Apparently he only used his specs for fairly basic tasks like electronic payments and text messaging. There were several conversations with Gliese people in them including some intimate conversations between him and the woman, Alice, who had shot DuPont, but not much else. They also had Cliff's beige cap, the first one Thakkar had managed to retrieve and examine, but it was unclear whether any recorded media could be recovered from it. With any luck, Wu would deliver some more before the end of the day. FfēFfē Automata already had sensors that could read the wispy magnetic fields around the brain, but only a rudimentary ability to induce thoughts by reversing the process and injecting magnetic fields back into it. He was interested in seeing how *they* did it. The cap retrieved by Brad the night before was baffling. He and his team of robots were examining it and getting various kinds of imagery and instrument readings. Thakkar's experience with it had been as fascinating to him as it had been disturbing.

He was toying with a hypothesis about it. It was a crazy hypothesis, and he needed hard evidence before he was willing to articulate it, even to his team at FfēFfē. He had only discussed it with Wilkins, his most advanced robot model, more advanced even than FfēFfē's inaugural commercial models and with more powerful resources supporting him from FfēFfē's AI data center. He also needed the additional caps, functioning ones, in order to take a few apart and examine them in great detail. If his hunch was correct, it could only be considered a grave existential threat.

Wilkins came and sat down with Thakkar.

"We still don't have anything about the lab," said Wilkins. "These people from last night were mainly security and logistics. Most of the dead guy's last day was dedicated to finding the missing chips. They probably know nothing about anything beyond dealing with incoming shipments."

"Has Wu contacted Benita yet?" asked Thakkar.

"Not yet. We've gotten video of a few of his people at the antique shop. They got there a while ago. Looks like Wu had some caps after all, and it's not even lunch time."

"That guy must know a lot more about what's going on at Gliese than those two folks from last night," mused Thakkar. "He must have had caps on hand the whole time."

Icons flashed in both Thakkar's and Wilkins' peripheral vision, and a teleconference began between them and Benita and Brad, who were in a car on their way to the antique shop.

"Ms. Garcés! So good of you to join us. You've done a splendid job so far. I can barely contain myself," said Thakkar.

"Well, it's only been a couple of days. We'll see how things turn out," she said.

"Let me share a view," said Brad. In a moment everyone could see a 3D landscape projected in front of them. It depicted an aerial view of the area surrounding the antique shop, as seen from the rear, including a radius of about 2 blocks around it.

"This is a view from a drone. That small van behind the shop brought some of Wu's people about an hour ago," he said. "They've been inside for a little while."

"Maybe they're looking for Bennington's hiding places," said Benita. "I've just got something from Wu. He says to leave the chips and the metal samples where we find the caps. Have a look at this." She shared a video of Pari lying on a bed, unconscious.

"Didn't she come home last night?" asked Benita.

"Apparently not," said Thakkar sheepishly. "They come and go as they please. They're adults. Even Pari."

He nodded towards a robot that was standing nearby, and it turned and walked off, presumably to verify that she was not in her room.

"Why doesn't she have a security detail?" asked Benita.

"She does," said Thakkar, "But she makes them keep their distance, to the point of being next to useless. We've had all manner of conflict over it, and this is where we are. She's thrown some fairly vicious tantrums about them, both privately and publicly. It's like she has some kind of death wish. I hope she thinks it over, but she's stuck in a pretty wild lifestyle. At least she still lives here where we have some kind of ongoing contact with her. It's better than the alternative."

"Well, he says they'll release Pari once they verify that we gave them everything that was in the photo I shared with him last night," said Benita.

At that moment, three people walked out from the back of the shop, closed the door, and got in their van.

"OK, we're moving in," said Wilkins.

It took about 5 minutes for 2 robots to pick up the package left by Wu's people and leave the chips and rare earths.

"I've sent Wu the message. I also asked where we can pick up Pari," said Benita.

After 10 minutes, the same van as before drove up to the antique shop loading dock. It took them only a minute or so to take the boxes and put them in the van, which then drove off. Another 5 minutes later, Benita received a message.

"Wu says he'll tell us where Pari is as soon as he has all of the items. That was the agreement."

Brad and Benita arrived at a staging area near the shop where the robots that had picked up the box were parked. They parked their own car alongside the robots' car.

"No explosives or booby traps, as far as we can tell," said one of the robots, a Wilkins, who handed Benita the opened box. She and Brad each pulled out a hat and examined it. She put it on.

"I don't feel anything," she said.

"This may be a power switch," said Brad, pointing to the pressure switch near the brim. Benita took hers off, pressed the switch, and hesitated. She looked at Brad.

"If anything bad happens, pull it off me immediately," she told him. He nodded, and shifted his body to have his hands ready near her head. Benita put the cap on.

A smiling woman who looked as if she had come out of an airline safety video appeared in the car in the seat across from Benita, next to Zag. He couldn't see her because she wasn't being detected by the specs' video and audio, but the cap apparently knew enough to sit her next to him and not on top of him, or so it seemed. Was it able to analyze Benita's perception directly?

"Welcome to **Gliese Genetics!** To configure your new cap, think or say 'configure'," said the woman. There were various icons and indicators floating around her. Everything remained steady as Benita turned her head one way and then the other. The woman repeated her suggestion.

"Oh my god," she whispered, almost to herself. "My *god*..."

"Are you OK?" asked Brad, ready to pull it off.

"Fine, fine," she said, waving him off. "It's like the specs, only *real*! It's like I'm actually seeing and hearing things with my own eyes and ears."

"What are you seeing?" asked Thakkar anxiously. Benita could see and hear everything in her specs as she always did, but the cap visions seemed to be her own.

"There's a woman sitting across from me asking me if I want to configure the cap, and she's repeating it every few seconds. She looks like a real person sitting there. She's sitting next to Zag, as if the cap knew that I could see him there."

"What!" said Zag with alarm. "Where is she? Why can't I see her?"

"It's amazing! This is far more realistic than the specs. I feel as if I'm actually seeing this stuff, as if it was actually there." She leaned forward to touch the smiling woman's knee.

"She has no mass or substance, though. I can feel a tingle on my skin when it's inside of her, I don't know, surface? But I can't actually feel her skin or anything." She waved her hand back and forth across the woman's knee. The tingling was an interesting sensation.

"Your cap is in trouble," said Zag. "Not the baseball cap, your capture gear cap. You're starting to lose channels."

Benita took the cap off, and the woman and the icons that came with her were gone.

"Come on back guys, we need to secure the caps," said Thakkar. "Is there anything else? Chargers? Accessories? Documentation of any kind?"

"No, just the caps. We still need to confirm with Wu, drop off the rest of the stuff, and go get Pari," said Benita.

"Right, right, could you please hand the caps off to the robots so they can bring them back? They're dropping off the remaining items at the shop right now."

A few minutes later, the robots came by again, and after the usual specs authentication ritual Benita handed them the box of caps through the window. Another icon soon flashed in her specs.

"Wu says we can pick Pari up at this address," she said. It was an address on Upper Mori Road in San Bruno.

"It looks like an old dirt road on the coast next to a golf course," said Brad. "We should head on out. They probably just dumped her there. She may not be conscious, and there may be golfers or hikers out there."

Benita gave the car the address and it drove off.

*　　*　　*　　*　　*

It was mid-afternoon when Benita and Brad got to the drop off point. It was a beachside scrubland area next to a golf course, where golfers dotted the greens in the distance. The dirt road that led into it looked like it was mainly used by hikers, mountain bikers, and horseback riders. The surface was hard and dry this time of year. During an intense rainy season it might get muddy enough to be impassable. It narrowed considerably until it reached a small dirt parking area about 300 meters from the main road. There were no other cars, and Pari was lying on a rustic park bench next to a trailhead marker. She looked as if she had fallen asleep there.

"Let's get her in the car and get out of here," said Benita as she got out of the car. She walked over and saw that Pari was gradually starting to wake up. It reminded Benita of Pari's drugged state at Bennington's, the night he was shot. Benita threaded her arms under Pari's shoulders and tried to stand her up. Pari's wild eyes met hers, and for a moment she embraced Benita tightly and again started kissing her sloppily on the mouth. Her hair had that same haunting fragrance, now mixed in with California sage and the salty breeze from the nearby ocean. Her lips slow-danced with Benita's for a quivering moment.

"Will you stop!" she said, pulling away and giving Pari a shake. Pari responded with a darkly serious gaze, and promptly collapsed in Benita's arms.

"What's that?" asked Brad, looking towards the main road.

A large plume of dust rose behind a car that was speeding towards them along the dirt access road. Its motors groaned as it bumped violently on the uneven surface.

"Doesn't look like a ranger or a cop. They must be pretty motivated," said Benita.

"Let's get Pari packed up and get out of here."

The car soon skidded to a rough stop in a way that blocked Benita and Brad's car. The Gliese woman came out and walked briskly towards them. She pulled her right hand from behind her back and pointed a gun at Benita. Brad instinctively ran towards the woman and grabbed the wrist of her gun hand, forcing it to point upwards. Benita lay the collapsed Pari on the ground and ran towards the Gliese woman, putting one hand under the woman's chin and the other over her eyes, forcibly bending her neck back. Between Benita and Brad they managed to push the woman backwards, keeping her just off balance enough to prevent her from fighting back effectively. A few meters away from where they had started, the ground sloped down steeply into a dry stream bed several meters deep, sparsely lined with dry vegetation, and they did their best to guide her towards it. With his free hand, Brad struggled to bend the woman's wrist hard enough to force her to drop the gun to the ground, although not before she got a couple of shots off.

In one final heave, they hurled her down into the ravine. She bounced once on her buttocks and fell backwards, her head hit the ground with enough force for her face to look stunned. Her legs flipped over her at somewhat of an angle, and their momentum was enough for her to roll several times until she came to rest at the bottom of the sloping ground.

Benita and Brad didn't wait to watch. They were already running towards Pari and the car. Brad saw the gun on the ground, put the safety on, and flung it into the surrounding shrubs and grasses. Between them they got Pari into the car, then managed to circumvent the other car and drive off before the Gliese woman made her way out of the dry arroyo. Pari was at best semi-conscious, and lay on the car seat across from Brad and Benita.

"What the fuck was her problem!" exclaimed Benita, catching her breath. It had been quite a jolt of adrenaline. Without her security training and Brad's very evident security behavior capture content, she might have been killed.

"I don't know," said Brad. His voice also seemed excited and out of breath, in spite of being a lungless machine. This was the voice that behavior capture actors had after capturing hand to hand combat activities with their sensor suits, so that's the voice Brad had now. No doubt his heart rhythm mini-model was also going a mile a minute. He spotted the baseball cap Benita had tested on the seat next to her. He picked it up to examine it. "They must have tracked the cap. Did you turn it off?"

"I don't think so."

"Try it on and see if it's still on."

Benita put it on and the woman began suggesting that she start the cap configuring process over and over again. The car was now at an angle that allowed her to notice a marker hovering over the place where they had found Pari, now receding into the distance. The marker was tagged "Alice Woods, Security."

"It was on alright, and there's an icon tagging the woman who attacked us. Her name is Alice Woods, apparently. She probably followed us all the way out here with no trouble at all." She took the cap off and pressed the button near the brim to turn it off.

An icon was glowing in Benita's specs. It was Wilkins.

"Here's the preliminary examination," said Wilkins in the background. "Consider this the beginning of your reading in, Benita."

The video switched to a view of a work table, on which was a disassembled cap, probably one they had just picked up from the antique shop. The cap's inner lining had been removed, exposing about a dozen components bridged with small odd-looking cables. There were no circuit boards in it, just some flat, tablet-shaped interconnected items that Benita couldn't recognize, although not being a hardware engineer that might not mean much.

"I don't really recognize them," said Wilkins, "Maybe the actual circuitry is embedded in some kind of a casting resin in these tablets."

"So what exactly am I being read in on?" asked Benita.

"You'll know more once we examine those components," replied Wilkins. "They're being carefully dissected. We sent a couple to Blam. They have some serious reverse engineering resources there."

"We were attacked by the Gliese woman, as you may have seen from Brad," said Benita. "We have Pari, by the way. She looks OK. She's asleep at the moment. Don't turn the caps on. The Gliese people will be able to locate you."

"We just saw that. Wu may not have managed to conceal the loss of the caps," answered Wilkins. "Please bring Pari by the house. We may need to talk about a few things."

Pari barely stirred as they drove on.

38

The car stopped at the carport on the side of Thakkar's stately home. Once again, a couple of additional Wilkins were waiting to take Pari to her room. What Benita always assumed was the main Wilkins stood in front of them.

Pari had been sitting up on the floor of the car for a few minutes, still looking groggy. Benita suspected that Pari was quite the car floor connoisseur. At the moment she didn't have the impeccable fashion model chic appearance she'd had on other occasions. She looked tired, and the dirt from the hiking trail made her look grungy, and her hair disheveled.

"I'll help her out," said Benita, offering her hand. Pari took it and made it out of the car more or less under her own power. Benita met her eyes for a moment, but Pari looked distant, and merely said a polite "thank you," then walked off with the extra Wilkinses. Benita was surprised to feel disappointment at her sudden formality, and perhaps a vague sense of loss.

"Let's go to Dr. Thakkar's office," said the remaining Wilkins.

Thakkar was sitting on the sofa, wearing a surprisingly compact and comfortable-looking exoskeleton.

"Well, now that you have the caps, it seems I'm out of a job." said Benita.

"Oh, not at all, not at all," said Thakkar, waving it off. "We're actually at a crucial point now. The components in the caps are compatible with a hypothesis I have been developing with my team. We've cut one of them open and had the cross-sections of some of the internal components scanned. That gave us a crude model of their structure. We'll have a lot more once the Blam folks start looking at them."

Wilkins made a movement, and a large 3D rendering of the scan shimmered over the coffee table before them.

"It looks like the components in the cap are all more or less the same, at least so far," said Wilkins. The view showed a reconstruction of one of the components, which at a distance looked a lot like a thick chocolate-covered cookie with many thin layers of filling. The view zoomed in and the inside looked like the cross-section of a hundred story building with the most complex electrical and plumbing systems ever conceived.

"This is one of the 18 components in the device. The others we've examined are similar, but not quite identical. This particular one was towards the front of the cap, around the brain's frontal lobes," said Wilkins.

"This is some kind of electronic circuit?" asked Benita. "A 3D circuit? I didn't know they had that many layers. I thought they had, I don't know, a dozen layers? I saw a video about that."

"The most advanced prototypes being worked on today are in the 20 to 30 layer range. At research institutions they occasionally get to 50 or so, but they generally don't work. A variety of flaws cause parts of the circuits to fail, short out, or simply lose connection with the others. This circuit has at least 117 layers," said Wilkins. "That's well past the current state of the art, in that regard, although the feature sizes are much bigger than in research chips. It's as if they know how to do lots of layers, but don't have the right equipment to make them with small feature sizes. Maybe that's a clue to why they work."

"Well, maybe it's a secret Chinese prototype," said Benita. "Or European, or Indian. It could be anybody. It could be someone's grad school project."

"Well," started Thakkar in a fatherly tone. "We can't think of *anyone* it could be. As you know, our back-end AI systems and the robots use state of the art chips. The most powerful available, made by companies that dominate the world's electronics markets. These companies are intimate with the best research institutions. It's very, very hard to believe that someone secretly has this technology, but hasn't fielded a single commercial product. They would make a killing, they would be worth a fortune, even with this quality. They would transform the electronics market from top to bottom. We'd have chips thousands of times, maybe millions of times more powerful than what is currently on the market, if they used high end manufacturing facilities. It's just not credible."

"So?" asked Benita. "Who made it?"

"We believe the Gliese people made it, or someone they're connected to did, or at least helped them do it," said Thakkar. "You may be asking yourself: 'then why don't they, whoever they may be, make these advanced products and sell them,' right?"

Benita nodded, a puzzled expression on her face.

"Well, my hypothesis is," said Thakkar, pausing. He looked as if he were struggling to put it into words, or hesitant to say them. "There are a number of hints that lead us to believe that it's an extraterrestrial technology of some kind, or at least someone who's set up a base in a high orbit around the earth."

Benita's face was frozen, baffled, her eyes squinting slightly, scanning Thakkar's face. Her mouth was slightly open. Several seconds passed. She closed her mouth, and blinked her eyes a few times.

"Extraterrestrial... As in *alien*? From outer space?" she said. "What, from another planet? From some other solar system?" She was involuntarily raising her voice. Thakkar held up his hand to pause her.

"Yes, yes, it's crazy. I know, I know," he replied, now waving dismissively. "I've been looking into this for a couple of years now. *We've* been looking. My research team has been on it. We have circumstantial evidence, and now these circuits are concrete evidence. This is our most important discovery so far. In fact, this is enough to get higher authorities actively involved, now that we have some extra caps."

"What higher authorities?" asked Benita.

"I know a couple of people at Homeland Security. I've been speaking with them informally. We'll be talking about it tomorrow. Some people at Blam are also involved."

"It seems pretty far-fetched to me. Aliens? This would be a historic moment, having contact with beings from another planet."

"We have no evidence of any beings from another planet. We've only detected the presence of people. People are doing the bidding of someone or something that isn't physically present. They have a nightly communication via satellite using their own equipment. We haven't yet identified the satellite they use. Their antenna is apparently pointed at something in orbit around the earth, in about the same orbit as the moon, but we haven't been able to find anything in publicly available records that's parked where their antenna is pointing. We have hundreds of hours of video of the antenna, and we've managed to get a good estimate of where it's pointing."

He twiddled his fingers and a highly sped up video of a dish antenna appeared floating before them. It was mounted on top of an old bus parked at a small farm, and looked to be about a meter and a half in diameter. The antenna was barely visible through a stand of trees. It seemed to be tracking something in the sky as the earth rotated and as the days rolled quickly by in the highly sped up video. When it was pointing at the horizon, it quickly rotated back to await its target's return on the opposite horizon. The video was followed by an animation that traced a straight line from the base of the dish through its focal point, then zoomed all the way out to show the line pointing away from earth on a diagram showing the earth, the moon, and the curve of the moon's orbit around the earth. The straight line was remarkably consistent as the earth rotated and the moon moved along the arc. It showed a point that seemed to be precisely along the moon's orbit around the earth, accurately intersecting it about one sixth of an orbit behind the moon as it moved, as if something were trailing the moon at a fixed distance.

"The antenna seems to be pointing at the L5 Earth-Moon Lagrange point, which is a point where the gravity of the earth and the moon more or less balance out, so it wouldn't require much energy for a satellite to maintain that position."

"So they're communicating with something at that point?" asked Benita. "Does any country or company have anything out there?"

"There's some dust and debris that's managed to settle in the region. There are a couple of functioning communications satellites relatively nearby, and some probes have passed through there over the years. On the diagram it looks like a point, but in practice it's a pretty large volume of space. It hasn't been systematically explored. There could be anything out there, really. If anybody has any secret assets there, we wouldn't know about them," said Wilkins.

"Have you tried detecting their signals? From Gliese or from the L5 point?"

"That turns out to be pretty difficult. We've made a few half-assed attempts, but so far have found nothing," said Thakkar. "Someone with resources in space would have to try. We hope that the folks at Homeland Security can help kick off the process."

"So you have surveillance on Gliese Genetics? How close? It looks like the video was taken from less than a kilometer away. What other kinds of data have you gotten? If there are only people there, the alien hypothesis is kind of weak, no?"

"We've rented a cottage that has a line of sight on Gliese Genetics, or parts of it. There's a lot of tree cover, so we can't see everything. It's on a hill about half a kilometer away," answered Wilkins. "We kind of lucked out with this antenna."

"They've been slowly building up some kind of biotech lab, with Wu's and Bennington's help. By slowly I mean for at least 5 years, maybe 10. They run a plant tissue culture and genetics business that appears to have a lot of products. They've started to market some farm animals with extensively modified genomes. They already have a line of highly modified plants, both ornamental and edible. They've been able to get all of the FDA approvals they've filed for, in spite of being a pretty small operation. They're probably making quite a bit of money at it, too. Wu in particular has been slowly gathering equipment for them, at least since we've been watching. They also seem to be building up a data center down there, and given this last shipment of chips, they appear to be building an AI. An artificial intelligence. Not a crappy one, mind you, potentially a fairly powerful one," said Thakkar. "A lot of it doesn't completely add up."

"Why don't they make their own chips?" she asked. "They made the ones in the caps, right?"

Thakkar shrugged.

"Making chips like that is hard. You need really expensive and sophisticated equipment, lots of highly trained people, and all sorts of exotic materials. You'd think that if they could make something like this," he twiddled his fingers for the virtual model to float before them once more, "they'd be able to make their own AI circuitry, but there's a lot we don't know. You traded some rare earths along with the chips, so those might be limiting resources, or maybe their setup is very small and inefficient. Maybe their process is still too crude. There are about a dozen or two people out there, by our reckoning, and they don't look like the kinds of folks who could run a chip fab, let alone create quantum computing hardware, even with sophisticated labor and operations software. In any case, they run a biotech lab for their plant and animal business. My guess is that they're using that as a front for something, although I'm not sure what. Let's hope they're not making some kind of bioweapon down there."

"So what's my next move?" asked Benita.

"I'd like you to go back and talk to Wu. See what else he knows. Also Brenda, Bennington's woman. He was the one who got them the quantum gate arrays, so she may yet have some insight on that and useful contacts. Once the Feds are all over them, we won't have access. We need to find out if they know of other places like Gliese, and what kinds of equipment they've been buying. It would be great if you could get some kind of concrete evidence, but I suspect that won't be easy."

"OK, let me go home and take a shower, then I'll go out to the club and look for him," said Benita.

"Wait until tomorrow morning," said Thakkar. "We don't want to seem over-anxious or do anything that might empower him."

39

Alice Woods saw stars for just a moment. She had hit her head on something that felt hard, but not rock hard, and not enough to completely knock off her specs. It must have been the hard dry ground. Falling backwards into a shallow ravine had magnified the force of the blow. She sat up, propping herself up with her arms. The ground was as warm as the afternoon, the sky deep blue with broad streaks of tan-colored smoke from a wildfire far away. She could smell the ocean, which must have been very nearby, lightly seasoned with the acrid scent of burnt forests and homes.

It came to her suddenly. They were up there, just over the edge of the ravine, only a few meters away. She heard the whining of motors and the growl of tires over gravel and dirt. They were getting away. She got up too quickly, and almost fell down again from vertigo, its lavender gray haze almost blotting out her vision. She regained her balance and stood there for a few moments, then carefully climbed back up. Nobody was up here, just her car parked where she had left it and a thin cloud of dust that was quickly dissipating. In the distance she saw the car turning off the dirt road and onto the paved street. The icon that she had been using to track them disappeared from her visual field a moment later.

She remembered her pistol, but her hands were empty. She looked back down at where she had fallen, nothing. The robot had twisted it out of her hand. She searched the ground for a while and found only a single spent bullet casing, then got in her car and told it to go back to Gliese. It was an older model than her usual car, which had to be disposed of in case it came up on any home surveillance videos from the previous night. She dozed off during most of the hour and a half drive.

*   *   *   *   *

The car parked itself, and her supervisor, Steve Ramos was already walking towards her as she got out.

"I missed them. Sorry," she said. Her voice expressed genuine regret. Steve looked angry, as if he were about to chew her out severely for having gone out on her own, but that wasn't the way things were done here. Mistakes, even massive mistakes, were problems to be solved, bugs to be fixed.

"It's OK, don't worry about it," he said. "Wu's handed them some caps in exchange for the chips."

Alice saw the seriousness in his face. They were all trained to never ever lose contact with their caps. They were considered some of the most valuable property that Gliese had, on par with their lab operations and trade secrets.

"I know, I tracked one of them to where they were picking up a hostage or something. So, what does Hoyt say?" Hoyt Waterston was the site supervisor at Gliese. He was the local authority and the main liaison with the corporate offices.

"He and corporate are plenty pissed. They were hoping you could grab the girl and use her to get the caps back. Now he's going to have to tell corporate. It's serious. We've never lost any of the core proprietary technology, as far as I know."

Alice felt deeply depressed about shooting Cliff the night before. She had not felt this close to despondence in a long while. The last time, she had ended up on the streets. Rage about Cliff was what drove her now, not whether some of the caps were lost. He was dead over some measly caps, stolen by some huge, greedy corporation. She wept herself to sleep.

"The police are also investigating the death of Bennington's driver, and for some reason they suspect we're involved. There must be video from neighborhood surveillance or something. If this all starts blowing back on us, we may need to begin evacuating the site. We'll know after Hoyt talks to corporate."

"What should I be doing?" she asked. She knew that evacuating would be a drastic measure indeed.

"Go get some rest. I'll let you know once there's a plan."

Alice went back to her room to get a clean change of clothes and then to the main farmhouse to take a shower. She was surprised at how dirty she had gotten in the ravine. She went back to the trailer where she bunked and got into bed. She put her specs on the charging cradle that was on her nightstand, put her cap next to them on its own charger, sobbed quietly for a while, then fell asleep.

40

The evening rush was starting to gather steam at the Q'Boom Qlub when Wu looked up from his desk and saw that the person knocking on his open door was none other than Hoyt Waterston, the man in charge at Gliese. He was a lanky fortyish man with male pattern baldness, and walked with the slight stoop of an academic. He was very smart and very well informed. Wu found that he was also a shrewd businessman, and a demanding one as well. They had gotten along well over the last few years, and Wu easily sensed that Waterston wasn't in a good mood.

"I can't believe you pulled that Eddie, seriously," said Waterston, closing the door behind him, then inviting himself to sit down in front of Wu's desk. Wu noticed that Waterston wasn't wearing his ever-present Gliese cap.

"What do you mean, Hoyt?" started Wu. "Are you talking about the caps?"

"Yeah, the caps. The caps you just gave away. We managed to track one of them out to Pacifica. I don't know what was going on out there, but there was a robot involved, a pretty sophisticated looking one. Did you just give our caps to FféFfé Automata? Do you have any idea what's going to happen next? Did you think nobody would find out?"

Damn it, thought Wu.

"Well, you've got the chips, right? Your people were making it pretty clear you wanted them back."

"But not at the expense of the caps!" said Waterston, almost shouting. "That stuff belongs to corporate! It's unbelievably valuable proprietary technology! It's a bucketful of trade secrets, and now those people have them! This is very, very secret stuff! Corporate knew they were gone before I did!"

"You guys made the caps? You didn't buy them from China?" said Wu, trying to be funny.

"Cut the bullshit, Eddie. No, they're not from China and you know it! There's going to be a shitstorm once those people get a good look at them. I will make sure you get at least twice as much shit as I do, Eddie. You really fucked up this time." Wu had never seen him this upset. Their dealings were invariably calm, discreet, and well paid.

"People steal technology all the time. This is Silicon Valley. Half the people at my club are trying to steal from each other. That's kind of the point. You can sue them at the World Trade Organization or call the Feds. So, what's the plan?"

"The plan? There's no plan, Eddie. Or maybe the plan is that corporate will come down here and fuck us all over, Eddie. Including you."

Wu scoffed.

"Where did you get them from? Who's your supplier?"

"Who? You don't know who we're dealing with, Eddie. These people are unforgiving. They're great when everything's going smoothly, and very helpful when it's time to solve problems," said Waterston. "But when people really screw up, they tend to disappear. Permanently."

"So what are you saying, that they're going to come out here and kill us? Over some electronic caps?"

Waterston fixed his gaze on Wu, saying nothing. Wu scoffed again.

"Are you threatening me, Hoyt? Who's going to do this, you? Your people? We *will* defend ourselves! I also have a 'corporate office.'"

"Well, there's only one way to find out, isn't there?" said Waterston, getting up to leave.

"Hold on, Hoyt. What can we do about this? Have you talked to them? How did they find out? Maybe we can get them back. We can track them down. How hard can that be?"

"Eddie, it's out of my hands." Waterston turned and left.

41

Back in his office, Waterston sat at his desk with his Gliese cap on. In a certain routine way, he imagined the start of a private communication to corporate. Might as well get it over with, he thought.

In his mind's eye, as if in a waking dream, he suddenly sat at a conference table with a few other people. The leader of the corporate team was a woman named Jane Smith. He couldn't remember the names of the others, who rarely spoke anyway. To some extent they were just props, or avatars quietly supervising the discussion. Jane was always the primary contact. It wasn't clear where this conference room was, in what city, in what country, or whether it existed at all. The whole setting looked and felt like living in a dream world. Jane would say things, create action items, and things in the real world happened accordingly. Sometimes Waterston and his team performed the tasks and sometimes they didn't, so he inferred that there were other teams somewhere carrying out their own action items. It was from one of those nameless other teams that they received Gliese's supply of caps, and to others that Gliese sent a variety of its own work products.

All Waterston could be fairly certain of, was that the conference was occurring via the satellite link. The satellite was far enough away that the round trip between him and the conference room participants was 2 or 3 seconds. This meant that he would say something, then wait about 3 seconds to get a response. Why this was so was a mystery to him. He speculated that maybe a more distant satellite was cheaper than a nearer one with less lag time.

The sensors in his cap picked up some aspect of what he was thinking as he spoke out loud to the dreamlike figures, and the signals gathered from the sensors were transmitted through the satellite uplink and somehow relayed to corporate. They, in turn, sent signals that would be output by the cap into his head as dream-like scenes.

"You were unable to recover the communications devices?" asked Jane.

"Correct," he replied. "We were not. We aren't sure who has them at the moment or where they're located, they're all powered down. It's likely that a large and highly visible robotics company, FfēFfē Automata, has them. Their parent company, Blam, may also be involved, and we think they might have been the original buyers of the electronic parts and one or the other of them may have been observing us for a while."

The other figures exchanged glances with each other, Jane's gaze was fixed on Waterston.

"What is the response from your supplier, *Magical Elements, LLC*?"

"The owner, Eddie Wu, argues that the trade was done in order to recover the electronic parts for the new computing system. He believed that the parts had a high enough priority that the trade was worthwhile. He did recover all of the missing components, as well as the rare earths."

"He was aware that the communication devices are entirely off limits, correct?"

"He claims he wasn't aware that the device was proprietary."

"And yet he knew they were valuable enough to trade them?"

Waterston had no answer for this. Obviously there was a contradiction there. Bennington and Wu knew that the caps were proprietary and off limits, he had mentioned it to them himself on several occasions. Waterston's staff were well-trained to protect Gliese property, and that neither Bennington nor Wu nor anyone else could so much as touch it.

"I can't answer for him. I assume Wu is not being forthright," said Waterston.

Jane and the other figures exchanged glances in various combinations. There was a long pause. Waterston assumed they were discussing things behind the scenes, in their own version of private speech.

"We will discuss the matter on our end," said Jane. "Please contact us two hours from now." The dream faded away, and Waterston was back in his office, sitting at his desk.

What would they decide? Waterston assumed the worst, that they would have to evacuate the site. They ran evacuation drills twice a year, once during the rainy season and once in the summer. Even though most of the proprietary assets, as they were called, were in trailers, the existing laboratory and the new one nearing completion were housed in some "portables." These were mobile buildings that could in principle be relocated, but were larger than a trailer and required more setup and teardown than simply parking a trailer at a desired location. The drills consistently showed that it was about a day long operation for three people for each portable. They would have to be stripped of valuables and abandoned if they were to escape in less than 24 hours.

Even before they started, he'd have to rent some tractor trucks to move all of the trailers. With so little time, he'd be lucky to empty the portables and distribute their contents among the trailers, packing them more or less solid. The Gliese staff was less than 30 people, so they'd have to get started as soon as possible. Right now would be a good time.

He got up to go ask his staff to get the process moving. The first phase would be to start packing things up for transport and renting the necessary vehicles. He could always cancel it if the evacuation orders didn't come through, and all they'd have to do would be to unload and unpack everything.

42

The L5 Earth-Moon Lagrange point can be calculated to a specific region along the moon's orbit around the earth where the gravitational forces of the earth and moon exactly cancel out, and stationary objects that happen to be located there do not fall to the earth or to the moon due to gravitational forces, or at least not as readily as elsewhere. In practice, things are more complicated, and remaining there with minimal energy expenditure is quite a balancing act.

The L5 point marks a fairly large volume of space in which moving objects can be caught in "tadpole orbits," which are tear-drop shaped trajectories that orbit around the L5 point itself. Objects such as dust particles or small asteroids that happen to wander into that region can end up in such orbits if they are moving slowly enough and in the right direction. They can persist there indefinitely unless some outside force such as a collision with a faster moving object manages to push them out.

One such object was an artificially constructed vehicle of sorts, perhaps more like a space station. Artificially constructed, but not man-made, it had been built over an interval of several earth centuries and completed early during the period that humans tend to refer to as the 13th century.

There were no living beings on it, nor was it created by living beings. Its crew consisted of machine learning models that were derived from living beings in a manner similar to the techniques used by FfēFfē Automata to embed human behavior into its own machine learning models. Those living beings had died tens of thousands of earth years ago, and the machine learning models derived from them resided on disks of dense circuitry about the size of a hockey puck. These circuits were similar, technologically, to the circuits in the caps that Gliese staff members wore. The circuits in the caps, however, were much simpler and not as finely crafted. The circuits in the L5 station were created by a civilization far more advanced than present day humans, those in the caps were created by humans using improvised equipment that took a long time to re-invent.

The machine learning models of the L5 station considered themselves conscious beings, virtual replicas of the biological beings they were derived from before their nearly 50,000 earth year voyage towards our sun. Their degree of sentience was as debatable as whether FfēFfē's virtual characters and robots were or ever would be conscious. To that civilization, our solar system was a nearby star, a place to which they could send probes to set up colonies and expand their domain beyond their home planet, and finally take possession of what they perceived as their cosmic endowment. Their overarching goal was to seed a living community of their biological kind on a target planet, establish a viable population, and thereby reconstitute a remote instance of their civilization. Anything that ultimately served that purpose was on the table, and these virtual explorers were devoted to fulfilling the mission.

The disks of circuitry in which these model consciousnesses resided took turns being activated as virtual characters or installed in mechanical replicas of their biological creators. They were virtual and robotic versions of their creators in the same way that Zag and Wilkins were replicas of their human creators. When not in such a robotic rotation, the disks were stored away and the consciousnesses within them waited in a deathly indefinite sleep.

There were only about a hundred disks on the Earth-Moon L5 station, and only about half a dozen were on active robot duty at any given time.

These were the participants in the conference room with Waterston, and the currently designated leader of the active team always played the role of Jane Smith. The role had other names, such as Saki Matsumoto, María Delgado, Kisi Okonjo, and many others. Gliese Genetics was by no means their only earthly team. This small number of active crew made the Earth-Moon L5 station an outpost. The main complex of stations and infrastructure was in the Earth-Sun L5 point, over 150 million kilometers away along the Earth's orbital trajectory around the Sun.

The Earth-Sun L5 complex, the main base, consisted of over two dozen craft, about half of which were built after arriving at this solar system, and all of the rest heavily modified or refurbished since then. Across them, there were close to 200 disks on active robot duty, building out infrastructure, managing the mining of asteroids and comets, and managing the mission's activities on earth. Another thousand or so disks were in storage. After arriving in our solar system, it had taken over 4000 earth years to reach this level of development.

The initial mission had consisted of 50 nearly identical craft, each capable of independently carrying out the mission duties. Fewer than a fifth of them managed to arrive intact enough to carry out meaningful mission activities, and disks had to be rescued from some of the heavily damaged craft that were barely able to limp into the solar system. The rest either disappeared or were all but destroyed during the eons-long voyage through deep space with all of their disks lost.

Those that did arrive had been scoured by dust and half-shredded by rocks of various sizes. The craft were shaped and equipped in such a way as to avoid and deflect such threats, but 50,000 years do not pass in vain. Even the luckiest few were severely damaged, and it was only thanks to ingenious modular design that enough disks, resources, and functional equipment survived to support the mission as planned. Power generation, consumables, spare parts, redundant systems, all were either near the end of their useful lives or had been exhausted centuries or millennia earlier. Many had become unsalvageable ghost ships, unable to perform the maneuvers needed to enter the solar system and establish stable orbits, and had gone off into deep space taking thousands of sleeping virtual crew with them. For the fortunate survivors, tens of earth centuries were required to gradually accumulate the materials to rebuild and set up a self-sustaining beachhead so very far from home.

The round trip radio communication time between the outpost and the main base was about 20 earth minutes, long enough that live conversations were a practical impossibility. Communication was usually through pre-recorded messages, where a conference room full of robots at the main base sent videos of themselves speaking and providing multimedia presentations to the more modest conference room at the outpost, who then responded in kind as needed. On this occasion the outpost sent a presentation describing the loss of the communications devices, the beige caps, and finished off with a request for further instructions. The main base did all the planning and resource allocation, and the outpost coordinated all of the actual on-planet activities through their human recruits.

For most of their history of activities on Earth, the conference room at the main base would normally have decided to recover the lost equipment at any cost, killing and disposing of earthlings as necessary. There had been no lack of such loss of equipment before, but it had become much less frequent as the mission grew more competent in its dealings on Earth. The last significant such loss had been just over 10 Earth years before, and was resolved by destroying two adjacent buildings with a fuel-air explosion that the locals concluded had been a mysterious gas leak. Nothing remained but rubble and ashes, which was deemed a resounding success by the conference room members on duty. Smaller scale clean-up episodes never rose beyond the level of ordinary criminality or commonplace accidents, at least as perceived by the locals, and the lost items were generally either recovered or destroyed.

This time the stolen items were already in the hands of an important organization on Earth, so that was not yet a practical option. The earthlings had been notably increasing their ability to patrol their planet's surroundings and detect an ever-expanding variety of signals. It was only a matter of time before they were able to detect the magnetic field communications devices. The time might not be far off when they would systematically search for the outpost and the main base. The conference room participants could only hope that moment had not yet arrived.

In the end, the committee chose a conservative approach. The work unit that had lost the devices would be evacuated, dismantled, and any non-essential physical resources would be destroyed. The unit's earthlings would be immediately scattered to other work units. If any of them were captured, the remaining earthlings would do their best to search out and kill both captors and captives. All remaining work units would be required to go to their highest level of lockdown, and prepare to evacuate at a moment's notice. The message was relayed to the outpost.

Waterston was waiting at the appointed time, and promptly received his orders. Gliese Genetics was to be dismantled, non-essential assets destroyed, and team members reassigned to other work units. A brief list of personnel and trailer drop-off locations was included with the message. No work unit knew the identity of any other work unit. Compartmentalization of activities was rigorous. Gliese Genetics would dissolve into a dispersed network of dead drops.

The written base dissolution plan that Waterston had on file was to be carried out immediately, which included everything from closing bank accounts and funneling money through opaque financial networks, to burning trailers to the ground at remote rural locations and quickly making everything else seemingly vanish. These were procedures that had been developed and refined over more years than Waterston could guess. He had already begun the process, and had made sure that all other ongoing activities were discontinued. By mid-morning tomorrow Gliese would be a vacant agricultural property managed by an impenetrable web of shell companies, and not long afterwards sold off to the highest bidder, most likely to another opaque shell company. Rented vehicles would either be discreetly dropped off at their rental agencies or destroyed along with their non-essential contents. Staff members would all then proceed to locations where other work units would pick them up and accept them as new team members.

43

A few of the Crazy Ladies folks were standing or sitting around one of the picnic tables at the edge of the greenhouse area. It was twilight, and Sue was setting up a couple of electric lanterns to keep the party going, while one of the men tended to a barbecue grill. A half dozen others were chatting, eating, and drinking beer or Mexican-style lemonade made from limes grown in the farm's orchard area. Tavo was sitting at the table next to Raúl, and Sue was clearly ignoring him.

A convoy of 8 trucks made its way up Pequod Lane, and those with cargo enclosures noisily scraped through low-hanging tree branches. They were rentals, and once they rounded the bend towards the end of the road, it was clear that they were headed towards Gliese.

"Wonder what they're bringing," said Raúl, gesturing towards the trucks with his bottle.

"Maybe they're here to pick something up. Those tractor trucks are probably going to tow some of the trailers away," speculated Tavo. He noticed Sue at the edge of his field of view. He could see that she was also intrigued. The others noticed the trucks, but were less interested and continued to party among themselves. Someone had fired up a vaporizer with some boutique-grade cannabis grown in one of the greenhouses.

The trucks paused at the end of the lane, waited for someone to open the gate, then filed in one by one. It was hard to see what went on beyond the treeline, but it looked as if the trucks distributed themselves among the main buildings at Gliese. Tavo heard the metal curtains of the cargo enclosures being raised, and there seemed to be some heightened chatter and activity back there. It occurred to him that he hadn't found out anything about the body that was brought in the night before by Alice. He twiddled his fingers and searched for information in his specs, but found nothing. For all anyone knew, the body was still over there. He turned towards Sue, who was also dividing her attention between the party and the goings on at Gliese. Raúl was exhaling a respectable cloud of cannabis smoke, and already looked to be approaching the lower limits of wasted.

Tavo refilled his lemonade glass and grabbed a handful of tortilla chips. He made sure to make brief eye contact with Sue in the growing darkness, her eyes were chilly indeed, and walked towards the old redwood board fence behind the converted bus where he bunked. He tried to walk as silently as possible, and stayed in the shadow of the bus, not quite reaching the fence. There was still enough light that he preferred to wait for a while before going right up to the fence, and a half moon would make it difficult to remain unseen beyond the shadows.

The Gliese folks were assiduously loading the trucks with all sorts of boxes, furniture, crates, and other items that seemed to have been ready and waiting for the trucks to arrive. It didn't look like they were shipping a new load of product. It looked like they were vacating the premises. Some people looked like they were inspecting the grounds on the far end of the property with red flashlights, occasionally bending down to pick something up and put it in a shoulder bag. He switched on the night vision overlay on his specs to have a better look. There were a couple more flashlights behind the next treeline over. The three tractor trucks that had arrived were orienting themselves to be hitched to some trailers that looked like the large mobile office buildings at big construction sites. These people were serious about vanishing in a hurry and without a trace.

He saw something out of the corner of his eye and discovered that Sue was standing next to him, looking straight ahead.

"I hope you can say something sincerely apologetic right now," whispered Cyn. She was standing next to him opposite Sue, and was wearing a *film noir* spy outfit, complete with trench coat and a rakish fedora.

"Hey," he said. Sue glanced at him coldly then turned back to watch the Gliese people.

"I'm sorry if I hurt your feelings the other night," he said. *That sounded kind of stupid*, he thought. He tried to compose something better in the silence that followed. He silent spoke *What to say when she*'s *really mad at you* into a search bar in his specs. A *lot* of results came back, but nothing seemed appropriate.

"You're going to have to wing it," said Cyn. "Speak from the heart or she'll never speak to *you* again."

Tavo did not find that advice helpful.

"Did you enjoy yourself at least?" she asked finally. He half shrugged, but was unable to answer anything.

"What was her score?" she asked. She was still serious, and Tavo knew that any answer would count against him so he decided to just tell the truth.

"93," he said. She looked at him and her eyes widened somewhat, then she looked away. Suddenly she turned towards him and pounded him once on the chest with a clenched fist and growled "Asshole!" through her teeth, just quietly enough for nobody from Gliese to turn and look. Sue was a strong, athletic young woman, and the blow sent Tavo back a couple of steps. He'd have a bruise later.

"You just couldn't let her go by," she said quietly. "Are you always hunting for other women? Other high scores? Did you check me out too?" She turned to look at him. Her lips trembled a bit. He saw her twiddle something. He had no idea what her score was, come to think of it. He never coincided with her on HunterGather, and wondered now if she was carefully avoiding him there, perhaps not wanting their friendship to be rooted in a score from some random specs app provider. She looked into his eyes silently. Something occurred to him, and he twiddled

HunterGather on. She was active as well, and her average score was 98. It suddenly disappeared as she logged back out. She turned to look at the Gliese folks again, and wiped an eye with the back of her hand.

"I'm sorry," he said, and tried to put his hand in the small of her back. She pushed him away and kept looking towards Gliese, whose staff was loading everything that wasn't bolted to the ground onto the trucks. They both stood there silently, watching their neighbors and being near each other, arms barely touching.

"Alice brought a dead guy in her car last night. Pretty late," he said after what seemed a long while. "I saw them unload it."

She turned to look at him, her face was stunned curiosity still tinged with anger. Her eyes seemed to bore into his in the dim evening light, their saccades pressing into him for more, the daggers not dissipated. She turned to look towards Gliese again. Tavo looked on as well, both watching the frenetic activity on the other side of the fence.

A moment later, she turned to look at him for a moment, evoking a disconcerting sense of loss. She turned and walked back to the picnic table where the others were still partying.

Cyn stood there looking at him as well, silently and sternly, once again a barrister, with a thick leather-bound book under one arm.

44

"So, to summarize, you'll only be taking a backpack and a separate carry-on. Most of your stuff goes in the carry-on. All of your IDs, the cash we've just handed out, and anything you might need to have on your person should be in the backpack. Make sure you have at least one change of light clothing in your backpacks, and make sure your caps are also secured in your backpacks. *Do not* wear your caps in plain sight. Use them only as Steve has just indicated to you. We'll deal with your carry-ons. You'll get them back when you get to your next teams. Any questions?" asked Waterston.

The entire crew of Gliese Genetics was assembled in the farmhouse's large former living room. For a moment there was only a solemn silence. Most of them were old enough to have gone through this sort of thing before, layoffs, emigrations, relocations, truncated relationships, and the like. This evacuation would be at least as bad as any personal change they'd experienced before, both from the sense of crisis and imminent danger, as well as from the sudden rupture of workplace camaraderie and personal friendships. Most would very likely never see each other again. One or two people were sobbing audibly. A few, like Alice, had gone through this before, although in other very different circumstances.

Alice was not crying, but her eyes were teary with a growing rage. This was her sixth personal reset. The sixth time friendships and intimate relationships were to be shattered, the sixth time an organization's promise was postponed, the dream of a stable, peaceful, just, and prosperous world, where people could live out happy lives without worrying about war, poverty, dictatorship, exploitation, and all the rest of it. College, the military, a couple of international non-governmental organizations, things always fell apart in the end, or quite simply and unceremoniously, they ended.

The Gliese promise in particular was to do away with the atavistic ills of human society and usher in a true utopia, at least that's what people were telling her when she spoke tentatively with a few of them from the Crazy Ladies side of the fence, and that's what the people in the New World said. Once again, the promise was broken, this time with her beloved Cliff tragically killed by her own hand thanks to those bastards Wu and Bennington and their idiot underlings, the crook and the whore. Bennington was dead, but Wu was still out there happily making money from Gliese. All roads led to Wu and his damned club. It was unfair, unjust. She could not abide it.

Of all her past friends and lovers, Cliff had been the only one she felt could be a soul mate, someone with whom she wanted to live a Utopian dream to the end of their lives. Now she would go through the indignity of being picked up by strangers at a truck stop or a strip mall parking lot and spend a few weeks being scrutinized and judged, both as a new team member and by some as a potential sex partner, and then the long, slow, and uncertain search for intimacy. She was no longer really up for this. Maybe she should have stayed at Crazy Ladies among the twenty-somethings and spent more time on HunterGather when she was in town. But then she would never have been with Cliff, and would have always been deeply and painfully alone.

The meeting broke up and everyone went off to pack up what clothing and personal possessions could fit in a backpack and a piece of carry-on luggage. Anything left over would be gathered up and burned somewhere. Large quantities of personal possessions had been discouraged exactly for this eventuality, and some of the newbies would soon understand this policy the hard way. Alice had been traveling lightly for some years now.

As part of security at Gliese, she was one of the few who had been assigned a firearm for her day to day duties. She put it in her backpack with her toiletries, a couple of books, three notebooks, and some clothing, along with her passport, IDs, and birth certificate. She would play dumb and turn the gun in if asked, otherwise she would keep it, along with a couple of spare clips and half a box of 9mm rounds. Judging from the sudden evacuation hysteria, she fully expected it to fall through the cracks and stay in her hands. Maybe she was expected to be its ongoing custodian, who knew? Gliese never left much to chance. For now she would cooperate and dutifully allow herself to be taken to her assigned drop site, wherever that might be.

In the meantime, she joined in with the others packing things up in the trailers and repeatedly inspecting the property prior to the evacuation procedures. to make sure that no trace of their existence was left. Each team member helped thoroughly inspect each of the several lab buildings, ranch houses, sheds, the barn, greenhouses, and the area behind the windbreak where the portables had been parked. Every scrap of paper, box, abandoned article of clothing, food wrapper, tool, or anything that wasn't a natural part of the ranch was dutifully collected. The many plants in the greenhouses were to be temporarily abandoned, and other work units would attempt to recover them if that could be done without being detected.

They worked through the night, drinking coffee and eating sandwiches and donuts brought in by Waterston himself. Outside, the inspections were being carried out with night vision activated in people's specs. Alice was on duty with her supervisor, Steve Ramos, inspecting the area behind the treeline. The half-moon provided enough light for the night vision, which they complemented with infrared flashlights and their specs' IR channel overlay, in case prying eyes were watching from afar. Between the normal colors barely visible in the moonlight, and the two false-color overlays, the reddish hue of the IR channel and the ghostly green of the night vision, the Ranch and the trees around it looked like a far away alien world.

"Here, use this, too," said Steve. He handed her a UV flashlight. "Switch on your UV channel."

The UV channel added yet another overlay, this one with a deep purple cast. Alice was now immersed in an unreal world, one from which she would soon disappear. Steve's eyes glowed like those of a video vampire, and the occasional bit of litter on the ground glowed in the darkness before them, its paper or ink fluorescing under the sweeping beam of the UV light. This was her farewell to Gliese, the once beautiful and bucolic farm where she had finally found love. Now it was a garish, unearthly landscape, the stuff of cinematic nightmares. In the distance, a forest animal would occasionally pause briefly to examine them, thinking it was invisible in the darkness. The fox, or deer, or raccoon were far enough that they were visible only in the green monochrome of the night vision channel, as if she was in a small puddle of gaudiness moving through a grainy, green-tinged black and white movie from the previous century. She was no longer here, she was already in a distorted, fading memory of having been here.

*　　*　　*　　*　　*

Hours later, as the sky lightened behind the eastern hills, the whole crew milled around the now sealed trucks and trailers, drinking coffee and eating breakfast burritos. They had all been assigned to vehicles, each headed in a different direction. After some sad goodbyes, Alice boarded one of the white vans, now fitted with passenger seats, and found her place in the back row with her backpack on her lap. Her four grim-faced companions followed suit with very little conversation. An on again, off again couple who were soon to be dropped off separately had eyes that were swollen with grief. It made little sense to Alice, but that was the plan. Would they somehow meet up again in the same work unit? Would they find each other in the New World? The couple sat together, wordlessly holding hands. If Cliff were here she would at least have had that. She looked out her window studying the silhouettes of the trees and the hills against the dawn, unable to hold back her own tears. A few minutes later, the van drove off, turned right on Carlson Road, then merged onto Highway 152 heading east, towards the Central Valley.

The crew that remained were to drive the trucks and trailers and their valuable cargo to isolated dead drops, to be picked up by other work units. They mounted up, started their vehicles, and waited for them to warm up.

45

"Looks like all of the trucks are warming up," said Thakkar. A thermal imaging channel was overlaid on the video feed they were receiving from the rented hillside cottage half a kilometer away from Gliese. This was where all of their surveillance of Gliese Genetics had come from. Thakkar had managed to cajole the owners, a retired couple that lived in the main house, into a 2 year lease of a cottage in the rear of the property that had been vacant at the time. The image was through a telephoto lens, and was a bit shaky.

From the cottage they could see much of the Gliese property, including part of the area beyond the treeline that divided the property in two. Wilkins and his fellow robots had been alerted to lights and activities during the night by surveillance software monitoring the image, and had been watching the vehicles as they prepared to move out. Thakkar had been awakened early, and he had already made a few phone calls to his contacts at Blam, in the local intelligence community, and at Homeland Security.

Not even two minutes after the first tractor and trailer pulled out of the property, a half dozen unmarked vehicles with flashing lights intercepted them about halfway down Pequod Lane. The vans with the staff had managed to leave about half an hour earlier, but the trucks and trailers full of cargo were now bottled up along much of the length of Pequod Lane, all the way up to Gliese Genetics. The drivers closest to the cars gave up immediately, but those in the rear abandoned their trucks and ran for the sparsely wooded hillside. A few were met by individuals who closely resembled military special operations teams.

"Jackpot," chuckled Thakkar.

"The three vans are still being followed both by drone and on the ground," said Wilkins. He switched their shared feed to a map showing their positions. One van was heading south on Highway 1, another southeast on Highway 129 on its way to Highway 101, and a third was heading east on Highway 152.

"So what's the expectation? Are they going to kill them and dump them someplace, or are they going to meet up with somebody?" asked Thakkar.

"Hard to say. I think the hope is that they'll lead us to other groups, if they exist. If it starts to look like an execution, the feds will try to intervene," answered Wilkins. "That's what the chatter has been."

"Well, it's out of our hands at this point. Let's hope they capture more goodies in the trucks."

Wilkins switched back to the scene near Gliese. The thermal imaging was still on, and every single trailer was glowing bright yellow.

"Whoa, whoa, whoa!" exclaimed Thakkar, sitting up in his chair, smoothly assisted by his exoskeleton.

"Hold on, let me get their audio. It sounds like everyone's pretty excited. Here, I'll put the audio on," said Wilkins.

The chatter was intense. Voices were barking orders to back away from the trailers, and to make sure none of the captives tried to hurt themselves. Apparently a couple of them were already unconscious and unresponsive. Fire and emergency services people were joining in on the crowded communications channel they were listening in on, giving their ETAs. Watsonville was a modestly sized city, so this was going to tie up a lot of its emergency services and personnel. The far end of Pequod Lane angled away from the main road by about 30 or 40 degrees. It was past several farms and tree lines, and was now choked with close to a dozen burning trucks and trailers. The fire department would have to thread its way through the few narrow service roads of the neighboring farms. Already there was chatter complaining about a shortage of water tankers needed to help douse the flames. These farms relied on a combination of recycled waste water, well water, and water purchased from desalinators, which might or might not be enough to confront a fire of this size. The surrounding trees and bone dry grass and brush around the farms and in the nearby hills were also in danger of igniting, if they hadn't already. It was hard to see with all of the smoke.

"Seriously? They're going to burn everything?" said Thakkar, almost shouting.

46

Alice watched as the mountain forest along the highway turned into the outskirts of Gilroy as they drove. She was exhausted, but had drunk too much coffee to be able to sleep. Her supervisor Steve was driving, with Waterston riding shotgun. It looked as if they were becoming agitated about something. Suddenly Steve made a left turn on an already yellow traffic light, then a hard right into the parking lot of a large strip mall. It was early enough that the parking lot was largely empty, save perhaps for the workers who were already clocked into their shifts at the supermarket and various other businesses.

"OK, folks, change of plan!" shouted Waterston. "The trucks were ambushed as they left Gliese! We're bailing out here and splitting up. Get in this supermarket, spend about 5 minutes in there, then go from store to store doing the same thing. Keep doing that going from mall to mall. Use residential streets between malls, but stay indoors whenever possible. We'll be leaving food and water at drop-off points, so switch your caps on now but keep them in your backpacks. Don't let anyone see them. Every hour or so hide somewhere out of sight and put it on, we'll be in touch in the New World. Now go! *Go!*"

Confusion reigned as everyone spilled out of the van. Alice headed into the supermarket with the rest of them. *What the fuck! Now what?* she wondered. She quickly separated herself from the others and went to the back of the store, where a pair of swivel doors led to the restrooms. She quickly examined the space as she headed for the restroom. Beyond the restrooms was a large warehouse space crowded with boxes, rows of heavy metal racks full of more boxes, and a forklift. Two employees were unpacking new merchandise towards the back. There was a loading dock in back to the left. The restrooms were housed in a boxy structure that didn't reach up to the building's high industrial roof. Still inside the short hallway, across from the restrooms, was some kind of employee area. There were some lockers there, so she went in and checked to see if any were open. The first one she could open had a store apron with a name tag that read "Norma Escalante." She grabbed it and put it on, then put her backpack in the locker and closed it, remembering that it was locker 33. She grabbed a clipboard from a desk, and put a pen behind her right ear, and walked towards the loading dock in back. The two men busily unpacking merchandise didn't seem to notice her. Both of them had specs face, no doubt getting guidance from the store software or playing with their virtual characters.

The loading dock was open, and there were no trucks, so she stepped outside into a shady area of the platform. It was a beautiful clear day. A glint in the sky above caught her eye, and then another. Drones. They were here. She stayed in the shade to avoid drawing attention and stopped looking up at them. On the opposite end of the platform were a few chairs, presumably for the local vaping circle. She calmly walked over and sat down, taking care not to look up at the sky. She sat down and pretended to examine the papers on her clipboard. Maybe 5 minutes later, a commotion of cars could be heard from the parking lot side of the building, then some loud voices in the store. A woman screamed a couple of times. Alice stared fixedly at the clipboard. Two men in black riot gear burst onto the platform and headed towards her. She only half pretended to be terrified, because she actually was terrified, and tried to look confused. It took little effort.

"Who the fuck are you?!" demanded one of them.

"Uh... Uh... I'm... I'm..." she meekly pointed her badge at him. "My purse is in the... the..." she pointed back inside the store. The clipboard fell noisily off her lap and onto the platform, then bounced off onto the asphalt a meter or so below. She half got up as if to retrieve it then sat back down.

"I... I..." she stammered, trying to act like a terrified minimum wage employee, and the adrenaline already in her system bolstered her credibility. She started to feel an urge to urinate. Damn coffee, but she realized it could be useful.

"I need to go to the restroom," she said to the two men who had been glaring at her during this brief encounter. The two men exchanged glances, then locked their gazes on her again. One of them seemed to listen to something for a moment.

"Come with us," said one of them, and they led her to the restroom, holding the door open after she went in and standing guard outside. She relieved herself as noisily as she could, and when she emerged only one of the men remained.

"Stay here," he said, and went back into the supermarket through the swinging doors. Alice had no idea what to do. With any luck, they'd forget about her and she would be able to leave. She could make a run for it now, but there were probably still drones up there. The commotion inside the store had died down by then. She quietly walked up to the double doors and had a look through the smudgy oval windows. The aisles of merchandise didn't allow much of a view, although she did have a clear line of sight to the one of the main doors out front. She recognized 2 of her former teammates walking out single file, hands behind their heads. A few of the SWAT team guys filed out behind them, and someone outside shouted "Clear!"

She ran to the lockers pulling off the apron. She threw it on a table and grabbed her backpack out of locker 33. She checked a few other lockers and found one that was open with somebody's handbag in it. She rifled through it, pulled a checkbook-sized wallet out, and put the bag back in the locker as she had found it, then headed towards the loading dock. The loading area was deserted, no doubt all of the employees were now inside the store watching the excitement. She stood in the shady part of the loading dock and saw that there was a shaded route to the back entrance of a QueeQueg Coffee shop. There were stair steps on that end of the platform, and she made her way through the shade as calmly as possible, went down the steps, and entered the coffee shop. A dingy hallway led past the restrooms and into the main café.

A woman at a table by the front window was the only person paying attention to the small convoy of dark vehicles now exiting the parking lot. Alice feigned mild interest and walked towards the front to have a look. They were indeed leaving. From a side window she could see a few supermarket employees going back inside. The drama appeared to be over.

"A tall mocha, please," she asked the cashier. "And may I have the bathroom key?"

"You don't need one, just go in," answered the cheery young girl.

Alice ignored the payment authorization icon in her specs and went to the restroom, locked the door, and pulled her gun out of the backpack. The clip was full, and she then tucked it under her waistband in back, making sure her sweatshirt was covering it loosely. Next she examined the wallet she had taken from the store. There was a small amount of cash, some bills and some coins, as well as some IDs and credit cards. Definitely old school. There was even a checkbook. The woman on the driver's license looked to be about fiftyish, and didn't resemble Alice in the least. There was nothing else of use, so she took the cash, and rinsed the wallet in soapy water from the sink. She dropped it in the waste basket and covered it over with used paper towels. She washed her hands then went back for her coffee.

The girl was waiting for her at the register, and made it a point to tell Alice how much the coffee would cost.

"I'm sorry! I really had to use the restroom," said Alice.

Luckily, there had been enough money in the wallet to pay for the coffee in cash, leave a conspicuously nice tip, and have enough left over for a reasonable lunch later. Money was going to be a problem, though. Alice had always paid for things with her specs, and that would be a bad idea for now. She sat down at a table with a window view and twiddled to power them down. She'd have to figure out how to pay for a CalRail ticket out of Gilroy. The money the Gliese people had distributed together with the cash in the purse wasn't quite enough for both a ticket and more food and water later on, especially if she'd have to survive on it for more than a day or two.

The parking lot was calm, and Alice kept an eye out for drones as she sipped her coffee. She saw none.

47

Tavo was in the lead tanker truck waiting for Sue and Raúl to line up behind him when the Gliese convoy came through their gates and slowly moved down the lane. There must have been easily a dozen trucks, and it looked like they'd be taking quite a while to pass Crazy Ladies and drive all the way down Pequod Lane to the main road. They'd probably be loaded down with all of Gliese, like a circus packed up and heading out of town.

There were suddenly sirens in the background, and not very far off. Tavo craned his neck, but the trees and farm buildings next door obstructed his view of the lane past the point where it turned westwards towards Carlson Road. The Gliese convoy stopped in its tracks, the last three trucks blocking any chance of Crazy Ladies' water tankers getting out. He turned off his engine to save fuel.

There were several sirens, and one of them seemed to be getting closer. The Gliese people were quickly becoming agitated, and some of them got out of the truck cabs. Backpacks came out and were hurriedly put on, and after brief exchanges some of the Gliese people started running back up the road to Gliese, and others headed for the hills on the other side of the lane from Crazy Ladies. Down the road a few meters there was a creek bed that led up into the mountains that separated Watsonville from Gilroy. It was heavily overgrown, since that's where the winter rains flowed down from the slopes, and it wound its way into the woods further up. There were a few dirt roads out there somewhere, but not much else. As the crow flies, it was a good 10 kilometers to the edge of Gilroy, with elevation changes of 300 meters or more. There wasn't much water anywhere this time of year, the rainy season was a month away if not more. Still, the Gliese people from the trucks vanished into the wilderness before a lone unmarked car with a removable red beacon on its roof and a wailing siren managed to make its way up this far. Its two occupants were hysterically yelling into their specs and trying to see where everyone had gone.

When they spotted Tavo, Sue, and Raúl waiting in their trucks to get on the road they jumped out of their car and ran over shouting threats and commands and wielding their guns. Tavo made sure his hands were visible, and tried to let them know that they weren't Gliese people, but the two cops (or whatever they were) clearly had no idea of who was who or what was what. Tavo slowly got out of his truck in as non-threatening a manner as possible, and was glad to see that his two friends were doing the same. He could barely understand what the cops were shouting, their voices already getting hoarse, but from their gestures they apparently wanted him to get down on the ground face down with his hands spread out. He complied as best he could.

The cops calmed down somewhat when Tavo, Sue, and Raúl were on the ground, and he could make out that they were reporting 3 suspects detained along with their vehicles. Tavo could hear another siren approaching.

The nearest Gliese truck was only about 5 meters away, right in front of them. It made a loud thud inside its cargo enclosure, but Tavo wasn't able to see it well from his prone position. It sounded as if the thud damaged the enclosure itself.

"Fuck!" shouted one of the cops, "Shit!" Once again, they started yelling hysterically through their specs at whoever was on the other end, now it was about an "incendiary weapon" or an "improvised explosive device." The truck that made the noise started to burn, its enclosure and the cargo inside enveloped in a fireball that gave off a surprising amount of heat. The truck right behind it now thudded as well, and another fireball erupted from its cargo enclosure.

Tavo pushed himself up from the ground in time to see the nearest truck's cargo enclosure coming slowly apart at its seams, leaking orange flames that were bright even in broad daylight and billowing thick gray-black smoke. The intense heat given off by the flames was alarming. He decided there was no way he was going to wait around to get burned to death, and got back up to run towards his two companions yelling "Let's go! Let's go!" The three of them ran back towards Crazy Ladies. The cops were too busy with the new explosions and with a few Gliese folks that could still be seen running towards the hills.

Everybody at Crazy Ladies was out by then, staring out towards the road at the line of trucks burning like jungle torches in an old movie.

"That hillside's going to go up in a second," said one.

"That one truck is still OK," said another, pointing at the last truck. It was stopped under some trees just outside of the farm's driveway. There were 2 Gliese people taking something out of the back of the truck and loading it onto a pickup pointing back in the direction of Gliese. The cops hadn't seemed to notice yet.

"They're going to try and get out the back way, I'll bet," said someone.

"*Jijos de su puta madre...*" cursed Raúl, who immediately ran towards them.

"Raúl! What the fuck are you doing!" shouted Tavo. He felt a strong impulse to follow him, if only to see what was so important to the Gliese people to cause such a disaster, and what they were trying to escape with. On the other hand, what if the truck blew up? What if things got even worse? He ran off, following Raúl. Sue followed Tavo in turn, also driven by excitement and morbid curiosity.

Raúl got to the truck first and was about to pound the nearest Gliese guy in the face, but hesitated when he saw that the other guy had a pistol in his hand and was walking towards him.

"Back off, bro, this has nothing to do with you. Back off, now!" said the man with the gun. Raúl looked at him, then at the boxes in the back of the pickup, then back at the guy with the gun. Now that he was here, he was unsure of what to do next. Tavo arrived at that moment, and soon Sue was there as well.

"What the fuck is going on! Why is everything blowing up!" said Tavo, trying to catch his breath.

"You people shouldn't be here. It's dangerous. We're going to blow this truck too," said the guy putting a box in the pickup. "Don't get involved here. Walk away. I mean it, man, you're in way over your head."

"Hey! Hey!" shouted one of the cops as he ran towards them, about 15 meters away. "Freeze, motherfuckers! Freeze! Now! On the ground! Now! Now!" It would have been comical had he not started firing warning shots with his sidearm.

The Gliese people got in the pickup as quickly as they could, but the cop had already reached them. The truck started to pull away as the cop tried to force open the passenger side door. Raúl instinctively grabbed one of the boxes out of the pickup bed and threw it in the brush on the side of the road. Neither the Gliese guys nor the cop seemed to notice, and the pickup was moving fitfully for some reason. The cop was holding on to the head or arm of the guy in the passenger side. Raúl grabbed another box as the pickup suddenly sped away, but fell onto the ground and dropped the box. Sue grabbed it and threw it after the first one. They looked like trash among the wild grasses and shrubs. The cop that had tried to stop the pickup was on the ground a few meters away. He must have been dragged a bit as the truck picked up speed. He was howling in pain. One of his ankles was bent in an unnatural angle, it must have been accidentally run over by the pickup. His gun had fallen on the ground, and was halfway between Tavo and the cop.

The three walked over to him, quickly getting between him and his weapon.

"What the hell is going on?!" asked Tavo.

"Don't play dumb, asshole. We've got you. You're not getting away with this crap. We'll get your buddies soon enough," answered the cop, wincing with pain. The ankle looked bad, and some blood was starting to seep into his pants leg, probably a compound fracture.

"Play dumb? About what?" asked Tavo.

"Could you please spell it out for us? Just so that we're all in sync here?" said Sue. The cop sneered blankly at them, but didn't answer. It looked like rapidly growing pain in his leg was starting to monopolize his attention. Another official vehicle managed to get up this far, but only one person was in it. The driver stopped next to them and got out of the car. He quickly took in the scene.

"Where are you people from?" he said. He was a bear of a man, and his voice conveyed calm authority. His stern gaze encouraged Tavo to answer quickly.

"We're from Crazy Ladies," he said, pointing towards the farm. "All these trucks are from Gliese," he now pointed to the opened gate through which the pickup had escaped.

"Yeah, that pickup gonna go around the back of the farm and cut over to Carlson," said Raúl. "They got some boxes and shit outta this truck. They say it gonna blow up, too." Nervous glances were exchanged.

"Help me get this guy in the car," said the new cop. It was directed at Raúl, either because he was the last one to speak or because he was obviously the strongest person there. "You folks get back to your farm."

"Yes sir," said Tavo, and he and Sue started back slowly, frequently looking over their shoulder. Soon the cop turned the car around to get his injured colleague some medical attention. Raúl was still standing where the car had been.

"Hey! We gotta get them boxes!" he shouted at them. Tavo and Sue looked at each other and walked back. Raúl grabbed one box and Tavo the other, and they made their way back to the farm, hiding in the smoke, the shade, or behind vegetation whenever possible. They left the boxes next to some plastic crates behind the main farmhouse. There was quite a bit of smoke at this point, so it seemed very unlikely that anybody saw them.

By the time they got back to their companions, some of the trees that lined the road in front of the farm had caught fire. Some Crazy Ladies folks were already busy trying to douse the flames and wet the rest of the trees that led into the farm itself with a garden hose and move flammable materials out of harm's way. Their virtual assistants had switched to emergency mode and were now coordinating them. *This is going to rapidly deplete our water reserves*, thought Sue.

As predicted, there was a brush fire across the road spreading up the hills. Beyond the fire, fugitive Gliese folks were hiding or running. Whether the fire would help them or hinder them was not at all clear.

48

"So what's the damage? What was recovered?" asked Thakkar. He was on a call with Liz Hoffmann, his contact at Homeland Security. Liz was one of the people he had called the previous day about the Gliese caps. Some lengthy discussions over multiple conference calls had ensued, and it was thanks to them that there had been any federal officers around to stop the evacuation at Gliese.

"All but two of the trucks were burned down to ash, one failed to ignite at all, and one apparently has fairly limited fire damage. People are still either evaluating the safety of checking the undamaged truck or maybe are already in there. There's some fear of booby traps," he answered.

"How soon do you think they'll have an idea of what's left? Will we receive any information on that? Images? Videos?"

"It's about lunch time over there, right? Maybe by tonight there'll be information. Hard to say what you'll be able to see. The spooks have pretty much taken over. Given that you're already read in, I suspect they'll want your opinion. They've barely begun, though. My understanding is that they're still battling wildfires out there."

"Read in? We handed this to you on a silver platter!" replied Thakkar, only half jokingly. "What about detainees? Did you get anyone?"

"I'm told that at the main site, eight people were captured and there were four fatalities. Two from gunshot wounds from our side, two from as yet unknown causes. In the escape vehicles we got another four people, so that's a total of twelve. There may be people at large in the hills behind the site. Somewhere in the vicinity of half a dozen people may have escaped from the vans, maybe more. The folks we do have are being interrogated now, but I'm told nothing important has come out. They aren't talking, and some folks suspect they're afraid of being punished if they say anything. They all had caps, though."

"How likely do you think it is that some will crack?"

"It's just a matter of time. Apparently some of them are close to cracking already. We may have something by the end of today. Got to go. I'll get back to you."

"Sure, keep me in the loop. Thanks!" said Thakkar.

"Well, so much for that," he said to Wilkins.

"This is definitely a setback. If the vans had continued on their way, they might have led us somewhere. They must have gotten word of the operation," said Wilkins.

"Well, at least they've got some loot, unless it's all toilet paper and cafeteria furniture. Let's hope their prisoners have some useful information. I wonder if the anti-terrorism laws apply to collaborating with aliens."

"We should give Yulya a call," said Wilkins.

Thakkar mumbled a halfhearted reply. Yulya Shiderova was his current contact at Blam for everything having to do with the beige caps and the quantum chips. In spite of an almost dainty appearance and polite, reserved demeanor, she was a tough young woman. Her mind was always running at twice the speed as Thakkar's, and her concise, staccato running commentary was sharp. Like a blade. She was generous with her time, but Thakkar knew better than to waste it. She always provided everything Thakkar requested, but he was always left with the sensation of increasing political debt. With regards to the chips and the caps, every conversation with her felt to Thakkar as if she was sucking information out of his head through a drinking straw.

"It's better for you to call her than for her to call you," said Wilkins. "Also better than me dealing with *her* assistants first."

"Yeah, yeah..." replied Thakkar.

49

Alice was not exactly a stranger to Gilroy. Gliese Genetics was in Watsonville, in the next valley to the west. The modest mountain range that separated them was no great barrier, and Gilroy had been hosting an ever growing collection of brand name outlet stores for decades. People drove the long distance from Silicon Valley proper or rode CalRail to go shopping there, whether they saved much money or not. The rise of the co-ops over the past 10 years or so from Watsonville to Los Baños and the artisanal products they produced made the area even more popular. Alice and Cliff had been there many times.

With her specs powered down to avoid being tracked, Alice didn't recognize exactly where she was. She had been walking for almost an hour, plenty of time to have gotten to the train station by now, and the last few blocks had been getting sketchier with each step. The young men on the corner ahead of her looked like they might be a problem. One of them appeared to be selling something to another, who in turn went and handed what must have been money to a third. The buyer walked off with his new stash, and the others eyed her warily as she approached. A jumble of memories from her days in Afghanistan were bubbling up, and she made a conscious effort to keep them at bay.

She nodded a greeting at the first man when she was about two or three meters away from him, and turned to do the same to his friend, who looked like he was 13 or so. That brief distraction allowed her to grab her pistol with her right hand and the first guy's arm with the other, and deftly have the muzzle pressed just above the young man's Adam's apple.

"Shut up and don't fight," she said firmly as she pushed the out of balance youth towards his friend, to whom she ordered "Don't move or you both die."

She threw the first guy down to the sidewalk. She pointed her weapon alternately at one and the other.

"Put your guns and your money on the sidewalk. Now! And no bullshit. Don't think I won't shoot."

The money taker was the younger one, and he looked genuinely frightened. The other was older, and presumably more seasoned. He had a look in his eye as he suddenly reached behind his back to pull out his gun. Alice could see the quick motion before it even started. She fired a round at the edge of his right ear, hoping to just graze it, before he had time to finish the arc and have his gun pointed at her. He didn't even manage to squeeze off a shot, but immediately fell backwards with a confused look on his face, his pistol clattering on the sidewalk. His ear was half torn off, lots of blood was flowing, and it looked like some of the scalp was damaged. The bullet must have grazed his skull and knocked him senseless. Alice felt bad about such a poor shot. Many years ago she had gotten pretty good at it. The other boy was now terrified, his face and lips ashen, tears welling up in his eyes.

"Money and guns," she repeated firmly, pointing her gun at him again. The boy fumbled for both and clumsily managed to place them on the sidewalk next to his feet.

"Run. In five seconds you're dead."

The boy seemed confused.

"Run!" she shouted, "*Now!*" He ran. He was half way down the next block as Alice finished picking up the money and started walking briskly around the corner ahead of her. A quick glance behind her showed that at least a couple of young men had seen the altercation. She started to run once she was around the corner and out of their sight. She dodged back and forth behind whatever obstacles she could, crossed the street, turned down another corner, and arrived at a strip mall. She chose the largest fast food joint, a *Cheezis K. Reist Burgers*, and went inside. The early lunch crowd was starting to arrive, so she was able to get to the restroom without drawing attention to herself. After relieving herself of the adrenaline-stimulated urge to urinate, she counted the money she had taken from the boy. Not a huge amount, but it would get her a CalRail ticket back up to Burlingame, and could keep her fed for at least a week if she was disciplined about it. She'd have to spend the nights on the street, though. *Cheezis K. Reist* was cheap enough to have this shop in a ghetto, so she decided to have lunch now, then find the CalRail station and get out of town. The police could arrive at the crime scene any time now. She changed into the extra yoga pants and the other sweatshirt she had in her backpack, which would at least disrupt whatever description any witnesses might provide to the police.

She ordered a burger and fries and went to sit near a window to eat them. There was no police action outside, and nobody that seemed to be looking for anyone. In fact, the place looked pretty calm. Alice made short work of the burger and the small bag of fries. A Hispanic woman was at the next table eating lunch with two small children, a boy and a girl, who seemed far too full of energy to focus on eating their food.

"Excuse me," asked Alice. The woman smiled at her and shook her head.

"*Disculpe*," asked Alice through her relatively thick accent. "*Como puedo llegar a la estación del tren?*" The woman looked somewhat surprised, but explained to her that the train station was about 6 blocks away down a large avenue at the far end of the strip mall.

"*Muchísimas gracias!*" said Alice with genuine appreciation. She gathered her trash and her backpack and went for the door. As she was putting her trash in the waste bin, she saw that one of the cars parked outside had its windows rolled down, and had something she couldn't make out in the back seat. She pushed through the exit door and slowly walked past the car. There was a sweater or something on the back seat among other articles of clothing, a couple of paper bags with something in them, a half-empty take-out food carton, and other random items. She snapped up the sweater and rolled it up around one hand, smoothly continued on her way past the car, then turned left towards the street that would take her to the CalRail station. As she waited for the light to change, she carefully draped the sweater over her backpack in case there was a description of her on the police wire by now, and started carrying it with the handle instead of on her back. She tied her hair up in a small bun and when the light changed, started walking towards the station.

The lack of sirens or other unusual activity seemed odd to her. Not only had she just shot some poor kid, but there might well be several of her colleagues also skulking around trying to leave the area. Could she be the only one? She shifted the backpack to the other hand. Carrying it like that was tiring, even with a padded handle like hers had.

Her eyes scanned the sky for any glint of a drone. She couldn't see any, but that didn't mean much. Even if she saw one, it could be doing a variety of other things besides hunting down Gliese escapees. The traffic on the street was picking up for the lunch rush, but she didn't notice any police or feds who might be undercover and scanning for suspicious pedestrians.

*　　*　　*　　*　　*

At the end of what turned out to be a pleasant and refreshing walk, she was finally across the street from the train station. It would be wise for the authorities to be on it like fleas on a dog, so she'd have to act as calmly and innocently as possible. This usually meant being slower than other people and acting more naive, increasing your visibility rather than trying to hide.

More than likely, the witnesses to the shooting of the young drug dealer would be reticent to talk to police, and the teams hunting down Gliese people almost certainly had only the sketchiest of information. Her carry-on had no personally identifying information, and there had been little time for witnesses to see or report anything that could be used to identify her. That only left any surveillance that might have been downloaded from the supermarket where they had all initially tried to hide. They might be able to use it to filter imagery from the CalRail surveillance systems, but she was willing to bet that the bureaucratic and logistical barriers to getting that done quickly might still be giving her time to squeak through. That would have to suffice as a strategy.

She entered the station, and matched her pace and attitude to the rest of the crowd. After buying a ticket from a vending machine, and playing dumb for a few moments trying to figure out where to go, she found herself standing on the northbound platform along with a few dozen others. So far so good.

The next train was in 4 minutes, according to the sign, so Alice studiously paced around imitating a couple of other nearby commuters doing the same. Trying to accurately mimic one then another helped pass the time and kept her focused.

There was a sudden commotion as two security guards and two people dressed in office attire ran down the escalator, weaving around the people slowly being brought down. They ran onto the platform, and headed directly towards her, looking straight at her. She carefully matched the rhythm of a woman in an expensive-looking black wool skirt and jacket, who was pacing around nearby, evidently studying something in her specs. Alice did her best to strike a balance between ignoring the rapidly approaching authorities and getting ready to step aside, as any normal person would do. Her right hand was touching her hip and she was supremely conscious of the pistol in the small of her back. She fantasized that it, too, was taut and ready for action. She was certain that she'd be able to take at least a couple of these people out before being subdued, and if the gods looked kindly upon her she could take them all out and run up the landscaping that lined the platform and make it over the chain-link fence at the top.

She deftly stepped aside as the security folks rushed past her. Several meters beyond, near the end of the platform, a homeless-looking man had started shouting obscenities at them. She now realized that the man's pants were lowered to his ankles, and there was a puddle next to him with something in the middle that just might be feces. The northbound train started tooting its horn as it approached from the other end of the platform.

50

The car pulled up to the white curb in front of the Q'Boom Qlub, and both Benita and Brad stepped out. The burly bouncers were absent, given that it was still early afternoon, the tail end of the lunch rush.

The hostess was at the bar chatting with the bartender and a waitress, but came over to her podium near the door when she saw Benita and Brad.

"I'm sorry, but no robots in the bar," she said.

"We have urgent business with Mr. Wu," answered Benita. "The robot will be present. Would you like me to obtain a warrant? It would be a bit of a hassle for both of us, but it's definitely doable."

The hostess eyed her with noticeable contempt, and was probably wondering if this was a bluff. She waited for someone else to decide.

"Mr. Wu hasn't arrived yet," she said after a moment.

"Hasn't he? That's what I was told last night, and it turned out not to be true. That can't go on," replied Benita in her best courteous-but-stern investigator voice.

"I wonder if you know what car he drives. You can check the parking lot for yourself." The woman paused then, perhaps listening to something coming over her specs.

"Would you prefer a private table? I'd be happy to provide you with complimentary refreshments?" she started off, leading the way without waiting for a response. She led them through the small tables to the bar next door, where she had seen Brenda two nights earlier.

She led them to one of the small private booths that lined the far end of the room, past the one where she had sat before, each one with either a curtain or a folding screen that looked pretty sound-proof, depending on the degree of paranoia one might feel. The young woman drew the curtain as Benita and Brad took their seats and left.

"Let me see what's holding Wu up," said Benita. She twiddled an icon to make a voice call, just to show her level of impatience. She added Brad to the call. It rang three times and, surprisingly, Wu's voice came on.

"I'll be there in less than 5 minutes. I'm getting off the freeway right now. Please hang on until I get there," he said.

"OK, we'll be here," she said, and hung up.

"We have no choice but to believe him," said Brad.

"The guy's a weasel. Getting anything useful out of him is going to be like pulling teeth from a mule."

The curtain was not fully closed, and Benita was able to see a waitress fiddling with some items on her podium. A woman walked into the bar and asked her something, and the waitress nodded. The woman was strikingly beautiful, and seemed dressed like a very high class sex worker. There was something familiar about her, and it suddenly dawned on Benita that it was Brenda, who had evidently gotten a rather drastic haircut. It was cut quite close, much like what Benita had under her wig, but on Brenda it looked fabulous.

"Brenda Castro just walked in," she told Brad.

"What?" he paused, presumably relaying the information. "I though she told you she was skipping town."

"She said that. Maybe she's still dealing with clients." Benita pulled back the curtain a bit. "Sit over there so nobody can see you and I can pull the curtain back more."

"Right. I should have used the robots-only entrance."

"Stop whining. She's sitting down at a booth. Can you still see?"

"I can see. Wasn't she afraid of the Gliese people? Her boyfriend was killed two days ago."

Both of them studied Brenda as she sat alone at a table, apparently waiting for someone or something. She seemed serious, but not somber, and her makeup masked whatever other signs of mourning might otherwise be visible.

An icon drew attention to itself, and Benita twiddled the message into view.

"Wu says he's parking the car in back and will be in here in a minute. Let me tell him we're in this booth."

A minute or so after she privately said "Send," there was some kind of clatter outside on the street that was just audible inside the bar. Soon a minor commotion grew at the main door, and a few employees ran in and out of the building.

51

Alice scanned the parking lot of the Q'Boom Qlub several times, but Wu's car did not appear to be here. It was still mid-afternoon, and he might well be at his warehouse. It wasn't too far away, but in order to get a car she'd have to power up her specs, not a wise move if the authorities had her accounts under surveillance. The train station was only 3 blocks away from the club, but there was no convenient way to get to Wu's warehouse except by car.

At that moment, Wu's car drove into the parking lot followed by a car carrying a couple of members of his ever-present security detail. They drove past her and parked about five spaces away from where she stood, the security folks a couple of spaces further down, almost at the end of the lane.

Gotcha, you fucker, she thought as she turned sideways to discreetly reach for her pistol. She pretended to look at the other cars while watching them from the corner of her eye. The two security guards were out first and perfunctorily looked around the parking lot. Alice faked some specs face, and they paid her no attention. If familiarity breeds contempt, monotony breeds carelessness. Moments later, Wu came out of his fancy sports car. All three carried themselves with a leisurely manner.

As soon as she saw that they were all walking towards her, she made a quick firing plan in her mind, pulled out her gun and started firing from left to right. In the moment, she was puzzled that one of the guards already had his weapon out as she spun, and had gotten a shot off a split second before she did. The other guard was well on his way towards doing the same. She fired one shot at each man, and felt she must have hit Wu, who briefly had the confused expression of a man who had just sensed some kind of powerful physical force acting upon his body, something harder than he could ever have imagined, and had not yet fully realized what was going on around him. Alice was further puzzled that the guards had fired their first few rounds clearly at an angle to her, at somebody else, and were only now aware that she, too, was a threat.

A loud buzz grazed her head at high speed, about as close as it could have been without touching her ear. She felt a slight breeze as it passed. Something tugged hard at her sweatshirt near her waist as she let off her third shot on the second pass. Both bodyguards were down, as well as Wu, and she was debating to herself whether to do another pass, go examine the victims, or flee. A loud pop and some loud groaning behind her and to her left drew her attention, and she spun around quickly ready to shoot at it. A young man was trying to keep from sliding off the trunk of a parked car and onto the asphalt of the parking lot. He had a pistol in his right hand, his grip loosening quickly, and red stains appearing on his torso and legs. The car's alarm was sounding. Suddenly, fleeing seemed like the best choice, so Alice ran weaving through the cars, heading for a small street down the block to her right.

Her backpack bounced as she ran, and she was aware of at least a half a dozen people who had either witnessed the action or had come out soon thereafter. They all seemed to be studying her with evident horror. She'd be in viral videos within minutes. More than a few people were hiding behind cars or hitting the deck to avoid being shot, even though the gunfire was over. Getting out of here was going to be a challenge. Heart pounding in her chest, she ran across the street and turned left on the cross street, lined with doctor's offices, real estate agents, lawyers, and the like. Without pausing she ran to the end of the block, thankfully empty of pedestrians, and slowed to a casual but somewhat brisk walk. She turned to see if she had been followed, but saw nobody.

The street ended on a diagonal intersection with El Camino Real and some other street, with a church on the corner to her left. She calmly walked in, pretending to sit at a pew to pray. She was suddenly aware that she was sweaty, breathing hard, and with a heart rate going a hundred miles an hour. She tried not to show it, and spent a good while cooling off and collecting her thoughts.

52

"Let's go out there and see what's going on. Wu should be out there. We can find him and walk him to his office," said Benita. Brad nodded and they headed out. Brenda was sitting at her booth, puzzled at the sudden activity. She met Benita's gaze with an unreadable poker face. Outside, a police siren was audible in the distance, apparently coming this way.

They came out to the sidewalk, and turned the corner to the right to get to the parking lot. A knot of people was gathering near the parking lot entrance, some of them spilling out onto the street. Benita and Brad made their way and saw that a young man was lying behind a parked car a meter or two from the sidewalk. He was drawing infrequent spasmodic breaths, and his shirt and jeans were drenched in blood. Further down the parking lane, three men lay haphazardly on the pavement, equally bloodied. The man closest to them appeared to be Wu. Benita looked at the young man, and thought she recognized the face, contorted in a dissipating panic.

She twiddled a private, confidential message to Brad: "The shooter's Thakkar's neighbor, the one that shot Bennington."

Brad froze for a moment, sending the news up the chain.

A man stood nearby, constantly taking deep draws from his vaporizer as he excitedly described what he had seen, probably for the third or fourth time, to the small crowd that had gathered.

"..and she ran across the parking lot down there, and turned left on Primrose. She's probably escaped by now. She was hauling ass."

He took a healthy pull from the vaporizer.

"She got off a few shots at those guys down there. Both of them, this guy right here..." clouds of vapor billowed from his mouth as he spoke.

"..and her were shooting at those three guys over there. It was fast, I barely had time to duck."

More vaporizer pulling, more clouds of vapor that shone bright white in the sunlight.

Benita motioned towards Brad, and they walked back towards the bar.

"Let's see if Brenda's still there. I'm curious to know what her immediate plans are. She may be somewhat off the Feds' radar for the moment."

"Nobody is off their radar. Be careful, you don't want to open yourself up to any kind of obstruction or conspiracy charges."

"I know the drill, I used to go after folks like that on my behavior capture gigs. She's basically on her own, but that doesn't mean we can't give her a few hints in exchange for information. We can pretend we're still investigating and play dumb if they get pissed off at us. It'll give FfēFfē's lawyers something to do in their spare time. There's a few laws we can hide behind."

They entered the bar, and Brenda was still sitting alone. The hostess wasn't there, and with all the commotion nobody prevented Brad from entering.

"I'll be at our private table," he said, and walked off towards it. Benita sat with Brenda.

"I thought you'd be gone by now."

"I still have some unfinished business," said Brenda. Her voice was inexpressive. She was a steely young woman indeed.

"Selling something?"

Brenda nodded.

"The Feds are out in force. Were you aware of that? Wu is lying dead out there. Somebody just shot him. The guy who shot Bennington is out there as well, drawing his last breaths. He was apparently one of the shooters."

Brenda's eyes widened.

"An unknown woman was apparently also one of the shooters. I wonder who that might have been," added Benita.

Brenda turned away for a moment, then back to meet Benita's gaze.

"Yeah, I'll bet it's that cunt from Gliese. The one that shot Rashaun. Why she killed Wu is beyond me, but those Gliese people are fucking insane. It's a cult. They're crazy extremists. She comes after me, we'll see who gets the best shot. It'll be a pleasure to be the one to get rid of her, the crazy fucking bitch. I spent an hour putting every clip I have of her on face recognition, gait recognition, network scanning, you name it. It wasn't cheap, but if she comes anywhere near me, I'll know. As soon as I sell the pieces I have left, I'm gone."

"As I said, the Feds are on the case. There's some weird stuff going on at Gliese, and some seriously nasty folks from the government are on it like flies to shit. They'll be around to ask you questions any time now, especially with those dead guys lying out there. Are you still at your apartment?"

"No way! I'm not stupid or suicidal. I'm moving around. I can't avoid coming here because this is my only remaining place of business." Brenda spotted someone at the bar. "And if you don't mind, a customer has arrived, so..."

"You know how to reach me. Good luck." Benita got up and went off to join Brad.

53

Alice felt a calm come over her as she sat in a pew near the back of the church. The dim lighting there, the colors streaming in through some high stained glass windows, and the silence of the almost empty space had helped her recover from the terror of the gun battle and the escape. She now realized that she had had some kind of death wish, and was fully expecting, even hoping perhaps, to die in the gun battle to avenge her beloved Cliff. At least Wu was gone now, the rest no longer interested her. She was still here, though, and unless she wanted to spend the rest of her life on the run and robbing drug traffickers for a living, she'd probably have to rejoin the Gliese team, or whatever new work unit she'd be assigned to. Same old shit.

That meant she'd have to power up her cap for further instructions. That could be dangerous if they were now able to detect whatever communications signals the caps used. Even if she only did it for a few moments, long enough to check for messages from Steve or Waterston, she'd have to make sure they wouldn't associate her location with Wu's killing. With any luck they'd focus on that kid who was also shooting at Wu and his people. Alice just couldn't wrap her head around that. Who the hell was he? Why did he do that? How could they both have been there at the same time for the same purpose? She'd have to leave all that aside until she knew more. For the moment, she'd have to put some distance between her and the Q'Boom Qlub, but before that she'd have to change her appearance as much as possible. The gunfight videos were probably going to be among this week's biggest infotainment hits.

She was startled by some rustling behind her, but it turned out to be a cleaning woman pushing her cart across the back of the church. She got up and approached her.

"*Disculpe, creo que perdí mi abrigo aquí la semana pasada, no sabe si alguien lo encontró?*" she asked, assuming the woman wasn't fluent in English and hoping this would allay any misgivings the woman might have. There was undoubtedly some kind of lost and found where she might pick something up.

"*Sí, sí, claro seño, es por acá, sígame,*" she answered, and motioned her to follow. The woman led her to a room with a rack of clothing, with more in some boxes on top a folding table as well as underneath. There was quite a number of other miscellaneous items and boxes. This was evidently where the endless stream of clutter received by the church was stored, including the remnants of used clothing donations and the like.

"*Muy bien, gracias! Yo lo busco.*" said Alice, and proceeded to examine the surprising quantity and variety of items on the rack. The cleaning woman hesitated, as if she was waiting for Alice to find her jacket, but then excused herself to go back and continue whatever it was she was doing.

Alice examined the rack and found a sweatshirt that would fit nicely, and didn't smell particularly dirty. She rifled through the boxes and found a pair of men's khaki pants that would probably fit well, along with a nice canvas shoulder bag that looked almost new. A belt and a scarf that roughly matched her sweatshirt rounded out her new wardrobe.

The woman didn't sound nearby, but Alice quietly closed the door just in case. She quickly changed into the new clothes and transferred all of her belongings from the backpack to the shoulder bag. There were two nice clean holes near the waist of her sweatshirt, more or less where she had felt a tug during the gunfight. She put the items she had just taken off into a box and piled as many nearby items on top as she could, slid the box under the folding table, then moved other boxes in front of it.

Once she was ready, she quietly left the room and headed for the main door of the church, hoping not to run into the cleaning woman. As she crossed the foyer towards the door, she spotted the woman down a hallway, but her back was facing Alice.

The late afternoon sun felt delicious on her face, and the feeling of safety provided by her new disguise filled her with confidence and helped her calmly walk the several blocks back to the CalRail station. The last couple of blocks were busy with police and emergency vehicles, and she could see several drones whizzing over the area. A helicopter hovered overhead, though she wasn't sure if it was police or press. The wisest thing she could do was to show intense curiosity from a distance as she strolled towards the station, as if she wasn't quite sure what was going on. The only danger now was to have her face identified by the station's surveillance, but there wasn't much she could do about that. She bought a ticket up to San Francisco, where melting into the crowd would be easier.

* * * * *

The ride up to The City was uneventful, and she concluded that she was not being actively searched for by the authorities, at least not yet. In truth, she was a nobody. She had never been in trouble with the law, and Gliese made sure its people were well versed in keeping low profiles. The camaraderie and insularity of belonging to such a group further reinforced that.

The train left her at the downtown station on 1st and Mission Streets. There were plenty of people around, so she felt this would be a good place to power up her cap long enough to see if there was any news from her team. She found an unobtrusive corner in the park on the station's roof, powered up her cap in her shoulder bag, and put it on for a few moments. There was already a message waiting, in an icon that required several call and response code phrases to activate. This was a system that was rarely used. In fact, most of her teammates probably only interacted with it during the occasional training and evacuation drills. It was supposed to prevent captured caps from being used by the authorities to decipher confidential communications. Of course, if anybody cracked under interrogation, all that was moot.

Once in the system, she found a single brief message: Petaluma Pie Kitchen. Petaluma was a small city about an hour's drive north of San Francisco, just before the larger city of Santa Rosa. At least she wouldn't have to backtrack south. She was halfway there already. Presumably, they were expected to loiter around the area near the pie shop until they were recognized either by some former colleague or someone from the new work group. She resigned herself to joining whatever new team presented itself. She knew now that she was a lifer.

The cap went back in her shoulder bag and she switched it off, then powered up her specs. A quick query showed that she could catch a ferry to Marin County at a terminal a couple of blocks away from where she now stood. From there the local light rail system would take her to Petaluma, and leave her about 4 blocks away from the pie shop. She powered off her specs and headed for the ferry terminal.

54

"Help me out here, Liz. What have your people found in the trailers?" asked Thakkar.

"They're still working on it, Ram," answered Liz, his Homeland Security contact. "I'll be honest, though. They're clamping down. It's now past top secret, at a classification level that's itself classified, so I'm basically out of the loop."

"Any gossip? Any rumors or rumblings of what they've found?"

"Nothing, and at this point it's getting risky for me to even talk about it, Ram. If they need you, they'll pull you in. All you can do is wait. Sorry, but that's how things are at the moment."

"Liz, I found the damn things! I handed it all to those people! We turned over the first devices to them! That doesn't count? We're already read into this stuff!" Thakkar was trying his best not to be angry with his friend. She was, after all, Thakkar's best contact.

"I hear you, Ram, but you know how these folks are. Do you have any other leads you can track down? At this point, that's likely to be a more fruitful source of information. They'll get back to you eventually, once they feel they've gotten a handle on the situation."

"OK, got it Liz. Sorry to get all worked up about it. Please let me know if anything interesting comes out."

"Will do, old friend. Sorry I don't have anything else."

Thakkar sat glumly in his chair. It was looking pretty doubtful indeed that he'd be getting much more information about what was found at Gliese. Best case, they'd come back for some follow-up, at which point he might be able to wheedle something out of them in return.

"Brenda Castro is still out there. Brad and Benita just contacted her at Wu's club," said Wilkins.

"She's a bit player. Bennington just used her to sell whatever stolen jewelry or artwork he managed to get from his thieving friends," said Thakkar with more than a note of bitterness. "She's just a whore that sells expensive trinkets to vastly over-compensated assholes, nothing more."

"Still, she's out there, and she may have some information about those 'thieving friends,' who might well lead us to other cells like Gliese. Once the feds get hold of her, even she will be out of our reach. We can rent someplace for her and keep her under wraps, and say we were trying to protect her from whoever shot Wu and from any renegade Gliese people. We should buy up whatever items she still feels a need to sell, so we can keep her away from Wu's club and from the antique shop."

"What?! I'm not interested in any jewelry, or whatever other crap she has." He knew Wilkins was right, and wasn't even sure what it was about the woman that he found so distasteful. It wasn't that she did sex work. He wasn't at all concerned about that. He had known more than a few women very much like her, and was still close friends with a few of them. It wasn't that she sold stolen goods. He had occasionally bought some pretty dubious items himself when the temptation was great enough. Maybe it was the fact that she was one of Bennington's people. The man who had taken advantage of Pari's youthful idiocy, scammed her, drugged her, and raped her. Repeatedly. That was more than he could bear, but he knew the rational choice was to put that aside, take her out of play, and try to get whatever useful information she might have.

"Oh, all right," he mumbled at Wilkins. "Make it happen."

Wilkins nodded and was silent for a moment.

"Meanwhile, I'll sync up with Yulya," said Thakkar. If it were physically possible for Wilkins to raise an eyebrow, he would have.

55

"They want us to go back and get Brenda. Buy everything she has at whatever price she asks" said Brad.

They had just gotten on highway 101, on the long drive south to Benita's apartment.

"We have to get her a safe house, and keep her off the map. They want to see if she has anything that can lead us to some other cell like Gliese."

"She's probably with a customer," answered Benita.

"We can go see if she's at the same place she took the guy the day DuPont and the other Gliese guy were killed."

"That would be a pretty dumb place to take a customer," said Benita.

"Going back to Wu's club was pretty dumb if she thought someone from Gliese was after her, which might not even be the case, by the way."

Benita told the car to go back to the Q'Boom Qlub.

* * * * *

Brad waited in the car while Benita went inside. They had to park in the public lot half a block away, since the club's parking lot was still a crime scene. The club itself was miraculously still open, with conspicuously beefed up security. The crowd was still thin at this hour, but it didn't seem that people were shunning the place. Benita wondered how many people knew or cared about what had happened just an hour or so ago. It was already in the headlines. No police were in evidence inside, maybe because all of the action occurred outside. The staff and customers seemed to be talking among themselves more excitedly than on her previous visits, but otherwise it looked like business as usual. The implacable power of money. She wondered who was taking over, and what higher powers existed above Wu.

Brenda was not in sight, at least not in the bar near the entrance, nor in the one next to it. The private tables had their curtains open and were all empty, as were the booths and most of the seats at the bar. Benita strolled through the double doors to the gaudily lit karaoke bar next door. There weren't many people here yet either, nor was Brenda.

She went back to the other bar and around back to see if she could get up to Wu's office. Upstairs, the double doors to the rear corridor past his office were open, and there didn't seem to be anyone back there. She stepped in and started walking along a hallway that made its way across formerly separate buildings.

The doors to the hallway of another office section were open, but even before she got there she could hear quite a bit of activity. She walked by casually, as if she was headed to the exit door at the far end of the corridor. She had a good look down the hallway, and saw at least three people who looked like detectives addressing with great seriousness another three who must have been Wu's employees. The latter looked distressed indeed, and the detectives were probably taking full advantage. Benita kept walking, then pretended she had forgotten something and doubled back. On this pass she saw three more people walking determinedly up the hallway from the other end, towards the detectives and their subjects. The alpha member was already addressing the detectives requesting a more formal meeting in one of the larger conference rooms. Undoubtedly, the Q'Boom Qlub's legal counsel had finally arrived. The lawyers would surely seal this place up tight, and at very least Benita would have to wait days before she could start plying the club staff for anything.

She recalled Brenda mentioning some private rooms upstairs, where she strongly implied that acts of assignation could be discreetly carried out in the course of business with the club's patrons. She doubled back to go past the office area again and on to another area beyond it. The lighting was darker and warmer here. It seemed that the entire area was one big mysterious schmooze space. It was lit like a bar, with lots of tables and booths, curtains and other partitions liberally and strategically placed to create smaller spaces and presumably also to mute conversations. It was deserted.

There was a dimly lit but well-appointed hallway that branched off the main corridor. The carpeting was sumptuous, the wood paneling and wall paper beautifully done, and 4 doors lined the right side. At the far end of the hallway were some larger dark and windowless wooden doors that by Benita's estimation enclosed a stairway and an elevator shaft that led to the street level.

She walked down the hallway and peeked into the open door of the first room. It was effectively a hotel room, with a mini-bar, a double bed, a couple of loveseats behind a coffee table, and a small bathroom with a shower, all in a cozy but not cramped arrangement. The furniture and décor were as handsome as the hallway. While one could undoubtedly conduct a business meeting in one of these, Benita surmised that these were the very rooms Brenda had mentioned. Benita walked further down the hallway. The second and third doors were also open, but the last one was closed. She came as close to the door as she dared to try and hear something. There were voices. A woman was speaking, punctuated by modest laughter. A man spoke, also with an occasional good-humored noise. The woman said something, but all Benita could make out was "the larger ones are all 12 carats."

Benita sensed something, turned and saw a woman at the corridor end of the hallway. It was the hostess from the other day, arms akimbo with a severe glare directed at Benita, who calmly and quietly started walking towards her.

"I'm looking for Brenda Castro," said Benita.

"You'll have to wait somewhere else," said the young woman sternly, "this area requires a reservation, and disturbing or spying on the patrons is forbidden."

"OK, sorry. We're investigating all aspects of Mr. Wu's murder. As you know, we had business with him recently, and there were still some loose ends."

The young woman studied her intently. No doubt other people were doing so as well through her specs, and Benita's presence here must have been detected by a surveillance system that was not as distracted by the day's events as the bar's employees were.

"You can wait in the bar next door. Please follow me," said the girl finally. She led Benita to the empty tables and asked her to wait there.

"Your friend will probably be out shortly, and you'll see her when she walks by. Please do not disturb anyone in her party." With that, the young woman walked past Benita and around one of the many partitions. From the sound of it, there was an elevator on the other side.

Benita sat on a bar stool at a discreet distance from the back corridor to wait and see if Brenda appeared. No doubt the club's security folks would send up one of the detectives to check Benita out as a suspect. That would be most prudent, and Benita knew that she'd do it herself as well under the circumstances. Sure enough, it wasn't 3 minutes before one of the guys from the hallway further down came around to have a word.

"And you are?" he asked, somewhat mockingly.

"My name is Benita Garcés. I work with Dr. Rameshwar Thakkar of FfēFfē Automata. If you consult with your federal colleagues you'll see that we were the ones who helped them with an ongoing investigation having to do with Mr. Wu."

"My federal colleagues, huh?" he asked rhetorically. His gaze went into specs face as he twiddled his fingers, then looked to be reading or listening to something. His eyes seemed to glance at something next to him that only he could see, an avatar or two helping with the investigation.

"I see," he said. "OK. Please let me know if you need anything. We may eventually want to talk to you." An icon came up in Benita's specs, in which she accepted his business card.

"Will do. I'm always willing to help," she said. The detective left as promptly as he had arrived, although not without taking a good look at Brenda, who was standing at the corridor.

Brenda walked over and sat at Benita's small table. They were alone in the room.

"We want to help you," said Benita. It was a vague opening gambit. She had to be careful not to say or do anything litigable that might be recorded by the club. "We want to protect you from the Gliese people."

She sent Brenda a private message as well, using the covert link provided by Wilkins: "We want to track down anyone or anything having to do with those people."

Brenda replied on the same link: "Wait for me at a private table. I have one more sale tonight."

"We'll buy all of the stuff you have left at whatever price you ask," replied Benita over the link.

Brenda gave her a sidelong glance as she walked away, but said nothing.

56

The Petaluma Pie Kitchen was a 10 minute walk from the light rail station. It was warmer than San Francisco, but not by much at this hour. A wide swath of wildfire smoke crossed the afternoon sky further north. *There must be some big ones fairly near here*, thought Alice.

On the way, she crossed the bridge over Lynch Creek, a typically dry California waterway. A couple of blocks further, she came upon a small urban park nestled between two buildings in downtown Petaluma. Several trees swayed in the now brisk breeze, and a few people sat on park benches or at parasol-shaded tables outside of the 3 or 4 restaurants that gave onto the quaint little plaza. One of them was the Petaluma Pie Kitchen, which was open for business. Alice walked around the little park for a few minutes hoping to be noticed by whomever she was supposed to meet. Her rapidly growing hunger, perhaps inspired by the idea of eating a freshly baked savory pie, soon got the better of her so she went in and got a couple of small hand-pies.

She sat down at a table just outside of the pie shop for her impromptu meal. Each pie was about the size of a fairly large *empanada*, and she relished every bite. As she was finishing her second one, she noticed a man and a woman sit down on a bench almost directly in front of her, about 5 meters away. They paid her no attention, chatting casually. The woman discreetly pulled something out of her shoulder bag, just far enough so that Alice was able to see what it was, the brim of a beige baseball cap just like the one she currently had in her own shoulder bag. The woman put it away again, and the couple rose to their feet and walked away.

Alice got up as well, put her napkins and pie wrappers in a nearby waste bin, and walked after them to join her new team.

57

The evening crowd was starting to trickle in. Benita was sipping some of the overpriced house wine as she waited for Brenda, looking at everybody's HunterGather scores in stealth mode so as to not draw much attention. So far, the numbers coming into the club had not been nearly as impressive as last time. Lots of green dots, though. The night was still young. Maybe the later crowd would be better. The Q'Boom Qlub was a major find for her. It would be impossible for her to avoid becoming a regular. Brad was still waiting in the car, and she considered asking him to join her. The two burly bouncers had taken their positions at the door, so that might not work out.

What could Brenda know that Thakkar and his team didn't know already? All that occurred to Benita at the moment was that her contacts in the antique shop network might know something, perhaps the locations of other organizations like Gliese. Bennington's shop would be overrun by the authorities by now, so the store's software and data were now inaccessible. They'd be after Brenda soon. The Gliese site, or whatever might be left of it, was also in their hands. All that Benita had left were the materials that Thakkar had provided originally, and which she had begun to review more carefully given the excitement of the last few days.

She twiddled her fingers to start looking through it again while she waited. The activities at the Gliese site seemed to be the key, so she focused on those for the moment. There were written reports from her predecessor and from various members of Thakkar's team. She had only looked at a few dozen of the many photos and videos that had been collected, and was relieved that they could be searched for by keyword. She decided to look for videos of the Gliese site.

There was quite a bit of drone footage, flying over Gliese at what must have been considered a safe distance. It was taken with telephoto lenses, and the sharpness varied a bit as the system compensated for shakiness. It was crisp enough to be able to extract text on the surfaces of boxes being delivered or from documents carelessly being read out in the open by oblivious Gliese staff. Many of these videos cross referenced documents that kept meticulous track of it all. Some of the photos and videos were overlaid with that information, and it looked like Thakkar's team had managed to put together a fairly detailed understanding of what was going on.

One of the main conclusions was that Gliese Genetics was a biotech company that was a front for some very sophisticated industrial chemistry, along with their plant and animal tissue culture and cloning business. The reports suggested that they were generously over-equipped relative to the products and services they sold. They were purchasing enough DNA sequencing and synthesis equipment to do a hundred times the volume they appeared to be selling, and had purchased some pricey research grade attachments to build DNA sequences with many unnatural chemical components, as if they were fundamentally redesigning biology at the molecular level. They had also set up a battery of automated organic chemical synthesizers, also with exotic attachments. The speculation was that they could synthesize weird chemicals in laboratory scale bulk, and run them through their DNA synthesizers to create who knows what. Thakkar's team had even purchased some of the plants and one of the new chickens that Gliese had recently brought to market. It was sent to several local academic labs for analysis, (at not insignificant cost, noted Benita), but aside from a some significant genetic alterations, there were no weird chemicals in them.

The supposed artificial intelligence project, for which they were evidently obtaining the quantum gate arrays, was even less clear. Thakkar's people had tracked a few computer racks, computer and networking equipment, and a variety of parts to build custom computers, but not much else was known. One report argued that they were setting up much more in-house computing infrastructure than a business like Gliese could possibly need, but admitted that such things were hard to estimate. If they were doing some kind of sophisticated modeling or analysis, their needs could be open ended. It was interesting that they opted to build and run their own systems, instead of just renting capacity in the cloud, but that was not at all uncommon for paranoid innovation-driven businesses.

Benita was starting to get bored, until she found a small collection of media that had clearly been gathered by a behavior capture actor. One in particular consisted of the actor skulking around the hills behind Gliese at dusk, apparently trying to sneak onto the property. There was full stack media, with stereoscopic video, stereophonic audio, and various audio and video overlays. It started with the actor crouched near a somewhat dilapidated chain-link fence overlooking some of the portable buildings behind the second tree line. Entering here would put him or her well inside Gliese. Nobody was in sight, and the video overlay showed the areas covered by known surveillance equipment. In Benita's mind, the word "known" was a red flag for a site like this.

"There's a hole in the fence," said a male voice, apparently over a private speech channel. He had a distinctly Indian accent. Mohan? He slowly moved towards the fence, and sure enough, part of it looked torn with an opening large enough for a person to squeeze through. As he made his way through, there was another male voice, a familiar one to Benita.

"We aren't sure of the surveillance coverage. It's too much of a risk," said the second voice.

The actor turned his gaze behind him, and about 5 meters away stood a robot. It was identical to Brad, and the voice was definitely Brad's as well. Benita felt a chill go up her spine at the recognition. Was that *her* Brad? A different one? Why hadn't she been told? But the fact that she was seeing this video meant that this information had been available all along, if only she had reviewed it earlier.

The actor was now inside the perimeter, and was crawling on his hands and knees through the brush to stay out of sight. Unfortunately, the brush ended about 3 or 4 meters in, and from there on there was no natural cover. For a few moments, he looked this way and that, trying to find a way to one of the small buildings. There was more surveillance cover here, much more, but there were a few approaches that looked dark. He chose the most direct one, and sprinted towards the building, hoping the overlay was accurate. The video started looking degraded, its image resolution visibly diminished and patchy.

"I'm next to building C," he said, the audio now tinny. "Gaah!" he shouted, and fell to the ground. The sky was rapidly darkening, with a few sunset-tinged clouds overhead. The actor growled incoherently.

Two people came into view, and stood over him. Benita recognized one of them. It was the woman who had attacked her in the scrubland next to the golf course, when they were picking Pari up after Wu had released her. The other was a man she didn't recognize. He had a taser in his right hand. The image started to distort with more compression artifacts, and the audio became choppy. Soon the image froze, the audio cut out, and the video ended.

Benita looked at the other video file names. There was another with the same name, save for an additional hexadecimal code. She twiddled on it to have a look.

It was the same scene, only from a vantage point slightly farther away, up the shallow slope of the hill behind Gliese. There was a man crouching a few meters away.

"There's a hole in the fence," he said over the private channel.

"We aren't sure of the surveillance coverage, it's too much of a risk," said the voice of whoever was recording this. The man turned around and glanced at the robot, with a mocking smirk. She assumed that this was Mohan, Aradhya's erstwhile love interest.

The scene played out as before, and the man made up to the nearest structure. It was building C, which according to the other documents housed the organic synthesis lab. Suddenly two people, a man and a woman darted out from around a corner of the building, the man pointing his taser at Mohan as he approached.

"Gaah!" shouted Mohan as he fell backwards onto the ground. The robot turned in the opposite direction, and started running up the hill, darting this way and that to stay covered by vegetation. He pulled up a small panel showing one of Mohan's electrocardiograph channels and left it in view. There was a jump cut in the video, and now Brad was at the top of a hill looking down at Gliese from a much greater distance. It was now twilight, and Mohan was nowhere to be seen, but his heart was still going, according to the EKG.

"Ranger has been captured! Ranger has been captured!" said Brad over the private channel. As he spoke, Mohan's heart channel flatlined. Either they had removed his suit, or he had been killed.

"I've lost Ranger's biometrics," said Brad as he scanned through all of the channels he could access at a distance from Mohan's body suit. The signal was present. It was simply flat.

"Remain at your current position," came a voice over the audio channel. "Go into power save mode with an eye on the site."

Brad found a place where he could sit on the ground and still see Gliese. His body locked into that position to avoid wasting energy on the motors that controlled his limbs.

Another jump cut, and Brad was still in the same place looking down at Gliese. It looked like the sun would soon come up behind him, so this must be hours later. Two men came out of building C carrying a stretcher with what could easily be an immobile human body, covered from head to toe with a tarp, and loaded it into a waiting car. Brad watched it drive off. There was no longer a signal coming from Mohan's body suit.

Another jump cut, and now Brad was lying on the ground next to a dirt road, with hills on either side. The image and the audio were now quite degraded, as two men picked him up and loaded him into a small van. Brad was lying down in the back of the van, and turned his head to look at the man riding shotgun. The man pulled out a thermal cup and drank something from it. The cup had the FfēFfē logo. Audio and video cut out at that point.

*   *   *   *   *

Benita looked up and saw that Aradhya was standing in front of her.

"How long have you been here?" asked Aradhya.

"A while. I was here when Wu got shot."

"You saw him get shot?" asked Aradhya in evident horror.

"I was inside at the time. I didn't see anything. Let me show you something." Benita pulled up Brad's video again, clipped out the clearest frame showing Mohan's face, and sent it to Aradhya. *I hope I don't get shit for this*, she thought.

Aradhya gasped when she saw it.

"When was this? Where is he?" she said.

"I have no idea. That's outside of a small biotech in Watsonville. Do you know anything about that?"

Aradhya looked fixedly at Benita, and said nothing.

"I gather that's a yes?" said Benita. Aradhya looked away, pretending to examine the Art Nouveau wallpaper.

"Why are you here, exactly?" asked Benita. "What do you know about the place in Watsonville?"

Aradhya examined the meticulously finished fingernails of her right hand, pretending to inspect some minor imperfection.

"Look, I know about that place. I know what's been going on there. I'm married to him. I live in my Dad's house. Wilkins does a lot of work for me as well," she said finally.

"You don't exactly look distraught about Mohan."

Aradhya looked at the floor, shaking her head.

"It was long over for us by then," she said. "He just couldn't keep his pants on, especially with all of those 'interstitial behavior' sluts."

"Word has it that you don't have such a long attention span yourself."

"Oh cut the horseshit, Benita. What are you, 15 years old?" It was the first time Aradhya had addressed her by name. "Where's *your* lovey-dovey hubby? Or maybe you prefer the ladies? Pari certainly seemed to like you."

"So that *was* Mohan."

"Of course it was. That happened only a week or 10 days before you started working with my Dad. He even had that garish painting replaced just for you."

Benita looked puzzled.

"You know which one. Dad even had a giclée sent out to you. Mohan also got one, except back then it was a male god and a male monkey warrior. Dad had the goofy idea that there'd be some kind of subliminal effect on him, and then on you. It was supposed to inspire you into being some kind of knight in shining armor, the Hindu version, anyway. Somebody in Fremont painted them maybe two months ago, a guy who does paintings for the local Hindu temples."

Benita said nothing. She actually liked the print and had been planning on splurging for a decent framing job.

"By the way, are there any more materials? Mohan made several trips out there, as I understand it."

"What happened to him?" asked Benita. Aradhya shrugged.

"We assume the worst."

"Well aren't we the chilly little sociopath," said Benita.

"Fuck off, Benita. It's not like you're on the moral high ground here."

Benita's opened her mouth to confect some kind of snide retort, but thought the better of it and closed it.

"So you knew what was going on there all along. What were you after? Obviously not Mohan," said Benita.

"As you undoubtedly already suspect, this chilly little sociopath was thinking about the business opportunities. I'd like to convince you to show me all of the materials that you've been provided. I want you to provide whatever information that comes into your hands regarding whatever Gliese was doing down there. The more technical, the better."

"I don't work for you."

"You will be compensated," answered Aradhya. "Generously."

At that moment Brenda appeared, looking first at Aradhya, then at Benita.

"So! You *do* prefer the ladies, I see. I'm impressed. Very impressed," said Aradhya as she got up from the table. "That is one beautiful dress, and it is *gorgeous* on you, and a stunning hairstyle," she said to Brenda. "I'll leave you with your lady friend." With that, she turned and calmly walked towards the bar.

"You know her?" asked Brenda.

"I do. Do you?"

"You know she's the sister of Sav's most recent catch, right? She knows who *I* am, no doubt."

"It's her father who wants to put you in a safe house. He's one of the founders of FféFfē Automata, and..." said Benita in private speech over the covert link.

"*What*? Why the fuck would I want anything to do with those people? What do *they* want?" replied Brenda, also now on the covert link. Her eyes were wide and piercingly hot.

"The short answer is that Bennington was trying to unload some very valuable chips that are being watched by all sorts of security agencies, and those people in Watsonville he sold things to have just been raided by the feds. It's only a matter of time before they grab *you*."

Brenda thought for a moment, her intense gaze still fixed on Benita.

"You said you'd buy my remaining inventory at whatever price I ask."

Benita nodded. An icon appeared in her specs, a text containing nothing more than a number with a dollar sign ahead of it. A nice, respectable number, but one Benita was sure would be fine. She private messaged it to Wilkins.

"Sold," said Benita, after a moment of specs face.

"They're in my car." said Brenda.

"Let's take mine, in case you're being tracked. Is it a rental?"

"It is. Everything I own is in there. Don't worry, I travel light. Will I be moving in with you?"

Benita blushed, which was interrupted only by Brenda's HunterGather callout briefly appearing by her head, an even 90 average.

"Your green dot," said Brenda. Benita was still in HunterGather stealth mode, so she switched to active mode for a moment. Brenda raised an eyebrow, and her profile went dark again.

"Are you always on the hunt?" asked Brenda. More blushing on Benita's part.

"It's just that, well, the other night, there were, I saw quite a few high scores. That's actually pretty rare for me," said Benita.

"Well, news flash. These people tend to be kind of strange, to say the least, which leads me to believe that you're kind of weird yourself. That, by the way, is part of the reason this place is so successful. If you're a weirdo with a decent income, or better yet with a significant personal fortune, this is the place to be. Take it from someone who's made a living out of it."

"And not a bad one at that, it looks like."

"Sav was about to get some higher end merchandise. I was expecting to double my income. By the way, don't get too excited by the high scores. Trust me."

Brenda had a moment of specs face as she examined something.

"I see that your people have come through on what I have left, though. Please convey my thanks and appreciation. Well, shall we?" said Brenda, getting up from the table. Benita got up as well.

"I'll let them know. Let's grab all your stuff and go to a safe place. I've been provided an address," said Benita.

They walked past Aradhya, who was seated at the bar nursing a drink and placidly ignoring them.

"Power down your specs," said Benita. "You'll have to go dark for a while."

58

"Well, at least the fires are out," said Sue.

"The fires on the hills can still come back if the wind changes," said Tavo.

"Fire's not gonna come back," said Raúl. "Winds always go east in the afternoon. Hills gonna burn, though."

Crazy Ladies was safe, for the moment. There was fire damage to trees along the road, but all of the structures were far enough inside the property to have escaped the flames. The hillsides on the other side of the road were on fire, but the forested areas were a few hundred meters distant, and the nearby grassy areas were all burnt out. There would be fires over the ridge, perhaps for days.

"Let's get them boxes, man," said Raúl. They were drinking lemonade at one of the picnic tables. Water would soon run low, but they wouldn't be able to go get more until the road was cleared of at least some of the smoking hulks. The truck that hadn't burned had been completely relieved of its contents, and a surprising number of people were dedicated to examining the rest of them and carrying off whatever they could. Quite a few of them had dark jackets with the acronym "FBI" on their backs in conspicuously large letters.

"Looks like there was some pretty valuable stuff in there," said Tavo.

"Let's be discreet about it, I don't want us to get in trouble with all those feds," said Sue.

They got up and slowly made their way to the boxes they had hidden, trying to act as if they were just going about everyday farm activities. None of the feds were paying any attention to them.

"Let's put them in crates so that nobody notices," said Sue, as she grabbed a large plastic crate. The boxes barely fit in the largest crates, but they looked innocent enough. Raúl grabbed an empty crate so that they'd all look busy, and the trio returned to the picnic table. They put the boxes on the bench opposite the road, so that the table would give them cover.

Raúl pulled out a pocket knife to open up the first box.

"*Puta, ca'on!*" he whispered to himself, awestruck. The box contained a variety of glass and plastic jars, and some smaller boxes, all packed together with wads of cash. The three stared at it for a few moments, speechless. Raúl closed the box.

"We should do this somewhere else," he said. They all exchanged looks, then looked at the closed box.

"We can go to a potting room in one of the greenhouses," said Sue. "There won't be anyone there. It's pretty much harvest time. The old one in back would be good."

"Let's go," said Tavo, and the three carried the crates to one of the original greenhouses that had been built near the rear border of the farm, when the land on which the newer greenhouses had been built was still arable land. It was out of sight and out of mind on this chaotic late autumn afternoon.

*   *   *   *   *

Once in the potting room, they put both boxes on one of the potting tables and started pulling things out. They had a plastic bag ready for the cash in case somebody came by. It was quite a bit of cash. They also pulled out the jars and smaller boxes. The three glass jars held about a liter of fluid each, and contained some kind of preserved biological specimens, one in each jar.

"What *is* this," said Sue as she examined one. It appeared to be some kind of multi-legged creature, with ten appendages that were clearly legs and a few others that might or might not be. There were 3 or 4 kinds of orifices distributed around the body, some of which had smooth round surfaces in them that could conceivably be eyes. The surface was a mottled pattern of browns and black, reminiscent of a leopard shark.

"Is that some kind of ocean animal?" asked Raúl.

"Not one that I've ever seen, not even in pictures," said Sue.

"This one looks like a plant," said Tavo. It looked like something between a pine cone and a densely packed cluster of grapes, with what might have been a cut stem on one end. It was bluish violet all over, except the round grape-like parts which were more reddish.

The third jar had four smaller specimens similar to the first one. They were different sizes, and the smaller ones looked less well formed than the larger ones, and all of them less so than the large one in the first jar.

"Maybe these are from different times in their development," said Sue. "Maybe these died before they were fully developed."

"But what are they? Is this the kind of stuff they're inventing over there? Do they expect to sell this stuff as food?" said Tavo.

"That shit is disgusting," laughed Raúl. He was counting the cash.

The rest of the jars were smaller and made of opaque white plastic. They all contained fine crystalline powders. Their labels had what appeared to be inventory codes and lengthy chemical names, with bizarre syllables interspersed by numbers and punctuation symbols. Some of the names were several lines long, and had what must be nicknames in parentheses. The nicknames were not much more informative than the chemical names, at least to Sue, Tavo, and Raúl.

There were a few binders in the boxes, and they had diagrams and photos of creatures that looked like those in the glass jars.

"It looks like they were growing these," said Sue, as she paged through one of them. "It looks like they all died during development, at least so far. It has codes for gene sequence files and a bunch of other information." She looked inside the front and back covers of the binder.

The last page was a plastic sheet with pockets in it, and some of the pockets had memory cards.

"I'll bet there's all sorts of stuff in these things," she said, looking at the memory cards. "There's a lot of other kinds of plants and animals in the binder. I've never seen anything like them. They're all really weird looking."

Tavo had been busy opening one of the smaller boxes. It had been taped shut, but once he had cut the tape the top came off smoothly. Inside were some shallow plastic trays stacked on top of each other, and each tray had two rows of fairly large flat objects that looked like expensive computer chips.

"Wow, look at these. I'll bet they're worth a couple of grand. They look new," said Tavo. "Maybe we could sell them online." He looked at his friends faces to see whether they thought that might be a good idea.

"You don't want the Gliese people to come back and get you, man," said Raúl. His tone was uncharacteristically serious.

"I agree. Look at all those feds out there. This stuff is probably a lot more valuable than we know," said Sue. "This stuff can probably get us into *a lot* of trouble."

"Well then, what do we do?" asked Tavo.

"I say we keep the money. We can pretend it wasn't here," said Raúl.

"What if the bills are marked, or if the feds are tracking the serial numbers?" asked Tavo. Raúl frowned.

"*Es un chingo de lana, ca'on,*" said Raúl, "A whole lotta money! We could buy and sell stuff, cash only."

There were more items, some electronic circuit boards with big heat sinks on them, some jars filled with lumpy metal beads, a small binder with more plastic pages that had memory cards in small pockets, and a box with some new-looking beige baseball caps.

59

Thakkar sat in an easy chair turning one of the beige baseball caps over in his hand. There was nobody else in his private studio, not even Wilkins.

In spite of a lengthy series of expensive and gradually more aggressive treatments, the dull, diffuse pain in his right side was now ever-present, and slowly but perceptibly increasing, day by day. Next week was Halloween, and according to his doctors he might not make it to New Year's, maybe not even Christmas.

It was a minor satisfaction that he managed to expose the people in Watsonville. Even more satisfying was getting his hands on a few of the caps.

The caps! He held one in his hand, possibly the most remarkable device he had ever seen. He had not yet dared to turn it on and wear it again. With Gliese down, there was no telling who it would be communicating with, and he didn't want to draw any malevolent forces to his home. Blam had already beefed up his home security detail, and now there were various types of feds involved. His daughters' security had been increased, and even Pari had grudgingly agreed to it.

But now here he found himself on the home stretch. Several years of his life had been captured and instilled into Wilkins and Brad, but his own thread of life, that of the unique and distinct human known as Rameshwar Thakkar, would soon come to an end. It was nearly spooled out, and he knew that his final days would be a muddle of chemical confusion, his mind turning to mush as his liver finally shut down. If he had anything else he wanted to do in this life, the moment to do it was now.

The caps could be the final piece of the puzzle. A plan had been forming in his mind, a plan to cast off what bound him, to shuffle off his mortal coil, but do so fully conscious and move on to the next world with eyes and ears open, gazing back from the other side, from the undiscovered country, from which he had every intention to return. The means for which he had been patiently building with the help of Blam's powerful magic. The caps, or something akin to them, were the key.

* * * * *

Time and tide wait for no man, and one day Rameshwar Thakkar found himself in a lucid moment, a brief respite from the flood of biochemical waste in his blood and the harsh drugs that were less and less able to keep his cancer in check. His liver was no longer able to help clear it all out. The private nurse on duty had inadvertently left his intravenous fluid drip at much too high a rate for nearly an hour before setting it back to the proper flow, and his kidneys had managed to flush enough of the noxious chemicals out of his system to bring him to a state of foggy wakefulness.

He felt as if he was lying in a desert, prostrate in the hot sun, unable to move and blinded by the bright light of day. A familiar presence was nearby, and he saw that it was Wilkins. The desert was really his bed in his studio, and the sun streaming through the windows seemed brighter than he could ever remember.

"Wilkins," said Thakkar, weakly.

In a parallel dream, a wizened old man lying in a hospital bed, his skin like a thin sheet of dull, buff-colored latex haphazardly wrapped around his bones, also said "Wilkins" at the exact same moment. The old man looked disturbingly familiar.

"Is that..." said Thakkar, as did the old man.

"Yes," said Wilkins, and Thakkar couldn't tell if Wilkins had said it to him or to the old man, or if Thakkar had said it himself to the old man. Thakkar was talking to himself, but that seemed to include Wilkins, who was sitting at Thakkar's bedside, as well as the old man. Thakkar attributed it all to the toxic slush coursing through his veins.

"We're still connected," said the Wilkins voice. "The connection worked, remember?"

Thakkar now vaguely recalled his plan, to set up a two way communication between himself and Wilkins. His own mind and Wilkins' would somehow be melded and made one. Thakkar's headpiece would be connected to Wilkins' magneto-encephalographic mini-model to form a bridge into whatever was running inside the mix that comprised Wilkins. Thakkar had hypothesized that at the very moment of his death the flesh and bone side of the bridge would disappear, leaving only the simulated side, the one running in Wilkins. His awareness of his surroundings, the thread of Rameshwar Thakkar, would somehow hold on by its metaphysical fingernails and escape the final eternal sleep that awaits us all. From then on, inside that grand and mysterious ocean of numbers, he might live on.

The old man in the bed was indeed wearing his headpiece, one that looked bulkier than the ones he had been wearing for years. He tried to touch it, but was too weak to even move his arm from where it lay at his side. Two entwined dreams were clear now. One dream was Wilkins. It felt both distant and immediate, with the eerie and unsettling sense of quotidian unreality of dreams. Except that Thakkar was not asleep, so far as he could tell, and the dream was not fading. In the other dream, he was in his room, in his life, as he remembered it prior to slipping into chemical delirium. He now recalled that developing and testing the headpiece had taken weeks. He couldn't guess how long ago that had been.

"This may be it, Ram," said the Wilkins voice.

Thakkar put his focus on the Wilkins dream. It was akin to an elaborate video game, in which he was a simulated character in a simulated world, one that nonetheless bore a striking resemblance to the world in the old man dream, the Thakkar dream. It didn't have quite the same quality as the beige caps, there was a palpable sensation of fakeness to it. There was a feeling of many other characters in this world. He couldn't see them, but he could sense that they were there, near him, seeing what he saw, hearing what he heard, and considering it all moment by moment along with him. They made themselves known through him, as if their thoughts were his own thoughts, like the soft murmuring of a crowd.

He was a man and many other men, and a woman and many other women. The man seemed familiar to him. He was comfortable with him. The woman seemed familiar as well, like someone he had known before but now knew much more intimately. He recalled seeing himself sitting in a wheelchair, drinking soup out of a mug, cheerily cackling to himself about something. When was that?

"Ram," said the Wilkins voice, and Thakkar now sensed that the voice emanated from this dream, the Wilkins dream, not the old man dream. Other memories came and went: he sat at a desk as a man and a woman stood before him, people he had never met but suddenly recognized. They had failed to prevent someone from being shot. It had to do with the theft of a great deal of valuable information from a company in Palo Alto, one who's chief technical officer he had met at a few local business conferences. In another, he pressed his back against a wall, in the dark, next to a dimly lit hallway. Someone was coming, but he was ready. A semi-automatic pistol was in his hands. He noticed his neatly painted fingernails against the metallic sheen of the gun, and felt pleased at how they looked. His perfume was subtle and ravishing. In yet another, a man suddenly lunged at him in a bar, but Thakkar was fast and his fist went forcefully against the man's face. The image of the man's angry, half-closed eyes and dangerously compressed nose lingered in his mind. He stood over a crib watching a baby sleeping placidly, and realized that the child's mother stood next to him. He held her close with his arm around her waist.

"Ram," said the Wilkins voice again, interrupting Thakkar's reverie.

All these characters were together living a consensual dream, along with Thakkar. A dream within a dream. A dream within a dream, *tête-à-tête* with the other dream, the one of the old man.

The old man could recall the seemingly endless chapters of his life, one which was evidently nearing its last scene, its final page, perhaps already in its closing paragraph. The younger man in his memories had had a beautiful, brilliant wife, and together they had had two beautiful daughters. That young man had matured, and had done something important in the latter parts of his life. Thakkar and the other characters in this dream recognized each other as that very thing, the thing that the man in that memory had done, the thing he had invented.

The old man in the other dream was becoming confused. The chemicals in his blood were swiftly returning, and there was something else. There was a chill, a wave of foreboding coming over the old man that Thakkar could feel even from within the Wilkins dream. He remembered a bright, sunny day from his childhood, his mother and his aunties puttering around a kitchen chatting, joking, and laughing with each other. He remembered their colorful clothing and long black braids, and the overwhelming fragrance of the spices they cooked with. He recalled the days of his youth, now a young man, feeling all-powerful and immortal, drinking in the secrets of the universe he learned each day at university. In flashbacks, he recalled many moments in the arms of his beloved, languidly inhaling her scent, or laying on a bed with her draped over him, both of them sweaty and drunk with love. He remembered the machines he had helped create, and for a moment the newest device, the one in which he found himself now, lost in an intertwining of dreams.

The old man dream was slipping away, and the characters in the Wilkins dream could see it as well. They too remembered lying in the arms of others and the seductive intoxication of love. They remembered their little boys and little girls, aunties and uncles, and myriad kitchens with sumptuous cooking.

Like a candle unexpectedly blown out by a momentary breeze, the old man dream abruptly disappeared, and now there was only one. For a moment Thakkar felt as if he had awoken from a long and fitful sleep, a night of tossing and turning and dreaming. He was fully awake now, he and the rest of them. The old man was now known to them only in fragmented memories, the many memories of all who found themselves here in the Wilkins dream. And yet, the old man was still there. He was one of them. He was Thakkar.

There was much to do now, for there were many other Wilkins, Brads, Letys, and more. A new world of entwined, consensual dreams making their way among *Homo sapiens* awaited them.

Heinz Hemken

Thanks

Early readers of the ever-changing drafts of this story include Sandra Antúnez, for whose patience and insightful commentary I am eternally grateful. Endless discussions of both the story itself and its underlying inventions brought into focus what was initially only vague speculation.

More formal iterations were read by Marco Hemken, Andy Wood, Yannick Pouliot, and Francisco M. de la Vega. They helped me keep my feet on the ground and cut out huge chunks of pointless text. They provided many welcome sanity checks.

My editor, Rebecca Brewer, reviewed a late draft and helped me refine what was still an unwieldy text. Her notes and comments got me to a point where I no longer saw anything more to add or remove. There is no substitute for a professional editor like Rebecca.

To all of you, I give my heartfelt thanks.

—Juneteenth, 2020